Dear Readers,

Many years ago, when I was a kid, my father said to me, "Bill, it doesn't really matter what you do in life. What's important is to be the *best* William Johnstone you can be."

I've never forgotten those words. And now, many years and almost 200 books later, I like to think that I am still trying to be the best William Johnstone I can be. Whether it's Ben Raines in the Ashes series, or Frank Morgan, the last gunfighter, or Smoke Jensen, our intrepid mountain man, or John Barrone and his hard-working crew keeping America safe from terrorist lowlifes in the Code Name series, I want to make each new book better than the last and deliver powerful storytelling.

Equally important, I try to create the kinds of believable characters that we can all identify with, real people who face tough challenges. When one of my creations blasts an enemy into the middle of next week, you can be damn sure he had a good reason.

As a storyteller, my job is to entertain you, my readers, and to make sure that you get plenty of enjoyment from my books for your hard-earned money. This is not a job I take lightly. And I greatly appreciate your feedback— you are my gold, and your opinions *do* count. So please keep the letters and e-mails coming.

Respectfully yours,

William Johnstone

WILLIAM W. JOHNSTONE

TRAIL OF THE MOUNTAIN MAN

REVENGE OF THE MOUNTAIN MAN

PINNACLE BOOKS
Kensington Publishing Corp.
http://www.kensingtonbooks.com

PINNACLE BOOKS are published by

Kensington Publishing Corp.
850 Third Avenue
New York, NY 10022

Copyright © 2007 by Kensington Publishing Corp.
Trail of the Mountain Man copyright © 1987 by William W. Johnstone
Revenge of the Mountain Man copyright © 1988 by William W. Johnstone

All rights reserved. No part of this book may be reproduced in any form or by any means without the prior written consent of the Publisher, excepting brief quotes used in reviews.

If you purchased this book without a cover, you should be aware that this book is stolen property. It was reported as "unsold and destroyed" to the Publisher and neither the Author nor the Publisher has received any payment for this "stripped book."

This novel is a work of fiction. Names, characters, places, and incidents are either the product of the author's imagination, or are used fictitiously. Any resemblance to actual persons, living or dead, or events is entirely coincidental.

All Kensington Titles, Imprints, and Distributed Lines are available at special quantity discounts for bulk purchases for sales promotions, premiums, fund-raising, and educational or institutional use. Special book excerpts or customized printings can also be created to fit specific needs. For details, write or phone the office of the Kensington special sales manager: Kensington Publishing Corp., 850 Third Avenue, New York, NY 10022, attn: Special Sales Department, Phone: 1-800-221-2647.

Pinnacle and the P logo Reg. U.S. Pat. & TM Off.

First Pinnacle Books Printing: January 2007

10 9 8 7 6 5 4 3 2 1

Printed in the United States of America

TRAIL OF THE
MOUNTAIN MAN

Dedicated to Caroline Gehman.
Have a nice day—or night—whatever.

BOOK ONE

This will remain the land of the free only so long as it is the home of the brave.
—Elmer Davis

I seen my duty and I done it.
—Anonymous

1

As gold strikes go, this particular strike was nothing to really shout about. Oh, a lot of the precious metal was dug out, chipped free, and blasted from the earth and rock, but the mines would play out in just over a year. The town of Fontana would wither and fade from the Western scene a couple of years later.

But with the discovery of gold, a great many lives would be forever changed. Livelihoods and relationships were altered; fortunes were made and lost; lives were snuffed out and families split, with the only motive greed.

Thus Fontana was conceived only to die an unnatural death.

Dawn was breaking as the man stepped out of the cabin. He held a steaming cup of coffee in one large, callused hand. He was tall, with wide shoulders and the lean hips of the horseman. His hair was ash-blond, cropped short, and his eyes were a cold brown, rarely giving away any inner thought.

The cabin had been built well, of stone and logs. The floor was wood. The windows held real glass. The cabin had been built to last, with a hand pump in the kitchen to bring up the water. There were curtains on the windows. The table and chairs and benches were hand-made and carved; done with patience and love.

And all about the house, inside and out, were the signs of a woman's touch.

Flowers and blooming shrubs were in colored profusion. The area around the house was trimmed and swept. Neat.

It was a high-up and lonely place, many miles from the nearest town. Below the cabin lay a valley, five miles wide and as many miles long. The land was filed on and claimed and legal with the Government. It belonged to the man and his wife.

They had lived here for three years, hacking a home out of the high, lonesome wilderness. Building a future. In another year they planned on building a family. If all stayed according to plan, that is.

The man and wife had a couple hundred head of cattle, a respectable herd of horses. They worked a large garden, canning much of what they raised for the hard winters that lashed the high country.

The man and woman stayed to themselves, socializing very little. When they did visit, it was not to the home of the kingpin who claimed to run the entire area, Tilden Franklin. Rather it was to the small farmers and ranchers who dotted the country that lay beneath the high lonesome where the man and woman lived.

There was a no-name town that was exclusively owned by Tilden Franklin. The town held a large general store, two saloons, a livery stable, and a gunsmith.

But all that was about to change.

Abruptly.

This was a land of towering mountains and lush, green valleys, sparsely populated, and it took a special breed of men and women to endure.

Many could not cope with the harshness, and they either moved on or went back to where they came from.

Those that stayed were the hardy breed.

Like Matt and Sally.

Matt was not his real name. He had not been called by his real name for so many years he never thought of it. There were those who could look at him and tell what he had once been; but this was the West, and what a man had once been did not matter. What mattered was what he was now. And all who knew Matt knew him to be a man you could ride the river with.

He had been a gunfighter. But now he rarely buckled on a short gun. Matt was not yet thirty years old and could not tell you how many men he had killed. Fifty, seventy-five, a hundred. He didn't know. And neither did anyone else.

He had been a gunfighter, and yet had never hired out his gun. Had never killed for pleasure. His reputation had come to him as naturally as his snake-like swiftness with a short gun.

He had come West with his father, and they had teamed up with an old Mountain Man named Preacher. And the Mountain Man had taken the boy in tow and begun teaching him the way of the mountains: how to survive, how to be a man, how to live where others would die.

Preacher had been present when the boy killed his first man during an Indian attack. The old Mountain Man had seen to the boy after the boy's dying father had left his son in his care. Preacher had seen to the boy's last formative years. And the old Mountain Man had known that he rode with a natural gunslick.*

It was Preacher who gave the boy the name that would become legend throughout the West; the name that would be whispered around ten thousand campfires and spoken of in a thousand saloons; the name that would be spoken with the same awe as that of Bat Masterson, Ben Thompson, the Earp boys, Curly Bill.

*The Last Mountain Man

Smoke.

Smoke's first wife had been raped and murdered, their baby son killed. Smoke had killed them all, then ridden into the town owned by the men who had sent the outlaws out and killed those men and wiped the town from the face of Idaho history.*

Smoke Jensen then did two things, one of them voluntarily. He became the most feared man in all the West, and he dropped out of sight. And then, shortly after dropping out of sight, he married Sally.

But his disappearance did nothing to slow the rumors about him; indeed, if anything, the rumors built in flavor and fever.

Smoke had been seen in Northern California. Smoke had gunned down five outlaws in Oregon. Smoke had cleaned up a town in Nevada. Since his disappearance, Smoke, so the rumors went, had done this and that and the other thing.

In reality, Smoke had not fired a gun in anger in three years.

But all that was about to change.

A dark-haired, hazel-eyed, shapely woman stepped out of the cabin to stand by her man's side. Something was troubling him, and she did not know what. But he would tell her in time.

This man and wife kept no secrets from each other. Their lives were shared in all things. No decisions were made by one without consulting the other.

"More coffee?" she asked.

"No, thank you. Trouble coming," he said abruptly. "I feel it in my gut."

A touch of panic washed over her. "Will we have to leave here?"

Smoke tossed the dregs of his coffee to the ground.

*Return of the Mountain Man

"When hell freezes over. This is our land, our home. We built it, and we're staying."

"How do the others feel?"

"Haven't talked to them. Think I might do that today. You need anything from town?"

"No."

"You want to come along?"

She smiled and shook her head. "I have so much to do around the house. You go."

"It'll be noon tomorrow before I can get back," he reminded her.

"I'll be all right."

He was known as Matt in this part of Colorado, but at home Sally always called him Smoke. "I'll pack you some food, Smoke."

He nodded his head. "I'll saddle up."

He saddled an appaloosa, a tough mountain horse, sired by his old appaloosa, Seven, who now ran wild and free on the range in the valley Smoke and Sally claimed.

Back in the snug cabin, Smoke pulled a trunk out of a closet and opened the lid. He was conscious of Sally's eyes on him as he removed his matched .44s and laid them to one side. He removed the rubbed and oiled gun belts and laid them beside the deadly colts.

"It's come to that, Smoke?" she asked.

He sighed, squatting before the trunk. He removed several boxes of .44 ammo. "I don't know." His words were softly spoken. "But Franklin is throwing a big loop nowadays. And wants it bigger still. I was up on the Cimarron the other day—I didn't tell you 'cause I didn't want you to worry. I made sign with some Indians. Sally, it's gold."

She closed the trunk lid and sat down, facing her husband. "Here? In this area?"

"Yes. Hook Nose, the buck that spoke English, told me that many whites are coming. Like ants toward honey was his words. If it's true, Sally, it's trouble. You know

Franklin claims more than a hundred and fifty thousand acres as his own. And he's always wanted this valley of ours. It's surprising to me that he hasn't made a move to take it."

Money did not impress Sally. She was a young, high-spirited woman with wealth of her own. Old money, from back in New Hampshire. In all probability, she could have bought out Tilden Franklin's holdings and still had money.

"You knew about the gold all along, didn't you, Smoke?"

"Yes," he told her. "But I don't think it's a big vein. I found part of the broken vein first year we were here. I don't want it."

"We certainly don't need the money," she reminded him.

Smoke gave her one of his rare smiles, the smile softening his face and mellowing his eyes, taking years from the young man's face. "That's right. I keep forgetting I married me a rich lady."

Together, they laughed.

Her laughter sobered as he began filling the cartridge loops with .44 rounds.

"Does part of it run through our land, Smoke?"

"Yes."

"I'll pack you extra food. I think you're going to be gone longer than you think."

"I think you're probably right. Sally? You know you have nothing to fear from the Indians. They knew Preacher and know he helped raise me. It's the white men you have to be careful of. It would take a very foolish man to bother a woman out here, but it's happened. Stay close to the house. The horses will warn you if anyone's coming. Go armed at all times. Hear me?"

"Yes, Smoke."

He leaned forward and kissed her mouth. "I taught you to shoot, and know you can. Don't hesitate to do so. The pot is boiling, Sally. We're going to have gold-hunters coming up against Franklin's gunhands. When Franklin learns of the gold, he's going to want it all. Our little no-name town is going to boom. For a time. Trouble is riding our way on a horse out of Hell. You've never seen a boom town, Sally. I have. They're rough and mean and totally violent. They attract the good and the bad. Especially the bad. Gamblers and gunhawks and thieves and whores. We're all going to be in for a rough time of it for a while."

"We've been through some rough times before, Smoke," she said quietly.

"Not like this." He stood up, belted the familiar Colts around his lean waist, and began loading the .44s.

"Matt just died, didn't he?" she asked.

"Yes. I'm afraid so. When Smoke steps out of the shadows, Sally—and it's time, for I'm tired of being someone else—bounty hunters and kids with dreams of being the man who killed Smoke Jensen will be coming in with the rest of the trash and troublemakers. Sally, I've never been ashamed of what I was. I hunted down and destroyed those who ripped my life to shreds. I did what the law could not or would not do. I did what any real man would have done. I'm a Mountain Man, Sally. Perhaps the last of the breed. But that's what I am.

"I'm not running anymore, Sally. I want to live in peace. But if I have to fight to attain that peace . . . so be it. And," he said with a sigh, "I might as well level with you. Peyton told me last month that Franklin has made his boast about running us out of this valley."

"His wife told me, Smoke."

The young man with the hard eyes smiled. "I might have known."

She drew herself up on tiptoes and kissed him. "See you in two or three days, Smoke."

2

"Word is out, boss," Tilden's foreman said. "It's gold, all right. And lots of it."

Tilden leaned back in his chair and looked at his foreman. "Is it fact or rumor, Clint?"

"Fact, boss. The assay office says it's rich. Real rich."

"The Sugarloaf?"

Clint shrugged his heavy shoulders. "It's a broken vein, boss. Juts out all over the place, so I was told. Spotty. But one thing's for sure: all them piss-ant nesters and small spreads around the Sugarloaf is gonna have some gold on the land."

The Sugarloaf was Smoke's valley.

Tilden nodded his handsome head. "Send some of the crew into town, start stakin' out lots. Folks gonna be foggin' in here pretty quick."

"What are you gonna call the town, boss?"

"I knew me a Mex gal years back, down along the Animas. Her last name was Fontana. I always did like that name. We'll call 'er Fontana."

Tilden Franklin sat alone in his office, making plans. Grand plans, for Tilden never thought small. A big bear of a man, Tilden stood well over six feet and weighed a good two hundred and forty pounds, little of it fat. He was forty years old and in the peak of health.

He had come into this part of Colorado when he was twenty-five years old. He had carved his empire out of the wilderness. He had fought Indians and outlaws and the elements . . . and won.

And he thought of himself as king.

He had fifty hands on his spread, many of them hired as much for their ability with a gun as with a rope. And he paid his men well, both in greenbacks and in a comfortable style of living. His men rode for the brand, doing anything that Tilden asked of them, or they got out. It was that simple.

His brand was the Circle TF.

Tilden rose from his chair and paced the study of his fine home—the finest in all the area. When that Matt What's-His-Name had ridden into this part of the country— back three or four years ago—Tilden had taken an immediate dislike to the young man.

And he didn't believe Matt *was* the man's name. But Tilden didn't hold that against anyone. Man had a right to change his own name.

Still, Tilden had always had the ability to bully and intimidate other men. He had always bulled and bullied his way through any situation. Men respected and feared him.

All but that damned Matt.

Tilden remembered the first day he'd come face to face with Matt. The young man had looked at him through the coldest eyes Tilden had ever seen—a rattler's. And even though the young man had not been wearing a short gun, there had been no backup in him. None at all. He had looked right at Tilden, nodded his head, and walked on.

Tilden Franklin had had the uncomfortable and unaccustomed sensation that he had just been graded and found wanting. That, and the feeling that he had just been summarily dismissed.

By a goddamned saddle-bum, of all people!

No, Tilden corrected himself, not a saddle-bum. Matt might be many things, but he was no saddle-bum. He had to have access to money, for he had bought that whole damned valley free and clear. Bought most of it, filed on the rest of it.

And that woman of his, Sally. Just thinking of her caused Tilden to breathe short. He knew from the first day he'd seen her that he had to have her. One way or the other—and she was never far from his thoughts.

She was far and above any other woman in the area. She was a woman fit to be a king's queen. And since Tilden thought of himself as a king, it was only natural he possess a woman with queen-like qualities.

And possess her he would. It was just a matter of time.

Whether she liked it, or not. He feelings were not important.

Three hours after leaving his cabin, Smoke rode up to the Colby spread. He halloed the house from the gate and Colby stepped out, giving him a friendly wave to come on in.

Colby's spread was a combination cattle ranch and farm, something purists in the cattle business frowned on. Colby and his family were just more of them "goddamned nesters" as far as the bigger spreads in the area were concerned. Colby had moved into the area a couple of years before Smoke and Sally, with his wife Belle, and their three kids, a girl and two boys. From Missouri, Colby was a hardworking man in his early forties. A veteran of the War Between the States, he was no stranger to guns, but was not a gunhand.

"Matt," he greeted the rider. His eyes narrowed at the sight of the twin Colts belted around Smoke's waist and tied down. "First time I ever seen you wearin' a pistol, much less two of them."

"Times change, Colby. You heard the gold news?"

"Last week. People already movin' in. You wanna come in and talk?"

"Let's do it out here. You ever seen a boom town, Colby?"

"Can't say as I have, Matt." The man was having a difficult time keeping his eyes off the twin Colts. "Why do you ask?"

"There's gold running through this area. Not much of it—a lot of it is iron and copper pyrites—but there's enough gold to bring out the worst in men."

"I ain't no miner, Matt. What's them pyrites you said?"

"Fool's gold. But that isn't the point, Colby. When Tilden Franklin learns of the gold—if he doesn't already know—he'll move against us."

"You can't know that for sure, Matt. 'Sides, this is our land. We filed on it right with the Government. He can't just come in and run us off."

The younger man looked at Colby through hard, wise eyes. "You want to risk your family's lives on that statement, Colby?"

"Who are you, Matt?" Colby asked, evading the question.

"A man who wants to be left alone. A man who has been over the mountain and across the river. And I won't be pushed off my land."

"That don't tell me what I asked, Matt. You really know how to use them guns?"

"What do you think?"

Colby's wife and kids had joined them. The two boys were well into manhood. Fifteen and sixteen years old. The girl was thirteen, but mature for her age, built up right well. Sticking out in all the right places. Adam, Bob, Velvet.

The three young people stared at the Colts. Even a fool could see that the pistols were used but well taken care of.

"I don't see no marks on them handles, Mister Matt,"

Adam said. "That must mean you ain't never killed no one."

"Adam!" his mother said.

"Tinhorn trick, Adam," Smoke said. "No one with any sand to them cuts their kills for everyone to see."

"I bet you wouldn't say that to none of Mister Franklin's men," Velvet said.

Smoke smiled at the girl. He lifted his eyes to Colby. "I've told you what I know, Colby. You know where to find me." He swung into the saddle.

"I didn't mean no offense, Matt," the farmer-rancher said.

"None taken." Smoke reined his horse around and headed west.

Colby watched Smoke until horse and rider had disappeared from view. "Thing is," he said, as much to himself as to his family, "Matt's right. I just don't know what to do about it."

Bob said, "Them guns look . . . well, *right* on Mister Matt, Dad. I wonder who he really is."

"I don't know. But I got me a hunch we're all gonna find out sooner than we want to," he said sourly.

"This is our land," Belle said. "And no one has the right to take it from us."

Colby put his arm around her waist. "Is it worth dyin' for, Ma?"

"Yes," she said quickly.

On his ride to Steve Matlock's spread, Smoke cut the trail of dozens of riders and others on foot, all heading for Franklin's town. He could tell from the hoofprints and footprints that horses and men were heavily loaded.

Gold-hunters.

Steve met him several miles from his modest cabin in the high-up country. "Matt," the man said. "What's going on around here?"

"Trouble, I'm thinking. I just left Colby's place. I couldn't get through to him."

"He's got to think on it a spell. But I don't have to be convinced. I come from the store yesterday. Heard the rumors. Tilden wants our land, and most of all, he wants the Sugarloaf."

"Among other things," Smoke said, a dry note to the statement.

"I figured you knew he had his eyes on Sally. Risky to leave her alone, Matt. Or whatever your name is," he added acknowledging the Colts in a roundabout manner.

"Tilden won't try to take Sally by force this early in the game, Steve. He'll have me out of the way first. There's some gold on your land, by the way."

"A little bit. Most of it's fool's gold. The big vein cuts north at Nolan's place, then heads straight into the mountains. Take a lot of machinery to get it out, and there ain't no way to get the equipment up there."

"People aren't going to think about that, Steve. All they'll be thinking of is gold. And they'll stomp on anyone who gets in their way."

"I stocked up on ammo. Count on me, Matt."

"I knew I could."

Smoke rode on, slowly winding downward. On his way down to No-Name Town, he stopped and talked with Peyton and Nolan. Both of them ran small herds and farmed for extra money while their herds matured.

"Yeah," Peyton said. "I heard about the gold. God-damnit, that's all we need."

Nolan said, "Franklin has made his boast that if he can run you out, the rest of us will be easy."

Smoke's smile was not pleasant, and both the men came close to backing up. "I don't run," Smoke said.

"First time I ever seen you armed with a short gun,"

Peyton said. "You look . . . well, don't take this the wrong way, Matt . . . *natural* with them."

"Matt," Nolan said. "I've known you for three years and some months. I've never seen you upset. But today, you've got a burr under your blanket."

"This vein of gold is narrow and shallow, boys," Smoke said, even though both men were older than he. "Best thing could happen is if it was just left alone. But that's not going to happen." He told them about boom towns. "There's going to be a war," he added, "and those of us who only wanted to live in peace are going to be caught up in the middle of it. And there is something else. If we don't band together, the only man who'll come out on top will be Tilden Franklin."

"He sure wants to tan your hide and tack it to his barn door, Matt," Peyton said.

"I was raised by an old Mountain Man, boys. He used to say I was born with the bark on. I reckon he was right. The last twelve–fifteen years of my life, I've only had three peaceful years, and those were spent right in this area. And if I want to continue my peaceful way of life, it looks like I'm gonna have to fight for them. And fight I will, boys. Don't make no bets against me doing that."

Nolan looked uncomfortable. "I know it ain't none of my business, Matt, and you can tell me to go to hell if you want to. But I gotta ask. Who are you?"

"My Christian name is Jensen. An old Mountain Man named Preacher hung a nickname on me years back. Smoke."

Smoke wheeled his horse and trotted off without looking back.

Peyton grabbed his hat and flung it on the ground. "Holy Christ!" he yelled. "Smoke Jensen!"

Both men ran for their horses, to get home, tell their families that the most famous gun in the entire West had been their neighbor all this time. And more importantly, that Smoke Jensen was on *their* side.

3

When Smoke reached the main road, running east to west before being forced to cut due south at a place called Feather Falls, he ran into a rolling, riding, walking stream of humanity. Sitting astride his horse, whom he had named Horse, Smoke cursed softly. The line must have been five hundred strong. And he knew, in two weeks, there would probably be ten times that number converging on No-Name.

"Wonderful," he muttered. Horse cocked his ears and looked back at Smoke. "Yeah, Horse. I don't like it either."

With a gentle touch of his spurs, Smoke and Horse moved out, riding at an easy trot for town.

Before he reached the crest of the hill overlooking the town, the sounds of hammering reached his ears. Reining up on the crest, Smoke sat and watched the men below, racing about, driving stakes all over the place, marking out building locations. Lines of wagons were in a row, the wagons loaded with lumber. Canvas tents were already in place, and the whiskey peddlers were dipping their homemade concoction out of barrels. Smoke knew there would be everything in that whiskey from horse-droppings to snakeheads.

He rode slowly down the hill and tied up at the railing

in front of the general store. He stood on the boardwalk for a moment, looking at the organized madness taking place all around him.

Smoke recognized several men from out of the shouting, shoving, cursing crush.

There was Utah Slim, the gunhand from down Escalante way. The gambler Louis Longmont was busy setting up his big tent. Over there, by the big saloon tent, was Big Mamma O'Neil. Smoke knew her girls would not be far away. Big Mamma had a stable of whores and sold bad booze and ran crooked games. Smoke had seen other faces that he recognized but could not immediately put names to. They would come to him.

He turned and walked into the large general store. The owner, Beeker, was behind the counter, grinning like a cream-fed cat. No doubt he was doing a lot of business and no doubt he had jacked up his prices.

Beeker's smile changed to a frown when he noticed the low-slung Colts on Smoke. "Something, Matt?"

"Ten boxes of .44s, Beeker. That'll do for a start. I'll just look around a bit."

"I don't know if I can spare that many, Matt," Beeker said, his voice whiny.

"You can spare them." Smoke walked around the store, picking up several other items, including several pairs of britches that looked like they'd fit Sally. In all likelihood, she was going to have to do some hard riding before all this was said and done, and while it wasn't ladylike to wear men's britches and ride astride, it was something she was going to have to do.

He moved swiftly past the glass-enclosed showcase filled with women's underthings and completed his swing back to the main counter, laying his purchases on the counter. "That'll do it, Beeker."

The store owner added it up and Smoke paid the bill.

"Mighty fancy guns you wearin', Matt. Never seen you wear a short gun before. Something the matter?"

"You might say that."

"Don't let none of Tilden's boys see you with them things on. They might take 'em off you 'less you know how to use them."

Beeker did not like Smoke, and the feeling was shared. Beeker kowtowed to Tilden; Smoke did not. Beeker thought Tilden was a mighty fine man; Smoke thought Tilden to be a very obnoxious SOB.

Smoke lifted his eyes and stared at Beeker. Beeker took a step backward, those emotionless, cold brown eyes chilling him, touching the coward's heart that beat in his chest.

Smoke picked up his purchases and walked out into the spring sunlight. He stowed the gear in his saddlebags and walked across the street to the better of the two saloons. In a week there would be fifty saloons, all working twenty-four hours a day.

As he walked across the wide dirt street, his spurs jingling and his heels kicking up little dust pockets, Smoke was conscious of eyes on him. Unfriendly eyes. He stepped up onto the boardwalk and pushed through the swinging doors. Stepping to one side, giving his eyes time to adjust to the murky interior of the saloon, Smoke sized up the crowd.

The place was filled with ranchers and punchers. Some of those present were friends and friendly with Smoke. Others were sworn to the side of Tilden Franklin. Smoke walked to the end of the bar.

Smoke was dressed in black pants, red and white checkered shirt, and a low crowned hat. Behind his left-hand Colt, he carried a long-bladed Bowie knife. He laid a coin on the bar and ordered a beer.

The place had grown very quiet.

Normally not a drinking man, Smoke did occasionally enjoy a drink of whiskey or a beer. On this day, he simply wanted to check out the mood of the people.

He nodded at a couple of ranchers. They returned the silent greeting. Smoke sipped his beer.

Across the room, seated around a poker table, were

half a dozen of Tilden's men. They had ceased their game and now sat staring at Smoke. None of those present had ever seen the young man go armed before—other than carrying a rifle in his saddle boot.

The outside din was softened somewhat, but still managed to push through the walls of the saloon.

"Big doings around the area," Smoke said to no one in particular.

One of Tilden's men laughed.

Smoke looked at the man; he knew him only as Red. Red fancied himself a gunhand. Smoke knew the man had killed a drunken Mexican some years back, and had ridden the hoot-owl trail on more than one occasion. But Smoke doubted the man was as fast with a gun as he imagined.

"Private joke?" Smoke asked.

"Yeah," Red said. "And the joke is standin' at the bar, drinkin' a beer."

Smoke smiled and looked at a rancher. "Must be talking about you, Jackson."

Jackson flushed and shook his head. A Tilden man all the way, Jackson did all he could to stay out of the way of Tilden's ire.

"Oh?" Smoke said, lifting his beer mug with his left hand. "Well, then. Maybe Red's talking about you, Beaconfield."

Another Tilden man who shook in his boots at the mere mention of Tilden's name.

Beaconfield shook his head.

"I'm talkin' to you, Two-Gun!" Red shouted at Smoke.

Left and right of Smoke, the bar area quickly cleared of men.

"You'd better be real sure, Red," Smoke said softly, his words carrying through the silent saloon. "And very good."

"What the hell's that supposed to mean, nester?" Red almost yelled the question.

"It means, Red, that I didn't come in here hunting trouble. But if it comes my way, I'll handle it."

"You got a big mouth, nester."

"Back off, Matt!" a friendly rancher said hoarsely. "He'll kill you!"

Smoke's only reply was a small smile. It did not touch his eyes.

Smoke had slipped the hammer thong off his right-hand Colt before stepping into the saloon. He placed his beer mug on the bar and slowly turned to face Red.

Red stood up.

Smoke slipped the hammer thong off his left-hand gun. So confident were Red's friends that they did not move from the table.

"I'm saying it now," Smoke said. "And those of you still left alive when the smoke clears can take it back to Tilden. The Sugarloaf belongs to me. I'll kill any Circle TF rider I find on my land. Your boss has made his boast that he'll run me off my land. He's said he'll take my wife. Those words alone give me justification to kill him. But he won't face me alone. He'll send his riders to do the job. So if any of you have a mind to open the dance, let's strike up the band, boys."

Red jerked out his pistol. Smoke let him clear leather before he drew his right-hand Colt. He drew, cocked, and fired in one blindingly fast motion. The .44 slug hit Red square between his eyes and blew out the back of his head, the force of the .44 slug slamming the TF rider backward to land in a sprawl of dead, cooling meat some distance away from the table.

The other TF riders sat very still at the table, being very careful not to move their hands.

Smoke holstered his .44 in a move almost as fast as his draw. "Anybody else want to dance?"

No one did.

"Then I'll finish my beer, and I'd appreciate it if I could do so in peace."

No one had moved in the saloon. The bartender was so scared he looked like he wanted to wet his long handles.

"Pass me that bowl of eggs down here, will you, Bea-confield?" Smoke asked.

The rancher scooted the bowl of hard-boiled eggs down the bar. Smoke looked at the bartender. "Crack it and peel it for me."

The bartender dropped one egg and made a mess out of the second before he got the third one right.

"A little salt and pepper on it, please," Smoke requested.

Gas escaped from Red's cooling body.

Smoke ate his egg and finished his beer. He wiped his mouth with the back of his hand and deliberately turned his back to the table of TF riders. "Any back-shooters in the bunch?" he asked.

"First man reaches for a gun, I drop them," a rancher friendly to Smoke said.

"Thanks, Mike," Smoke said.

He walked to the batwing doors, his spurs jingling. A TF rider named Singer spoke, his voice stopping Smoke. "You could have backed off, Matt."

"Not much backup in me, Singer." Smoke turned around to once more face the crowded saloon.

"I reckon not," Singer acknowledged. "But you got to know what this means."

"All it means is I killed a loud-mouthed tinhorn. Your boss wants to make something else out of it, that's his concern."

"Man ought to have it on his marker who killed him." Singer didn't let up. "Matt your first or last name?"

"Neither one. The name is Jensen. Smoke Jensen."

Singer's jaw dropped so far down Smoke thought it might hit the card table. He turned around and pushed open the doors, walking across the street to his horse. As he swung into the saddle, he was thinking. Should get real interesting around No-Name . . . real quick.

4

As Smoke was riding out of the town, one of Tilden's men, who had been in the bar around the card table, was fogging it toward the Circle TF, lathering a good horse to get the news to Tilden Franklin.

Tilden sat on his front porch and received the news of the gunfight, a look of pure disbelief on his face. "Matt killed Red? What'd he do, shoot him in the back?"

"Stand-up, face-to-face fight, boss," the puncher said. "But Matt ain't his real name. It's Smoke Jensen."

Tilden dropped his coffee cup, the cup shattering on the porch floor. "Smoke Jensen!" he finally managed to blurt out. "He's got to be lyin'!"

The puncher shook his head. "You'd have to have been there, boss. Smoke is everything his rep says he is. I ain't never seen nobody that fast in all my life."

"Did he let Red clear leather before he drew?" Tilden's voice was hoarse as he asked the question.

"Yessir."

"Jensen," Tilden whispered. "That's one of his trademarks. Okay, Donnie. Thanks. You better cool down that horse of yours."

The bowlegged cowboy swaggered off to see to his horse. Tilden leaned back in his porch chair, a sour sensation in his stomach and a bad taste in his mouth. Smoke Jensen . . . *here*! Crap!

What to do?

Tilden seemed to recall that there was a murder warrant out for Smoke Jensen, from years back. But that was way to hell and gone over to Walsenburg; and the men Smoke had killed had murdered his brother and stolen some Confederate gold back during the war.*

Anyway, Tilden suddenly remembered, that warrant had been dropped.

No doubt about it, Tilden mused, with Smoke Jensen owner of the Sugarloaf, it sure as hell changed things around some. Smoke Jensen was pure hell with a gun. Probably the best gun west of the Mississippi.

And that rankled Tilden too. For Tilden had always fancied himself a gunslick. He had never been bested in a gunfight. He wondered, as he sat on the porch. Was he better than Smoke Jensen?

Well, there was sure one way to find out.

Tilden rejected that idea almost as soon as it popped into his mind.

He did not reject it because of fear. The big man had no fear of Smoke. It was just that there were easier ways to accomplish what he had in mind. Tilden had never lost a fight. Never. Not a fistfight, not a gunfight. He didn't believe any man could beat him with his fists, and damn few were better than Tilden with a short gun.

He called for his Mexican houseboy to come clean up the mess made by the broken cup and to bring him another cup of coffee.

The mess cleaned up, a fresh cup of steaming coffee at hand, Tilden looked out over just a part of his vast holdings. Some small voice, heretofore unheard or unnoticed, deep within him, told him that all this was enough. More

The Last Mountain Man

than enough for one man. You're a rich man it said. Stop while you're ahead.

Tilden pushed that annoying and stupid thought from his mind. No way he would stop his advance. That was too foolish to even merit consideration.

No, there were other ways to deal with a gunhawk like Jensen. And a plan was forming in Tilden's mind.

The news of the saloon shooting would soon be all over the area. And the small nester-ranchers like Nolan and Peyton and Matlock and Colby would throw in with Smoke Jensen. Maybe Ray and Mike as well. That was fine with Tilden.

He would just take them out one at a time, saving Jensen for last.

He smiled and sipped his coffee. A good plan, he thought. A very good plan. He had an idea that most of the gold lay beneath the Sugarloaf. And he'd have the Sugarloaf. And the mistress of Sugarloaf too.

Sally.

Sally had dressed in boys' jeans and a work shirt. Her friends and family back in New Hampshire would be horrified to see her dressed in male clothing but there came a time when practicality must take precedence over fashion. And she felt that time was here.

She looked out the window. Late afternoon. She did not expect Smoke to return for another day—perhaps two more days. She was not afraid. Whenever Smoke rode in for supplies it was a two- or three-day trek— sometimes longer. But those prior trips had been in easier times. Now, one did not know what to expect.

Or from which direction.

As soon as Smoke had gone, she had saddled her pony, a gentle, sure-footed mare, and ridden out into the valley. She had driven two of Smoke's stallions, Seven and Drifter, back to the house, putting them in the corral. The mountain horses were better than any watchdog she had ever seen. If anyone even came close to the house, they would let her know. And, if turned loose, the stallion Drifter would kill an intruder.

He had done so before.

The midnight-black, yellow-eyed Drifter had a look of Hell about him, and was totally loyal to Smoke and Sally. Sally had belted a pistol around her waist, leaned a rifle against the wall, next to the door, and laid a double-barreled express gun on the table. She knew how to use all the weapons at hand, and would not hesitate to do so.

The horses and chickens fed, the cow milked, all the other chores done, Sally went back into the house and pulled the heavy shutters closed and secured them. The shutters had gun slits cut into them, which could be opened or closed. She stirred the stew bubbling in the blackened pot and checked her bread in the oven. She sat down on the couch, picked up a book, and began her lonely wait for her man.

Smoke put No-Name Town far behind him and began his long trip back to Sugarloaf. He would stop at the Ray ranch in the morning, talk to him. The fat was surely in the fire by now, and the grease would soon be flaming.

Some eight high-up and winding miles from the town, just as purple shadows were gathering in the mountain country, Smoke picked a spot for the night and began making his lonely camp. He did not have to picket Horse, for Horse would stay close, acting as watcher and guard.

Smoke built a small fire for coffee, and ate from what Sally had fixed for him. Some cold beef, some bread with a bit of homemade jam on it. He drank his coffee, put out the fire, and settled into his blankets, using his saddle for a pillow. In a very short time, he was deep in sleep.

* * *

In the still unnamed town, Utah Slim sat in a saloon and sipped a beer. Even though hours had passed since the shooting of Red, the saloon still hummed with conversation about Smoke Jensen. Utah Slim did not join in the conversations around the bar and the tables. So far, few knew who he was. And that was the way he liked it—for a time. When it was time for Utah Slim to announce his intentions, he'd do so.

He was under no illusions; he'd seen Smoke glance his way riding into town. Smoke recognized him. Now it was just a waiting game.

And waiting was something Utah was good at. Something any hired gun had better be good at, or he wouldn't last long in this business.

Louis Longmont stepped out of his canvas bar and game room and glanced up and down the street. A lean, hawk-faced man, with strong, slender hands and long fingers, the nails carefully manicured, the hands clean, Louis had jet-black hair and a black pencil-thin mustache. He was dressed in a black suit, with white shirt and dark ascot—the ascot something he'd picked up on a trip to England some years back. He wore low-heeled boots. A pistol hung in tied-down leather on his right side; it was not for show alone. For Louis was snake quick with a short gun. A feared, deadly gunhand when pushed.

Louis was not an evil man. He had never hired his gun out for money. And while he could make a deck of cards do almost anything except stand up and sing "God Save the Queen," Louis did not cheat at poker. He did not have to cheat. A man possessed of a phenomenal memory, Louis could tell you the odds of filling any type of poker hand; and he was also a card-counter. He did not consider that cheating, and most agreed with him that it was not.

Louis was just past forty years of age. He had come to the West as a mere slip of a boy, with his parents, arriving from Louisiana. His parents had died in a shanty-town fire, leaving the boy to cope the best he could.

Louis had coped quite well, thank you.

Louis had been in boom towns all over the West, seeing them come and go. He had a feeling in his guts that this town was going to be a raw bitch-kitty. He knew all about Tilden Franklin, and liked none of what he'd heard. The man was power-mad, and obviously lower class. White trash.

And now Smoke Jensen had made his presence known. Louis wondered why. Why this soon in the power-game? An unanswered question.

For a moment, Louis thought of packing up and pulling out. Just saying the hell with it! For he knew this was not going to be an ordinary gold-rush town. Powerful factions were at work here. Tilden Franklin wanted the entire region as his own. Smoke Jensen stood in his way.

Louis made up his mind. Should be a very interesting confrontation, he thought.

He'd stay.

Big Mamma O'Neil was an evil person. If one could find her heart, it would be as black as sin itself. Big Mamma stepped out in front of her gaming room and love-for-sale tent to look up and down the street. She nodded at Louis. He returned the nod and stepped back inside his tent.

Goddamned stuck-up card-slick! she fumed. Thought he was better than most everyone else. Dressed like a dandy. Talked like some highfalutin' professor—not that Big Mamma had ever known any professor; she just imagined that was how one would sound.

Big Mamma swung her big head around, once more looking over the town. A massive woman, she was strong as an ox and had killed more than one man with her huge, hard fists. And had killed for money as well as pleasure; one served her interests as much as the other.

Big Mamma was a crack shot with rifle or pistol, having grown up in the raw, wild West, fighting Indians and hooligans and her brothers. She had killed her father with an axe, then taken his guns and his horse and left for Texas. She had never been back.

She had brothers and sisters, but had no idea what had ever become of any of them. She really didn't care. The only thing she cared about was money and other women. She hated men.

She had seen Smoke Jensen ride in, looking like the arrogant bastard she had always thought he would be. So he had killed some puncher named Red—big deal! A nothing rider who fancied himself a gunhand. She'd heard all the stories about Jensen, and discounted most of them as pure road apples. The rumors were that he had been a Mountain Man. But he was far too young to have been a part of that wild breed.

As far as she was concerned, Smoke Jensen was just another overrated punk.

As the purple shadows melted into darkness over the no-name town that would soon become Fontana, Monte Carson stepped out of the best of the two permanent saloons and looked up and down the wide, dusty street. He hitched at the twin Colts belted around his waist and tied down low.

This town, he thought, was shaping up real nice for a hired gun. And that's what Monte was. He had hired his guns out in Montana, in the cattle wars out in California, and had fought the sheep farmers and nesters up in Wyoming. And, as he'd fought, his reputation had grown. Monte felt that Tilden Franklin would soon be contacting him. He could wait.

On the now-well-traveled road beneath where Smoke slept peacefully, wagons continued to roll and rumble along, carrying their human cargo toward No-Name Town. The line of wagons and buggies and riders and walkers was now several miles long. Gamblers and would-be shop-owners and whores and gunfighters and snake-oil salesmen and pimps and troublemakers and murderers and good solid family people . . . all of them heading for No-Name with but one thought in their minds. Gold.

At the end of the line of gold-seekers, not a part of them but yet with the same destination if not sharing the same motives, rattled a half a dozen wagons. Ed Jackson was new to the raw West—a shopkeeper from Illinois with his wife Peg. They were both young and very ideal-istic, and had no working knowledge of the real West. They were looking for a place to settle. This no-name town sounded good to them. Ed's brother Paul drove the heavily laden supply wagon, containing part of what they just knew would make them respected and secure citizens. Paul was as naive as his brother and sister-in-law concerning the West.

In the third wagon came Ralph Morrow and his wife Bountiful.They were missionaries, sent into the godless West by their Church, to save souls and soothe the sinful spirits of those who had not yet accepted Christ into their lives. They had been looking for a place to settle when they had hooked up with Ed and Peg and Paul. This was the first time Ralph and Bountiful had been west of Eastern Ohio. It was exciting. A challenge.

They thought.

In the fourth wagon rode another young couple, mar-ried only a few years, Hunt and Willow Brook. Hunt was a lawyer, looking for a place to practice all he'd just been taught back East. This new gold rush town seemed just the place to start.

In the fifth wagon rode Colton and Mona Spalding. A doctor and nurse, respectively. They had both graduated their schools only last year, mulled matters over, and de-cided to head West. They were young and handsome and pretty. And, like the others in their little caravan, they had absolutely no idea what they were riding into.

In the last wagon, a huge, solidly built vehicle with six mules pulling it, came Haywood and Dana Arden. Like the others, they were young and full of grand ideas. Haywood had inherited a failing newspaper from his father back in Pennsylvania and decided to pull out and head West to seek their fortunes.

"Oh Haywood!" Dana said, her eyes shining with excitement. "It's all so wonderful."

"Yes," Haywood agreed, just as the right rear wheel of their wagon fell off.

5

Smoke was up long before dawn spread her shimmering rays of light over the land. He slipped out of his blankets and put his hat on, then pulled on his boots and strapped on his guns. He checked to see how Horse was doing, then washed his face with water from his canteen. He built a small, hand-sized fire and boiled coffee. He munched on a thick piece of bread and sipped his coffee, sitting with his back to a tree, his eyes taking in the first silver streaks of a new day in the high-up country of Colorado.

He had spotted a fire far down below him, near the winding road. A very large fire. Much too large unless those who built it were roasting an entire deer—head, horns, and all. He finished the small, blackened pot of coffee, carefully doused his fire, and saddled Horse, stowing his gear in the saddle bags.

He swung into the saddle. "Steady now, Horse," he said in a low voice. "Let's see how quiet we can be backtracking."

Horse and rider made their way slowly and quietly down from the high terrain toward the road miles away using the twisting, winding trails. Smoke uncased U.S. Army binoculars he'd picked up years back, while traveling with his mentor, the old Mountain Man Preacher, and studied the situation.

Five, no—six wagons. One of them down with a busted back wheel. Six men, five women. All young, in their early twenties, Smoke guessed. The women were all very pretty, the men all handsome and apparently—at least to Smoke, at least at this distance—helpless.

He used his knees to signal Horse, and the animal moved out, taking its head, picking the route. Stopping after a few hundred twisting yards, Smoke once more surveyed the situation. His binoculars picked up movement coming from the direction of No-Name. Four riders. He studied the men, watching them approach the wagons. Drifters, from the look of them. Probably spent the night in No-Name gambling and whoring and were heading out to stake a gold claim. They looked like trouble.

Staying in the deep and lush timber, Smoke edged closer still. Several hundred yards from the wagon, Smoke halted and held back, wanting to see how these pilgrims would handle the approach of the riders.

He could not hear all that was said, but he could get most of it from his hidden location.

He had pegged the riders accurately. They were trouble. They reined up and sat their horses, grinning at the men and women. Especially the women.

"You folks look like you got a mite of trouble," one rider said.

"A bit," a friendly-looking man responded. "We're just getting ready to fulcrum the wagon."

"You're gonna do *what* to it?" another rider blurted.

"Raise it up," a pilgrim said.

"Oh. You folks headin' to Fontana?"

The wagon people looked at each other.

Fontana! Smoke thought. Where in the hell is Fontana?

"I'm sorry," one of the women said. "We're not familiar with that place."

"That's what they just named the town up yonder," a

rider said, jerking his thumb in the direction of No-Name. "Stuck up a big sign last night."

So No-Name has a name, Smoke thought. Wonder whose idea that was.

But he thought he knew. Tilden Franklin.

Smoke looked at the women of the wagons. They were, to a woman, all very pretty and built-up nice. Very shapely. The men with them didn't look like much to Smoke; but then, he thought. they were Easterners. Probably good men back there. But out here, they were out of their element.

And Smoke didn't like the look in the eyes of the riders. One kept glancing up and down the road. As yet, no traffic had appeared. But Smoke knew the stream of gold-hunters would soon appear. If the drifters were going to start something—the women being what they wanted, he was sure—they would make their move pretty quick.

At some unspoken signal, the riders dismounted.

"Oh, say!" the weakest-jawed pilgrim said. "It's good of you men to help."

"Huh?" a rider said, then he grinned. "Oh, yeah. We're regular do-gooders. You folks nesters?"

"I beg your pardon, sir?"

"Farmers." He ended that and summed up his feelings concerning farmers by spitting a stream of brown tabacco juice onto the ground, just missing the pilgrim's feet.

The pilgrim laughed and said, "Oh, no. My name is Ed Jackson, this is my wife Peg. We plan to open a store in the gold town."

"Ain't that nice," the rider mumbled.

Smoke kneed Horse a bit closer.

"My name is Ralph Morrow," another pilgrim said. "I'm a minister. This is my wife Bountiful. We plan to start a church in the gold town."

The rider looked at Bountiful and licked his lips.

Ralph said, "And this is Paul Jackson, Ed's brother.

Over there is Hunt and Willow Brook. Hunt is a lawyer. That's Colton and Mona Spalding. Colton is a physician. And last, but certainly not least, is Haywood and Dana Arden. Haywood is planning to start a newspaper in the town. Now you know us."

"Not as much as I'd like to," a rider said speaking for the first time. He was looking at Bountiful.

To complicate matters, Bountiful was looking square at the rider.

The woman is flirting with him, Smoke noticed. He silently cursed. This Bountiful might be a preacher's wife, but what she really was was a hot handful of trouble. The preacher was not taking care of business at home.

Bountiful was blonde with hot blue eyes. She stared at the rider.

All the newcomers to the West began to sense something was not as it should be. But none knew what, and if they did, Smoke thought, they wouldn't know how to handle it. For none of the men were armed.

One of the drifters, the one who had been staring at Bountiful, brushed past the preacher. He walked by Bountiful, his right arm brushing the woman's jutting breasts. She did not back up. The rider stopped and grinned at her.

The newspaperman's wife stepped in just in time, stepping between the rider and the woman. She glared at Bountiful. "Let's you and I start breakfast, Bountiful," she suggested. "While the men fix the wheel."

"What you got in your wagon, shopkeeper?" a drifter asked. "Anything in there we might like?"

Ed narrowed his eyes. "I'll set up shop very soon. Feel free to browse when we're open for business."

The rider laughed. "Talks real nice, don't he, boys?"

His friends laughed.

The riders were big men, tough-looking and seemingly

very capable. Smoke had no doubts but what they were all that and more. The more being troublemakers.

Always something, Smoke thought with a silent sigh. People wander into an unknown territory without first checking out all the ramifications. He edged Horse forward.

A rider jerked at a tie-rope over the bed of one wagon. "I don't wanna wait to browse none. I wanna see what you got now."

"Now see here!" Ed protested, stepping toward the man.

Ed's head exploded in pain as the rider's big fist hit the shopkeeper's jaw. Ed's butt hit the ground. Still, Smoke waited.

None of the drifters had drawn a gun. No law, written or otherwise, had as yet been broken. These pilgrims were in the process of learning a hard lesson of the West: you broke your own horses and killed your own snakes. And Smoke recalled a sentiment from some book he had slowly and laboriously studied. When you are in Rome live in the Roman style; when you are elsewhere live as they live elsewhere.

He couldn't remember who wrote it, but it was pretty fair advice.

The riders laughed at the ineptness of the newcomers to the West. One jerked Bountiful to him and began fondling her breasts.

Bountiful finally got it through her head that this was deadly serious, not a mild flirtation.

She began struggling just as the other pilgrims surged forward. Their butts hit the ground as quickly and as hard as Ed's had.

Smoke put the spurs to Horse and the big horse broke out of the timber. Smoke was out of the saddle before Horse was still. He dropped the reins to the ground and faced the group.

"That's it!" Smoke said quietly. He slipped the thongs from the hammers of his .44s.

Smoke glanced at Bountiful. Her bodice was torn,

exposing the creamy skin of her breasts. "Cover yourself," Smoke told her.

She pulled away from the rider and ran, sobbing, to Dana.

A rider said, "I don't know who you are, boy. But I'm gonna teach you a hard lesson."

"Oh? And what might that be?"

"To keep your goddamned nose out of other folk's business."

"If the woman had been willing," Smoke said, "I would not have interfered. Even though it takes a low-life bastard to steal another man's woman."

"Why, you . . . *pup!*" the rider shouted. "You callin' me a bastard?"

"Are you deaf?"

"I'll kill you!"

"I doubt it."

Bountiful was crying. Her husband was holding a handkerchief to a bloody nose, his eyes staring in disbelief at what was taking place.

Hunt Brook was sitting on the ground, his mouth bloody. Colton's head was ringing and his ear hurt where he'd been struck. Haywood was wondering if his eye was going to turn black. Paul was holding a hurting stomach, the hurt caused by a hard fist. The preacher looked as if he wished his wife would cover herself.

One drifter shoved Dana and Bountiful out of the way, stepping over to join his friend, facing Smoke. The other two drifters hung back, being careful to keep their hands away from their guns. The two who hung back were older, and wiser to the ways of gunslicks. And they did not like the looks of this young man with the twin Colts. There was something very familiar about him. Something calm and cold and very deadly.

"Back off, Ford," one finally spoke. "Let's ride."

"Hell with you!" the rider named Ford said, not taking his eyes from Smoke. "I'm gonna kill this punk!"

"Something tells me you ain't neither," his friend said.

"Better listen to him," Smoke advised Ford.

"Now see here, gentlemen!" Hunt said.

"Shut your gawddamned mouth!" he was told.

Hunt closed his mouth. Heavens! he thought. This just simply was not done back in Boston.

"You gonna draw, punk?" Ford said.

"After you," Smoke said quietly.

"Jesus, Ford!" the rider who hung back said. "I know who that is."

"He's dead, that's who he is," Ford said, and reached for his gun.

His friend drew at the same time.

Smoke let them clear leather before he began his lightning draw. His Colts belched fire and smoke, the slugs taking them in the chest, flinging them backward. They had not gotten off a shot.

"Smoke Jensen!" the drifter said.

"Right," Smoke said. "Now ride!"

6

The two drifters who had wisely elected not to take part in facing Smoke leaped for their horses and were gone in a cloud of galloping dust. They had not given a second glance at their dead friends.

Smoke reloaded his Colts and holstered them. Then he looked at the wagon people. The Easterners were clearly in a mild state of shock. Bountiful still had not taken the few seconds needed to repair her torn bodice. Smoke summed her up quickly and needed only one word to do so: trouble.

"My word!" Colton Spaiding finally said. "You are very quick with those guns, sir."

"I'm alive," Smoke said.

"You *killed* those men!" Hunt Brook said, getting up off the ground and brushing the dust from the seat of his britches.

"What did you want me to do?" Smoke asked, knowing where this was leading. "Kiss them?"

Hunt wiped his bloody mouth with a handkerchief. "You shall certainly need representation at the hearing. Consider me as your attorney."

Smoke looked at the man and smiled slowly. He shook his head in disbelief. "Lawyer, the nearest lawman is about three days ride from here. And I'm not even sure this area is in his jurisdiction. There won't be any hearing, Mister. It's all been settled and over and done with."

Haywood Arden was looking at Smoke through cool eyes. Smoke met the man's steady gaze.

This one will do, Smoke thought. This one doesn't have his head in the clouds. "So you're going to start up a newspaper, huh?" Smoke said.

"Yes. But how did you know that?"

"Me and Horse been sitting over there," Smoke said, jerking his head in the direction of the timber. "Listening."

"You move very quietly, sir," Mona Spalding said.

"I learned to do that. Helps in staying alive." Smoke wished Bountiful would cover up. It was mildly distracting.

"One of those ruffians called you Smoke, I believe," Hunt said. "I don't believe I ever met a man named Smoke."

Ruffians, Smoke thought. He hid his smile. Interesting choice of words to describe the drifters. "I was halfway raised by an old Mountain Man named Preacher. He hung that name on me."

The drifter called Ford broke wind in death. The shopkeeper's wife, Peg, thought as though she might faint any second. "Could someone please do something about those poor dead men?" she asked.

Dawn had given way to a bright clear mountain day. A stream of humanity had begun riding and walking toward Fontana. A tough-looking pair of miners riding mules reined up. Their eyes dismissed the Easterners and settled on Smoke. "Trouble?" one asked.

"Nothing I couldn't handle," Smoke told him.

"'Pears that way," the second miner said drily. "Ford Beechan was a good hand with a short gun." He cut his eyes toward the sprawled body of Ford.

"He wasn't as good as he thought," Smoke replied.

"'Pears that's the truth. We'll plant 'em for four bits a piece."

"Deal."

"And their pockets," the other miner spoke.

"Have at it," Smoke told them. "The pilgrims will pay."

"Now see here!" Ed said starting to protest.

"Shut up, Ed," Haywood told him. He looked at the miners. "You gentlemen may proceed with the digging."

"Talks funny," one miner remarked, getting down and tying his mule. He got a shovel from his pack animal and his partner followed suit.

"You live and work in this area, Mister Smoke?" Mona asked.

One miner dropped his shovel and his partner froze still as stone. The miner who dropped his shovel picked it up and slowly turned to face Smoke. "Smoke Jensen?"

"Yes."

"Lord God Almighty! Ford shore enuff bit off more than he could chew. Smoke Jensen. My brother was over to Uncompahgre, Smoke. Back when you cleaned it up. He said that shore was a sight to see."*

Smoke nodded his head and the miners walked off a short distance to begin their digging. "How deep?" one called.

"Respectable," Smoke told them.

They nodded and began spading the earth.

"Are you a gunfighter, Mister Smoke?" Willow asked.

"I'm a rancher and farmer, Ma'am. But I once had the reputation of being a gunhawk, yes."

"You seem so young," she observed. "Yet you talk as if it was years ago. How old were you when you became a . . . gunhawk?"

"Fourteen. Or thereabouts. I disremember at times." Smoke usually spoke acceptable English, thanks to Sally; but at times he reverted back to Preacher's dialect.

"He's kilt more'un a hundred men!" one of the miners called.

The wagon people fell silent at that news. They looked

*The Last Mountain Man

at Smoke with a mixture of horror, fascination, and revulsion in their eyes.

It was nothing new to Smoke. He had experienced that look many times in his young life. He kept his face as expressionless as his cold eyes.

Smoke cut his eyes to Bountiful. "Lady," he said, exasperation in his voice, his tone hard. "Will you please cover your tits!"

Smoke had seen the remainder of the rancher-farmers in the mountain area and then headed for home. He almost never took the same trail back to his cabin. A habit he had picked up from Preacher. A habit that had saved his life on more than one occasion.

Even though he was less than five miles from his cabin when dark slipped into the mountains, he decided not to chance the ride in. He elected to make camp and head home at first light.

He caught several small fish from a mountain stream and broiled them over a small fire. That and the remainder of Sally's bread was his supper.

Twice during the night Smoke came fully awake, certain he had heard gunshots. He knew they were far away, but he wondered about it. The last shot he heard before he drifted back to sleep came from the south, far away from Sally and the cabin.

He was up and moving out before full dawn broke. Relief filled him when he caught a glimpse of the cabin, Sally in the front yard. Smoke broke into a grin when he saw how she was dressed . . . in men's britches. His eyes mirrored approval when he noted Seven and Drifter in the corral. As he rode closer, he saw the pistol belted around her waist, and the express gun leaning against the door frame, on the outside of the cabin.

Man and wife embraced, each loving the touch and

feel of the other. With their mouths barely apart, she saw the darkness in his eyes and asked, "Trouble?"

"Some. A hell of a lot more coming, though. I'll tell you about it. You?"

"Didn't see a soul."

They kissed their love and she pushed him away, mischief in her hazel eyes. "I missed you."

"Oh? How much?"

"By the time you see to Horse and get in the house, I'll be ready to show you how much."

Fastest unsaddling and rub-down in the history of the West.

Passions cooled and sated, she lay with her head on Smoke's muscular shoulder. She listened as he told her all that had happened since he had ridden from the ranch. He left nothing out.

"Sec anyone that you knew in town? Any newcomers, I mean?"

"Some. Utah Slim. I'm sure it was him."

"I've heard you talk of him. He's good?"

"One of the best."

"Better than you?"

"No," Smoke said softly.

"Anyone else?"

"Monte Carson. He's a backshooter. Big Mamma O'Neil. Louis Longmont. Louis is all right. Just as long as no one pushes him."

"And now we have Fontana."

"For as long as it lasts, yes. The town will probably die out when the gold plays out. I hope it's soon."

"You're holding just a little something back from me, Smoke."

He hesitated. "Tilden Franklin wants you for his woman."

"I've known that for a long time. Has he made his desires public?"

"Apparently so. From now on, you're going to have to be very careful."

She lay still for a moment, silent. "We could always leave, honey."

He knew she did not wish to leave, but was only voicing their options. "I know. And we'd be running for the rest of our lives. Once you start, it's hard to stop."

In the corral, Seven nickered, the sound carrying to the house. Smoke was up and dressed in a moment, strapping on his guns and picking up a rifle. He and Sally could hear the sounds of hooves, coming hard.

"One horse," Sally noted.

"Stay inside."

Smoke stepped out the door, relaxing when he saw who it was. It was Colby's oldest boy, and he was fogging up the trail, lathering his horse.

Bob slid his horse to stop amid the dust and leaped off. "Mister Smoke," he panted. So the news had spread very fast as to Smoke's real identity.

"Bob. What's the problem?"

"Pa sent me. It's started, Mister Smoke. Some of Tilden's riders done burned out Wilbur Mason's place, over on the western ridge. Burned him flat. There ain't nothing left no where."

"Anybody hurt over there?"

"No, sir. Not bad, leastways. Mister Wilbur got burned by a bullet, but it ain't bad."

"Where are they now?"

"Mister Matlock took the kids. Pa and Ma took in Mister Wilbur and his missus."

"Where's your brother?"

"Pa sent him off to warn the others."

"Go on in the house. Sally will fix you something to eat. I'll see to your horse."

Smoke looked toward the faraway Circle TF spread. "All right, Franklin," he muttered. "If that's how you want it, get ready for it."

7

Leaving Bob Colby with Sally, Smoke saddled Drifter, the midnight-black, wolf-eyed stallion. Sally fixed him a poke of food and he stashed that in the saddlebags. He stuffed extra cartridges into a pocket of his saddlebags, and made sure his belt loops were filled. He checked his Henry repeating rifle and returned it to the saddle boot.

He kissed Sally and swung up into the saddle, thinking that it had certainly been a short homecoming. He looked at Bob, standing tall and very young beside Sally.

"You stay with Sally, Bob. Don't leave her. I'll square that with your Pa."

"Yes, sir, Mister Smoke," the boy replied.

"Can you shoot a short gun, Bob?"

"Yes, sir. But I'm better with a rifle."

"Sally will loan you a spare pistol. Wear it at all times."

"Yes, sir. What are you gonna do, Mister Smoke?"

"Try to organize the small farmers and ranchers, Bob. If we don't band together, none of us will have a chance of coming out of this alive."

Smoke wheeled Drifter and rode into the timber without looking back.

He headed across the country, taking the shortest route to Colby's spread. During his ride, Smoke spotted men staking out claims on land that had been filed on by small farmers and ranchers.

Finally he had enough of that and reined up. He stared hard at a group of men. "You have permission to dig on this land?"

"This is open land," a man challenged him.

"Wrong, mister. You're on Colby land. Filed on legally and worked. Don't be here when I get back."

But the miners and would-be miners were not going to be that easy to run off. "They told us in Fontana that this here land was open and ready for the takin'."

"Who told you that?"

"The man at Beeker's store. Some others at a saloon. They said all you folks up here were squattin' illegal-like, that if we wanted to dig, we could; and that's what we're all aimin' to do."

So that was Tilden's plan. Or at least part of it, Smoke thought. He could not fault the men seeking gold. They were greedy, but not land-greedy. Dig the gold, and get out. And if a miner, usually unarmed, was hurt, shot in any attempt to run them off, marshals would probably be called in.

Or . . . Smoke pondered, gazing from Drifter to the miners, Tilden might try to name a marshal for Fontana, hold a mock election for a sheriff. Colorado had only been a state for a little over two years, and things were still a bit confused. This county had had a sheriff, Smoke recalled, but somebody had shot him and elections had not yet been held to replace the man. And even an illegally elected sheriff would still be the law until commissioners could be sent in and matters were straightened out.

Smoke felt that was the way Tilden was probably leaning. That's the way *he* would play it if Smoke was as amoral as Tilden Franklin.

"You men have been warned," he told the miners. "This is private property. And I don't give a damn what you were told in town. And don't think the men who own the land won't fight to keep it, for you'll be wrong if you do. You've been warned."

"We got the law on our side!" a miner said, considerable heat in his voice.

"What law?"

"Hell, man!" another miner said. "They's an election in town comin' up tomorrow. Gonna be a sheriff for a brand-new town. You won't talk so goddamned tough with the law lookin' over your shoulder, I betcha."

Smoke gazed at the men. "You're all greedy fools," he said softly. "And a lot of you are going to get hurt if you continue with this trespassing. Like I said, you've been warned."

Smoke rode on, putting his back to the men, showing them his contempt.

An hour later, he was in Colby's front yard. Wilbur Mason had joined Colby by the corral at the sound of Drifter's hooves. A bloody bandage was tied around Wilbur's left arm, high up, close to the shoulder. But Smoke could tell by looking at the man that Wilbur was far from giving up. The man was angry and it showed.

"Boys," Smoke said. "You save anything, Wilbur?"

"Nothing, Matt . . . Smoke. You really the gunfighter?"

"Yes." He swung down and dropped Drifter's reins on the ground. "Do any of you know anything about an election coming up tomorrow in town?"

"No," they said together. Colby added. "What kind of election, Smoke?"

"Sheriff's election. Tilden may be a greedy bastard, but he's no fool. At the most, there is maybe twenty-five of us out here in the high country. There is probably two or three thousand men in Fontana by now. Our votes would be meaningless. And for sure, there will be Tilden men everywhere, ready to prod some of you into a fight if you show up by yourselves in town. So stay out until we can ride in in groups."

"Who's runnin' for sheriff?" Wilbur asked.

"I don't know. A TF man for sure, though. I'll check it out. Bob is staying with Sally, Colby. That all right with you?"

"Sure. He's a good boy, Smoke. And he'll stand fast facin' trouble. He's young, but he's solid."

"I know that. He said Adam was riding out to check the others . . . what's the word so far?"

"They're stayin', Smoke. Boy's asleep in the house now. He's wore out."

"I can imagine." His eyes caught movement near the house. Velvet. "Keep the women close by, Colby. This situation is shaping up to be a bad one."

"Velvet's just a kid, Smoke!" her father protested. "You don't think . . ." He refused to even speak the terrible words.

"She looks older than her years, Colby. And a lot of very rough people are moving into this area. Tilden Franklin will, I'm thinking, do anything to prod us all into something rash. He's made his intentions toward my wife public. So he's pulling out all the stops now."

Both Colby and Wilbur cursed Tilden Franklin.

Smoke waited until the men wound down. "How's your ammo situation?"

"Enough for a war," Colby said.

"Watch your backs." Smoke swung into the saddle and looked at the men. "A war? Well, that's what we've got, boys. And it's going to be a bad one. Some of us are not going to make it. I don't know about you boys, but I'm not running."

"We'll all stand," Wilbur said.

Smoke nodded. "The Indians have a saying." His eyes swept the land. "It's a good place to die."

8

Smoke touched base with as many small ranchers and farmers as he could that day, then slowly turned Drifter's head toward the town of Fontana. There was no bravado in what he was about to do, no sense of being a martyr. The area had to be checked out, and Smoke was the most likely candidate to do that.

But even he was not prepared for the sight that greeted him.

Long before he topped the crest overlooking the town of Fontana, he could see the lights. Long before the rip-roaring town came into view he could hear the noise. Smoke topped the crest and sat, looking with amazement at the sight that lay beneath and before him.

Fontana had burst at the seams, growing in all directions within three days. From where he sat, Smoke could count fifty new saloons, most no more than hurriedly erected wooden frames covered with canvas. The town had spread a half mile out in any direction, and the streets were packed with shoulder-to-shoulder humanity.

Smoke spoke to Drifter softly and the big, mean-eyed stallion moved out. Smoke stabled Drifter in the oldest of the corrals—a dozen had suddenly burst forth around the area—and filled the trough with corn.

"Stay away from him," he warned the stable boy. "If anyone but me goes into that stall, he'll kill them."

"Yes, sir," the boy said. He gazed at Smoke with adoration-filled eyes. "You really the gunfighter Smoke Jensen?"

"Yes."

"I'm on your side, Mister Smoke. Name's Billy."

Smoke extended his hand and the boy gravely shook it. Smoke studied the boy in the dim lantern-light of the stable. Ragged clothes, shoes with the soles tied so that they would not flop.

"How old are you, Billy?"

"Eleven, sir."

"Where are your folks?"

"Dead for more years than I can remember."

"I don't recall seeing you before. You been here long?"

"No, sir. I come in a couple weeks ago. I been stayin' down south of here, workin' in a stable. But the man who owned it married him a grass widow and her kids took over my job. I drifted. Ol' grump that owns this place gimme a job. I sleep here."

Smoke grinned at the "ol' grump" bit. He handed the boy a double eagle. "Come light, you get yourself some clothes and shoes."

Billy looked at the twenty-dollar gold piece. "Wow!" he said.

Smoke led the boy to Drifter's stall and opened the gate, stepping inside. He motioned the boy in after him. "Pet him, Billy."

Billy cautiously petted the midnight-black stallion. Drifter stopped eating for a moment and swung his big head, looking at him through those yellow, killer-cold, wolf-like eyes. Then he resumed munching at the corn.

"He likes you," Smoke told the boy. "You'll be all right with him. Anyone comes in here and tries to hurt you, just get in the stall with Drifter. You won't be harmed."

The boy nodded and stepped back out with Smoke.

"You be careful, Mister Smoke," he warned. "I don't say much to people, but I listen real good. I hear things."

They walked to the wide doors at the front of the stable. "What do you hear, Billy?"

Several gunshots split the torch- and lantern-lit night air of Fontana. A woman's shrill and artificial-sounding laughter drifted to man and boy. A dozen pianos, all playing different tunes, created a confusing, discordant cacophony in the soft air of summer in the high-up country.

"Some guy name of Monte Carson is gonna be elected the sheriff. Ain't no one runnin' agin him"

"I've heard of him. He's a good hand with a gun."

"Better than you?" There was doubt in Billy's voice at that.

"No," Smoke said.

"The boss of this area, that Mister Tilden Franklin, is supposed to have a bunch of gunhands comin' to be deputies."

"Who are they?"

"I ain't heard."

"What have you heard about me?"

"I heard two punchers talkin' yesterday afternoon, over by a tent saloon. Circle TF punchers. But I think they're more than just cowboys. They wore their guns low and tied down."

Very observant boy, Smoke thought.

"If they can angle you in for a backshoot, they'd do it. Talk is, though, this Mister Franklin is gonna let the law handle you. Legal-like, you know?"

"Yeah." Smoke patted the boy's shoulder. "You take good care of Drifter, Billy. And keep your ears clean and open. I'll check you later."

"Yes, sir, Mister Smoke."

Smoke stepped out of the stable and turned to his left. His right hand slipped the thong off the Colt's hammer. Smoke was dressed in black whipcord trousers, black shirt, and dark hat. His spurs jingled as he walked, his boots kicking up little pockets of dust as he headed for the short boardwalk that ran in front of Beeker's General Store, a saloon, and the gunsmith's shop. Smoke's eyes were in constant motion, noting and retaining everything he spotted. Night seemed to color into day as he approached the boom-town area.

A drunk lurched out from between two tents, almost colliding with Smoke.

"Watch where you're goin,' boy," the miner mush-mouthed at him.

Smoke ignored him and walked on.

"A good time comes reasonable," a heavily rouged and slightly overweight woman said, offering her charms to Smoke.

"I'm sure," Smoke told her. "But I'm married."

"Ain't you the lucky one?" she said, and stepped back into the shadows of her darkened tent.

He grinned and walked on.

Smoke walked past Beeker's store and glanced in. The man had hired more help and was doing a land office business, a fixed smile on his greedy, weasel face. His hatchet-faced wife was in constant motion, moving around the brightly lighted store, her sharp eyes darting left and right, looking for thieving hands.

Other than her own, Smoke mentally noted.

He walked on, coming to the swinging doors of the saloon. Wild laughter and hammering piano music greeted his ears. It was not an altogether offensive sound. The miners, as a whole, were not bad people. They were here to dig and chip and blast and hammer the rock, looking for gold. In their free time, most would drink and gamble and whore the night away.

Smoke almost stepped inside the saloon, changing his mind just at the very last moment. He stepped back away from the doors and walked on.

He crossed the street and stepped into Louis

Longmont's place. The faro and monte and draw and stud poker tables were filled; dice clicked and wheels spun, while those with money in their hands stared and waited for Lady Luck to smile on them.

Most of the time she did not.

Smoke walked to the bar, shoved his way through, and ordered a beer.

He took his beer and crossed the room, dodging drunks as they staggered past. He leaned against a bracing and watched the action.

"Smoke." The voice came from his left.

Smoke turned and looked into the face of Louis Longmont. "Louis," he acknowledged. "Another year, another boom town, hey?"

"They never change. I don't know why I stay with it. I certainly don't need the money."

Smoke knew that was no exaggeration on the gambler's part. The gambler owned a large ranch up in Wyoming Territory. He owed several businesses in San Francisco, and he owned a hefty chunk of a railroad. It was a mystery to many why Louis stayed with the hard life he had chosen.

"Then get out of it, Louis," Smoke suggested.

"But of course," Louis responded with a smile. His eyes drifted to Smoke's twin Colts. "Just as you got out of gunfighting."

Smoke smiled. "I put them away for several years, Louis. Had gold not been found, or had I chosen a different part of the country to settle, I probably would never have picked them up again."

"Lying to others is bad enough, my young friend, But lying to one's self is unconscionable. Can you look at me and tell me you never, during those stale years, missed the dry-mouthed moment before the draw? The challenge of facing and besting those miscreants who would kill you or others who seek a better and more peaceful way? The so-called loneliness of the hoot-owl trail? I think not, Mister Jensen. I think not."

There was nothing for Smoke to say, for Louis was right. He had missed those death-close moments. And Sally knew it too. Smoke had often caught her watching him, silently looking at him as he would stand and gaze toward the mountains, or as his eyes would follow the high flight of an eagle.

"Your silence tells all, my friend," Louis said. "I know only too well."

"Yeah," Smoke said, looking down into his beer mug. "I guess I'd better finish my beer and ride. I don't want to be the cause of any trouble in your place, Louis."

"Trouble, my friend, is soniething I have never shied away from. You're safer here than in any other place in this woebegotten town. If I can help it, you will not be backshot in my place."

And again, Smoke knew the gambler was telling the truth. Smoke and Louis had crossed trails a dozen times over the years. The man had taken a liking to the boy when Smoke was riding with the Mountain Man Preacher. In the quieter moments of his profession, Louis had shown Smoke the tricks of his gambler's trade. Louis had realized that Smoke possessed a keen intelligence, and Louis liked those people who tried to better themselves, as Smoke had always done.

They had become friends.

Hard hoofbeats sounded on the dirt street outside the gambling tent. Smoke looked at Louis.

"About a dozen riders," Smoke said.

"Probably the 'deputies' Tilden Franklin called in from down Durango way. They'll be hardcases, Smoke."

"Is this election legal?"

"Of course not. But it will be months before the state can send anyone in to verify it or void it. By then, Franklin will have gotten his way. Initial reports show the gold, what there is of it, assays high. But the lode is a narrow one. I suspect you already knew that."

"I've know about the vein for a long time, Louis. I never wanted gold."

A quick flash of irritation crossed Louis's face. "It is well and good to shun wealth while one is young, Smoke. But one had best not grow old without some wealth."

"One can have wealth without riches, Louis," Smoke countered.

The gambler smiled. "I believe Preacher's influence was strong on you, young man."

"There could have been no finer teacher in all the world, Louis."

"Is he alive, Smoke?"

"I don't know. If so, he'd be in his eighties. I like to think he's still alive. But I just don't know."

Louis knew, but he elected to remain silent on the subject. At least for the time being.

Boots and jangling spurs sounded on the raw boards in front of Louis's place. And both Louis and Smoke knew the time for idle conversation had passed.

They knew before either man sighted the wearers of those boots and spurs.

The first rider burst into the large tent.

"I don't know him," Louis said. "You?"

"Unfortunately. He's one of Tilden's gunhands. Calls himself Tay. I ran into him when I was riding with Preacher. Back then he was known as Carter. I heard he was wanted for murder back in Arkansas."

"Sounds like a delightful fellow," Louis said drily.

"He's a bully. But don't sell him short. He's hell with a short gun."

Louis smiled. "Better than you, Smoke?" he asked, a touch of humor in the question.

"No one is better than me, Louis," Smoke said, in one of his rare moments of what some would call arrogance; others would call it merely stating a proven fact.

Louis's chuckle held no mirth. "I believe I am better, my friend."

"I hope we never have to test that out of anger, Louis."

"We won't," Louis replied. "But let's do set up some cans and make a small wager someday."

"You're on."

The gunfighter Tay turned slowly, his eyes drifting first to Louis, then to Smoke.

"Hello, punk!" Tay said, his voice silencing the piano player and hushing the hubbub of voices in the gaming tent.

"Are you speaking to me, you unshaven lout?" Louis asked.

"Naw," Tay said. The leather thongs that secured his guns were off, left and right. "Pretty boy there."

"You're a fool," Smoke said softly, his voice carrying to Tay, overheard by all in the gaming room.

"I'm gonna kill you for that!" Tay said.

Those men and women seated between Tay and Smoke cleared out, moving left and right.

"I hope you have enough in your pockets to bury you," Smoke said.

Tay's face flushed, both hands hovering over the butt of his guns.

He snarled at Smoke.

Smoke laughed at him.

"A hundred dollars on the Circle TF rider," a man seated at a table said.

"You're on," Louis said taking the wager. "Gentlemen," he said to Smoke and Tay. "Bets are down."

Tay's eyes were shiny, but his hands were steady over his guns.

Smoke held his beer mug in his left hand.

"Draw, goddamn you!" Tay shouted.

"After you," Smoke replied. "I always give a sucker a break whenever possible."

Tay grabbed for his guns.

9

"Your behavior the other day was disgusting!" Ralph Morrow would not let up on his wife. "Those men are dead because of you. You do realize that, don't you?"

Bountiful tossed her head, her blond curls bouncing around her beautiful face. Her lips were set in a pout. "I did nothing," she said defending her actions.

"My god, I married an animal!" Ralph said, disgust in his voice. "Can't you see you're a minister's wife?"

"I'm beginning to see a lot of things, Ralph. One of which is I made a mistake."

"In coming out West? Did we have a choice, Bountiful? After your disgraceful behavior in Ohio, I'm very lucky the Church even gave me another chance."

She waved that off. "No, Ralph, not that. In my marrying such a pompous wee-wee!"

Ralph flushed and balled his fists. "You take that back!" he yelled at her.

"You take that back!" she repeated mimicking him scornfully. "My God, Ralph! You're such a flummox!"

Man and wife were several miles from the town of Fontana. They were on the banks of a small creek. Ralph sat down on the bank and refused to look at her. A short distance away at their camp, the others tried without much success not to listen to their friends quarrel.

"They certainly are engaged in a plethora of flapdoodle," Haywood observed.

"I feel sorry for him," Dana said.

"I don't," Ed said. "It's his own fault he's such a sissypants."

All present looked at Ed in the dancing flames of the fire. If there was a wimp among them, it was Ed. Ed had found a June bug in his blankets on the way West and, from his behavior one might have thought he'd discovered a nest of rattlers. It had taken his wife a full fifteen minutes to calm him down.

Haywood sat on a log and puffed his Meerschaum. Of them all, Haywood was the only person who knew the true story about Ralph Morrow. And if the others wanted to think him a sissy-pants . . . well, that was their mistake. But Haywood had to admit that, from all indications, when Ralph had fully accepted Christ into his life, he had gone a tad overboard.

If anyone had taken the time to just look at Ralph, they would have noticed the rippling boxer's muscles; the broad, hard, flat-knuckled fists; the slightly crooked nose. It had always amazed Haywood how so many people could look at something, but never see it.

Haywood suppressed a giggle. Come to think of it, he mused, Ralph *did* sort of act a big milquetoast.

But it should be interesting when Ralph finally got a belly full of it.

Smoke cleared leather before Tay got his pistols free of their holsters. Smoke drew with such blinding speed, drawing, cocking, firing, not one human eye in the huge tent could follow the motion.

The single slug struck Tay in the center of the chest and knocked him backward. He struggled up on one elbow and looked at Smoke through eyes that were already glazing over. He tried to lift his free empty hand; the hand was so heavy he thought his gun was in it. He began squeezing his trigger finger. He was curious about the lack of noise and recoil.

Then he fell back onto the raw. rough-hewn board floor and was curious no more.

"Maybe we won't set up those tin cans," Louis muttered, just loud enough for Smoke to hear it.

"Tie him across a saddle and take him back to Tilden Franklin," Smoke said, his voice husky due to the low-hanging cigarette and cigar smoke in the crowded gaming tent. "Unless some of you boys want to pick up where Tay left off."

The riders appeared to be in a mild state of shock. They were all, to a man, used to violence; that was their chosen way of life. They had all, to a man, been either witnesses to or participants in stand-up gunfights, back-shoots, and ambushes. And they had all heard of the young gunslick Smoke Jensen. But since none had ever seen the man in action, they had tended to dismiss much of what they had heard as so much pumped-up hoopla.

Until this early evening in the boom town of Fontana, in Louis Longmont's gaming tent.

"Yes, sir, Mister Jensen," one young TF rider said. "I mean," he quickly corrected himself, "I'll sure tie him across his saddle."

Until this evening, the young TF rider had fancied himself a gunhawk. Now he just wanted to get on his pony and ride clear out of the area. But he was afraid the others would laugh at him if he did that.

Smoke eased the hammer down with his thumb. A very audible sigh went up inside the tent with that action. There was visible relaxing of stomach muscles when Smoke holstered the deadly Colt.

Smoke looked at the young puncher who had spoken. "Come here," he said.

The young man, perhaps twenty at the most, quickly crossed the room to face Smoke. He was scared, and looked it.

"What's your name?" Smoke asked.

"Pearlie."

"You're on the wrong side, Pearlie. You know that?"

"Mister Smoke," Pearlie said in a low tone, so only Smoke and Louis could hear. "The TF brand can throw two hundred or more men at you. And I ain't kiddin'. Now, you're tough as hell and snake-quick, but even you can't fight that many men."

"You want to bet your life, Pearlie?" Louis asked him. The man's voice was low-pitched and his lips appeared not to move at all.

Pearlie cut his eyes at the gambler. "I ain't got no choice, Mister Longmont."

"Yes, you do," Smoke said.

"I'm listenin'."

"I need a hand I can trust. I think that's you, Pearlie."

The young man's jaw dropped open. "But I been ridin' for the TF brand!"

"How much is he paying you?"

"Sixty a month."

"I'll give you thirty and found."

Pearlie smiled. "You're serious!"

"Yes, I am. Have you the sand in you to make a turn-around in your life?"

"Give me a chance, Mister Smoke."

"You've got it. Are you quick with that Colt?"

"Yes, sir. But I ain't nearabouts as quick as you."

"Have you ever used it before?"

"Yes, sir."

"Would you stand by me and my wife and friends, Pearlie?"

"'Til I soak up so much lead I can't stand, Mister Smoke."

Smoke cut his eyes at Louis. The man smiled and nodded his head slightly.

"You're hired, Pearlie."

"Pearlie did *what*?" Tilden screamed.

Clint repeated his statement, standing firm in front of the boss. Clint was no gunhawk. He was as good as or better with a short gun than most men, but had never fancied himself a gunfighter. He knew horses, he knew cattle, and he could work and manage men. There was no backup in Clint. He had fought Indians, outlaws, nesters, and other ranchers during his years with Tilden Franklin, and while he didn't always approve of everything Tilden did, Clint rode for the brand. And that was that.

"Goddamned, no-good little pup!" Tilden spat out the words. He lifted his eyes and stared into his foreman's eyes. "This can't be tolerated, Clint."

Clint felt a slight sick feeling in his stomach. He knew what was coming next. "No, sir. You're right."

"Drag him!" Tilden spat the horrible words.

"Yes, sir." Clint turned away and walked out of the room. He stood on the porch for a long moment, breathing deeply. He appeared to be deep in thought.

Louis shut the gaming room down early that evening. And with Louis Longmont, no one uttered any words of protest. They simply got up and left. And neither did anyone take any undue umbrage, for all knew Louis's games were straight-arrow honest.

He closed the wooden door to his gaming-room tent, extinguished most of the front lights, and set a bottle of fine scotch on the table.

"I know you're not normally a hard-drinking man, my young friend," Louis said, as he poured two tumblers full of the liquid. "But savor the taste of the Glenlivet. It's the finest made."

Smoke picked up the bottle and read the label. "Was this stuff made in 1824?"

Louis smiled. "Oh, no. That's when the distillery was founded. Old George Smith knew his business, all right."

"Knew?"

"Yes. He died six—no, seven years ago. He was on the Continent at the time."

Smoke sipped the light scotch. It was delicate, yet mellow. It had a lightness that was quite pleasing.

"I had been to a rather obscure place called Monte Carlo." Louis sniffed his tumbler before sipping.

"I never heard of that place."

"I own part of the casino," Louis said softly.

"Make lots of money?"

Louis's reply was a smile.

It silently spoke volumes.

"Prior to that, I was enjoying the theater in Warsaw. It was there I was introduced to Madame Modjeska. It was quite the honor. She is one of the truly fine actresses in the world today."

"You're talking over my head, Louis."

"Madame Mudrzejeweski."

"Did you just swallow a bug, Louis?"

Louis laughed. "No. She shortened her name to Modjeska. She is here in America now. Performing Shakespeare in New York, I believe. She also tours."

Smoke sipped his scotch and kept his mouth shut.

"When I finally retire, I believe I shall move to New York City. It's quite a place, Smoke. Do you have any desires at all to see it?"

"No," Smoke said gently.

"Pity," the gambler said. "It is really a fascinating place. Smoke?"

The young rancher-farmer-gunfighter lifted his eyes to meet Louis's.

"You should travel, Smoke. Educate yourself. Your wife is, I believe, an educated woman. Is she not?"

"School teacher."

"Ah . . . yes. I thought your grammar, most of the time, had improved since last we spoke. Smoke . . . get out while you have the time and opportunity to do so."

"No."

"Pearlie was right, Smoke. There are too many against you."

Smoke took a small sip of his scotch. "I am not alone in this, Louis. There are others."

"Many of whom will not stand beside you when it gets bad. But I think you know that."

"But some of them will, Louis. And bear this in mind: we control the high country."

"Yes, there is that. Tell me, your wife has money, correct?"

"Yes. I think she's wealthy."

"You *think*?"

"I told you, Louis, I'm not that interested in great wealth. My father is lying atop thousands and thousands of dollars of gold."

Louis smiled. "And there are those who would desecrate his grave for a tenth of it," he reminded the young man.

"I'm not one of them."

Louis sighed and drained his tumbler, refilling it from the bottle of scotch. "Smoke, it's 1878. The West is changing. The day of the gunfighter, men like you and me, is coming to a close. There is still a great rowdy element moving westward, but by and large, the people who are now coming here are demanding peace. Soon there will he no place for men like us."

"And? So?"

"What are you going to do then?"

"I'll be right out there on the Sugarloaf, Louis, ranching and farming and raising horses. And," he said with a smile, "probably raising a family of my own."

"Not if you're dead, Smoke." The gambler's words were softly offered.

Smoke drained his tumbler and stood up, tall and straight and heavily muscled. "The Sugarloaf is my home, Louis. Sally's and mine. And here is where we'll stay. Peacefully working the land, or buried in it."

He walked out the door.

10

Smoke made his Spartan camp some five miles outside of Fontana. With Drifter acting as guard, Smoke slept soundly. He had sent Pearlie to his ranch earlier that night, carrying a hand-written note introducing him to Sally. One of the older ranchers in the area, a man who was aligned on neither side, had told Smoke that Pearlie was a good boy who had just fallen in with the wrong crowd, that Pearlie had spoken with him a couple of times about leaving the Circle TF.

Smoke did not worry about Pearlie making any ungentlemanly advances toward Sally, for she would shoot him stone dead if he tried.

Across the yard from the cabin, Smoke and Sally had built a small bunkhouse, thinking of the day when they would need extra hands. Pearlie would sleep there.

Smoke bathed—very quickly—in a small, rushing creek and changed clothes: a gray shirt, dark trousers. He drank the last of his pot of coffee, extinguished the small fire, and saddled Drifter.

He turned Drifter's head toward Fontana, but angling slightly north of the town, planning on coming in from a different direction.

It would give those people he knew would be watching him something to think about.

About half a mile from Fontana, Smoke came up on a small series of just-begun buildings; tents lay behind the construction site. He sat his horse and looked at Preacher Morrow swinging an axe. The preacher had removed his shirt and was clad only in his short-sleeve undershirt. Smoke's eyes took in the man's heavy musculature and the fluid way he handled the axe.

A lot more to him than meets the eyes, Smoke thought. A whole lot more.

Then Smoke's eyes began to inspect the building site. Not bad, he thought. Jackson's big store across the road, and the offices of the others in one long building on the opposite side of the road. The cabins would be behind the offices, while Jackson and his wife and brother would live in quarters behind but connected to the store.

Smoke's eyes caught movement to his left.

"Everything meet with your approval, Mister Jensen?"

Smoke turned Drifter toward the voice. Ed Jackson. "Looks good. The preacher's a pretty good hand with an axe, wouldn't you say?"

"Oh . . . him? 'Bout the only thing he's good at. He's a sissy."

Smoke smiled, thinking: Shopkeeper, I hope you never push that preacher too hard, 'cause he'll damn sure break you like a match stick.

Hunt, Colton, Haywood, and their wives walked out to where Smoke sat Drifter. He greeted the men and took his hat off to the ladies. Bountiful was not with the group and Smoke was grateful for that. The woman was trouble.

Then he wondered where the shopkeeper's brother was. He wondered if Bountiful and Paul might be . . .

He sighed and put his hat back on, pushing those thoughts from him. He dismounted and ground-reined Drifter.

"Going into town to vote, Mister Jensen?" Hunt asked.

"No point in it. One-sided race from what I hear."

"Oh, no!" Colton told him. "We have several running for mayor, half a dozen running for sheriff, and two running for city judge."

"Tilden Franklin's men will win, believe me."

"Mister Franklin seems like a very nice person to me," Ed said, adding, "not that I've ever met the gentleman, of course. Just from what I've heard about him."

"Yeah, he's a real prince of a fellow," Smoke said, with enough sarcasm in his voice to cover hotcakes thicker than molasses. "Why just a few days ago he was nice enough to send his boys up into the high country to burn out a small rancher-farmer named Wilbur Mason. Shot Wilbur and scattered his wife and kids. He's made his boast that he'll either run me out or kill me, and then he'll have my wife. Yeah, Tilden is a sweet fellow, all right."

"I don't believe that!" Ed said, puffing up.

Smoke's eyes narrowed and his face hardened. Haywood looked at the young man and both saw and felt danger emanating from him. He instinctively put an arm around his wife's shoulders and drew her to him.

Smoke said, his eyes boring into Ed's eyes, "Shopkeeper, I'll let that slide this one time. But let me give you a friendly piece of advice." He cut his eyes, taking in, one at a time, all the newcomers to the West. "You folks came here from the East. You do things differently back East. I didn't say better, just different. Out here, you call a man a liar, you'd better be ready to do one of two things: either stand and slug it out with him or go strap on iron.

"Now you all think about that, and you'll see both the right and wrong in it. I live here. Me and my wife been here for better than three years. We hacked a home out of the wilderness and made it nice. We fought the hard winters, Indians a few times, and we know the folks in this area. You people, on the other hand, just come in here. You don't know nobody, yet you're going to call me a liar. See what I mean, Shopkeeper?

"Now the wrong of it is this: there are bullies who take advantage of the code, so to speak. Those types of trash will prod a fellow into a fight, just because they think that to fight is manly, or some such crap as that. Excuse my language, ladies. But the point is, you got to watch your mouth out here. The graveyards are full of people ignorant of the ways of the West."

Ed Jackson blustered and sweated, but he did not offer to apologize.

He won't make it, Smoke thought. Someone will either run him out or kill him. And mankind will have lost nothing by his passing.

"Why is Franklin doing these things, Mister Jensen?" Haywood asked.

"Smoke. Call me Smoke. Why? Because he wants to be king. Perhaps he's a bit mad. I don't know. I do know he hates farmers and small ranchers. As for me, well, I have the Sugarloaf and he wants its."

"The Sugarloaf?" Hunt asked.

"My valley. Part of it, that is."

"Are you suggesting the election is rigged?" Haywood inquired.

"No. I'm just saying that Tilden's people will win, that's all."

"Has Mister Franklin offered to buy any of the farmers' or ranchers' holdings?" Hunt asked.

Smoke laughed. "Buy? Lawyer, men like Tilden don't offer to buy. They just run people out. Did cruel kings offer to buy lands they desired? No, they just took it, by force."

Preacher Morrow had ceased his work with the axe and had joined the group. His eyes searched for his wife and, not finding her present, glowered at Ed Jackson.

Maybe I was right, Smoke thought.

"Are you a Christian, Mister Jensen?" he asked, finally taking his eyes from the shopkeeper.

Bad blood between those two, Smoke thought. "I been to church a few times over the years. Sally and me was married in a proper church."

"Have you been baptized, sir?"

"In a little crick back in Missouri, yes, sir, I was."

"Ah, wonderful! Perhaps you and your wife will attend services just as soon as I get my church completed?"

"I knew a lay preacher back in Missouri preached on a stump, Preacher Morrow. Look around you, sir. You ever in all your life seen a more beautiful cathedral? Look at them mountains yonder. Got snow on 'em year-round. See them flowers scattered around, those blue and purple ones? Those are columbines. Some folks call them Dove Flowers. See the trees? Pine and fir and aspen and spruce and red cedar. What's wrong with preaching right in the middle of what God created?"

"You're right, of course, sir. I'm humbled. You're a strange man, Mister Jensen. And I don't mean that in any ugly way."

"I didn't take it in such a way. I know what you mean. The West is a melting pot of people, Preacher. Right there in that town of Fontana, there's a man named Louis Longmont. He's got degrees from places over in Europe, I think. He owns ranches, pieces of railroads, and lots of other businesses. But he follows the boom towns as a gambler. He's been decorated by kings and queens. But he's a gambler, and a gunfighter. My wife lives in a cabin up in the mountains. But she's worth as much money as Tilden Franklin, probably more. She's got two or three degrees from fancy colleges back East, and she's traveled in Europe and other places. Yet she married me.

"I know scouts for the Army who used to be college professors. I know cowboys who work for thirty and found who can stand and quote William Shakespeare for hours. And them that listen, most of them, can't even read or write. I know Negroes who fought for the North and white men who wore the Gray who now work side by side and who would die for each other. Believe it."

"And you, Smoke?" Hunt asked. "What about you?"

"What about me? I raise cattle and horses and farm. I mind my own business, if people will let me. And I'll harm no man who isn't set on hurting me or mine. We need people like you folks out here. We need some stability. Me and Sally are gonna have kids one day, and I'd like for them to grow up around folks like you." He cut his eyes to Ed Jackson. "Most of you, that is." The store-owner caught the verbal cut broadside and flushed. "But for a while yet, it's gonna be rough and rowdy out here." Smoke pointed. "Ya'll see that hill yonder? That's Boot Hill. The graveyard. See that fancy black wagon with them people walking along behind it, going up that hill? That wagon is totin' a gunhawk name of Tay. He braced me last night in Louis's place. He was a mite slow."

"You killed yet *another* man?" Ed blurted out.

"I've killed about a hundred men," Smoke said. "Not counting Indians. I killed twenty, I think, one day up on the Uncompahgre. That was back in '74, I think. A year later I put lead into another twenty or so over in Idaho, town name of Bury. Bury don't exist no more. I burned it down.*

"People, listen to me. Don't leave this area. We got to have some people like you to put down roots, to stay when the gold plays out. And it will, a lot sooner than most folks realize. And," Smoke said with a sigh, "we're gonna need a doctor and nurse and preacher around here . . . the preacher for them that the doc can't patch up."

The newcomers were looking at Smoke, a mixture of emotions in their eyes. They all wanted for him to speak again.

*Return of the Mountain Man

"Now I'm heading into town, people," Smoke said. "And I'm not going in looking for trouble. But I assure you all, it will come to me. If you doubt that, come with me for an hour. Put aside your axes and saws and ride in with me. See for yourself."

"I'll go with you," Preacher Morrow said. "Just let me bathe in the creek first."

All the men agreed to go.

Should be interesting, Smoke thought. For he planned to take Preacher Morrow into Louis's place. Not that Smoke thought the man would see anything he hadn't already seen . . . several times before, in his past.

11

Ralph Morrow was the first one back to where Smoke stood beside Drifter. "Where is your wife, Preacher?"

The man cut his eyes at Smoke. Smoke could see the faded scars above the man's eyes.

A boxer, Smoke thought. He's fought many times in the ring.

"Walking along the creek over there," he said, pointing. "I suppose she's safe. From hostiles," he added, a touch of bitterness in his voice.

"I'd think so. This close to town. Preacher? Anytime you want to talk, I'm available."

The man looked away, stubbornness setting his chin.

Smoke said no more. The others soon joined them and they made their way into Fontana. The newspaper man carried a note pad and had a breastpocket full of pencils. Smoke stabled Drifter with Billy and smiled at the boy. Billy was dressed in new britches and shirt, boots on his feet. "Give him some corn, Billy."

"Yes, sir. I heard that was some show last night over to Longmont's place."

Smoke nodded. "He was a tad slow."

Billy grinned and led Drifter into his stall, the big outlaw stallion allowing the boy to lead him docilely.

"What a magnificent animal," Colton remarked, looking at Drifter.

"Killed the last man who owned him," Smoke said.

The doctor muttered something under his breath that Smoke could not quite make out. But he had a pretty good idea what it was. He grinned.

The town was jammed with people, bursting at its newly sewn seams. American flags were hung and draped all over the place. Notices that Tilden Franklin was going to speak were stuck up, it seemed, almost everywhere one looked.

"Your fine man is going to make a speech, Jackson," Smoke said to the shopkeeper, keeping his face bland. "You sure won't want to miss that."

"I shall make every attempt to attend that event," Ed announced, a bit stiffly.

Several of the miners who had been in Louis's place when Tay was shot walked past Smoke, greeting him with a smile. Smoke acknowledged the greetings.

"You seem to have made yourself well known in a short time, Smoke," Hunt said.

"I imagine them that spoke was some that made money betting on the outcome of the shooting," the lawyer was informed.

"Barbaric!"

"Not much else to do out here, Lawyer. Besides, you should see the crowds that gather for a hanging. Folks will come from fifty miles out for that. Bring picnic lunches and make a real pleasurable day out of it."

The lawyer refused to respond to that. He simply shook his head and looked away.

The town was growing by the hour. Where once no more than fifty people lived, there now roamed some five thousand. Tents of all sizes and descriptions were going up every few minutes.

Smoke looked at Ed Jackson. "I'm not trying to pry

into your business, Shopkeeper, so don't take it that way. But do you have any spare money for workmen?"

"I might. Why do you ask?"

"You could get your store up and running in a few days if you were to hire some people to help you. A lot of those men out there would do for a grubstake."

"A what?"

"A grubstake. You give them equipment and food, and they'll help you put up your building and offer you a percentage of what they take out of the ground. I'd think about it—all of you."

"I thought you didn't care for me, Mister Jensen," the shopkeeper said.

"I don't, very much. But maybe it's just because we got off on the wrong foot. I'm willing to start over."

Ed did not reply. He pursed his perch-mouthed lips in silence. "I thank you for your suggestion," he said, a moment later. "I shall . . . give you a discount on your first purchases in my store for it."

"Why, thank you very much," Smoke replied, a smile on his lips. "That's right generous of you, Ed."

"Yes," Ed said smugly. "It is, isn't it?"

The other men turned their heads to hide their smiles.

"How do I go about doing that?" Ed questioned.

"Just ask somebody," Smoke told him. "Find a man who is afoot rather than riding. Find one carrying everything on his back or pushing a cart. You'll probably get some refusals, but eventually you'll find your people."

Ed, Colton, Hunt, and Haywood walked off into the pushing, shoving hubbub of humanity, leaving Smoke and Preacher Morrow standing alone.

"You have no spare money, Preacher?" Smoke asked.

Ralph's smile was genuine. "Find me one who does have spare money. But that isn't it. I want to build as much of my church as possible myself. It's . . . a personal thing."

"I understand. I'm a pretty good hand with an axe myself. I'll give you a hand later on."

Ralph looked at the gunfighter. "I do not understand you, Mister Jensen."

Before Smoke could reply, the hard sounds of drumming hooves filled the air. "Tilden Franklin," Smoke said. "The king has arrived."

"Pearlie!" Sally called. "Come take a break and have some coffee. And I made doughnuts."

"Bearsign!" the young puncher shouted. "Yes, ma'am. I'm on my way."

Sally smiled at that. She had learned that cowboys would ride a hundred miles for home-cooked doughnuts . . . something they called bearsign. It had taken Sally a time to learn why they were called bearsign. When she finally learned the why of it, she thought it positively disgusting.

"You mean! . . ." she had puffed to Smoke. "These people are equating my doughnuts to . . . that's disgusting!"

"Bear tracks, Sally," Smoke had told her. "Not what you're thinking."

She had refused to believe him.

And Smoke never would fully explain.

More fun letting her make up her own mind.

"My husband must have thought a lot of you, Pearlie," she said, watching the puncher eat, a doughnut in each hand. "He's not normally a trusting person."

"He's a fine man, Miss Sally," Pearlie said around a mouthful of bearsign. "And got more cold nerve than any man I ever seen."

"Can we win this fight, Pearlie?"

The cowboy pushed his battered hat back on his head. He took a slug of coffee and said, "You want a straight-out honest answer, ma'am?"

"That's the only way, Pearlie."

Pearlie hesitated. "It'll be tough. Right off, I'd say the odds are slim to none. But there's always a chance. All depends on how many of them nester friends of yourn will stand and fight when it gets down to the hardrock."

"A few of them will."

"Yes'um. That's what I mean." He stuffed his mouth full of more bearsign.

"Matlock will, and so will Wilbur. I'm pretty sure Colby will stand firm. I don't know about the others."

"You see, ma'am, the problem is this: them folks you just named ain't gunhands. Mister Tilden can mount up to two hundred riders. The sheriff is gonna be on his side, and all them gun-slingin' deputies he'll name. Your husband is pure hell with a gun—pardon my language—but one man just can't do 'er all."

Sally smiled at that. She alone, of all those involved, knew what her husband was capable of doing. But, she thought with a silent sigh, Pearlie was probably right . . . it would be unreasonable to expect one man to do it all.

Even such a man as Smoke.

"What does Mister Franklin want, Pearlie . . . and why?"

"I ain't sure of the why of it all, ma'am. As for me, I'd be satisfied with a little bitty part of what he has. He's got so much holdin's I'd bet he really don't know all that he has. What does he want?" The cowboy paused, thinking. "He wants everything, ma'am. Everything he sees. I've overheard some of his older punchers talk about what they done to get them things for Tilden Franklin. I wouldn't want to say them things in front of you, ma'am. I'll just say I'm glad I didn't have no part in them. And I'm real glad Mister Smoke gimme a job with ya'll 'fore it got too late for me."

"You haven't been with the Circle TF long, then, Pearlie?"

"It would have been a year this fall, ma'am. I drifted down here from the Bitterroot. I . . . kinda had a cloud hangin' over me, I guess you'd say."

"You want to talk about it?"

"Ain't that much to say, ma'am. I always been mighty quick with a short gun. Not nearabouts as quick as your man, now, but tolerable quick. I was fifteen and workin' a full man's job down in Texas. That was six year ago. Or seven. I disremember exact. I rode into town with the rest of the boys for a Saturday night spree. There was some punchers from another spread there. One of 'em braced me, called me names. Next thing I recall, that puncher was layin' on his back with a bullet hole in his chest. From my gun. Like I said, I've always been mighty quick. Well, the sheriff he told me to light a shuck. I got my back up at that, 'cause that other puncher slapped leather first. I tole the sheriff I wasn't goin' nowheres. I didn't mean to back that sheriff into no corner, but I reckon that's what I done. That sheriff was a bad one, now. He had him a rep that was solid bad. He tole me I had two choices in the matter: ride out or die.

"Well, ma'am, I tole him I didn't backpaddle for no man, not when I was in the right. He drew on me. I kilt him."

Pearlie paused and took a sip of coffee. Sally refilled his cup and gave him another doughnut.

"Whole place was quiet as midnight in a graveyard," Pearlie continued. It seemed to Sally that he was relieved to be talking about it, as if he had never spoken fully of the events. "I holstered my gun and stepped out onto the boardwalk. Then it hit me what I'd done. I was fifteen years old and in one whale of a pickle. I'd just killed two men in less than ten minutes. One of them a lawman. I was on the hoot-owl trail sure as you're born.

"I got my horse and rode out. Never once looked back. Over in New Mexico two bounty hunters braced me outside a cantina one night. I reckon someone buried both of them next day. I don't rightly know, seein' as how I didn't stick around for the services. Then I was up in Utah when this kid braced me. He was lookin' for a rep, I guess. He didn't make it," Pearlie added softly. "Then the kid's brothers come a-foggin' after me. I put lead in both of them. One died, so I heard later on.

"I drifted on over into Nevada. By this time, I had bounty hunters really lookin' for me. I avoided them, much as I could. Changed my name to Pearlie. I headed north, into the Bitterroot Range. Some lawmen came a-knockin' on my cabin door one night. Said they was lawmen, what they was was bounty hunters. That was a pretty good fight. I reckon. Good for me, bad for them. Then I drifted down into Colorado and you know the rest."

"Family?"

Pearlie shook his head. "None that I really remember. Ma and Pa died with the fevers when I was eight or nine. I got a sister somewheres, but I don't rightly know where. What all I got is what you see, ma'am. I got my guns, a good saddle, and good horse. And that just about says it all, I reckon."

"No, Pearlie, you're wrong," Sally told him.

The cowboy looked at her, puzzlement in his eyes.

"You have a home with us, as long as you want to ride for the brand."

"Much obliged, ma'am," he said, his voice thick. He did not trust himself to say much more. He stood up. "I better get back on the Sugarloaf East, ma'am. Things to do."

Sally watched him mount up and ride off. She smiled, knowing she and Smoke had made yet another friend.

12

Surprisingly, Smoke noted, the election went smoothly. There was one central voting place, where names were taken and written down in a ledger. There was no point in anyone voting more than once, and few did, for Tilden Franklin's men were lopsidedly out in front in the election count, according to the blackboard tally.

By noon, it was clear that Tilden's people were so far ahead they would not be caught.

Hunt, Haywood, Colton, and Ed had voted and vanished into the surging crowds. Preacher Morrow stayed with Smoke.

"You're not voting, Preacher?" Smoke asked.

"What's the point?" Ralph summed it up.

"You're a quick learner."

"It's not Christian of me, Smoke. But I took one look at that Tilden Franklin and immediately formed an acute dislike for the man."

"Like I said, a quick learner."

"The man is cruel and vicious."

"Yes, he is. All of that and more. Insane, I believe."

"That is becoming a catch-all phrase for those who have no feelings for other men's rights, Smoke."

Smoke was beginning to like the preacher more and more as time went by. He wondered about the man's past, but would not ask, that question being impolite. There were scars on the preacher's knuckles, and Smoke knew they didn't get there from thumping a Bible.

Then the call went up: the other candidates had withdrawn. Tilden Franklin's men had won. Within minutes, Monte Carson was walking the streets, a big badge pinned to his shirt.

Smoke deliberately stayed away from the man. He knew trouble would be heading his way soon enough; no point in pushing it.

He felt someone standing close to him and turned, looking down. Billy.

"What's up, Billy?"

"Trouble for you, Smoke," the boy said gravely.

Preacher Morrow stepped closer, to hear better. Haywood and Hunt were walking toward the trio. Smoke waved them over.

"Listen to what the boy has to say," Smoke said.

Billy looked up at the adults standing about him. "Some of the Circle TF riders is gonna prod you, Smoke. Push you into a gunfight and then claim you started it. They're gonna kill you, Smoke."

"They're going to try," Smoke said softly correcting him.

"Where did you hear this, boy?" Hunt asked.

"I was up in the loft getting ready to fork hay down to the horses when the men came inside the barn. I hunkered down in the loft and listened to them talk. They's five of them, Smoke. Valentine, Suggs, Bolton, Harris, and Wright."

"I've heard of Valentine," Smoke said. "He's a gunhawk. Draws fighting wages from Franklin."

"His name was mentioned too," the boy continued. "They said Mister Franklin told them to nip this matter in the bud and end it. If you was to die, they said, the other nests would crumble like a house of cards. They said the new law was on their side and Mister Franklin told them they didn't have nothin' to worry about from that end."

"I suggest we go see the new sheriff immediately," Hunt said. "Let him handle this matter."

Billy shook his head. "I don't know who you are, mister. But you don't understand the way things are. Monte Carson is Franklin's man. Franklin says frog, Carson jumps. Judge Proctor is an old wine-head from over the Delores way. Franklin brung him in here to stick him in as judge. It's all cut and dried. All made up agin Smoke."

"Incredible!" Haywood said. "Oh, I believe you, son." He looked at Billy. "Activities of this sort are not confined solely to the West."

Billy blinked and looked at Smoke. "What'd he say?"

"Happens in other places too."

"Oh."

"If that is the case, Smoke," Hunt said, "then you must run for your life."

Smoke's eyes turned icy. He looked at the lawyer. "I don't run, Lawyer."

"Then what are you going to do?" Haywood asked. "You've all three heard Billy's statement. A newspaper man, a lawyer, a minister." Smoke smiled with a grim wolf's baring of his teeth. "Take Billy's story down. I see a way to make Tilden Franklin eat crow on this matter and backpaddle."

"What are you going to do, Smoke?" Preacher Morrow inquired.

"Fight," Smoke said.

"But there's *five* of them!" Hunt protested. "Five against one of you."

"I've faced tougher odds, Lawyer." He looked at Billy. "Where is it going down, Billy?"

"They're gonna brace you in the stable."

Smoke nodded his head. "After these gentlemen take your story on paper, Billy, you get the horses out of there. I don't want to see a good horse die on account of trash like Tilden's men."

"Yes, sir!"

Smoke looked at the three men. "I'll be heading down that way in about an hour, boys. I would suggest you all hunt a hole."

Sally looked toward the eastern slopes of the Sugarloaf. Pearlie was not in sight. Bob Colby was working inside the barn, cleaning it out. She called for him.

"Yes'um?" He stuck his head out of the loft.

"Bob, look and see if you can spot Pearlie. He should be over there." She pointed.

Bob searched the eastern slopes of the Sugarloaf. "Nothing, ma'am," he called. "I can't spot him."

"All right, Bob. Thanks. He's behind a hill, I guess." She put Pearlie out of her mind and thought about what to fix for dinner—supper, as they called it out here, although she had never gotten used to that.

"Now what, boys?" Pearlie asked the half-dozen Circle TF riders facing him.

"I guess you know what, Pearlie," a puncher said. He shook out a loop in his rope.

"You boys is wrong," Pearlie said. "A man's gotta right to ride for the brand he chooses."

"You a turncoat, Pearlie. You should have knowed that no one shows his ass-end to Mister Franklin."

"He ain't God, Lefty."

"He is around here," Lefty responded.

"Then let him bring you back to life," Pearlie said. He jerked iron and blew Lefty out of the saddle, the slug taking the TF rider in the right shoulder, knocking him to the ground.

Pearlie spun his cutting horse and tried to make a run for it. He was just a tad slow. He felt the loop settle around him, and then another circled him and jerked him out of the saddle. He hit the ground hard, the breath knocked out of him.

Pearlie struggled to free himself of the stiff ropes, but he knew he was fighting a losing fight. He lifted his six-gun and thumbed the hammer back. He hated to do it, but he had to leave some proof of who had done this to him.

He shot a TF horse. The animal dropped almost immediately as the slug entered behind its left shoulder and shattered the heart. The rider cursed and jumped free, kicking the six-gun out of Pearlie's hand.

"Drag the son of a bitch!" the horseless rider yelled.

Pearlie was jerked along the ground. Mercifully, his head struck a rock and he was dropped into the darkness of unconsciousness.

"Did you hear a shot?" Sally called.

"Yes'um!" Bob called back. "Probably Pearlie shootin' a rattler, is all."

"Maybe," Sally muttered. She went back into the house and strapped on a pistol. She picked up a rifle and levered a round into the chamber of the Henry. Back outside, she called, "Bob! Are you armed?"

"Yes'um. Got a short gun on and my rifle is right down there." He pointed.

"Get your rifle and stay in the loft. Keep a look-out for riders. I think we're in for some trouble."

"Yes'um!"

"While you're getting your rifle, close and bar all the barn doors. I'll bring Seven inside and put him in a stall."

"Yes'um, Miss Sally."

Sally hurriedly fixed containers of water and a basket of food for the boy. She put in several boxes of ammunition and carried it to him in the barn. "We might be in for a long day, Bob," she told him. "And you might have to stay out here by yourself tonight."

"I ain't skirred, Miss Sally. I can knock the eye out of a squirrel at a hundred yards with a rifle. If anybody comes to fight, we'll stand 'em off."

"Good boy. I'll be in the house. Let them come close, we'll catch them in a crossfire."

Bob grinned. "Yes, *ma'am!*"

It was as if some invisible messenger had passed the word. The town of Fontana grew quiet, then hushed almost entirely. Smoke walked across the street and stepped into the tent of Louis Longmont. Louis waved him to the bar.

"A pall has fallen over us, my young friend," Louis said. "I'm sure it concerns you. Am I correct?"

"Uh-huh. Some of Franklin's men are setting me up for a killing."

"And naturally, you're going to leave town in a cloud of dust, right?"

"Sure, Louis. You know that."

"How many?"

"Five." Smoke named them.

"Valentine is a bad one. I know him. He's a top gun from down near the Tex-Mex border. Watch him. He's got a border roll that's fast as lightning."

"Yeah, I've heard he's good. How good?"

"Very good," the gambler said softly. "He beat Johnny North."

A smile passed Smoke's lips. "But Johnny North is still alive."

"Precisely."

So Valentine was cat-quick, hut couldn't shoot worth

a damn. Many quick-draw gunhands were blindingly fast, but usually missed their first shots.

Smoke almost never missed.

"I'll back you up if you ask, Smoke," Louis offered.

"It'll come to that, Louis. But not yet. Speaking of Johnny North, where is he?"

"A question I've asked myself a few times since coming here. He'll be here. But he's a strange one, Smoke. He hates Monte Carson."

"So I hear. I've never heard of him teaming up with anyone."

"Lone wolf all the way. Johnny must be . . . oh, about my age, I suppose. But age has not slowed him a bit. When do you meet these gentlemen, and where?"

Smoke opened his watch. "In about fifteen minutes. Down at the stables."

"Anything you need?"

"A shotgun and a pocketful of shells."

Louis reached over the bar and pulled out a sawed-off twelve-gauge express gun. He handed Smoke a sack of shells.

"I loaded these myself," the gambler said. "Full of ball bearings."

Smoke loaded the express gun. "Got a taste of that scotch handy?"

Louis walked behind the long, deserted bar and poured two fingers of scotch for each of them. He lifted his glass. "To your unerring marksmanship."

"And hope I shoot straight too," Smoke said needling the man.

13

Pearlie opened his eyes. He could have sworn he opened his eyes. But he couldn't see a thing. Slowly, painfully, he lifted one hand and wiped his eyes. There. He could see . . . a little bit, at least.

He hurt all over. He wriggled his toes. Something was wrong. His boots were gone. He could feel the cool earth against his skin. His jeans were ripped and his shirt was gone. He carefully poked at himself. He was bruised and cut and torn from head to toes, but he didn't feel any broken bones sticking out. Lucky. Damn lucky.

Pearlie turned his head and felt something flop down over one ear. He carefully inspected his fingertips. A flap of skin was torn loose. He pressed it back against his head and took his bandana from around his neck, tying it around his head. Hurt like hell.

Only then did he think of the danger he might still be in. What if the TF riders were still hanging around?

He looked around him.

Nothing and nobody in sight.

He slowly drew himself up to his knees and looked around. He could clearly see where he had been dragged. He looked down where he had lain. A hole in the hard ground, blood beside it. He stuck a finger into the hole and pulled out the dirt. His fingers touched something hard. Pearlie dug it out and looked at it. A battered and mangled .44 slug. The bastards had shot him. They thought they'd killed him with a gunshot to the head. That would account for the flap of skin hanging down.

"Boy, you was lucky," he croaked, pushing the words out of a dry throat.

He looked back along the torn path he'd been dragged on. It ran for a ways back toward the cabin. He could see one boot standing all alone in the mangled path. He rose unsteadily to his feet and staggered back toward the boot, one solid mass of aches and pains and misery.

And mad.

Goddamn, was he mad!

He picked up the boot and wandered off in search of his other boot. Pearlie fell down more times than he cared to recall. He banged and bruised and battered his knees and hands each time he fell, but each time he hit the ground, his anger increased. He began cursing Tilden Franklin and all the TF riders who had dragged him and then left him for dead.

The verbal barrage seemed to help.

He found his other boot and sat down to rest, slipping on both his boots. Now he felt better. He could see, just barely, the fallen horse of the TF man. He walked and staggered and stumbled toward it. The animal had fallen on its left side; no way Pearlie could get to the rifle in the saddle boot. But he could salvage the canteen full of water. He sat on the rump of the dead horse and drank his fill. His eyes swept the immediate area. He spotted his six-gun and walked to it, picking it up. He brushed off the dirt, checked the action and the loads, and holstered the weapon. Now he felt better than ever. He dug in the saddlebags of the fallen horse and found a box of .44s, distributing them in his pockets.

Now, by God, just let me find some TF punchers! he thought. He managed to pull the other saddlebag from under the dead horse and rummage through it. Some cold biscuits and beef. As tired and as much as he hurt, he knew he had to have something to eat. Them bear-sign was good eatin', but they didn't stay with a man.

He ate the beef and biscuits and washed them down with water. He looked toward the direction of the ranch. A good four or five miles off. With an explosive oath, Pearlie stood up and began walking. Miss Sally and the boy was probably in for a rough time of it. And by *God*, Pearlie was gonna be there to help out.

He put one boot in front of the other and walked and staggered on.

Drops of blood marked his back trail.

Smoke didn't know where all the people had gone, but the streets of Fontana were empty and silent as he walked along, keeping to the near side of the long street, advancing toward the stable.

But he could feel many eyes on him as he walked.

He slipped the thongs from his Colts as he walked, shifting the sawed-off express from right hand to left hand. He looked up as the batwing doors of a saloon swung open. Tilden Franklin and his foreman, Clint, stepped out to stare at Smoke. The new sheriff, Monte Carson, stood beside them, his large, new, shiny badge catching the late-morning rays of the sun.

"We don't like troublemakers in this town, Smoke," Monte said.

Smoke stopped and turned to face the men. With his eyes on Monte, he said, "What trouble have I caused, Sheriff?"

That took Monte aback. He stared at Smoke. Finally, he said, "Man walks around carrying a shotgun like that one there you got must be lookin' for trouble."

Smoke grinned. "Why, Sheriff, I'm just going down to the stables to see about my horse. Any law against that?"

Monte shook his head.

"Thanks. If there is nothing else, I'll just be on my way."

Tilden grinned at Smoke. His mean eyes shone with evil and power.

Smoke met the man's eyes. "How about you, Franklin? You got anything to say?"

"You talk mighty big standing there with that express gun in your hands," Tilden replied.

"Insurance, Franklin," Smoke said. "Since you're afraid to move without your trained dogs with you."

That stung Clint. His eyes narrowed and his hands balled into fists. But he knew better than to prod Smoke; the gunfighter's rep was that his temper was volatile, and that express gun would turn all three of them into chopped meat at this distance.

"That's right, Clint," Smoke said, a nasty tone to his words. "I forgot. You'd rather make war against farmers and women and kids, wouldn't you?"

"Stand easy, Clint," Tilden quietly warned his foreman.

Smoke laughed and turned, continuing his walk down the street.

Billy darted from the corral and pressed against the side of a newly erected building. "They're all over the place, Smoke," he called in a stage whisper. "Two of 'em up in the loft."

Smoke nodded his thanks and said, "Get out of here, Billy. Hunt a hole."

Billy took off as if the devil was howling and smoking at his heels.

Smoke looked toward the corral. Horse was watching him, his ears perked up.

Smoke walked to the huge open doors and paused. He knew he would be blind for a few seconds upon entering the darkened stable. Out of habit, he rechecked the loads in the express gun and took a deep breath.

He slipped the thongs back on the hammers of his Colts and jumped inside the stable, rolling to his right, into an open stall.

Gunfire blasted the semi-darkness where Smoke had first hit the floor.

"Riders comin', Miss Sally!" Bob called from the barn loft.

"How far off, Bob?" she called from the house.

"'Bout a mile, ma'am. I can't make out no brand yet."

"If they're Circle TF, Bob," she called, "we'll blow them out of the saddle."

"Yes, *ma'am!*"

Woman and boy waited, gripping their rifles.

Pearlie found Lefty's horse and gently approached the still-spooked animal. The horse shied away. Pearlie sat down on a large rock and waited, knowing that the horse would eventually come to him, desiring human company. In less than five minutes, while Pearlie hummed a low tune, the animal came to him and shoved at the puncher with its nose. Pearlie petted the animal, got the reins, and swung into the saddle. Lefty's rifle was in the boot and Pearlie checked it. Full. Pearlie pointed the animal's nose toward the ranch.

"Let's go boy," Pearlie said, just as the sounds of gunfire reached him. "I wanna get in a shot or two myself."

Sally's opening shot knocked a TF rider out of the saddle. Bob squeezed off a round, the slug hitting a TF gunhawk in the center of his chest. The puncher was dead before he hit the ground. With only three gunslicks left out of the original half a dozen, those three spun their horses and lit a shuck out of that area.

They ran right into Pearlie, coming at them at full

gallop. With the reins in his teeth, his right hand full of Colt and his left hand full of Henry rifle, Pearlie emptied two saddles. The last TF rider left alive hunched low in the saddle and made it over a rise and out of range. He then headed for the ranch. They'd been told they were going up against Pearlie and one little lady. But it seemed that Pearlie was as hard to kill as a grizzly and that that little lady had turned into a bobcat.

Meanwhile, Pearlie reined up in a cloud of dust and jumped out of the saddle. "You folks all right?" he yelled.

"My God, Pearlie!" Sally rushed out of the house. "What happened to you?"

"They roped and drug me," Pearlie said. "Then shot me. But they made a bad mistake, ma'am."

She looked at him.

"They left me alive," Pearlie said, his words flint hard.

Smoke darted into the darkness of the first stall just as the lead tore smoking holes where he'd first hit. Rolling to one side, Smoke lifted the sawed-off express gun and eared back both hammers and waited.

"Got the punk!" someone hissed.

"Maybe," a calmer voice spoke from just above Smoke.

Smoke lifted the sawed-off and pulled both triggers. The express gun roared and bucked, and ball-bearing loads tore a great hole in the loft floor. The "maybe" man was flung out of the loft, both loads catching him directly in the crotch, almost tearing him in half. He lay on the stable floor, squalling as his blood stained the horse-shit-littered boards.

Smoke rolled to the wall of the stall, reloaded the express gun, and jumped over the stall divider, into the next stall. His ears were still ringing from the tremendous booming of the sawed-off.

Quietly, he removed his spurs and laid them to one side.

He heard someone cursing, then someone else said, "Jensen shot him where he lived. That ain't right."

The mangled man had ceased his howling, dying on the stable floor.

Smoke waited.

As he had expected, Sheriff Monte Carson was making no effort to interfere with the ambush.

So much for the new law and order in Fontana.

Smoke waited, motionless, his callused hands gripping the express gun. His mentor, Preacher, had taught Smoke well, teaching him, among other things, patience.

One of Tilden's gunhands lost his patience and began tossing lead around where he suspected Smoke to be. He was way off target. But Smoke wasn't.

Smoke blew the man out of the loft, the loads taking him in the belly, knocking him backward. He rolled and thrashed and screamed, the pain finally rolling him off the edge and dropping him to the ground floor.

Smoke heard one man jump from the loft and take off running. The others ran out the back and disappeared.

Smoke waited for a long ten-count, then slipped out the front door. He made sure all watching saw him reload the sawed-off shotgun. Then he walked straight up the dusty street to where Tilden and Monte were standing. Still in the street, Smoke wondered where Clint had gotten off to. No matter. Clint might ride for a sorry no-account, but the man was not a backshooter. Smoke knew that much about him.

Looking straight at Tilden, Smoke said, "Two of your men are on the stable floor. One is dead and I imagine the other won't live long the way he's shot. Your other hands lost their nerve and ran. Maybe you told them to ambush me, maybe you didn't. I don't know. So I won't accuse you of it."

Tilden stood still, smoking a thin cigar. But his eyes were filled with silent rage and hate.

Smoke looked at Monte. "You got anything you want to say to me, Sheriff?"

Monte wanted desperately to look at Tilden for some sign. But he was afraid to take his eyes off Smoke. He finally shook his head. "I reckon not."

"Fine." Smoke looked at Tilden. "See you 'round, Franklin." He knew the man despised to be called by his last name.

Smoke turned and walked to Louis Longmont's place. He handed Louis the shotgun and walked across the street to join the Easterners.

"Go get my horse, Billy. And stay out of the barn until someone cleans up the mess."

"Yes, sir!"

"Is that . . . it?" Hunt asked.

"That's it, Lawyer," Smoke told him. "Out here, for the time being, justice is very swift and short."

Smoke looked at Ed Jackson.

"I'd suggest you bear that in mind," Smoke told him.

14

Tilden sat at a table in a saloon. By himself. The kingpin rancher was in a blue funk and everybody knew it. So they wisely left him alone.

Those six gunhands he'd sent to ambush Jensen were among the best he'd had on his payroll. And they'd failed. And to make matters worse, Jensen had made Tilden look like a fool . . . in front of Monte and countless others who were hiding nearby.

Intolerable.

Tilden emptied his shot glass and refilled it from the bottle. Lifting the shot glass filled with the amber liquid to his lips, Tilden glanced down at the bottle. More than half empty. That too was intolerable. Tilden was not a heavy-drinking man, not a man who liked his thoughts muddled.

He set the shot glass on the table and pushed it from him. He looked up as one of his punchers—he couldn't remember the man's name and that irritated him further—entered the saloon and walked quickly up to Clint, whispering in the foreman's ear.

The foreman stiffened and gave the man a dark look, then cut his eyes to Tilden.

Tilden Franklin rose from the table and walked to Clint and the cowboy. "Outside," he said.

In the shade offered by the awning, the men stood on the boardwalk. "Say it," Tilden ordered the cowboy-gunhand.

"Lefty and five others went over to the Sugarloaf to drag Pearlie. Only one come back and he was shot up pretty bad. He said they drug Pearlie a pretty fair distance and then shot him in the head. But he ain't dead, boss. And they was two people at Jensen's spread. Both of them trigger-pullers."

"Son of a *bitch!*" Tilden cursed low.

"And that ain't all, boss. Billy was over to our western range drivin' the beeves back to the lower slopes. He seen a campfire, smelled beans cookin'. Billy took off over there to run whoever it was off the range. When he got there, he changed his mind. It was Charlie Starr."

Tilden thought about that for a few seconds. He didn't believe it. Last word he'd had of Charlie Starr was five, six years back, and that news had been that Starr had been killed in a gunfight up in Montana.

He said as much.

The puncher shook his head. "Billy seen Charlie over in Nevada, at Mormon Station, seven, eight years ago. That's when Charlie kilt them four gunslicks. Billy bought Charlie a drink after that, and they talked for nearabouts an hour. You've heard Billy brag about that, boss. It ain't likely he'd forget Charlie Starr."

Tilden nodded his head in agreement. It was not very likely. Charlie Starr. Mean as a snake and just as notional as a grizzly bear. Wore two guns, tied down low, and was just as good with one as the other. Charlie had been a number of things: stagecoach guard, deputy, marshal, gambler, outlaw, gunfighter, bounty hunter, miner . . . and a lot of other things.

Charlie was . . . had to be close to fifty years old. But

Tilden doubted that age would have slowed him down much. If any.

And Charlie Starr hated Tilden Franklin.

As if reading his thoughts, Clint said, "You don't think . . ."

"I don't know, Clint." He dismissed the cowboy and told him to get a drink. When the batwings had swallowed the cowboy, Tilden said, "That was more than fifteen years ago, Clint. Seventeen years to be exact. I was twenty-three years old and full of piss and vinegar. I didn't know that woman belonged to Charlie. Damnit, she didn't tell me she did. Rubbing all over me, tickling my ear. I had just ramrodded a herd up from Texas and was hard-drinkin' back then." He sighed. "I got drunk, Clint. I've told you that much before. What I haven't told you was that I got a little rough with the woman later on. She died. I thought she liked it rough. Lots of women do, you know. Anyway, I got the word that Charlie Starr was gunning for me. I ordered my boys to rope him and drag the meanness out of him. They got a little carried away with the fun and hurt him bad. He was, so I'm told, a long time recovering from it. Better part of a year. Word got back to me over the years that Charlie had made his brag he was going to brace me and kill me."

"I seen him up on the Roaring Fork nine, ten years ago," Clint said. "Luis Chamba and that Medicine Bow gunslick braced him. Chamba took a lot of lead, but he lived. The other one didn't."

"Where is Chamba?"

"Utah, last I heard."

"Send a rider. Get him."

"Yes, sir."

It was full dark when Smoke saw the lights shining from the windows of the cabin. He had pushed Horse hard, and the big stallion was tired, but game. Smoke rubbed him down, gave him an extra ration of corn, and turned him loose to roll.

When he opened the door to the cabin and saw Pearlie's battered and torn face, his own face tightened.

"He'll tell you over dinner," Sally said. "Wash up and I'll fix you a plate."

Over a heaping plate of beef and potatoes and gravy and beans flavored with honey, with bearsign for dessert, Pearlie told his story while Smoke ate.

"If there was any law worth a damn in this country I could have Tilden arrested," Smoke said, chewing thoughtfully.

"I don't even know where the county lines are," Pearlie said. He would have liked another doughnut, but he'd already eaten twenty that day and was ashamed to ask for another.

With a smile, Sally pushed the plate of bearsign toward him.

"Well," Pearlie said. "Maybe just *one* more."

"What county does our land lie in, Smoke?" Sally asked.

"I don't know. I'm not sure. It might be split in half. And that's something to think about. But . . . I don't know. You can bet that when it comes to little farmers and little ranchers up against kingpins like Tilden, the law is going to side with the big boys. Might be wiser just to keep the law out of this altogether."

"I thought you folks had bought most of your land and filed on the rest?" Pearlie said.

"We have," Smoke told him. "And it's been checked and it's all legal. But they surveyed again a couple of years ago and drew up new lines. I never heard anymore about it."

"Mister Smoke?" Bob asked, from a chair away from the adults.

"Yes, Bob?"

"Who is Charlie Starr?"

Smoke sopped up the last of his gravy with a thick hunk of bread and chewed for a moment. "He's a gunfighter, Bob. He's been a lot of things, but mostly he's a good man. But a strange one. I met him while I was riding with an old Mountain Man called Preacher. Why do you ask?"

"I heard them Jones boys talkin' last week. When we was all gathered over to the Matlocks' for Sunday services. That feller who sometimes works for Mister Matlock said Charlie Starr's been camped out around this country for a month or so."

"I can't believe Charlie is here to hire his gun out to Tilden. He never has hired his guns out against a little man. He's done a lot of things, but he kinda backed into his rep as a gunslick. Maybe that fellow was mistaken?"

"Maybe, Mister Smoke."

Charlie Starr shifted his blankets away from his fire and settled in for the night. He smiled in the darkness, the sounds of his horse cropping grass a somehow comforting sound in the night. Since that puncher had come up on him, he'd moved his location—out of, he thought, the TF range. High up in the mountains, where snow was still capping the crests, above some place called the Sugarloaf. Nice-sounding name, Charlie thought.

Louis Longmont sat at a table playing stud, winning, as usual. Winning even though his thoughts were not entirely on the game. He'd just that evening heard the rumors that Charlie Starr was in the area, and heard too that Tilden Franklin had sent a rider to Utah to get Luis Chamba, the Sonora gunslick. And he'd heard that Tilden was building up his own forces by half a hundred riders.

Louis pulled in his winnings and excused himself

from the game. His mind wasn't on it and he needed a breath of air. He walked outside, into the rambunctious, boom-town night air. The town was growing by hundreds each day. Most of the men were miners or would-be miners, but there was a lot of trash mixed in as well.

With this many people working the area, the town might last, Louis thought, six months—maybe less. There was a strong urge within the man to just fold his tent and pull out. Louis felt there would be a bloodbath before everything was said and done.

But Louis couldn't do that. He'd given his word to Preacher he'd look in on Smoke from time to time. Not that Smoke needed any looking after, Louis thought with a grin. But a man's word was his bond. So Louis would see it through. He tossed his cigar into the street and walked back into his gaming tent.

Tilden Franklin sat alone in his huge house, his thoughts as savage as much of the land that lay around him. His thoughts would have made a grizzly flinch. Tilden had never seen a woman that he desired more than Sally Jensen. Educated, aloof, beautiful. Tilden wondered how she'd look with her dress on the floor.

He shook that thought from him.

Then, with a faint smile curving his lips, he thought about the nester Colby. More specifically, Colby's daughter. Velvet.

Tilden laughed. He thought he knew how to get rid of that nester, and let his boys have some fun in the process.

Yeah. He'd give it some extra thought in the morning. But it seemed like a pretty good idea.

Billy lay on the hay in the loft, in his longjohns, his new clothing carefully folded and stored on a little ledge. His thoughts were of Smoke. Billy wondered how it would be to have a pa like Smoke. Probably real nice. There was a streak of gentleness in the gunfighter that few adults could see. But a kid could see it right off. Smoke for a pa. Well, it was something to dream about. One thing for sure, nobody would mess with you, leastways.

Ed Jackson lay by his wife's side and mentally counted all the money he was going to make. He'd hired some rough-looking men that day, promising them a grub-stake if they'd build his store for him. They had accepted. Ed Jackson dreamed of great wealth. Ed Jackson dreamed of becoming a very important person. Maybe even someone like Tilden Franklin.

Now there was a *really* important man.

Paul Jackson lay in his blankets under a wagon. He was restless, sleep was elusive. He kept thinking about the way Bountiful had looked at him. Something was building between them, he just knew it. And Paul also knew that he wasn't going to hang around here with his stupid, greedy brother any longer than necessary. If he could find gold, that would really make Bountiful sit up and take notice of him.

He grinned.

Or lay down and take notice of him.

Dana lay by her husband, listening to him breathe as he slept. She wondered if they'd made a mistake in coming out West. Haywood didn't think so, but she'd wondered often about it, especially during the last few days. These men out here, they took violent death so . . . so calmly. It frightened her.

* * *

Colton closed up his tent and put his money, some of it in gold dust, into a lockbox and carefully stowed it away in the hidden compartment under the wagon. He was tired, but he'd made more money in just two days than most physicians back East made in a month—maybe two months. If this kept up, he'd have enough to travel on to California and set up a practice in real style. In a place that had some class, with a theater and opera and all the rest that civilized people craved. At this rate, he'd have far more than enough in a year's time.

He washed his hands and made ready for bed.

Hunt was wide awake, his thoughts many and most of them confused. True, he'd been busy all day handling gold claims, but no one had come to him for any legal advice concerning the many fights and stabbings and occasional shootings that occurred within the town of Fontana. He simply could not understand that. Didn't these people understand due process? All those fistfights and gunfights. It was positively barbaric. And so needless. All people had to do was come see him; then they could handle it in a proper court of law.

If, Hunt thought with a grimace, they could find the judge when he was sober.

15

Leaving Pearlie with Sally, Smoke escorted Bob back to his home. For the first time since arriving in the area, Smoke saw both Wilbur Mason and Colby armed with short guns and rifles. Dismounting, Smoke ground-reined Drifter and faced the farmer-ranchers.

"Seen any of the others?" Smoke asked.

"Nolan rode by yesterday evenin'," Colby said. "He's scared and admitted it."

"Ray and Betty sent word that they're with us all the way," Mason said.

"How about Peyton?"

Both men shrugged.

"I think he'll stand," Smoke said. "Way he talked to me the other day, he'll stick. How's your food supply?"

"Plenty. The old woman canned enough last summer to last us for a good long time. Potato bin's half full. What's your plans, Smoke?"

Smoke brought them both up to date. Then he said, "I'm staying close to home. Shifting my cattle to a different graze. But if I need something in the way of supplies, nothing or nobody will keep me out of Fontana."

"When you decide to go in," Colby said, "I'll take my

wagon and go in with you. The two of us can get supplies
for everybody."

"Sounds good. We don't want to leave the whole area
without menfolk. I'm going to talk with the others today.
Get a better idea of where they stand. I'll see you both
later on."

Velvet came out of the house and walked to the well.
Smoke's eyes followed her. She was a young girl, but
built up like a grown woman. And that worried Smoke.
Tilden was ruthless, might do anything. And some of the
gunslicks riding for the TF brand were nothing more
than pure white trash. They'd do anything Tilden ordered. While most Western men would not bother a
good woman, there were always exceptions.

Colby had followed Smoke's eyes. "I still think you're
wrong, Smoke. She's just a child."

"Tilden Franklin is a sorry son of a bitch," Smoke told
the men. "Don't put anything past him." He swung into
the saddle. "See you boys later."

Smoke rode hard that day, stopping in to see all the
small outfits he thought might throw in with him and
the others. And he had been correct in his thinking.
Steve and Mike and Nolan and Ray all agreed to toss in,
forming an alliance among all the small spreads. If one
got hit, the others would respond.

Their lives and money were sunk deep into this land,
and with many, some of their blood as well. They were
not going to run.

"What's this talk about Charlie Starr, Smoke?" Nolan
asked.

"So far as I know, just that—talk." He told the man
what he knew about Starr. "I think, if he is in this area,
he's here to kill Tilden Franklin. Lots of bad blood between those two. Goes back years, so the story goes. I'm
going to try to pin the rumor down. When I do, I'll get

back with you. Stay loose, Nolan, and keep an eye on your womenfolk. I have no way of knowing exactly what Tilden has in mind, but whatever it is, it's bad news for us, that's for sure."

"I'm not going to put up with these miners tearing up my land, Smoke," the rancher said. "If I have to shoot two or three of them, I will."

"Check your land title, Nolan. You might not have mineral rights. Ever think about that?"

The farmer-rancher cursed. "I never thought about that. Could someone buy those rights without my permission?"

"I think so. The law is still kind of raw out here, you know that. I checked on my title last night. I own the mineral rights to my land."

"I just didn't think about it. I'll do just that. See you, Smoke."

Smoke spent a week staying close to home. He received no news about what might be happening in Fontana. Then, on a fine, clear, late spring day, Smoke decided to ride his valley. He found several miners' camps high up, and told the men to clear out—right then.

"And if we don't?" one bearded man challenged him.

"I'll kill you," Smoke told him, ice in the words.

"You talk big, mister," another miner said. "But I'm wonderin' if you got the sand to back up your words."

"My name is Smoke Jensen."

The miners cleared out within the hour.

With the sun directly over his head, Smoke decided to stop in a stand of timber and eat the lunch that Sally had prepared for him. He was just stepping down from the saddle when the smell of wood smoke reached him.

He swung back into the saddle and followed the invisible trail. It took him the better part of an hour to find the well-concealed camp, and when he found it, he knew he had come face to face with one of the most feared men in all the West.

Charlie Starr.

"Mind some company?" Smoke asked, raising his voice to be heard over the hundred yards or so that separated the men.

"Is this your land?" the man called.

"Sure is."

"Light and sit then. You welcome to share what I got."

"Thanks," Smoke said, riding in and dismounting. "My wife fixed me a bait of food."

Charlie Starr looked hard at Smoke, "Ain't I seen you afores?"

"Yes," Smoke told him, unwrapping the waxed paper Sally had used to secure his lunch. "Long time ago, up in Wyoming. I was with a Mountain Man called Preacher."

"Well, I'll just be damned if that ain't the truth! You've growed a mite, boy"

There was a twinkle in his eyes as he said it. And Smoke knew that Charlie Starr knew all about him.

Charlie's eyes flicked to Smoke's guns. "No notches. That's good. Only a tinhorn cuts his kills, and half of them are lies."

Smoke thought of Colby's boy, Adam. "I told that to a boy just the other day. I don't think he believed me."

"He might not live to be a man, thinking like that." Charlie's eyes lit up as he spotted the bearsign in Smoke's sack. "Say, now!"

Smoke halved his doughnuts and Charlie put them aside for dessert. "Much obliged, Smoke. Have some coffee."

Smoke filled his battered tin cup and settled back to enjoy his lunch among the mountain's flowers and trees and cool but pleasant breezes.

"You wonderin' why I'm squatted on your range?" Charlie asked.

"Stay as long as you're friendly, Charlie." Smoke spoke around a mouthful of beef and bread.

Charlie laughed. "And you'd brace me too, wouldn't you, young man?"

Younger eyes met older eyes. Both sets were flint hard and knowing.

"I'd try you, Charlie."

Charlie chuckled and said, "I killed my first man 'fore you was even a glint in your daddy's eyes, Smoke. Way before. How old do you think I am, Smoke?"

"You ain't no young rooster."

Again, the gunfighter laughed. "You shore right about that. I'm fifty-eight years old. I killed my first man when I was fourteen, I think it was. That's be, uh, back in '36, I reckon."

"I was fourteen when I killed an Indian. I think we were in Kansas."

"You don't say? I'm be damned. Some folks would say that an Injun don't count, but I ain't one of them folks. Injuns is just like us . . . but different."

Smoke stopped chewing and thought about that. He had to smile. "You don't look your age, Charlie."

"Thank you. But on cold mornin's I shore feel it. Seen me a bunch of boomers headin' this way. They made it to No-Name yet?"

"No-Name is now Fontana. Oh, yeah, the boomers made it and are still coming in."

"Fontana," Charlie said softly. "Right pretty name." His voice had changed, becoming low-pitched and deadly. "Fontana. Now what do you think about that."

Smoke said nothing. Preacher had told him the story about Charlie's girl, Rosa Fontana, and about Tilden Franklin killing the girl and dragging Charlie.

The men ate in silence for a time, silently enjoying each other's company. While they ate, they eyeballed each other when one thought the other wasn't looking.

Smoke took in Charlie's lean frame. The man's waist

was so thin he looked like he'd have to eat a dozen bear-sign just to hold his britches up. Like most cowboys, his main strength lay in his shoulders and arms. The man's wrists were thick, the hands big and scarred and cal-lused. His face was tanned and rugged-looking. Charlie Starr looked like a man who would be hard to handle in any kind of fight.

Then Smoke had an idea; an idea that, if Charlie was agreeable, would send Tilden Franklin right through the roof of his mansion in fits of rage.

"You always sit around a far grinnin', boy?" Charlie asked.

"No." Smoke had not realized he was grinning. "But I just had me an idea."

"Must have been a good'un."

"You lookin' for work, Charlie?"

"Not so's you'd notice, I ain't."

"My wife is one of the best cooks in the state."

"Keep talkin'." He picked up a doughnut and nibbled at it. Then he stuffed the whole thing in his mouth.

"Wouldn't be a whole lot to do. I got one hand. Name's Pearlie."

"Rat good with a gun, is he?"

"He'll do to ride the river with. Some of Tilden's boys hung a rope on him last week and dragged him a piece." Smoke kept his voice bland, not wanting Charlie to know that he knew about the bad blood between Starr and Franklin. Or why. "Then they shot him in the head. Pearlie managed to live and get lead in two of them. He's back working a full day now."

Charlie grunted. "Sounds like he'll do, all rat. What is he, half 'gator?"

"He's tough. I'll pay you thirty and found."

"Don't need no job. But . . ."

Smoke waited.

"Your wife make these here bearsign now and then, does she?"

"Once a week."

"I come and go as I please long as my work's caught up?"

"Sure. But I have to warn you . . . they'll probably be some shooting involved, and . . . well, with you getting along in years and all, I wouldn't blame you if you turned it down."

Charlie fixed him with a look that would have withered a cactus. Needles and all.

"Boy, are you out of your gawddamned mind or just born slow?"

"Well, no, Charlie . . . but they're gonna be broncs to bust, and with your age and all, I was just . . ."

Charlie threw his battered hat on the ground. "Gawddamn, boy, I ain't ready for no old folks' home just yet!"

"Now, don't get worked up, Charlie. You're liable to have a heart attack, and I don't know nothing about treating heart attacks."

Charlie turned blue around the mouth and his eyes bugged out. Then he began to relax and chuckle. He wiped his eyes and said, "Shore tell Preacher had a hand in your up-bringin', Smoke." He stuck a hard, rough hand across the hat-sized fire. "You got you a man that'll ride the river with you, Smoke Jensen."

Smoke took the hand and a new friendship was born.

16

On the slow ride back to the ranch, Smoke discovered that Charlie and Preacher shared one common bond. They both liked to bitch.

And like Preacher's had been, Charlie's complaints were numerous . . . and mostly made up.

"I stayed in a hospital a week one time," Charlie informed him. "Them doctors found more wrong with me than a human body ought to have to suffer. I swear, if I'd stayed in there another week, I'd have probably died. They told me that no human bein' could be shot twenty-two times and still live. I told them I wasn't shot no twenty-two times, it was twenty-five times, but three of them holes was in a place they wasn't about to look at.

"Boy, was I wrong!"

Smoke was laughing so hard he had to wipe his eyes with a bandana.

"Nurse come in that first day. That was the homeliest-lookin' female I ever did see. Looked like a buffalo. Told me to hike up that gown they had me in. I told her that her and no two others like her was big enough to make me do that.

"I was wrong agin.

"I want to warn you now, Smoke. Don't never get

around me with no rubber tubin'. Don't do it. I'm liable to go plumb bee-serk. Them hospitals, boy, they got a thing about flushin' out a man's system. Stay away from hospitals, boy, they'll kill you!"

Pearlie was clearly in awe. Not only was he working for Smoke Jensen, but now Smoke had done gone and hired Charlie Starr.

"Shut your mouth, boy," Charlie told him. "Afore you swaller a bug."

Pearlie closed his mouth.

Charlie was clearly taken aback when Sally came out of the cabin to meet him . . . dressed in men's jeans. With a pistol belted around her tiny waist.

Wimmin just didn't have no business a-runnin' around in men's pants. They'd be smokin' cigarettes 'fore long.

But he forgot all about that when she said, "Fresh apple pie for dessert, Mister Starr."

"Charlie, ma'am. Just Charlie."

The sun was just settling over the Sugarloaf when Sally called them in for dinner. Steaks, beans, potatoes, fresh-baked bread, and apple pie.

Smoke and Sally both noted that, for such a spare fellow, Charlie could certainly eat.

After Charlie had sampled his plate and pleased his palate, he said, "Bring me up to date, Smoke."

Smoke told him what he knew, and then what he guessed. Including Tilden's desires for Sally.

"That's his way, all right," Charlie said. Then he leveled with them, speaking slowly, telling them about Rosa. "Way I hear it, Tilden fancied that she was comin' up on him. But that was her job, hostess at a saloon. Rosa had part of the action, owned about twenty-five percent of it. When I come to in the hospital, after Tilden's boys drug me, Louis told me what really happened."

Smoke glanced at the man. "Louis!"

Charlie grinned grimly. "Louis Longmont. It was one of his places. And you know Louis don't tolerate no pleasure ladies workin' for him. That's more Big Mamma O'Neil's style. Louis was considerable younger then, and so was I. Louis said one of his bouncers saw it all . . . well, most of it. Tilden was so drunk he got it all wrong. And when Rosa tried to break a-loose from him, he started slappin' her around. Bad. The bouncers come runnin', but Tilden's hands held them at bay whilst he took Rosa in the back room and . . ." He paused, looking at Sally. ". . . had his way with her. Then he killed her. Broke her neck with his bare hands. You see, one of them doctors in that damnable hospital told me, once I got to trust the feller, that Tilden ain't quite right in the head. He's got the ability to twist things all around, and make the bad look good and so forth. He shapes things the way he wants them to be in his mind. I disremember the exact word the doc used. That buffler-faced nurse come by 'bout that time with some rubber tubin' in her hands and things kinda went hazy on me."

"What nurse?" Sally asked.

"I'll tell you later," Smoke said.

Charlie said, "Me and Rosa was gonna get married in the spring. I was unconscious for several days; didn't even get to go to her buryin'." He sighed deeply. "Course, by the time I got on my feet, Tilden and his bunch was long gone. I lost track of him for a time, but by then the fires inside me had burned low. I still hated the man, but I had to make a livin' and didn't have no idea where he might be. I been knowin' he was in this area for some years. I've drifted in and out half a dozen times, stayin' low, watching that low-life build his little kingdom. Then I had me an idea. I'd wait until he got real big, real powerful, real sure of himself. And then I'd kill him . . . slow."

Charlie laid down his knife and fork, pushed his empty plate from him, and stood up. "Bes' grub I've had in many a moon, ma'am. I thank you. Reckon I'll turn in now. Tomorrow I wanna start roamin' the range for a couple of days, learn all the twists and turns and ways in and out. I seen me a cookstove in the bunkhouse. I'll fix me a poke before I pull out in the mornin'. Night, folks."

After the door had closed softly and the sounds of Charlie's jingling spurs had faded, Pearlie said, "I think Tilden Franklin's string has just about run out."

"That hombre who just walked out the door," Smoke said, "I believe means every word he said.

"Story goes that Charlie's folks was kilt by Injuns when he was just a little boy. He was raised by the Cheyenne. If Charlie says he's gonna kill Tilden Franklin slow, that is exactly what he means."

For two days, Charlie prowled the Sugarloaf, getting his bearings and inspecting the cattle and horses that Smoke and Sally were raising.

"You want it known that you're working for me?" Smoke asked him upon his return to the ranch house.

"Don't make no difference to me, Smoke," the gunfighter said. "My bein' here ain't gonna make Tilden backpaddle none. Man sets out to be king, only thing that's gonna stop him is dyin'."

Smoke nodded his agreement. "I'll be gone for several days, Charlie. You and Pearlie stay close to the house, all right?"

"Will do."

Smoke pulled out early the next morning, riding Drifter. It was not like Tilden to wait, once his intentions became known; Smoke wanted to find out what the kingpin had up his sleeve.

As he rode, the sounds of drilling and hammers against rocks and occasional blasting came to him. The miners were in full swing. And they were paying no attention to the No Trespassing signs the farmer-ranchers had posted around their property. Bad trouble was building; the smell of it was in the air.

Smoke figured he'd better check in with Lawyer Brook as soon as he hit town.

"Smoke," the lawyer informed him, "there is nothing your friends can do, not legally."

"But it's their land!"

"But they don't hold the mineral rights to it. The holder of those rights has given the miners permission to mine. The miners get fifty percent, the holder of the rights gets fifty percent."

Smoke leaned back in his chair and built one of his rare cigarettes from the cloth pouch he carried in his vest pocket. He licked the tube and smoothed it, lighting and inhaling before speaking.

"Let me guess," Smoke said. "Tilden Franklin bought all the mineral rights."

"Well . . . if you don't hear it from me, you'll hear it from somebody else. Yes, that is correct."

"It's legal stealing, Hunt."

"I wouldn't phrase it quite like that," the lawyer said stiffly.

"I just did," Smoke told him. He walked out of the lawyer's new offices.

The long building containing the offices of the lawyer, the doctor, and the newspaper had been put up in a hurry, but it was well built nonetheless. Across the street, the big store of Ed Jackson was in business and doing quite well, Smoke observed, eyeballing the many heavily loaded wagons lined up behind it, waiting to be unloaded. And, surprisingly enough, Ralph Morrow's church was up—nearly completed. He walked across the small field to the church and located the minister.

"You do all this yourself, Ralph?" Smoke asked.

"Oh, no! Mister Franklin donated the money for the

church and paid the workmen to build it. He's really a very fine man, Smoke. I think you're wrong about him."

Slick, Smoke thought. Very slick on Tilden's part. "Well, I'm happy about your church, Ralph. I wish you a great deal of success."

"Thank you, Smoke." The minister beamed.

Smoke rode to the stable and located Billy. "Take care of him, Billy. Lots of corn and rub him down."

"Yes, sir!"

Smoke walked over to Louis's place and stepped inside. The gambler was sitting at a table, having breakfast. He waved Smoke over.

"Saw you ride in just as I was getting up. Care for a late breakfast?"

"Sounds good."

The gambler called for his cook and ordered breakfast for Smoke. Looking at Smoke, he asked, "Have you spoken to the minister yet?"

Smoke's smile gave him his silent reply.

"Nice move on Franklin's part, don't you think?"

"Very Christian of the man."

Louis enjoyed a laugh at the sarcasm in Smoke's voice. "Slick on his part about the mineral rights."

"I'll tell you the same thing I told Lawyer Brook—it's nothing but legal stealing."

"Oh, I agree with you, Smoke. But it is legal. Were I you, I'd advise the others to walk lightly and don't start any shooting."

"It's their land, Louis. They have a right to protect their herds."

Louis chewed for a moment, a thoughtful look on his face. "Yes, they do," he finally spoke. He took a sip of coffee out of one of the fanciest cups Smoke had ever seen. One thing about Louis Longmont. When he traveled, he went first class all the way, carrying a cook, a valet, and a huge bodyguard with him at all times. The bodyguard usually acted as bouncer in Louis's place, and was rarely seen—except when there was trouble. And then he was seen by the troublemaker only very briefly . . . seconds before the troublemaker died in Mike's bare hands. Providing Louis didn't shoot the troublemaker outright.

Louis buttered a piece of toasted bread and then spread preserves on top of that. The preserves, Smoke was sure, were imported. "Smoke, you know, or I hope you do, that I will back you to the hilt . . . in whatever you do. Regardless of whether I think you are right or wrong. Preacher saved my life a number of times, and besides that, you are a very good young man. But whether our newly elected law is worth a tinker's damn or not, in this mineral rights matter Tilden Franklin is legal. And the law is on his side. Smoke, the land can be repaired. Another hole in the ground is not worth a shooting or a hanging. Your herds? Well, that is quite another matter." He glanced at Smoke, a twinkle in his hard eyes. "There is no law out here that says a man can't hang or shoot a rustler or a horse thief—if you get my drift."

Smoke got it. And he would pass the word to the other small farmer-ranchers. Then they would ride out and advise the miners that there would be no trouble, providing the herds of cattle and horses were left alone. But trample over someone's garden, stampede one herd, cut out one beeve, or steal one horse, and someone was going to die.

And then, if any or all those things happened, they would have to have the raw nerve to carry the threat through.

The French chef placed a plate before Smoke. Smoke looked at the food on the plate. Damned if he knew what it was. He said as much.

Then the chef reached down with a lighted match, set fire to the stuff, and Smoke jumped out of his chair.

Louis had a good laugh out of that. "Sit down, Smoke. Enjoy your breakfast."

"Hell, I can't eat *fire!*"

The flames abated and the chef departed, chuckling. Louis smiled. "Those are *crepes suzette*, my young friend. This dish." He tapped another plate with a knife blade. "Is an *au jambon*."

"Do tell?"

"An omelette, with bits of ham," Louis explained. "Now eat and enjoy."

Them crap susies was a tad too sweet for Smoke's taste, but the omelette was tasty. He made a mental note to tell Sally about what he had had for a late breakfast. Maybe she'd heard of them; damned if he ever had.

"Either way," Smoke said, "I think we're all looking at a lot of trouble just up the road."

"I share your feelings, Smoke. But why not postpone it as long as possible. You know this strike is not going to last. In six months it will have seen its heyday."

"I can't figure you, Louis. I never . . ." He bit off the words just at the last possible second.

The gambler-gunfighter did not take umbrage at what he suspected Smoke had been about to say. Instead, he smiled and finished it for him. "Never knew me to back off from trouble, Smoke?"

"I apologize for thinking it, Louis."

Louis smiled and shook his head. "No need for any of that—not between friends." He sighed. "But you're right, Smoke. I am trying to avoid trouble. Not for my sake," he was quick to add. "But for yours."

Smoke laid down his fork. "My sake?"

"Listen to me, my young friend. How many guns do you have? A dozen? Maybe fifteen at the most? Tilden has seventy-five hardcases right now and can pull in two hundred more anytime he wishes, and will. Talk is that Luis Chamba is on his way here. And where Luis goes, Sanderson and Kane go with him. Think about it."

Smoke thought about it, and the more he thought about it the madder he got. Louis saw his expression change and tried to calm the young man down.

"No, Louis. No. Don't you see what Tilden is trying to pull?"

"Of course I do, boy! But give it time. In six months this area of the country will be right back where it was a month ago. Farm and ranch country. This town will dry up with only a few of the businesses remaining. I'm betting Tilden won't want to be king of nothing."

"He won't be king of nothing, Louis. For if we don't fight, he'll kill us all one by one. He'll make some grand gesture of buying out the widows or the kids—through some goddamned lawyer—and then he'll own this entire section of the state of Colorado. Everything!"

Louis nodded his head. "Maybe you're right, Smoke. Maybe you're right. If that's the case, then you've got to start hiring guns of your own. You and your wife have the means to do so; if you don't, let me advance you the money."

Suddenly, Smoke thought of something. In a way it was a cruel thought, but it was also a way for a lot of broke, aging men to gather in one final blaze of glory. The more he thought about it, the better he liked it, and his mood began to lighten. But he'd have to bounce it off Charlie first.

"Why are you smiling, Smoke?" Louis asked.

"Louis, you're one of the best gamblers around, aren't you?"

"Some say I am one of the best in the world, Smoke. I should think my numerous bank accounts would back up that claim. Why do you ask?"

"Suppose you suddenly learned you were dying, or suppose some . . . well, call it fate . . . started dealing you bad hands and you ended up broke and old—anything along that line—and then someone offered you the chance to once more live in glory. Your kind of glory. Would you take it, Louis, or would you think the offer to be cruel?"

"What an interesting thought! Say now . . . cruel? Oh,

no. Not at all. I would jump at the opportunity. But . . . what are you thinking of, Smoke? I'm not following this line of questioning at all."

"You will, Louis." Smoke stood up and smiled. His smile seemed to Louis to be rather mysterious "You will. And I think you'll find it to your 1iking. I really believe you will."

Long after Smoke had plopped his hat on his head, left the gaming room, and ridden out of town, Louis Longmont had sat at the table and thought about what his young friend had said.

Then he began smiling. Soon the smile had turned to chuckling and the chuckling to hard laughter.

"Oh . . ." he managed to say over the pealing laughter. "I love it!"

17

Smoke sat with Sally, Pearlie, and Charlie. Charlie listened to what Smoke had on his mind and then leaned back in his chair, a broad smile on his face. He laughed and slapped his knee.

"Smoke, that's the bes' idee I've heard of in a long, long time. Cruel? No, sir. It ain't cruel. What you're talkin' about is what they do bes'. You give me the wherewithal and I'll have an even dozen here in a week, soon as I can get to a telegraph and get hold of them and get some money to them."

"Name them, Charlie."

"Oh . . . well, there's Luke Nations, Pistol Le Roux, Bill Foley, Dan Greentree, Leo Wood, Cary Webb, Sunset Hatfield, Crooked John Simmons, Bull Flagler, Toot Tooner, Sutter Cordova, Red Shingletown . . . give me time and I'll name some more."

Pearlie said, "But all them old boys is *dead!*"

"No, they ain't neither," Charlie corrected. "They just retared is all."

"Well . . ." Pearlie thought a moment. "Then they mus' be a hundred years old!"

"Naw!" Charlie scoffed at that. "You jus' a kid, is all. They all in their sixties."

"I've met some of them. Charlie, I don't want to be responsible for any of them going to their deaths."

"Smoke . . . it's the way they'd want it. If they all died, they'd go out thankin' you for the opportunity to show the world they still had it in them. Let them go out in a blaze of glory, Smoke."

Smoke thought about it. That was the way Preacher would have wanted to go. And those old Mountain Men three years back, that's how they had wanted it. "All right, Charlie. We'll give you the money and you can pull out at first light. Me and Pearlie will start adding on to the bunkhouse. How many do you think will be here?"

"When the word gets out, I'd look for about twenty-five or so." Charlie said it with a smile. "You gonna have to hire you a cook to help Miss Sally. Or you'll work her to a frazzle, Smoke."

"All right. Do you know an old camp cook?"

"Shore do. Dad Weaver. He can cook and he can still pull a trigger too. One about as good as the other."

"Hire him. Oh, 'fore I forget." He looked at Sally. "I had a late breakfast with Louis Longmont. His chef fed me crap susies."

"Fed you *what*?" Sally said.

"The chef set it on fire before he served me. I thought he'd lost his mind."

"You didn't eat it, did you?" Pearlie asked.

"Oh, yeah! It was pretty good. Real sweet."

"*Crepes suzette*," Sally said.

"That's it," Smoke said. "Say it again."

"You pronounce it . . . *krehp sue-zeht*. You all try to say it."

They all tried. It sounded like three monkeys trying to master French.

"I feel like a plumb idiot!" Charlie said.

* * *

"What're those damned nesters up to?" Tilden Franklin asked his foreman.

"I can't figure it," Clint said. "They've all rode out and told the miners there wouldn't be no trouble as long as the miners don't spook their herds or trample their crops. They was firm, but in a nice way."

"Damn!" Tilden said. "I thought Jensen would go in shooting."

"So did I. You want us to maybe do a little night-ridin'?"

"No. I want this to be all the nesters' doing. Wait a minute. Yeah, I do want some night-riding. Send some of the boys out to Peyton's place. Rustle a couple head and leave thc butchered carcasses close to some miners' camps. Peyton is hot-headed; he'll go busting up in there and shoot or hang some of them. While we stand clear."

Clint smiled. "Tonight?"

"Tonight."

Sheriff Monte Carson and his so-called deputies kept only a loose hand on the rowdy doings in Fontana. They broke up fistfights whenever they could get to them in time, but rarely interfered in a stand-up, face-to-face shoot-out. Mostly they saw to it that all the businesses—with the exception of Louis Longmont, Ed Jackson, and Lawyer Hunt Brook—paid into the Tilden kitty . . . ten percent of the gross. And don't hold none back. The deputies didn't bother Doctor Colton Spalding either. They'd wisely decided that some of them just might need the Doc's services sooner or later . . . probably sooner.

And, to make matters just a little worse, the town was attracting a small group of would-be gunslicks; young men who fancied themselves gunfighters and looked to make a reputation in Fontana. They strutted about with their pearl-handled Colts tied down low and their huge

California spurs jangling. The young men usually dressed all in black, or in loudly colored silk shirts with pin-striped trousers tucked inside their polished boots. They bragged a lot about who they had faced down or shot, and did a lot of practicing outside the town limits. They were solid looking for trouble, and that trouble was waiting just around the corner for a lot of them.

The town of Fontana was still growing, both in businesses and population. It now could boast four hotels and half a dozen rooming houses. Cafes had sprung up almost as fast as the saloons and the hurdy-gurdy girls who made their dubious living in those saloons . . . and in the dirty cribs in the back rooms.

The mother lode of the vein had been located, and stages were rolling into town twice a day, to carry the gold from the assay offices and to drop off their load of passengers. Tilden Franklin had built a bank, The Bank of Fontana, and was doing a swift business. Supply wagons rolled and rattled and rumbled twenty-four hours a day, bringing in much-needed items to the various businesses.

To give the man a small amount of credit, Tilden Franklin had taken a hard look at his town and quietly but firmly begun rearranging the business district. There were now boundaries beyond which certain types could not venture during specific hours. The red-light district lay at one end of Fontana, and just behind a long row of saloons and greasy-spoon cafes. Those ladies who worked in the red-light houses—in God We Trust, All Others Pay Cash—were not allowed past the invisible line separating the good people from the less desirable people during the time between seven in the morning and four in the afternoon. Heaven forbid that a "decent woman" should have to rub shoulders with . . . that other kind of lady.

* * *

Peyton had found the butchered carcass of two of his beeves close to a miner's camp.

"Take it easy," Smoke said trying to calm the older man. "Those miners have hit a solid strike over there. No reason for them to have rustled any of your cows. Think about it, Peyton. Look here," Smoke said, pointing. "These are horse tracks around these carcasses."

"So?" Peyton angrily demanded. "What the hell has that got to do with it?"

"Those miners are riding mules, Peyton."

That news brought the farmer-rancher up short and silent. He walked over and sat down on a fallen log. He thought about that news for a moment.

"We're not actin' like Tilden would like," Peyton said softly. "So he's tryin' to prod us into doin' something to blow the lid off. I was about to play right into his game, and he would have sent those so-called deputies up to arrest me, wouldn't he, Smoke?"

"Probably." Smoke had told none of the others about the old gunfighters on their way in. Charlie had returned from his travels, all smiles and good news.

The aging gunfighters would begin arriving at any time, trickling in alone or in pairs as they linked up on the trails and roads.

"Go on home," Smoke told the older man, "I'll go see the miners."

Smoke watched the moan mount up and leave. He swung into the saddle and rode up toward the miners' camp. He hailed the camp and was told to come on in.

Briefly Smoke explained, but he made no mention of Tilden Franklin.

"Who would try to cause trouble, Smoke?" a burly miner asked.

"I don't know. But I just put the lid back on what might have been real trouble. You boys be careful from here on in. Tempers are frayed enough around here. The slightest thing could light the fuse."

"We will. Smoke, you reckon Peyton and some of the others would mind if me and the boys pitched in and kind of helped around their places? You know . . . we're all pretty handy with tools . . . maybe some repair work, such as that?"

"I think it would be a hell of a nice move on your part." Smoke grinned and the miners grinned back. "And it's gonna irritate whoever it is trying to stir up trouble. I'll tell the others to look for you. I bet y'all would like some home-cooked grub too, wouldn't you?"

That brought a round of cheers from the miners, many of whom had families far away.

Smoke wheeled his horse and rode back down the mountain. Smoke the gunfighter had suddenly become Smoke the peacemaker.

"Nothing," Clint told Tilden. "Smoke made peace with the miners. He figured it all out somehow."

"What's it going to take to prod those goddamned nesters into action?" Tilden asked. "I'm about out of ideas."

Clint didn't like what he was about to suggest, but Clint rode for the brand. Right or wrong. "The Colby girl."

Although it had originally been Tilden's idea, the more he thought about it, the less he liked it. Bother a good woman out West and a man was in serious trouble . . . and it didn't make a damn who you were or how much or how little you had.

"Risky, Clint." He met the man's eyes. "You have a plan?"

"Yes," the foreman said, and stepped across that narrow chasm that separated good from evil, man from rabid beast.

"How long will it take you to set it up?"

"A few days. Them nesters got to be going into town for supplies pretty soon."

Tilden nodded his head. "Do it."

"You better get some sort of platform, Boss," Pearlie told Smoke.

"Platform? What are you talking about?"

"Some of them old gunhands is pullin' in. I swear to God there oughta be a hearse followin' along behind 'em."

Smoke stepped out of the barn just as Charlie was riding up from the Sugarloaf range.

Smoke had never seen a more disreputable, down-at-the-heels-looking bunch in all his life. Some of them looked like they'd be lucky to see another morning break clear.

"See what I mean about that platform, Boss? I swear that them ol' boys is gonna hurt themselves gettin' off their horse."

Smoke had to smile. He was fondly recalling a bunch of Mountain Men who, at eighty, were as spry as many men half their age. "Don't sell them short, Pearlie. I got a hunch they're gonna fool us all."

"Hi, thar, Buttermilk!" Charlie called.

"Aaa-yeeee!" the old man hollered. "You get uglier ever' time I see you, Charlie."

"Talks funny too," Pearlie said.

"I seen now why he's called Buttermilk."

"Why?"

"That's probably all he can eat. He don't have any teeth!"

18

"*That* is The Apache Kid?" Sally said, speaking to Smoke. "I have heard stories about The Apache Kid ever since I arrived in the West. Smoke, he looks like he might topple over at any moment."

"That's him," Smoke said. "Preacher told me about him. And I'll make you a bet right now that that old man can walk all day and all night, stop for a handful of berries and take a sip of water, and go another twenty-four hours."

"I ain't dis-pootin' your word, Boss," Pearlie said. "But I'm gonna have to see it to believe it."

Smiling, Smoke bent down and picked up a small chunk of wood. "Apache!" he called.

The old, buckskin-clad man turned and looked at Smoke.

"A silver dollar says you can't knock it out of the air."

"Toss 'er, boy!"

Smoke tossed the chunk high into the air. With fifty-odd years of gunhandling in his past, Apache's draw was as smooth and practiced as water over a fall. He fired six times. Six times the hardwood chunk was hit, before falling in slivers to the ground.

"Jesus!" Pearlie breathed.

"That's six silver dollars you owe me," Apache said.

Smoke laughed and nodded his head. The Apache Kid turned to talk with Charlie.

"That Jensen?" Apache asked, as the other old gun-fighters listened.

"That's him."

"He as good as they say?" Bowie asked.

"I wouldn't want to brace him," Charlie said, paying Smoke the highest compliment one gunhand could pay to another.

"That good, hey?" Luke Nations asked.

"He's the best."

"I heared he was that," Dan Greentree said. "Rat nice of him to in-vite us on this little hoo-raw."

Smoke and Sally had gone into the cabin, leaving the others to talk.

Pearlie shyly wandered over to the growing knot of men. He was expecting to get the needle put to him, and he got just that.

"Your ma know you slipped away from the house, boy?" a huge, grizzled old man asked.

Pearlie smiled and braced himself. "You be Pistol Le Roux?"

"I was when I left camp this mornin'."

"I run arcost a pal of yourn 'bout three years ago—up on the Utah-Wyoming line. South of Fort Supply. Called hisself Pawnee."

"Do tell? How was ol' Pawnee?"

"Not too good. He died. I buried him at the base of Kings Mountain, north side. Thought you'd wanna know."

"I do and I 'preciate your plantin' him. Say a word over him, did you?"

"Some."

"This is Pearlie, Pistol."

"Pleased. Join us, Pearlie."

Pearlie stood silent and listened to the men talk. Charlie said, "This ain't gonna be no Sunday social, boys. And I'll come right up front and tell you that some of you is likely to be planted in these here mountains."

The sounds of horses coming hard paused Charlie. He waited until the last of the old gunslicks had dismounted and shook and howdied.

Charlie counted heads. Twenty of the hardest, most talked-about, and most legendary men of the West stood in the front yard of the sturdy little cabin. Only God and God alone knew how many men these randy old boys had put down into that eternal rest.

The Apache Kid was every bit of seventy. But could still draw and shoot with the best.

Buttermilk didn't have a tooth in his head, but those Colts belted around his lean waist could bite and snarl and roar.

Jay Church was a youngster, 'bout Charlie's age. But a feared gunhawk.

Dad Weaver was in his mid-sixties. He'd opened him a little cafe when he'd hung up his guns, but the rowdies and the punks hadn't left him alone. They'd come lookin' and he'd given the undertaker more business. He'd finally said to hell with it and taken off for the mountains.

Silver Jim still looked the dandy. Wearin' one of them long white coats that road agents had taken to wearing. His boots was old and patched, but they shined. And his dark short coat was kinda frayed at the cuffs, but it was clean. His Colts was oiled and deadly.

Ol' Hardrock. Charlie smiled. What could he say about Hardrock? The man had cleaned up more wild towns than any two others combined. Now he was aging and broke. But still ready to ride the high trails of the Mountain Men.

Charlie lifted his eyes and spotted Moody. Ol' Moody. Standin' away from the others, livin' up to his name.

Never had much to say, but by the Lord he was as rough and randy as they could come.

Linch. Big and hoary and bearded. Never packed but one short gun. Said he never needed but one.

Luke Nations. A legend. Sheriff, marshal, outlaw, gunfighter. Had books wrote about him. And as far as Charlie knew, never got a dime out of any of them.

Pistol Le Roux. A Creole from down in Louisiana. As fast with a knife as with a gun . . . and that was plenty fast.

Quiet Bill Foley. Wore his guns cross-draw and had a border roll that was some quick.

Dan Greentree. Charlie had ridden many a trail with Dan. Charlie wondered if these mountain trails around Fontana would be their last to ride.

Leo Wood. Leo just might be the man who had brought the fast draw to the West. A lot of people said he was. And a lot of so-called fast guns had died trying to best him.

Cary Webb. Some said he owned a fine education and had once taught school back East. Chucked it all and came West, looking for excitement. Earned him a rep as a fast gun.

Sunset Hatfield. Supposed to be from either Kentucky or Tennessee. A crack shot with rifle or pistol.

Crooked John Simmons. Got that name hung on him 'cause he was as cross-eyed as anybody had ever seen. Had a hair-trigger temper and a set of hair-trigger Colts.

Bull Flagler. Strong as a bull and just as dangerous. Carried him a sawed-off shotgun with a pistol grip on his left side, a Colt on the other.

Toot Tooner. Loved trains. Loved 'em so much he just couldn't resist holding them up back some years. Turned lawman and made a damn good one. Fast draw and a dead shot.

Sutter Cordova. His mother was French and his dad was Spanish. Killed a man when he was 'bout ten or eleven years old; man was with a bunch that killed his ma and pa. Sutter got his pa's guns, mounted up, and tracked them from Chihuahua to Montana Territory. Took him six years, but he killed every one of them. Sutter was not a man you wanted to get crossways of.

Red Shingletown. Still had him a mighty fine mess of flamin' red hair. He'd been a soldier, a sailor, an adventurer, a rancher . . . and a gunfighter.

And there they stood, Smoke thought, gazing at the men from the cabin. I'm looking at yet another last of a breed.

But did I do right in asking them to come?

Sally touched his arm. Smoke looked down at her.

"You did the right thing," she told him. "The trail that lies before those men out there is the one they chose, and if it is their last trail to ride, that's the way they would want it. And even though they are doing this for you and for Charlie, you know the main reason they're doing it, don't you?"

Smoke grinned, wiping years trom his face. He looked about ten years old. All except for his eyes. "Ol' Preacher."

"That's right, honey. They all knew him, and knew that he helped raise you."

"What do you plan on having for supper?"

"I hadn't thought. Why?"

"How about making some bearsign?"

"It's going to run me out of flour."

"Well, I think me and Charlie and some of those ol' boys out there just might ride into Fontana tomorrow. We'll stop by Colby's and get him to take his wagon. Stock up enough for everybody. 'Sides, I want to see Louis's face when we all come ridin' in."

"Uh-huh," she said, poking him in the ribs and tickling him, bending him over, gently slapping at her hands. "But mostly you want to see Tilden Franklin's face."

"Well . . . He suddenly swept her up in his arms and began carrying her toward the bedroom.

"Smoke. Not with all those . . ."

He kissed her mouth, hushing her.

". . . men out . . ."

He kissed her again and placed her gently on the bed.

"Who cares about those men out there?" she finally said.

It came as no surprise to Smoke to find the men up before he crawled out from under the covers. This high up, even the summer nights were cool . . . and this was still late spring. The nights were downright cold.

The men had gotten their bearsign the previous night, but Sally had been just a bit late with them.

Smoke dressed, belted on his Colts, and, with a mug of coffee in one hand, stepped out to meet the breaking dawn, all silver and gold as the sun slowly inched over the high peaks of Sugarloaf.

"Charlie, I thought a few of us would ride into town this morning and pick up supplies. We'll stop at Colby's place and he'll go with us in his wagon."

"Who you want to go in with you?"

"You pick 'em."

Adam Colby had been reading a dime novel about the life and times of Luke Nation, with a drawing of him on the cover, when he looked up at the sounds of horse's hooves drumming on the road. The boy thought he'd been flung directly into the pages of the dime novel.

He looked at the man on the horse, looked at the cover of the book, and then took off running for the house, hollering for his pa.

"Boy!" Colby said, stepping out of the house. "What in tarnation is wrong with . . ."

The man looked at the group of riders still sitting their horses in his front yard. Colby's eyes flitted from man to man, taking in the lined and tanned faces, the hard, callused hands, and the guns belted around the lean waists. Colby knew of most of the men . . . he just never imagined he'd see them in his front yard.

Adam approached Luke, the dime novel in his hand. He stood looking up at the famed gunfighter, awe in his eyes. He held out the book.

"Would you sign my book, Mister Nations?"

"I'd be right honored, boy," the gunfighter said. He grinned. "That's about all I can write is my name." He took the book and a stub of a pencil Adam held out to him and slowly printed his name, giving book and pencil back to the boy.

"Thank you, sir."

"You're welcome."

"We're riding into Fontana, Colby. Sally needs some supplies. Wanna get your wagon and come in with us?"

"Good idea. Wilbur and the boys will stay here. Give me a minute to get my shirt on. Adam, hook up the team, son."

Colby's wife Belle, daughter Velvet, and boys Adam and Bob stood with Wilbur and his wife Edna and watched the men pull out. They would stop at several other small spreads to take any orders for supplies. The men and women and kids left at Colby's place resumed their morning chores.

A mile away, hidden in the timber, a TF rider watched it all through field glasses. When the men had ridden and rumbled out of sight, the TF rider took a mirror from his saddlebags and caught the morning sun, signaling to another TF rider that everything was ready. He didn't know who them hard-lookin' old boys was with Jensen, but they didn't look like they'd be much trouble to handle. Most of 'em looked to be older than God.

* * *

Tilden Franklin wanted to make damn sure he was highly visible to as many people as possible until after Clint's plan was over. Tilden had taken to riding into Fontana every morning, early, with Clint and several of his hardcases for bodyguards. He and his foreman usually had breakfast at the best hotel in town and then took their after-meal cigars while sitting on the porch of the hotel, perhaps reading or talking or just watching the passing parade.

This morning, Tilden looked up from the new edition of the *Fontana Sunburst*, Haywood and Dana Arden's endeavor, just as a TF rider rode by. Without looking at either Tilden or Clint, the rider very minutely nodded his head as he passed.

With a slight smile, Tilden lifted the newspaper and once more resumed his reading.

In a way, Tilden thought, he was kind of sorry he was gonna miss out on the action with that built-up little gal of Colby's. Tilden would bet that, once she settled into the rhythm, Velvet would get to liking it. All women were the same when it came to that, Tilden felt. They liked to holler and raise sand, but they wanted it. They just liked to pretend they didn't for the look of things.

Women, to Tilden's mind, were very notional critters . . . and just like critters, not very bright. Pretty to have around, nice to pet, but that was about it.

One of Monte Carson's deputies rode up and looped the reins over the hitch rail in front of the hotel. Dismounting, he stood on the boardwalk facing Tilden.

"Charlie Starr ridin' in with that Smoke Jensen and the nester Colby, Mister Tilden."

Tilden felt his face stiffen and grow hot as the blood raced to flush his cheeks. He lowered the newspaper and stared at the deputy.

"Charlie *Starr?*"

"Yes, sir. And that ain't all. Smoke's got some mean ol' gunslicks with him, too. The Apache Kid, Sunset Hatfield, Bill Foley, Silver Jim, Moody, and Luke Nations. They ridin' like they got a purpose if you know what I mean."

A young, two-hit, half-assed punk, who thought himself to be a bad man, was hanging around near the open doors of the hotel. He smiled and felt his heart race at the news. The deputy had just mentioned half a dozen of the most famous gunslingers in all the West. And they were coming into town—here!

Right here, the punk who called himself The Silver Dollar Kid thought, is where I make my rep. Right here, right out there in that street, that's where it all starts. He smiled and walked through the lobby, slipping out the back way. He wanted to change clothes, put on his best outfit before he faced one of those old gunhawks. There was a picture-taker in town; might be a good idea to stop by his studio and tell him about the old gunslicks so's he could have all his equipment set up and ready to pop.

The punk ran back to his tent and began changing into his very finest.

The news of the approaching gunfighters, still several miles out of Fontana, swept through the town like wildfire through a dry forest. Haywood heard it and walked rapidly toward the main business district. He found himself a spot on the boardwalk across the street from where Tilden Franklin sat, surrounded by his hardcases.

Shopkeepers had shooed customers outside, where they stood, lining the boardwalks and packed-dirt sidewalks, waiting for the event of the day.

Louis Longmont came out of his gaming tent to stand on the boardwalk, watching as he smoked his first cigar of the morning. So Smoke had done it, he thought. A smile curved his lips. He'd actually pulled in some of the randiest old boys still living in the West.

"Going to be interesting," Louis murmured. "Very, very interesting."

19

Smoke halted his small group on the edge of town. He looked at Charlie. "A whole passel of two-bit young punks who'll be looking for a reputation in town. They'll be on the prod for a fight."

Charlie spat on the dirt beneath his horse's belly. "They'll damn sure get more than they bargained for with this bunch," he replied.

"We'll ride straight through," Smoke said. "Stopping at Jackson's Mercantile. Colby, pull your wagon up to the loading dock by the side. If there's going to be trouble, let the other side start it. Let's go, boys."

Smoke and Charlie took the point, with Apache and Sunset riding to the left of the wagon, Bill Foley and Silver Jim to the right, and Moody and Luke Nations taking the drag. Smoke rode slowly, so the wheels of the wagon would not kick up much dust. The town had virtually come to a halt, the streets lined with citizens. They stood silently, watching the riders make their way along the street. Trouble hung in the air, as thick as dust.

The riders could practically feel the hate from Tilden Franklin's eyes boring into them as they rode past where he sat like a king on the hotel boardwalk. Smoke met the man's eyes and touched his hat brim in a gesture of greeting.

Tilden did not return the greeting.

They passed Louis Longmont's gaming tent. Most of the old gunfighters knew the gambler and they greeted him. Louis returned the greeting and very minutely nodded his head in the direction Smoke was riding.

There was something or someone down there that Louis wanted Smoke to know about. Smoke's eyes searched both sides of the street. Then he saw them, the three of them, lounging in front of a newly erected tent saloon.

Luis Chamba, Kane, and Sanderson.

The Mexican gunfighter stood with his arms folded across his chest, his sombrero off his head, hanging down his back by the chin cord.

"See them?" Smoke whispered the words, just audible over the clop of hooves.

"I see them," Charlie returned the whisper. "That Chamba, he's a bad one. Kills for pleasure. Gets his kicks that way, you know?"

Smoke knew the type.

Then they were past the killers.

"Kane and Sanderson?" Smoke asked. He knew of them, but did not know them personally.

"Just as bad. They're all three twisted. And they'll kill anything or anybody for money."

"Look at them punks over to your left."

"Seen them too," Charlie said sourly. "Lookin' to make themselves a reputation. I hope they don't try none of this bunch. These guys are all on the shady side of their years, but Lord God, don't sell 'em short."

A young man with a smart-ass look to him and dressed like a San Francisco pimp stood glaring at the men. At least Smoke figured that's how a San Francisco pimp might dress, having never been there.

"Reckon it's time for us to start us a Boot Hill here in

Fontana, boys!" the loud-mouthed, loudly dressed young man said, raising his voice so the riders could all hear him.

The Apache Kid favored the young man with a glance and dismissed him just as quickly.

Sunset openly laughed at the dandy.

"Yeah," another duded-up, two-gun-totin' young man agreed, his voice loud. "And them old boys yonder ain't got long to go no ways. Might as well start with them. How 'bout it?"

None of the aging gunfighters even acknowledged the punk had spoken. They rode on.

"Hell!" another would-be gunslinger yelled, fanning the air with his fancy hat. "They so goddamned old they done lost their balls, boys!"

"That one is mine," Luke said, just so his friends could hear.

"He means it, Smoke," Charlie said. "Don't interfere none."

"Far be it for me to interfere," Smoke answered.

Back in the high country, Velvet Colby, her chores done for the morning, thought it would be nice to take a walk through the woods.

"Stay close, Velvet!" her mother called.

"Yes, ma'am, I will."

Adam watched her go. He stuck his dime novel in his back pocket and picked up his .22 rifle, following Velvet but staying back, knowing how his sister enjoyed being alone.

While Ed Jackson and his brother loaded the wagon with supplies, Colby walked with Smoke over to Louis Longmont's place. He introduced them and Louis invited them inside. Smoke had no intention of trying to shepherd and play check-rein on Charlie and the others. They'd been without his advice for a combination of about three hundred and fifty years. They didn't need it now.

"A taste of the Glenlivet, gentlemen?" Louis asked.

"Huh?" Colby asked.

"Fine scotch whiskey," Smoke told him.

Three tumblers poured three fingers deep, Louis lifted his glass. "Here's to a very interesting summer, gentlemen."

They clinked glasses and sipped.

Louis smiled. "Shall we adjourn to what laughingly passes for a veranda and watch the show, boys?"

"Sure going to be one," Smoke agreed, moving toward the door.

Luke Nations had broken off from the others and was walking toward the knot of would-be gunslicks, walking directly toward the duded-up punk with the fat mouth. Luke stopped about twenty-five feet from him. He stood with the leather thongs off the hammers of his Colts. He stood with his feet slightly spread. He was big and bent and old and mean-looking. And the look in his eyes would have warned off a puma.

"You made a comment a minute or so ago, kid," Luke said, his voice flat and hard. "Well, now is your chance to back up your mouth. Either that . . . or tuck your fancy tail between your legs and carry your ass!"

His name was Lester. But he called himself Sundance. At this moment, he felt more like Lester than Sundance.

The Silver Dollar Kid had backed up against a wall. Unlike Lester, he wasn't afraid; he just wanted to see if the old men still had it in them. When he had studied them, then he would make his move.

"Goddamn you, boy!" Luke's voice was so sharp, it hurt. "Do you hear me?"

"Yeah, I hear you." Sundance surfaced, pushing Lester out of the way.

Monte Carson had come on the run when he heard the news of the impending shoot-out. He came to an abrupt halt, almost falling as his high-heeled boots dug into the dirt of the street. One of his deputies ran into him, and they both almost fell.

"What the hell?" the deputy said.

"Shut up and look around you!" Monte whispered hoarsely.

The Apache Kid was just across the street, standing alone, both hands to his sides, the palms very close to the butts of his Colts.

The deputy cut his eyes. Old Sunset was standing behind them, about thirty feet away.

Bill Foley stood just to their right, poised and ready for anything that might come his way.

"Ssshhittt!" Monte hissed, the breath whistling between his slightly gapped front teeth. He was looking eyeball to eyeball with Silver Jim, his long white duster brushed back, exposing the butts of the Colts, the leather hammer thongs off.

Back of them, facing Tilden Franklin and Clint, stood Moody. Moody said, "You boys come to watch or get dealt in?"

Tilden chewed his cigar soggy in a matter of a heart-beat. He felt no fear, for there was no fear in him. But he had grown up hearing stories about these old gunfighters. And at this distance, everybody was going to get lead in them. And there was something else too. Tilden knew, from hard experience, that when dealing with ballsy old men you'd best walk lightly. With their best years behind them, they had nothing to lose. Old men did not fight fair. Tilden had learned that the hard way too.

Clint cut his eyes. Louis Longmont, his tailored jacket brushed back over the butts of his guns, stood to Clint's right. Smoke was facing Tilden's other hands, and the other hands were looking a little green around the mouth.

And the gunslinger Johnny North had finally made his appearance. The blond-haired Nevada gunhand stood in the street, facing Luis Chamba and his two side-kicks. Johnny was smiling. And those that knew Johnny knew Johnny was not the smiling type.

All in all, as the *Fontana Sunburst* would later say in a column by its editor, it was a most exhilarating and tense moment. These legends of the Wild West, captivating an entire town with their bigger-than-life presence. A moment from the fading past that would be forever etched in the minds of all who had the opportunity to witness this fortuitous encounter of the last of the Bad Men.

Haywood did, on occasion, get a tad bit carried away with his writing.

But since the written word was scarce in the West, folks would read and enjoy nearabout anything. They might not understand what the hell they were reading, but read it they would.

"Do it, punk!" Luke shouted. He began walking toward the dandy. Luke had felt all along the dandy didn't have the cold nerve to pull iron. When he reached the young man, who was beginning to sweat, he balled his left hand into a hard fist and knocked the loud-mouth to the dirt. Lester-Sundance fell hard. He lay on the dirt, looking up at Luke through wide, scared eyes.

Luke reached down and plucked the pearl-handled Colts from the young man's holsters. He stepped to one side and wedged one barrel between a support block and the boardwalk. With a swift jerk, he broke off first one barrel, and then the other. He tossed the ruined pistols to Lester-Sundance.

"I'll tell you something, boy," Luke said. "I wish some-body had done something like that to me when I was your age. I might have amounted to something."

Luke Nations turned his back to the sobbing, humili-ated young man and walked away.

"I'll kill him for that," Lester-Sundance sobbed, but not loud enough for Luke to hear. "You just wait and see. I'll get him for that."

The Silver Dollar Kid walked across the street, in the direction Luke had taken.

"Well, boys!" Louis said. "How about the drinks on me? What say you all?"

Smoke looked at Tilden Franklin. "That includes you too, Franklin. Join us?"

His face flushed with rage and hate, Tilden turned his back on the invitation and stomped back up the street, Clint following like a dog behind him.

The TF puppies followed Clint.

Louis watched Tilden wheel around and stalk off. The man is obviously of low degree," the gambler said.

Smoke, Colby, and the gunfighters had a laugh at that. Tilden had heard the remark, and his back stiffened with new anger. His rage was such that he could hardly see.

"Get the horses, Clint!" he snapped.

"Boss," Clint warned. "Hadn't we best stay in town?"

Tilden's big hands gripped a hitchrail and he trembled in his hot fury. "Yes. Yes," he repeated, then cleared his throat. "You're right. Order your boys to take off their gunbelts, Clint."

"*What?*"

"You heard me, Clint. We're going to take that invitation for a drink. And then I'm going to stomp Smoke Jensen's goddamned guts out. With my fists and boots!"

20

"What the hell?" Billy said, eyeballing Tilden and Clint and the other TF' rowdies removing their gunbelts and looping them on their saddle horns.

The livery stable-swamper darted across the street and into Louis Longmont's gaming place.

"Smoke!" he called. All heads turned toward the small boy in the doorway. "Tilden Franklin and them gunhands of his'n done dropped their gunbelts, and they're all headin' this way. I don't know what they're about, but I betcha it's bad trouble."

"I know what it is," Smoke said. He set his untouched tumbler on the bar. "Thanks, Billy."

"Come here, son," Louis said. "You get over there," he pointed, "and stay put. Andre!" he called for his chef. "Get this young man a sarsaparilla, *s'il vous plait*?"

"But *monsieur . . . ou*?"

"Reasonable question," Louis muttered. "Where indeed? Lemonade?"

Andre's face brightened. *"Oui!"*

A big glass of cool lemonade in front of him, Billy slipped from the table to the eggs-and-cheese-and-beef end of the bar and filled a napkin with goodies. Eating and sipping, Billy sat back to watch the show.

Louis watched the boy's antics and smiled. His big bouncer, Mike, stood close by Billy, his massive arms folded across his barrel chest,

The chef, Andre, had beat it back to his kitchen. Let the barbarians fight, he thought.

Boot heels drummed on the boardwalk and Tilden Franklin's bulk filled the doorway. "I thought I'd take you up on your offer, Gambler," he said.

"Certainly," Louis said. "Be my guest."

Tilden walked to the bar and poured a tumbler of whiskey. He toyed with the shot glass for a moment, then lifted the glass. "To the day when we rid the country of all two-bit nesters."

Tilden and his men drank. None of the others acknowledged the toast.

Tilden smiled. "What's the matter boys? None of you like my toast?"

Smoke lifted his glass. "To the day when farmers and ranchers all get along."

Smoke's friends toasted that. Tilden, Clint, and the other TF men did not.

"What's the matter, Tilden?" Smoke asked. "You don't like my toast?"

Tilden's smile was thin. Toying with his empty shot glass, his eyes on the polished bar, he said, "I've always had this theory, Jensen . . . or whatever your name is. My theory is that most gunslicks live on their reputations, that without a gun in their hand, they're mighty thin in the guts department. What do you think about that?"

"I think you're mighty thin between the ears, Tilden. That's what I think. I think you sit on your brains. Now what do you think about that?"

"I'm not armed, Jensen," Tilden said, still looking down at the bar.

Smoke unbuckled and untied. He handed his guns to Colby. "Neither am I, Tilden. So the next move is up to you."

Tilden looked at his riders. "Clear us a space, boys."

Gaming tables and chairs were pushed back, stacked against one wall. The barroom floor was empty.

Tilden's smile was ugly and savage. "I'm gonna break you in half, Jensen. Then your wife can see for herself what a real man can do . . . when she comes to my bed."

Smoke laughed at that. "You're a bigger fool than I first thought, Tilden. Now make your move or shut your goddamned flapping mouth."

Tilden spun away from the bar railing and charged Smoke. All two-hundred-forty-odd pounds of him, like an enraged bull, charging at the smaller man.

Smoke stepped to one side, stuck out a boot, and tripped the big man, sending him crashing and sprawling to the barroom floor. Smoke stepped in and kicked Tilden in the side, bringing a grunt of pain from the man. Before Smoke could put the boots to him again, Tilden rolled away and jumped to his feet.

Smoke, weighing some fifty-odd pounds less than Tilden, faced the bigger man. Both men lifted their hands and balled their fists.

"I'm taking bets on Smoke!" Louis announced. "Any takers?"

Clint and the TF men bet on their boss.

Haywood, Cohen, Hunt, Ralph, and Ed had quietly slipped into the gaming room, standing close to the front door.

Big Mamma O'Neil bulled her way past those at the door. "A hundred bucks on Tilden!" she yelled.

"Done!" Louis said.

"Barbaric!" Hunt muttered.

Big Mamma laughed and slapped the lawyer on the back, almost knocking him down. She stepped on past the men at the door and walked to a far wall.

Tilden flicked a right hand toward Smoke, a feeling-out punch. Smoke moved his head slightly, dodging the punch. He jabbed a hard left, catching Tilden in the mouth, snapping the man's head back.

With a roar, Tilden swung a roundhouse left that caught Smoke on the shoulder. A powerfully thrown punch, it brought a grunt of pain from the smaller man. Smoke countered with a right, hitting Tilden in the belly. It was like hitting a piece of hardwood. Tilden grinned at Smoke and the men went after each other, toe to toe, slugging it out.

Smoke realized that if he was to win this fight, and that was something he had to do, for morale's sake if nothing else, there was no way he could stand up and match Tilden punch for punch. The man was bigger and stronger, and in excellent physical shape.

Smoke jumped to one side and lashed out with one boot, the toe of the boot catching Tilden on the kneecap. Tilden howled in pain and, for a second, dropped his guard. A second was all that Smoke needed.

Smoke hit the man twice, a left-and-right combination to the jaw. His punches were savage, and they rocked the bigger man, bringing blood from one side of his mouth. Tilden staggered under the combination. Just for a second, his legs buckling.

Smoke hit the man flush on his mouth. Tildern's lips splattered under the hard-thrown punch, the blood spurting. Tilden grabbed Smoke in a bear hug, holding on until he could recover. Smoke experienced the man's massive strength as the air was crushed out of him. Tucking his head under Tilden's jaw, Smoke brought his head up savagely. Tilden's mouth snapped shut and he squalled in pain as the teeth caught his tongue and more blood was added to the flow from his battered mouth. The big man's grip eased and Smoke slipped out of the bear hug.

Pivoting, Smoke poured on the steam and hit Tilden in the gut with every ounce of strength he could muster. The right fist caught Tilden just above the belt buckle, and the wind whooshed out of the man as he involuntarily doubled over. Smoke stepped in close and grabbed Tilden's head and hair with both hands and brought the head down at the same time he was bringing a knee up. The knee caught Tilden smack on the nose and the nose crunched under the impact. Tilden was flung back against the bar.

The big man hung there, his eyes still wild but glazed over. Smoke stepped in close and went to work on the kingpin.

Smoke hammered at the man's belly and face with work-hardened fists. In seconds, Tilden's face was swollen and battered and bloody.

Clint stepped in to break up the fight and found himself suddenly lying on the barroom flour, hit on the back of the head by The Apache Kid's rifle stock. Clint moaned once and then lay still, out cold.

Smoke went to work on Tilden's belly, concentrating all his punches there, and they were thrown with all his strength. It was a savage, brutal attack on Smoke's part, but Smoke knew, from having the old Mountain Man Preacher as his teacher, that there was no such thing as a fair fight. There was only a winner, and a loser.

He hammered at Tilden's mid-section, working like a steam-driven pile-driver.

Twice, Tilden almost slumped to the floor. Twice, Smoke propped him back up and went to work on him. He shifted his attention to Tilden's face, his punches ruining the man's once-handsome features. Smoke's flat-knuckled fists knocked out teeth and loosened others. His fists completely flattened Tilden's nose. One punch to the side of Tilden's head ripped loose an ear, almost tearing it off the man's head. Still Smoke did not let up. His fists smashed into Tilden's sides and kidneys and belly and face.

Smoke was fighting with a cold, controlled, dark fury. His fists battered the man; this man who had boasted he would take Smoke's wife; this man who had sworn to run Smoke and the others out of this part of Colorado; this man who dared impose his will on all others.

Then Smoke realized he was battering and smashing an unconscious man. He stopped his assault and stepped back, his chest heaving and his hands hurting. Tilden Franklin, the bully of the valley, the man who would be king, the man who would control the destiny of all those around him, slipped to the floor to lie among the cigarette and cigar butts. His blood stained the trash on the floor.

He was so deep in his unconsciousness he did not even twitch.

"I'd have never believed it," Big Mamma O'Neil was heard to whisper. "But I seen it. Lord have mercy, did I ever see it."

"That's a hundred dollars you owe me, Big Mamma," Louis said. "You can give it to Billy over there."

Louis looked at the Tilden riders. "You TF riders can pay Big Mike."

"I have some medication at the office that will ease those swelling hands, Smoke," Colton said, "I'll be waiting for you."

Smoke leaned against the bar and nodded his head.

"Ain't you gonna see to Mister Franklin?" a TF rider asked.

"At the office," Colton said shortly. "I'll prepare a bed for him."

Smoke belted his guns around him and began working his fingers, to prevent them from stiffening any worse than he knew they would.

"Drag that cretin from my premises," Louis said, pointing at the prostrate Tilden Franklin.

Big Mamma O'Neil laid five twenty-dollar gold pieces on the table in front of Billy.

Billy looked up at her with a bit of egg sticking to his upper lip . . .

. . . and grinned!

BOOK TWO

Now this is the law of the jungle—as old and as true as the sky. And the Wolf that shall keep it may prosper, but the Wolf that shall break it must die.

—Kipling

1

Twice, Adam thought he heard something back in the timber behind the Colby house. He lifted his head and concentrated. Nothing. He returned to his reading of the dime novel about the adventures of Luke Nations.

He was just getting to the part about where Luke rides into the Indian camp, both six-guns blazing, to rescue the lovely maiden when he heard kind of a muffled, cut-off scream from in the timber.

"Velvet!" he called.

Only the silence greeted his call. And then it came to him. The silence. The birds and the small animals around the place were used to Velvet's walking through the woods. They seldom stopped their singing and chattering and calling simply because she came gently walking through.

The boy picked up his single-shot .22-caliber rifle and put his dime novel in the hip pocket of his patched and faded work pants. "Velvet!" he shouted.

Nothing.

Not the singing of a bird, not the calling or barking of a squirrel.

Something was wrong.

Adam hesitated, started to go back to the house for

Mister Wilbur. Then he shook his head. It would take too long, for Velvet had strayed a pretty good piece from the house.

There was movement from his left. Adam turned just as something hard slammed into the back of his head and sent him spinning into darkness. The darkness blotted out the sunlight filtering through the trees.

When he awakened, the first thing he noticed was that the sunlight through the limbs had changed somewhat, shifting positions. Adam figured he'd been out a good thirty to forty-five minutes. Painfully, he got to a sitting-up position. His head was hurting something fierce and things were moving around like they shouldn't oughta.

He sat very still for a few moments, until his head began to clear and settle down. He thought he heard some sort of grunting sounds. Adam couldn't figure out what they might be.

He got to his feet, swaying for a moment. When things settled down, he looked around for his .22 rifle. He checked it, brushing the dirt from it, and checked the load. He kept hearing that grunting sound. Slowly, cautiously, the boy made his way through the timber toward that odd sound.

He came to a little clearing—must be two miles from the house—and paused, peering through the branches.

What he saw brought him up short and mad.

It was Velvet, and she didn't have no clothes on; her dress was torn off and tossed to one side. And a bunch of them TF riders was standing around, some of them bare-assed naked, some in their long-handles.

And there was money all over the ground. Adam couldn't figure out what all them greenbacks and silver dollars was doing on the ground.

But he knew what them men was doing. He'd never done it with no girl hisself, but he wasn't no fool.

It looked like to him that Velvet wasn't having no good time of it. It looked like to him she was out cold. He could see bruises on her face and her . . . on her chest. And there was dark marks on her legs where them riders had gripped at her with hard hands. Like that one was doing now. Pokin' at her. From behind. Like an animal.

Adam lifted his rifle and sighted in. It was not going to be a hard shot, but he had the rifle loaded with little shorts for squirrels. He sighted in and pulled the trigger.

It was a good shot, the little chunk of lead striking the rapist in his right eye. The rapist just fell backward, off Velvet, and lay on his back, his privates exposed.

Velvet sort of rolled off the log they'd had her bent over and lay real still.

Adam quickly reloaded and sighted in again. But before he could pull the trigger, a short gun barked and something hard struck him in the chest. The slug knocked him backward. He lost his grip on his rifle. Adam knew he was bad hit, maybe going to die, but he lay still as the men ran up to him.

"Let's get outta here!" he heard one say.

"What about Steve?"

"Take him with us. We'll bury him proper."

"Little son of a bitch kilt him with a lousy .22," another spoke.

"Let's ride."

When the sounds of their horses had faded, Adam tried to reach his sister. He could not. The pain in his chest was getting worse and he was having a hard time seeing. He pulled his dime novel out of his pocket and took his worn stub of a pencil. Slowly, with bloody fingers, he began to print out a message.

A few minutes later, the boy laid his head down on the cool earth and closed his eyes. A moment later he was dead.

Smoke and the others arrived back a few hours before dark. They had pushed their horses hard. Colby and Charlie were about two hours behind.

Belle Colby met the men in the front yard.

"I can't find Velvet or Adam," she told Smoke. She had been crying, her eyes red-rimmed.

"Bob met us, Belle," Smoke said. "Charlie stayed with Colby just in case. They're a couple of hours behind us. Any idea where they might have gone?"

"No. The girl has her—what she calls her secret places in the timber where she goes to be alone."

The men dismounted. Smoke turned to The Apache Kid. "Apache, Preacher once told me you could track a snake over a flat rock."

"I'll find her trail," the old gunfighter said.

He moved out with a swiftness that belied his age. "Stay behind me," he called to the others. "Jist stay back till I locate some sign. And don't come up to me when I do find it. I don't want none of it all mucked up."

He began moving in a criss-cross manner, looking to anyone who did not understand tracking like a man who had lost his mind. In less than five minutes, he called out. "I got it. Stay behind me."

Apache was following the girl's sign, not Adam's, so they found the girl first.

"Good Jesus Christ!" Silver Jim said. He peeled off his duster and wrapped it around the girl. She was conscious, but in some sort of shock. She seemed unable to speak.

"What's all this money doing piled up here?" Moody asked. "I don't understand none of this."

"Twenty-one dollars," Smoke said, counting the coin and greenbacks. "This isn't making any sense to me."

Then Apache found the body of Adam and called out. The men gathered around.

"They's words writ on this page here," Apache said. "My readin' ain't good enough to make 'em out." He handed the dime novel to Smoke.

Smoke looked at the bloody, printed words. "IT WAS

TF RIDERS WHO DONE IT TO SIS. TF RIDERS WHO SHOT ME. GET THEM FOR ME LUKE. LUKE, GET"

Smoke read the message and then folded the book.

Luke Nations stood stony-faced. But there were tears running down his tanned, lined, leathery face.

"We play it legal-like, Luke, boys," Smoke said. "When that fails, then we go in shootin'."

"You play it legal-like, Jensen," Luke said, his words like chipped stone. "Me, I'll play my way."

He turned to go.

Smoke's hard voice stopped the old gunfighter. *"Luke!"*

The gunfighter turned slowly.

"Charlie told me when you signed on, you rode for the brand."

"I do."

"It's my brand."

That stung Luke. He stood for a moment, then slowly nodded his head. "Right. Boss. We play it legal-like. But you know damned well how it's gonna come out in the long haul."

"Yes, I do. Or at least suspect. But when all the shooting is over and the dust settled, we're going to have United States marshals in here, plus all sorts of lawyers and other big-worded people. I don't want anyone to point the finger at us and be able to prove that we started a damn thing. That make sense to you?"

"Put that way, I reckon it do."

"Fine. I hate to ask any of you boys to ride back to town. But we need the sheriff out here first thing in the morning."

Wilbur Mason had walked up. "I'll go," he said quietly.

Smoke nixed that. "You'd be fair game, Wilbur. And you're no hand with a gun. No, I'll go. I'll take the book and give it to Lawyer Brook and tell him the story in the presence of Sheriff Carson. Damn!" he said.

"What's wrong?" Silver Jim said.

"I'll have to take the girl into town to Doctor Spalding. She's in bad shape. Wilbur, hitch up a wagon and fill the back with hay for her comfort. Luke, ride like hell for my place and tell some other men to come hard. They can catch up with me on the way in."

Luke nodded and ran, in his odd, bowlegged, cowboy way, back to his horse.

"I've borrow a horse from Colby's stable and pick up mine on the way back. You boys tell Sally I'll be back when she sees me."

"You take 'er easy, Smoke," Silver Jim warned. "Them hands of yourn won't be fit for no quick draw for several days yet."

Smoke nodded and left.

Tilden Franklin had tried to sit a saddle. He fell off twice before he would allow himself to be taken back to his ranch in the back of a buckboard. If he was not blind crazy before, he was now. He knew it would be a week, maybe longer, before he was fit to do anything. He was hurt had, and he had enough sense to know it.

He also had enough sense to know, through waves of humiliation, that since he had started the fight, in front of witnesses, there was not a damn thing, legally, he could do about it.

Except lay in the back of the buckboard and curse Smoke Jensen.

Which he did, wincing with every bounce and jar along the rutted road.

Smoke had met Colby and Charlie on the trail and broken the news to the father. Colby and Wilbur had exchanged wagons and rolled on. Charlie had insisted on returning with Smoke. He didn't say it, but Smoke was glad the gunfighter was wth him, for his own hands were in no shape for any standup gunfight.

It was long after dark when they rolled into Fontana and up to the doctor's office. Velvet still had not spoken a word. Nor uttered any sound.

Colton looked at Velvet, looked at Smoke, and silently cursed. He ordered the girl taken into his examining room and called for his wife to be present.

"Tell me what happened," he told Smokes. "As succinctly as possible."

"As what?"

Colton sighed. "Make it short."

Lawyer Hunt made his appearance, with his wife Willow. Mona asked her to assist her with Velvet. The women disappeared into the examining room.

Smoke had sent Billy for the sheriff as they passed the livery stable. For once, Sheriff Carson seemed genuinely concerned. He knew for an ironclad fact that nobody, but *nobody*, messed with a good woman and came off easy. Monte Carson was a hired gun, true, but he respected good womanfolk.

With everyone present, Smoke told his story, handing the bloody, damning dime novel, autographed by Luke Nations, to Lawyer Hunt.

Nobody heard Louis Longmont enter the office. He stood off to one side, listening.

Lawyer Hunt read the message and looked at Monte. "Can you read, Sheriff?"

"Hell, yes!"

"Then read it and pick a side!" There was hard and genuine anger in the lawyer's voice. God*damn* people who would do this to a girl.

"Hey!" Monte said. "I don't pick sides. I'm the law around here."

"That remains to be seen, doesn't it?" Louis spoke from the darkness near the open door to the office.

Monte flushed and read the bloody words. Now, he thought, I *am* in a pickle.

Doctor Spalding stepped out of the examining room. "The girl's visible wounds will be easily treated. They're mostly superficial. But her mental state is quite another matter. She is catatonic."

Smoke lost his temper. He was tired, sore, hungry, disgusted, and could not remember when he wanted to kill anybody more than at this moment. "Now, what in the goddamn hell does all that jibber-jabber mean?"

"Settle down, Smoke," Louis said. Then the gambler explained the doctor's words.

Smoke calmed down and looked at Sheriff Carson. "You want a war on your hands, Monte?"

"Hell, no!"

"Somebody better hang for this, Monte," Smoke warned, his voice low and menacing. "Or that is exactly what you're going to have on your hands—a war."

Smoke stepped out into the night and walked toward the best of the hotels.

"You ever heard the expression 'caught between a rock and a hard place,' Sheriff?" Louis asked.

"Sure. Why?"

"Because that's where you are. Enjoy it." The gambler smiled thinly.

2

The news swept through the town of Fontana fast. Sheriff Monte Carson found Judge Proctor and jerked him away from the bottle on the bar, leading the whiskered man out of the batwings to the boardwalk.

Monte pointed a finger at the judge. He told him what had gone down, shaking his finger in the judge's face. "Not another drink until this is over," he warned the highly educated rummy. "If you don't think you can handle that, I can damn well put you in a cell and be shore of it."

Judge Proctor stuck out his chest and blustered. "You wouldn't dare!"

"Try me," Monte warned, acid in his voice.

Judge Proctor got the message, and he believed it. He rubbed a hand over his face. "You're right, of course, Sheriff. Goddamn Tilden Franklin! What was he thinking of authorizing something of this odious nature?"

Sheriff Carson shrugged. "Be ready to go at first light, Judge. No matter how the chips fall, we got to play this legal-like, all the way."

Judge Proctor watched the sheriff walk away into the night. "Should be interesting," he muttered. "A fair hearing. How quaint!"

* * *

Louis Longmont sat in his quarters behind his gaming room and sipped hot tea. At first, the news of the money near where the girl was found puzzled him. Then his mind began working, studying all angles. Louis felt he knew the reason for the money. But it was a thin rope Tilden had managed to grab onto. The man really must be quite insane to authorize such a plan. Colby and Belle and their kids were all deeply religious folk—most farmers were. And the sheriff and judge were going to be forced to handle this right by the law books.

But, the gambler thought with a sigh, there was always the jury to consider. And money, in this case, not only talked, but cursed.

Big Mamma sat at the back of her bar and pondered the situation. In a case like this, wimmin oughta be allowed to sit on the jury . . . but that was years in the future. Even though Big Mamma was as cold-hearted and ruthless as a warlord, something like this brought out the maternal instinct from deep within her. She would have scoffed and cursed at the mere suggestion of that . . . but it was true.

She looked around her. It wouldn't take near as long to tear all this down and get gone as it had to put it all up. Damned if she wanted to get caught up in an all-out shootin' war. But sure as hell, that was what was gonna happen.

That Smoke Jensen . . . well, she had revised her original opinion of that feller. He was pure straight out of Hell, that one. That one was no punk, like she first thought. But one-hundred-and-ten-percent man. And even though Big Mamma didn't like men, she could respect the all-man types . . . like Smoke Jensen.

* * *

Ralph Morrow lay beside his wife, unable to sleep. He was thinking of that poor child, and also thinking that he just may have been a fool where Tilden Franklin was concerned. After witnessing that fight in the gaming room this very day, and seeing the brutal, calculating madness in Tilden's eyes, the preacher realized that Tilden would stop at nothing to attain his goals.

Even the rape of a child.

Hunt sat in his office, looking at the bloody dime novel. Like the gambler, Louis Longmont, Hunt felt he knew why the money had been left by the raped child. And, if his hunch was correct, it was a horrible, barbaric thing for the men to do.

But, his lawyer's mind pondered, did Tilden Franklin have anything to do with it?

"Shit!" he said, quite unlike him.

Of course he did.

Colton dozed on his office couch. Even in his fitful sleep he was keeping one ear out for any noise Velvet might make. But he didn't expect her to make any. He felt the child's mind was destroyed.

He suddenly came wide awake, his mind busy. Supplies! He was going to have to order many more supplies. He would post the letter tomorrow—today—and get it out on the morning stage.

There was going to be a war in this area of the state—a very bad war. And as the only doctor within seventy-five miles, Colton felt he was going to be very busy.

Ed Jackson slept deeply and well. He had heard the news of the raped girl and promptly dismissed it. Tilden Franklin was a fine man; he would have nothing to do with anything of that nature. Those hard-scrabble farmers and small ranchers were all trash. That's what Mister Franklin had told him, and he believed him.

There had been no rape, Ed had thought, before falling asleep. None at all. The money scattered around the wretched girl proved that, and if he was chosen to sit on the jury, that's the way he would see it.

Sleep was elusive for Smoke. And not just for Smoke. In the room next to his, he could hear Charlie Starr's restless pacing. The legendary gunfighter was having a hard time of it too. Mistreatment of a grown woman was bad enough, but to do what had been done to a child . . . that was hard to take.

War. That word kept bouncing around in Smoke's head. Dirty, ugly range war.

Smoke finally drifted off to sleep . . . but his dreams were bloody and savage.

Not one miner worked the next day . . . or so it seemed at least. The bars and cafes and hotels and streets and boardwalks of Fontana were filled to overflowing with men and women, all awaiting the return of Judge Proctor and Sheriff Monte Carson from the sprawling TF spread.

Luke Nations had stayed at the Sugarloaf with Sally and most of the other gunslicks. Early that morning, however. Pistol Le Roux, Dan Greentree, Bull Flagler, Hardrock, Red Shingletown, and Leo Wood had ridden in.

And the town had taken notice of them very quickly. The aging gunhawks made Monte's deputies very nervous. And, to the deputies' way of thinking, what made it all even worse was that Louis Longmont was solidly on the side of Smoke Jensen. And now it appeared that

Johnny North had thrown in with Smoke too. And nobody knew how many more of them damned old gunfighters Smoke had brought in. Just thinkin' 'bout them damned old war-hosses made a feller nervous.

Just outside of town, Monte sat his saddle and looked down at Judge Proctor, sitting in a buckboard. "I ain't real happy about bringin' this news back to Fontana, Judge."

"Nor I, Sheriff. But I really, honestly feel we did our best in this matter."

Monte shuddered. "You know what this news is gonna do, don't you, Judge?"

"Unfortunately. But what would you have done differently, Monte?"

Monte shook his head. He could not think of a thing that could have been done differently. But, for the first time in his life, Monte was beginning to see matters from the *other* side of the badge. He'd never worn a badge before, never realized the responsibilities that went with it. And, while he was a long way from becoming a good lawman, if given a chance Monte might some day make it.

"Nothin', Judge. Not a thing."

Judge Proctor clucked to his team and rolled on.

Standing beside Smoke on the boardwalk, Lawyer Hunt Brook said, "Here they come Smoke. Two went out, two are returning."

"That's about the way I flgurcd it would be."

Judge Proctor halted his team in front of Hunt and Smoke. "Since you are handling this case for Miss Colby, Mister Brook," the judge said, "I'll see you in your offices in thirty minutes. I should like to wash up first."

"Certainly, your honor," Hunt said.

Smoke walked with the lawyer down the long, tightly packed street to his law office. Hunt went on into his personal office and Smoke sat out in the pine-fresh outer office, reading a month-old edition of a New York City newspaper. He looked up as Colby entered.

"It ain't good, is it, Smoke?" the father asked.

"It doesn't look good from where I sit. You sure you want to be here, listen to all this crap?"

"Yeah," the man said softly. "I shore do want to hear it. I left Belle with Velvet. This is hard on my woman, Smoke. She's talkin' hard about pullin' out."

"And you?"

"I told her if she went, she'd have to go by herself. I was stayin.'"

"She won't leave you, Colby."

"Naw. I don't think she will neither. It's just . . . whatever the outcome today, Smoke, we gotta get back, get Adam into the ground. You reckon that new minister, that Ralph Morrow, would come up to the high country and say a few words over my boy?"

The man was very close to crying.

"I'm sure he would, Colby. Soon as this is over, I'll go talk to him."

"I'd be beholden, Smoke."

Judge Proctor and Sheriff Carson entered the office. The judge extended his hand to Colby. "You have my deepest and most sincere condolences, sir."

"Thank you, Judge."

Monte stood with his hat in his hand, looking awfully uncomfortable.

Hunt motioned them all into his office. When they were seated, Judge Proctor looked at them all and said, "Well, this is a bit irregular, and should this case ever come to court, I shall, of course, have to bring in another judge to hear it. But that event appears highly unlikely."

Smoke's smile was ugly.

Monte caught the mocking smile. "Don't, Smoke," he said quietly. "We done our best. And I mean that. If you can ever prove we slacked up even a little, you can have my badge, and I'm sayin' that in front of witnesses."

For some reason, Smoke believed the man. Queer feeling.

"Here it is," Judge Proctor said. He looked at Colby. "This is highly embarrassing for me, sir. And please bear in mind, these are the words of the TF men who were . . . well, at the scene."

"Just say it," the rancher-farmer said.

"Very well. They say, sir, that your daughter had been, well, shall we say . . . *entertaining* the men at that location for quite some time. They say this has been going on since last summer."

"What's been goin' on?" Colby blurted. "I ain't understandin' none of this."

Smoke had a sudden headache. He rubbed his temples with his fingertips and wished all this crap would be over. Just get all the goddamned lies over and done with.

"Sir," Judge Proctor said. "The TF men claim that your daughter, Velvet, has been entertaining them with sexual favors for some time. For money."

Colby sat rock still for a moment, and then jumped to his feet. "That there's a damned lie, sir! My Velvet is a good girl!"

Smoke pulled the man back into the chair. "We know, Colby. We know that's the truth. It's all a pack of lies. Just like we figured it would be."

"Please, Mister Colby!" Judge Proctor said. "Try to control yourself, sir."

Colby put his face in his hands and began weeping.

Lawyer Brook wet a cloth from a pitcher on his desk and handed the cloth to Smoke, who handed it to Colby. Colby bathed his face and sighing, looked up. "Go on," he said, his voice strained.

The judge looked at the sheriff. "Would you *please* take a part in these proceedings, Sheriff? You explain. That's your job, not mine."

"Mister Colby," Monte said. "Them Harris brothers who ride for the TF brand, Ed and Pete? It was them and Billy and Donnie and Singer and . . . two or three more. I got their names writ down. Anyways, they claim that Miss Velvet was . . ." He sighed, thinking, Oh, shit! "Chargin' the men three dollars a turn. There would have been more than twenty-one dollars there this time except that not all the men got their turn."

"Dear God in Heaven!" Hunt Brook exclaimed. "Must you be so graphic, sir?"

"I don't know no other way to say it, Lawyer!" Monte said. "I'm doin' the bes' I can."

Hunt waved his hand. "I know, Sheriff. I know. Sorry. Please continue."

"They say Miss Velvet kep' her . . . earnin's in a secret place back in the timber. They told us where it was. We ain't been there, and you all know we ain't had the time to go to the ranch, into the high country, and back here by now. I'll tell y'all where they said it was. Y'all can see for yourselves.

"Anyways, Miss Velvet's brother come up there and started yellin' and hollerin' and wavin' that rifle of his'n around. Then he just up and shot Steve Babbin. That's for a fact. They buryin' Steve this afternoon. Shot him in the eye with a .22. Killed him. Little bitty hole. Had to have been a .22. Them ol' boys just reacted like any other men. They grabbed iron and started shootin'. Killed the boy. They kinda got shook about it and took off. That's about it, boys."

Monte leaned back in his chair and looked at the newly carpeted floor.

"And you believe their story, Sheriff?" Lawyer Brook asked.

"It ain't a question of' believin' or not believin', Lawyer. It's a matter of what can be proved. I don't like it, fellers. I just don't like it. But look at it like this: even if Miss Velvet could talk, which she cain't, it'd still be her word agin theirs. And that's the way it is, fellers."

Smoke stood up and put his hat on his head. "And that's it, huh, boys?"

"I'm afraid so, Mister Jensen," Judge Proctor said. "I don't like it. But we played this straight by the book. If you could bring me evidence to the contrary, I'd certainly listen to it and act accordingly."

"So will I, Smoke," Monte said softly. "Believe it."

"Oddly enough, I do believe you. Come on, Colby. Let's go."

Lawyer Hunt Brook was so angry he was trembling. "This is terrible!" He practically shouted the words. "This is not justice!"

"The lady is blind, Mister Brook," Judge Proctor said. "I shouldn't have to remind you of that." He stood up. "Come, Sheriff."

Stepping outside, the judge almost ran into Pistol Le Roux. "Good Lord!" Proctor said. "It's been years, Pistol. You're looking quite well."

"Thanks. How'd it go in yonder, Judge?"

"Not to anyone's liking, I'm afraid. Are you going to be in town long?"

"I work for Smoke Jensen."

"Oh, my!" the judge said. "How many of you, ah, men did Mister Jensen hire, Pistol?"

Pistol smiled. "Twenty or so."

Judge Proctor suddenly felt weak-kneed. "I see. Well, it's been nice seeing you, Pistol."

"Same here, Judge."

As they walked off, Monte asked. "How come it is you know that old gunslick, Judge?"

"I was up in the Wyoming country hearing a case of his when he was marshal of a town up there. Four pretty good gunhands braced him one afternoon."

"How'd it come out?"

"Pistol killed them all."

"And they's *twenty* of them old gunhawks workin' for Jensen?"

"Yes. Rather makes one feel inadequate, doesn't it, Sheriff?"

"Whatever that means, Judge."

The judge didn't feel like explaining. "You know, Monte, you could be a good lawman if you'd just try."

"Is that what I been feelin' lately, Judge?"

"Probably. But since you—we—are in Tilden Franklin's pocket, what are we going to do about it?"

"We wasn't in his pocket in this one, Judge."

"That is correct. And it's a rather nice feeling, isn't it, Sheriff Carson?"

"Damn shore is, Judge Proctor. Would you like to join me in a drink, Judge?"

"No, Sheriff. I think not. I just decided to quit."

3

When Smoke and Sally and Pearlie and most of the other aging gunhawks rode up to Colby's place the following morning, they were all amazed to see the hills covered with people

"What the hell?" Pearlie said.

"They're showin' Tilden Franklin how they feel," Luke said. "And rubbin' his nose in it."

"Would you look yonder?" Jay said. "That there is Big Mamma. In a *dress*!"

"Musta been a tent-maker move into town," Apache said.

"Who is that pretty lady beside the . . . large lady I presume you men are talking about?" Sally asked.

Smoke and Sally were in a buckboard, the others on horseback.

"That's Big Mamma's wife, Miss Sally," Silver Jim explained.

Sally looked up at him. "I beg your pardon, Silver Jim?"

"They was married 'bout three year ago, I reckon it was. Big Mamma had to slap that minister around a good bit 'fore he'd agree to do it, but he done 'er."

Sally turned her crimson face forward. "I do not

wish to pursue this line of conversation any further, thank you."

"No, ma'am," Silver Jim said. "Me neither."

The service was a short one, but sincerely given by Ralph. Adam's forever-young body was buried on a hillside overlooking the Colby ranch.

And while most knew the TF riders were watching from the hills, no TF rider showed his face at the funeral. The mood of the crowd was such that if any TF riders had made an appearance, there most likely would have been a hanging.

Belle Colby and Velvet sat in the front yard during the service. Velvet had yet to speak a word or utter any type of sound.

Tilden sat on the front porch of his fine ranch house. He hurt all over. Never, *never*, in his entire life, had he been so badly torn up. And by a goddamned two-bit gunslinger.

Clint walked up to the porch. "Twelve hands pulled out last night, Boss."

"You pay 'em off?" The words were hard to understand and even harder for Tilden to speak. His lips were grotesquely swollen and half a dozen teeth were missing. His nose had yet to be set because it was so badly broken and swollen hideously.

"No. They just packed it all up and rode off. Told Pete Harris they hired their guns to fight men, not to make war on little kids."

"How noble of them. Hell with them!"

"Some of the others say they'll ride for brand—when it comes to punchin' cows. But they ain't gettin' involved in no way."

"Hell with them too. Fire 'em!"

"Boss?"

"Goddamn you! I said fire them!"

Clint stood his ground. He put one boot up on the porch and stared square at Tilden. "Now you listen to me, Boss. We got a hell of a big herd out yonder. And we need punchers to see to that herd. Now I feel sick at my stomach over what I ordered them men to do to that Colby girl, but it's done. And I can't change it. I reckon I'll answer to the Lord for that. If so, that's 'tween me and Him. But for now, I got a herd to look after. Are you so crazy mad you can't understand that?"

Tilden took several deep breaths—as deeply as he dared, that is. For Smoke had broken several of his ribs. He calmed himself. "All right, all right, Clint! You've made your point. I want a tally of how many men are going to fight for me. Those that want to punch cows, do so. But for every one that won't fight, hire two that will. Is that understood?"

"Yes, sir."

"Let's face it. You made a mistake by suggesting what was done to the Colby bitch; I made a mistake by going along with it. All right. Like you say, it's done. I understand that Colby brat wrote in that stupid book about Luke avenging him, right?"

"Yes, sir."

"I figured by now that old bastard would have come storming in here, fire in his eyes and his guns smoking. Maybe he's lost his balls."

Clint shook his head. "You never knew Luke Nations, did you, Boss?"

"Can't say as I ever had the pleasure."

"I do," Clint said softly. "He's . . ." The foreman searched for a word. "Awesome. There ain't a nerve in his body, Boss. He'll be comin' in smokin', all right. Bet on that. But he'll pick the time and place."

"Hire the gunnies!" Tilden ordered, his voice

harsh. "And then tell our gunhawks it's open season on nesters."

Clint hesitated. "Can I say something, Boss?"

"What is it, Clint?"

"Why don't we just drop the whole damned thing, Boss? Call it off? If word of this war gets to the governor's ears, he's liable to send in the Army."

"Hell with the governor. We got the sheriff and the judge in our pockets; how's anything goin' to get out?"

"I don't know about Monte and the judge no more, Boss. They was both pushin' real hard yesterday about that Velvet thing."

"I got them elected, I can get them un-elected."

Clint's smile was rueful. "You're forgettin' something, Boss."

"What?"

"The *people* elected 'em, For four years."

Clint turned around and walked off, leaving Tilden alone on the porch . . . with his hurting body.

And his hate.

Two weeks passed with no trouble . . . none at all. Between Tilden and the smaller spreads, that is. There was still minor trouble in town. But Monte and his men put that down quickly and hard. And the now-sober Judge Proctor hit the offenders with such stiff fines and terms in the new jailhouse that it seemed to deter other potential lawbreakers.

And Monte stopped collecting graft from the saloons and other businesses. He was being paid a good salary as sheriff, and decided that was enough. Any deputy that didn't like the new rules could leave. A few did, most stayed. All in all, it was a good job.

Monte looked up as the front door to his office opened. Johnny North stood there, gazing at him.

"You decide to make your move now, Johnny?" Monte asked.

"I don't know," the gunfighter said. "Mind if I sit down?"

Monte pointed to a chair. "Help yourself."

Johnny first poured himself a cup of coffee. He sat and looked at the sheriff. "What the hell's the matter with you, Monte? You got religion or something?"

Monte smiled. "I ain't got religion, that's for sure. Maybe it's the something. Why do you ask?"

"I been waitin' for you to come brace me for two damn weeks. You forgot we're supposed to hate each other?"

"No, I ain't. But I'll tell you this: I can't remember what we're supposed to hate each other for!"

Johnny scratched his chin. "Come to think of it, neither can I. Wasn't it something about a gal?"

Monte started laughing. "I don't know! Hell, Johnny. Whatever it was it happened so many years ago, what difference does it make now?"

Johnny North joined in the laughter. "You et yet?"

"Nope. You buyin'?"

"Hell, why not? it's gettin' too damn hot outside for a gunfight anyways."

Laughing, the old enemies walked to a cafe.

A few of Tilden Franklin's hands were lounging in a tight knot outside a saloon. These were not the gunhawks employed by the TF brand, hut cowboys. And to show they were taking no sides in this matter, they had checked their guns with the bartender inside the saloon.

Monte Carson had made it clear, by posting notices around the town, that TF gunhawks had better not start any trouble in his town, or in any area of his jurisdiction. He'd had to get the judge to spell all the words.

The judge had done so, gleefully.

"Looks like Johnny North and the Sheriff done kissed and made up," one cowboy remarked.

"That's more trouble for Tilden," another observed. There was just a small note of satisfaction in the statement.

Another TF puncher sat down on the lip of a watering trough. "It's May, boys. Past time to move the herds up into the high country for the summer."

"I been thinkin' the same thing."

"I think I'll talk to Clint when we get back to the ranch. Kinda suggest, nice-like, that we get the herds ready to move. If he goes along with it, and I think he will, that'll put us some thirty-five miles from the ranch, up in the high lonesome. Take a hell of a pistol to shoot thirty-five miles."

"Yeah. That'd put us clean out of any war, just doin' what we're paid to do: look after cows."

Another cowboy sat down on the steps. He looked at the puncher who had suggested the high country. "You know, Dan, sometimes you can show some signs of havin' a little sense."

"Thank you," Dan said modestly. "For a fact, my momma didn't raise no fool for a son."

"Is that right?"

"Yeah," Dan said with a smile. "I had a sister."

The aging gunfighters were having the time of their lives. They were doing what most loved to do: work cattle. Smoke's bulls had been busy during the winter, and his herd had increased appreciably now that the calving was over. It was branding time, and the gunfighters were pitching in and working just as hard as Smoke or Pearlie. Some had gone to other small spreads in the area, helping out there, their appearance a welcome sight to the overworked and understaffed ranchers.

It appeared that the area was at peace. Smoke knew, from riding the high country, that Tilden Franklin's punchers were busy moving the TF herds into the high pastures, and doing so, he suspected, for many reasons, not all of them associated with the welfare of the cattle. That was another sign that Tilden had not given up in his fight to rid the area of all who would not bend to his will. Those TF hands who were not gunslicks but cowboys were clearing out of the line of fire.

He said as much to Charlie Starr.

The gunhand agreed. "It ain't even got started good yet, Smoke. I got word that Tilden is hirin' all the guns he can, and they're beginning to trickle in. It's shapin' up to be a bad one."

"They any good?"

"Some of them are bad hombres. Some of them are just startin' to build a rep. But they're alive, so they must be fair hands with a gun."

Smoke looked around him, at the vast, majestic panorama that nature had bestowed on this part of Colorado. "It's all so foolish," he said. "There is more than enough room for us all."

"Not to a man like Tilden," Luke Nations said, walking up, a tin cup of coffee in his hand. He was taking a break from the branding. "Tilden, least for as long as I've known of him, has always craved to be the bull of the woods. He's crazy."

All present certainly agreed with that.

"What'd Colby say or do when you give him that money we found in that holler tree?" Charlie asked Smoke.

"Sent it to Tilden by way of the Sheriff. Wrote him a note too. Told him where to put the money. Told him to put it there sideways."

Charlie and Luke both grinned at that, Luke saying, "I sure would have liked to seen the look on Tilden's face when he got that."

"How's his health?" Charlie asked.

"Coming along," Smoke said with a grin. "Doc Colton goes out there several times a week. 'Bout the only thing wrong with Tilden now—other than the fact he's crazy—is that he don't have any front teeth and his ribs is still sore."

"I figure we got two, maybe three more weeks before Tilden pulls all the stops out," Luke said. "He's not goin' to do nothin' until he's able to sit a saddle and handle a short gun. Then look out."

And they all agreed with that.

"I figure he'll save us for last," Smoke said. "I figure he'll hit Peyton first. That's the ranch closest to his range, and the furtherest from us. I've warned Peyton to be careful, but the man seemed to think it's all over now."

"Is he a fool?" Luke asked.

"No." Smoke said softly. "Just a man who tries to see the best in all people. He thinks Tilden has 'seen the light,' to use Peyton's own words."

"He's a fool then," Charlie opined. "There isn't one ounce of good in Tilden Franklin. That little trick with Velvet should have convinced Peyton."

"Speakin' of Velvet . . ." Luke let it trail off into silence.

"No change," Smoke said. "She eats, and sits. She has not uttered a sound in weeks."

"Her pa?"

"Colby has turned real quiet-like," Smoke told the men. "Never speaks of her. But I don't like the look in his eyes. Belle told me he takes his pistol out every day and practices drawing and firing."

"He any good?"

"No," Smoke said flatly. "He just doesn't have the eye and hand coordination needed to be any good. He's slow as molasses and can't hit jack-crap with a short gun."

"Then he's headin' for trouble," Luke said. "You want I should go talk to him?"

"Can if you want. But it won't do any good. I tried talking to him. He just turned his back and walked away."

Charlie spat on the ground. "The fool is diggin' his own grave, Smoke."

"Yeah. I know it. But he's all tore up with grief. I'm thinkin' he's gonna brace the Harris Brothers if he ever gets the chance."

"They'll kill him," Luke said. "Them boys is real good."

Smoke nodded his head. He summed up his feelings by saying, "I think Colby wants to die."

4

Paul Jackson walked into his brother's office at the general store and told Ed he was quitting.

Ed looked at his brother as if he was looking at a fool. "To do what?"

"I staked me out a claim. Looks promisin' too. You're makin' all the money here. Hell with you!"

"Fine. But remember this: you'll not get a penny's worth of credit from me."

"I got money of my own." He walked out of the office.

"You're a fool!" Ed shouted after his brother.

His brother turned around and made a very obscene gesture. It was intended for Ed, but Ed's wife caught it as well.

Peg stamped her foot.

Paul laughed and walked on out, feeling as though he had just had a great weight lifted from his shoulders. He swung into the saddle and trotted out, toward the high lonesome, where he had staked his claim.

Paul would show them all. He'd come back a rich man and take Bountiful from that namby-pamby preacher and then, just like in one of them dime novels, the both of them would ride off into the sunset, to be forever together.

Or something like that.

* * *

"What side of this fracus is Utah Slim on?" Johnny North asked Monte over coffee one bright early summer morning.

"I can't figure it, myself. He don't appear to be on neither side. And he ain't hurtin' for money. He's always got a wad of greenbacks."

"Gamble?"

Monte shook his head. "No. I ain't never seen nor heard of him gamblin'."

"He's on somebody's payroll," the gunslinger opined. "You can bet on that. Utah don't do nothin' for nothin'. He's here for a reason."

"You find out, you let me know?"

"Why not? I sure ain't got no axes to grind in this here fight."

"Tilden's hirin' you know."

"Screw Tilden Franklin. I got me a little claim staked out and got guys workin' it for shares. 'Bout five years back, I started puttin' back a little bit of money ever' time I had some to spare. Got it in a bank up in Boulder. With the gold I get out of this claim, I aim to start me a little ranch; maybe do a little farmin' too. Hang up my guns."

Monte started grinning.

"What are you grinnin' about, you ape?" Johnny asked.

"Gonna do a little bit of ranchin' and a little bit of farmin', hey?"

"Yeah! What's wrong with that?"

"Nothin'. Nothin' at all. But what happens if you run into some big rancher like Tilden when you decide to settle down?"

"Well . . . I reckon I'll fight."

Monte suddenly felt better. He started chuckling. "Oh, yeah, Johnny, you got an axe to grind in this war—you just ain't realized it yet."

Johnny thought about that, then he too started chuckling. "By God, Monte, you right. I think I'll go see if that feller Colby needs a hand. Might do me some good to do some hard work for a change."

"He can't pay you nothin'."

"I ain't askin' for nothin'."

Boot heels drummed on the boardwalk and someone was hollering for the sheriff.

Monte jumped up and headed for the door, Johnny right behind him. A wild-eyed miner almost collided with them both.

"Come quick, Sheriff! That nester Colby is about to draw down on a TF gunnie named Donnie. Hurry, Sheriff, hurry!"

"Crazy farmer!" Monte yelled, running toward a saloon. He could see a crowd gathered on both sides of a man standing out in the street. He recognized the man as Colby, and with a sick feeling realized he was not going to be able to stop it. He just knew that Colby had started it, and if that was the case, he would not interfere. It was an unwritten rule in the West—and would be for about a decade to come—that a man broke his own horses and killed his own snakes. If one challenged another to a gunfight, and it was a fair fight, few lawmen would interfere.

The gunslick, Donnie, was standing on the boardwalk, laughing at the farmer. Colby was standing in the street, cursing the TF rider.

Monte stopped some distance away, halting both Johnny and the miner. "Who started it?"

"That farmer. He called Donnie out and started cussin' him. Ain't you gonna stop it, Sheriff?"

"There is nothin' I can do, mister," Monte told the man. "If Colby wants to back off, I'll see that he gets that chance. But I can't stop it. There ain't no city or county law agin a one-on-one fight."

"Colby's gonna get killed," the miner said.

"I reckon," Monte agreed.

"What's the matter, Pig-farmer?" Donnie taunted the older man. "You done lost your nerve?"

"No," Colby said, his voice firm. "Anytime you're ready, draw!"

Donnie and his friends laughed. "Hell, Nester," Donnie said. "I ain't gonna draw on you. You called me out, remember?"

"You raped my Velvet and killed my boy."

"I didn't rape nobody, Nester. Your daughter was sellin' and we'uns bought. Cash money for merchandise. Your boy busted up in there and started throwin' lead around. We fired back. And that's the way it happened."

"You're a goddamned liar!" Colby shouted.

"Now that tears it, Nester," Donnie said, his hands over the butts of his guns. "You make your play." He grinned nastily. "Sorry 'bout Velvet, though. She shore liked it, the more the merrier."

Colby went for his old Navy Colt .36. Grinning, Donnie let the man fumble and then with a smooth, practiced motion drew, cocked, and fired, the slug taking Colby in the right shoulder. The farmer spun around, dropping his Navy Colt onto the dirt of the street.

Colby reached for the gun with his left hand and Donnie fired again, the slug striking Colby in the stomach. The farmer was tossed to one side and Donnie's Colt roared again, the slug raking Colby flush in the face, just above the nose and below the eye sockets. Colby's face was shattered. He trembled once and was still.

"That's it!" Monte shouted. "Holster your gun and ride out of town, Donnie. Right now. Git gone, boy, or face me. Make your choice."

"Hey, I'm leavin', Sheriff." Donnie grinned, returning his Colt to leather. "I mean, you saw it—I didn't start it."

Louis Longmont had watched the whole sickening show from across the street. But, like the sheriff, he had made no attempt to stop it. Such was the code demanded of those who braved the frontier.

Longmont tossed his cigar into the street and walked back to his gaming tent. Then a truth made its way into the light of his mind: he was sick of the whole damned mess. Tired of late hours and tired of taking other people's money—even if his games were honest—tired of sweat-stinking miners and cowboys, tired of the violence and dust and heat and intense cold. Tired of it all. Just plain tired of it.

The gambler realized then that this was to be his last boom town.

That thought made him immensely happy.

From his table in his gaming room, Louis watched the undertaker's black hack rumble past.

He heard a voice saying, "This poor wretch have any family?"

He could not hear the reply.

Louis poured a tumbler of scotch and lifted the glass, silently toasting the dead Colby.

"Not much money in his pockets." The undertaker's voice came to Louis.

"Mike!" Louis called.

The bouncer stuck his big head around the corner "Yeah, Boss?"

"Go tell the undertaker to prepare Colby's body and do it up nice—the best he can offer. I'm paying."

"Yes, sir."

"And tell Johnny North to come see me."

"Yes, sir."

A few minutes later, Johnny North stepped into the gaming tent. "You wanna see me, Louis?"

The two were not friends, but then neither were they enemies. Just two men who were very, very good with a gun and held a mutual respect for each other.

"You know where Colby's spread is located, Johnny?"

"I can probably find it."

"Someone needs to ride up there and tell his wife that she's a widow."

"You tellin' me to do it, Louis?"

"No." The gambler's left hand worked at a deck of playing cards on the table. His right hand was not visible. "But I am asking."

"If that's the case . . . fine. I'll go."

"Ask her . . . no, ride on to Smoke's place and tell him what happened, if you will, please. Ask him to arrange for a wagon to come for Colby's body."

"I'll do that too, Louis. Louis?"

The gambler looked at the gunfighter.

"It wasn't right . . . that shootin'. But we couldn't interfere."

"I know. But the West is changing, Johnny. Going to ranch and farm a bit with the savings you have up in Boulder, Johnny?"

That shook the blond-haired Nevada gunslick. "How in the hell . . ."

"I own part of the bank, Johnny," Louis said with a very slight smile.

Johnny returned the smile. "I think I might just ask the Widder Colby if she needs some help up there, Louis. Not today, now, that wouldn't be fitten. But later on."

"That would be a very decent act on your part, Johnny. I think Belle would appreciate that very much."

"I'll get goin' now. See you, Louis."

"See you. Thanks, Johnny."

As the sounds of Johnny's big California spurs faded on the boardwalk, Andre stuck his head out of the kitchen. "A snack, sir?" the chef asked.

"I think not, Andre. Just coffee, please."

The chef hesitated. "It is a dismal and barbaric place, is it not, *monsieur*?"

"For a while longer, Andre. But it will change as time passes, and time will pass."

"*Oui, monsieur.*"

* * *

Johnny North caught up with Donnie about five miles out of town. The young gunslick had several of his friends with him, but numbers had never bothered Johnny North before, and didn't this time.

Johnny North made all the gunslicks and so-called gunslicks of this group nervous. They all kept their hands in plain sight, and as far away from their guns as could be humanly arranged.

"I ain't lookin' for no truck with you, Johnny," Donnie said, his voice sounding a bit shrill.

"Peel off from your friends, Donnie," Johnny told him.

"Why?"

"We're gonna take a ride, just you and me."

"Where we goin'?"

"To deliver a death message"

"I'll be damned if I'm goin'!"

Johnny smiled grimly. "Do you prefer dead to damned, Donnie?"

"Huh?"

"You can either ride to the Colby place with me, and tell the widder how you gunned down her man, or you can be taken back to the TF spread . . . acrost your saddle. It's up to you, Donnie."

"They's five of us, Johnny," a TF gunhawk said.

"There won't be when the smoke clears."

Donnie and the others thought about that for a moment. "I reckon I'll ride with you, Johnny," Donnie said.

"Fine. You others hightail it back to the TF. You tell Tilden Franklin that from now on I'll be workin' out at Colby's place. Tell him to keep his ass and your asses off that range. You got all that?"

"Yes, sir, Johnny," a young TF gunnie said.

"Yes, sir, *Mister North*!"

"Yes, sir, Mister North!"

"Ride!"

The TF gunnies laid the spurs to their horses and left in a cloud of dust and drumming hooves. None of them was lookin' forward to delivering this news to Tilden Franklin. But none of them wanted to tangle with Johnny North neither. Lesser of two evils, they figured.

"You ride in front of me, Donnie," Johnny said. "Move out."

There was a lot of things Donnie wanted to say. Wisely, he said none of them. Just silently cussed.

5

"There was five of you!" Tilden shouted at the men. "Five of you! I'm paying you men good money, fighting wages. But so far, I've seen damn little fighting. But a hell of a lot of running. What does it take to put some backbone in you men?"

The gunslicks stood and took it in silence. Luis Chamba and his sidekicks, Kane and Sanderson, stood by the corner of the big house and smiled at the dressing-down Tilden was giving his gunhands.

When the chastised men had departed, Luis said, "Perhaps, *señor*, it is time for some night-riding, *si*?"

Tilden shifted his cold eyes to the Mexican gunfighter. "I'll pass the word, Luis. You're in charge. The others take orders from you. *Cooriente*?"

Luis smiled his reply.

"Make your plans, Luis."

"This game *señor* . . . what are the limits?"

"No limits, Luis. Let the chips fall."

"I like this game, *señor*," Luis said with a smile.

"I rather thought you would," Tilden said tightly.

Belle Colby stood in her front yard, Bob by her side, and listened to Donnie haltingly tell what had happened. The TF gunslick's face was flushed with anger, but he told it all, leaving nothing out.

When he had finished, Johnny said, "If I ever see you on this range, Donnie, I'll kill you. Now ride, punk— ride!"

Donnie wheeled his horse and galloped out.

Bob said, "Are you really Johnny North?"

"Yes. Ma'am?" He looked at Belle. "I'll be ridin' over to the Sugarloaf. I should be back by sundown. I'll bunk in the barn if that's all right with you."

"That will be fine, Mister North."

She had taken the news of her husband's death calmly. Too calmly for Johnny. He sat his horse and looked at her.

"You're wondering why I'm behaving in such a calm manner, Mister North?"

"The thought did pass my mind, ma'am."

"My husband told me before dawn this morning, as he was belting on a gun, that he was going into town. I felt then that I would never see him again. I did my grieving this morning."

Johnny nodded his head. He sat looking at the woman for a moment longer. Nice-looking woman; kind of trail worn, but that was to be expected, for this was a hard life for a woman. Then he thought of all the dance-hall floozies and hurdy-gurdy girls he had known down through the long and bloody years. Belle Colby, with her worn gingham dress, sunburned face, and work-hardened hands, seemed beautiful compared to them.

Johnny cleared his throat and plopped his hat back on his head. "You gonna need help around here, ma'am," he said. "If'n it's all right, I'll stick around and pull my weight and then some."

"That would be nice, Mister North," Belle said with a tired smile. "Yes. I'd like that."

Johnny returned the smile and wheeled his horse, heading to the Sugarloaf.

* * *

The crowd was respectable at Colby's burying, but not near so many people showed up as had Adam's planting. Most men, whether they would say it aloud or not—and it was the latter if they were married, felt that Colby had done a damn fool thing. And while most of them didn't condone what Donnie had done, they probably would not have interfered. They might have done something similar had they been in Colby's boots, but it would have been done with sawed-off express gun in their hands, not with a pistol in a fast-draw type of situation.

Out here, a man had damned well best know his limitations and capabilities.

And behave accordingly.

Once again the Reverend Ralph Morrow conducted the funeral services, and once again he and Bountiful and lots of others stayed for lunch. That was no problem, for everyone who attended the services had brought some sort of covered dish.

Like hangings, funerals also served as quite a social event.

Louis Longmont was there, all fancied up in a tailored black suit . . . carefully tailored to hide the shoulder-holster rig he wore under the jacket.

The aging gunfighters were all in attendance, gussied up in their best. They made no attempts to conceal their Colts, wearing them openly, low and tied down.

Pearlie had stayed behind at the Sugarloaf, just in case some TF riders decided to use the occasion to come calling. With a funeral of their own in mind.

Monte Carson and Judge Proctor were there, and so were Hunt and Willow Brook, Colton and Mona Spalding, Haywood and Dana Arden.

Ed Jackson did not show. He figured he might lose a dollar or so by closing down his store.

Besides, Ed felt that Colby had gotten exactly what he

deserved. And the next time he saw that Smoke Jensen, Ed just might give him a good piece of his mind about the totally uncalled-for beating of a fine man like Tilden Franklin. Well . . . he'd think about doing that, anyways.

"Going to stay on up here for a time?" Monte asked Johnny.

"Thought I might. Belle has her hands full all day just tryin' to look after Velvet, and I think me and Bob can pretty well handle it. And some of them old gunslingers come over from time to time, Belle says. Them old boys know a lot about farming and such."

Monte and Judge Proctor said their goodbyes to Belle and returned to Fontana.

By late afternoon, most of those attending had left for home, since many had traveled miles to get there. About half of the old gunslicks had left, returning to the Sugarloaf to give Pearlie a break.

Louis had returned with Monte and Judge Proctor, riding a magnificent black stallion.

"Like to ride over and spend the night at our place?" Smoke asked Reverend Morrow. "It's a lot closer than town, and we have the room. 'Sides, I'd like Sally and Bountiful to get to know each other."

After consulting with his wife, the young couple agreed. Those returning to the Sugarloaf made their way slowly homeward, Smoke and Sally and Ralph and Bountiful in buckboards, the rest on horseback.

"It's so beautiful up here," Bountiful said, squeezing her husband's arm. "So peaceful and lovely and quiet. I think I would like to live up here."

"Might have a hard time supporting a church up here, Bountiful."

"Yes, that's true. But you could do what you've always wanted to do, Ralph."

He looked at her, beautiful in the sunlight that filtered through the trees alongside the narrow road.

"You would be content with that, Bountiful? A part-time preacher and a full-time farmer?"

"Yes."

"You're sure?"

"I'm sure of several things, Ralph. One is that I'm not cut out to be a preacher's wife. I love you, but that isn't enough. Secondly, I'm not so sure you're cut out to be a preacher."

"It's that obvious, Bountiful?"

"Ralph, nothing happened back East. It was a harmless flirtation and nothing more. I think you've always known that. Haven't you?"

"I suspected. I should have whipped that scoundrel's ass while I was feeling like it."

He spoke the words without realizing what he had really said.

Bountiful started laughing.

"What is so . . ." Then Ralph grinned, flushed, and joined his wife in laughter.

"Ralph, you're a good, decent man. I think you're probably the finest man I have ever known. But you went into the ministry out of guilt. And I think that is the wrong reason for choosing this vocation. Look at us, Ralph. Listen to what we're saying. We've never talked like this before. Isn't it funny, odd, that we should be doing so now?"

"Perhaps it's the surroundings." And for a moment, Ralph's thought went winging back in time, back almost eight years, when he was a bare-knuckle fighter enjoying no small amount of fame in the ring, open-air and smokers.

The young man he'd been fighting that hot afternoon was good and game, but no match for Ralph. But back then, winning was all that Ralph had on his mind, that and money. And he was making lots of money, both fighting and gambling. The fight had gone on for more than thirty rounds, which was no big deal to Ralph, who had fought more than ninety rounds more than once.

And then Ralph had seen his opportunity and had

taken it, slamming a vicious left-right combination to the young man's head.

The young man had dropped to the canvas. And had never again opened his eyes. The fighter had died several days later.

Ralph Morrow had never stepped into another ring after that.

He and Bountiful had known each other since childhood, and it was taken for granted by all concerned that they would some day marry. Bountiful's parents were relieved when Ralph quit the ring. Bountiful was a bit miffed, but managed to conceal it.

Both had known but had never, until now, discussed the obvious fact that Ralph simply was not cut out to be a minister.

"What are you thinking, Ralph?"

"About the death I caused."

"It could just as easily have been you, Ralph," she reminded him. "You've told me a thousand times that the fight was fair and you both were evenly matched. It's over, Ralph. It's been over. Stop dwelling on it and get on with the matter of living."

Quite unlike the strait-laced minister, he leaned over and gave Bountiful a smooch on the cheek. She blushed while the old gunfighters, riding alongside the buckboards, grinned and pretended not to notice.

After supper, the young couples sat outside the cabin, enjoying the cool air and talking.

"How many acres do you have, Smoke?" Ralph asked.

"I don't really know. That valley yonder," he said, pointing to the Sugarloaf, "is five miles long and five miles wide. I do know we've filed on and bought another two thousand acres that we plan to farm. Right now we're only farming a very small portion of it. Hay and corn mostly. Right over there—" again he pointed, "is seven hundred and fifty acres of prime farm land just sittin' idle. I think we overbought some."

"That acreage is just over that little hill?" Bountiful asked.

"Yes," Sally said, hiding a smile, for it was obvious that the minister and his wife were interested in buying land.

"We'll ride over in the morning and take a look at it, if you'd like," Smoke suggested.

"Do you have a proper saddle for Bountiful?" Ralph asked.

"We're about the same size," Sally told him. "She can wear some of my jeans and ride astride."

Bountiful fanned her suddenly hot face. She had never had on a pair of men's britches in her life. But . . . this was the West. Besides, who would see her?

"I don't know whether that would be proper for a minister's wife," Ralph objected.

"Don't be silly!" Sally said, sticking out her chin. "If it's all right for a man, why should it be objectionable for a woman to wear britches?"

"Well . . ." Ralph said weakly. Forceful women tended to somewhat frighten him.

"Have you ever read anything by Susan B. Anthony, Bountiful?" Sally asked.

"Oh, yes! I think she's wonderful, don't you?"

"Yes. As well as Elizabeth Cady Stanton. You just wait, Bountiful. Some day women will be on an equal footing with men."

"Lord save us all!" Smoke said with a laugh. He shut up when Sally gave him a dark look.

"Do you think the time will come when women will be elected to Congress?" Bountiful asked.

Ralph sat stunned at the very thought.

Smoke sat grinning.

"Oh my, yes! But first we have to work very hard to get the vote. That will come only if we women band together and work very hard for it."

"Let's do that here!" Bountiful said, clapping her hands.

"Fine!" Sally agreed.

"But how?" Bountiful sobered.

"Well . . . my mother knows Susan B. very well. They went to school together in Massachusetts. I'll post a letter to Mother and she can write Miss Anthony. Then we'll see."

"Wonderful!" Bountiful cried. "I'm sure Willow and Mona and Dana would be delighted to help us."

Smoke rolled a cigarette and smiled at the expression on Ralph's face. The man looked as though he might faint at any moment.

The ladies rose and went chattering off into the cabin.

"My word!" Ralph managed to blurt out.

Smoke laughed at him.

"Boss!" Pearlie stilled the laughter and sobered the moment. "Look yonder." He pointed.

In the dusk of fast-approaching evening, the western sky held a small, faint glow.

"What is that?" Ralph asked. "A forest fire?"

"No," Smoke said, rising. "That's Peyton's place. Tilden's hands have fired it."

6

There was nothing Smoke could do. Peyton's spread was a good twenty-five miles away from Sugarloaf, his range bordering Tilden's holdings.

It was not long before the fire's glow had softened, and then faded completely out.

"Peyton refused our offer of help," Buttermilk said. "Some of us offered to stay over thar with him. But he turned us down flat."

"We'll ride over in the morning," Smoke said. "At first light. There is nothing we can do this evening."

"Except wonder what is happening over there," Ralph stated.

"And how many funerals you gonna have to hold," Luke added.

Peyton, his wife June, and their kids had been forced to retreat into the timber when it became obvious they were hopelessly outnumbered and outgunned. The family had made it out of the burning, smoking area with the clothes on their backs and nothing else.

They had lain quietly in the deep timber and watched their life's work go up, or down, in fire. They had watched as the hooded men shot all the horses, the pigs, and then set the barn blazing. The corral had been pulled down by ropes, the garden trampled under the hooves of horses. The Peyton family was left with nothing. Nothing at all.

They could not even tell what spread the men had come from, for the horses had all worn different or altered brands.

The family lay in the timber long after the night-riders had gone. They were not hurt, not physically, but something just as important had been damaged: their spirit.

"I tried to be friends with Tilden," Peyton said. "I went over to his place and spoke with him. He seemed to be reasonable enough, thanked me for coming over. Now this."

"They turned the wagon over," June said, her eyes peering into the darkness. "Broke off one wheel. But that can be fixed. There's lots of land to be had just north of here. I won't live like this," she warned. "I will not. And I mean that."

"I got a little money. I can buy some horses. We'll see what we can salvage in the morning."

"Nothing," June said bitterly. "Nothing at all."

"And you don't have any idea who they were?" Smoke asked Peyton.

Dawn had broken free of the mountains only an hour before. Smoke and some of his old gunhawks had left the Sugarloaf hours before first light, stopping along the way at the other small spreads.

"No," Peyton said, a note of surrender in his voice.

The Apache Kid returned from his tracking. "Headin' for the TF spread," he said. "Just as straight as an arrow that's where they're headin'."

"So?" June demanded, her hands on her hips. "So what? Prove that them riders come from the TF. And then even if you do that, see what the law will do about it."

"Now, June," Peyton said.

The woman turned around and walked off, her dress dirty and soot-covered.

"What are you gonna do?" Smoke asked Peyton.

"Pull out. What else is there to do?"

"We'll help you rebuild, just like we're doing with Wilbur Mason."

"And then what?" Peyton demanded. "What happens after that? I'll tell you," he blurted out. "The same thing all over again. No. I'll find me some horses, fix that busted wheel, and take off. This land ain't worth dyin' over, Smoke. It just ain't."

"That's not what you told me a few weeks back."

"I changed my mind," the man replied sullenly. "I don't feel like jawin' about it no more. My mind is made up. We're taking what we can salvage and pullin' out. Headin' up north of here. See you men." He turned and walked off, catching up with his wife.

"Let him go," Charlie said to Smoke. "He's not goin' to last anywhere out here. First time a drought hits him, he'll pack up and pull out. The locust come, he'll head out agin, always lookin' for an easy life. But he'll never find it. You know yourself it takes a hard man to make it out here. Peyton's weak, so's his woman. And them kids are whiners. He'll leave the land pretty soon, I'm figurin'. He'll get him a job in some little store, sellin' shoes and ribbons, and pretty soon he'll find something wrong with *that* job. But it ain't never gonna be his fault. It'll always be the fault of someone else. Forget him, Smoke. He ain't got no good sand bottom to him."

Smoke hated to say it, but he felt Charlie was right in his assessment of Peyton. Tilden had burned Wilbur Mason out; that had just made Wilbur and his family all the more determined to stay and fight.

"Good luck, Peyton!" Smoke called.

The man did not even turn around. Just waved his hand and kept on walking.

Somehow that gesture, or lack of it, made Smoke mad as hell. He wondered if he'd ever see Peyton or his family again. He thought, if he didn't, he wouldn't lose any sleep over the loss.

The few other small rancher-farmers in the high country met that afternoon on a plateau just about halfway between Smoke's Sugarloaf and the beginning of the TF range. And it was, for the most part, a quiet, subdued gathering of men.

Mike Garrett and his two hands; Wilbur Mason and Bob Colby; Ray Johnson and his hired hand; Nolan Edwards and his two oldest boys; Steve Matlock, Smoke and his gunhands.

And Reverend Ralph Morrow, wearing a pair of jeans and checkered shirt.

"Ralph is gonna buy some land from me," Smoke explained. "Farm some and ranch a little. Preach part time. The minister come up with a pretty good idea, I'm thinking. But we'll get to his idea in a minute. Anybody got any objections to Ralph joinin' our group?"

"I ain't got no objections," Ray said. "I'm just wonderin' if, him bein a preacher and all, will he fight?"

Ralph stepped forward. "Some of you might know me. For five years, I went by another name. I fought under the name of the Cincinnati Kid."

Matlock snapped his fingers. "I read about you in the Gazette. You kilt a man . . . ah . . ."

He trailed off into an uncomfortable silence.

"Yes," Ralph said. "I killed a man with my fists. I didn't mean to, but I did. As to whether I'll fight. Yes. For my family, my land, my friends. I'll fight."

And everyone there believed him. Still, one had to say, "But, Reverend Morrow, you're a minister; you can't go around shootin' folks!"

Ralph smiled . . . rather grimly. "Smoke and Charlie and some of the boys are going to help me build my cabin, first thing in the morning. You let some sucker come around and start trouble, you'll see how fast I'll shoot him."

The laughter helped to relieve the tension.

And Reverend Ralph Morrow suddenly became just "one of the boys."

"How about that other idea, Smoke?" Wilbur asked.

Smoke walked to the edge of the flats. He pointed down at the road. "That road, right there, connects Danner and Signal Hill. Seven, eight miles further down, you got to cut south to get to Fontana. Right?"

All agreed that was true. So?

"Pearlie is ridin' hard to the county seat right now. The Reverend and his wife, Bountiful, come up with this idea at noonin'. Right here, boys, right here on this plateau, but back yonder a ways, there's gonna be a town. We don't need Fontana. The land the town will be built on is gonna be filed on by Pearlie; he's carrying the money to buy some of it outright. When that surveyor was through here last year, he left a bunch of his markings and such at the house. Never did come back for them. Sally remembered 'em this morning. Everything is gonna be legal and right. My wife is puttin' up the money to build a large general store. I figure that once I explain it all to Louis Longmont, he'll see the humor in it and drop some of his money in. I'm hopin' he will. Pretty sure. Pearlie is carryin' a letter to the bank at the county seat; me and my wife have some money there." He grinned. "She has a heap more than I do. Wilbur Mason and his wife is gonna run the store for us. Wilbur owned a store back east of here at one time. So they both know what to do.

"Day after tomorrow, there's gonna be wagons rolling in here. Lumber, and a lot of it. We're gonna have several buildings here, including a sheriff's office and a jail."

Everybody was grinning now. Some of the men were laughing outright.

"We're gonna have a saloon, 'cause you all know that a saloon is just as much a meetin' place as it is a place to drink. We're gonna have us a cafe, with home-cookin'. The women will see to that. It'll bring in some money— and I know you all could use that. A church too, where we can all go to services come Sunday morning. And . . . a school. Both Sally and Bountiful are schoolmarms. And I'm gonna tell y'all something: once the wives of Beaconfield and Jackson hear about this town, with a church and proper schoolhouse, don't you think they won't be putting the pressure on their husbands to lean toward us."

"Who's gonna be the sheriff?" Matlock asked.

"Charlie Starr," Smoke said with a grin. "He's still got an old badge he wore some years back down close to Durango. I think he'd make a damned good one. Any objections?"

None.

"Now we want this to be kept secret as long as possible. Soon as the wagons start rolling in, though, the cat's gonna be out of the bag. But by that time, there won't be a damned thing Tilden Franklin can do about it except cuss. Now here is something else. There ain't no post office in Fontana. Never has been. We've always had to ride over to either Danner or Signal Hill to the post office. We can post a letter on the stage that comes through Fontana, but that don't always mean it'll get where it's goin'. Sally wrote a letter this morning to the proper people up in Denver and also to her folks who have a lot of high-up connections back East. So I think we'll get us a post office.

"Now the name. That come pretty easy too. Last evenin', as Ralph and Bountiful was ridin' along, talkin', they come to this point, right down there." He pointed. "And she said, 'Oh, look at that beautiful big rock'."

Smoke grinned. "Big Rock. Big Rock, Colorado!"

7

"The son of a bitch is doing *what*?" Tilden Franklin screamed the question at Clint.

"Buildin' a town," Clint said woefully. "Big Rock, Colorado."

Tilden sat down. "Well, he can't do that," he said with something very close to a pout. *"I* done built a town. A proper one."

"Maybe he can't, Boss. But somebody forgot to tell him that. Him and that goddamned preacher and their wives. And lemme tell you something about that preacher man. He's done up and bought some land from Smoke Jensen and his cabin is damn near complete. And maybe you oughta know this too: that preacher is more than just a preacher. He fought for some years under the name of the Cincinnati Kid."

Tilden stared at his foreman as if the man had lost his mind. Then he slowly nodded his head. "I read about him. He killed a man with his fists right before he was scheduled to fight . . . somebody big-named. Iron Mike or something like that. What's the point of all this, Clint? What does Jensen hope to prove by it?"

Clint sat down, rather wearily, and plopped his hat down on the floor beside the chair. "Damned if I know,

Boss. I figured with his reputation, when we burned Mason out, he'd come shootin'. He didn't. I figured when we . . . they done it to Velvet and killed Adam, Smoke would come a-shootin'. He didn't. Luis and his bunch burned out Peyton. And Smoke builds him a town. I can't figure it."

"I won't even ask if the town is legal."

"It's legal, and that Lawyer Hunt Brook and his wife done moved his practice out of Fontana and up to Big Rock. I spied on them some this morning. Then I nosed around Big Rock myself. That's a mighty fine store that's goin' up. And the smells from that cafe got my mouth waterin'. Some of the nesters' wives and older girls is doin' the cookin'. And them miners is swarmin' all over the place. They got 'em a saloon too. Big Rock Saloon. No games, no girls. A nice church and school combination goin' up too. And a jail."

"And I guess they elected themselves a sheriff, did they?"

"Shore did. Charlie Starr is the sheriff, and Luke Nations is his deputy."

Tilden pounded his fists on the desk and cursed. He looked and behaved like a very large, spoiled, and petulant child.

Clint waited patiently. He had seen his boss act like this before.

When Tilden had calmed down, Clint said, "Herds look good."

Tilden fixed him with a baleful look. "That's wonderful, Clint. I can't tell you how impressed I am. I'm making thousands of dollars a week on gold shares. I should be making several more thousands in kickbacks, except that goddamned sheriff I put into office has turned holy-roller on me. I am paying several thousands of dollars a month for some of the finest gunhands in the West, and they can't seem to rid the country of one Smoke Jensen. The son of a bitch rides all over the country, usually by himself, and my so-called gunslicks can't or won't, tackle him."

Clint sat quietly, knowing his boss was not yet through.

"Now Johnny North has taken up with a damned nester woman. Judge Proctor hasn't had a drink in weeks; he's turned just as righteous as Monte Carson. My men are afraid, *afraid,* to go into *my goddamn town!*"

Tilden rose from behind his desk to pace the study. He turned to face Clint's back.

"Turn around and look at me!" he ordered. "Tell Luis to take his men into town and rid it of Monte and Proctor. Right now, Clint. Right now!"

Clint retrieved his hat and stood up. "Boss," he said patiently. "Are you talkin' about treein' a town?"

"Exactly."

Clint sighed and shook his head. He wished Tilden would get Smoke Jensen out of his mind and just get on with the business of ranching. The big foreman wished a lot of things, but he knew that Smoke Jensen had become an obsession with Tilden. He wasn't even talkin' much about Sally no more. His hatred of Smoke had nearly consumed the man.

And Clint felt—no, *knew*—somehow that Tilden wasn't goin' to win this fight. Oh, he would succeed in runnin' out the nesters who were weak to begin with. Like Peyton. But Peyton was long gone. And them that remained was the tough ones. Not cold-eyed tough like Luis Chamba and Kane and Sanderson and Valentine and Suggs and them other gunslicks Tilden had on the payroll, but tough like with stayin' power.

And now Tilden wanted to tree a Western town. He lifted his eyes, meeting the just-slightly-mad eyes of Tilden Franklin.

"Are you not capable of giving those orders, Clint?"

"Don't push on me, Boss," Clint warned. "Don't do it."

Tilden's face softened a bit. "Clint . . . we've been together for years. We've spent more than a third of our lifetimes together. We've had rough times before. You own ten percent of this ranch. You could have taken your profits and left years ago, started your own spread, but you stayed with me. Just stay with me a while longer, you'll see. Things will be like they were years ago."

"Boss, things ain't *never* gonna be like they was. Not ever agin."

Tilden picked up a vase and hurled it against a far wall, breaking the vase, showering the carpet with bits of broken ceramic. "It will!" he screamed. "You'll see, Clint. Just get rid of Smoke Jensen and those nesters will fold up and slink away. Now get out, Clint. Carry out my orders. *Get out*, damn you!"

Crazy! Clint thought. He ain't just obsessed . . . he's plumb crazy. *He's* the one who's livin' in a house of cards. Not them nesters, but Tilden Franklin.

"All right, Boss," Clint said. There was a different note in his voice, a note that Tilden should have picked up on. But he didn't. "Fine. I'll get out."

Clint left the big house and stood for a moment on the front porch. His eyes swept the immediate holdings of Tilden Franklin. Thousands and thousands of acres. Too goddamn much for one man, and that silly bastard isn't content with it. He wants more.

But not with my help.

Clint walked to his own quarters and began packing. He would take only what he had to have to travel light. One pack horse. Clint had money. Being a very frugal man, he had banked most of his salary and the profits from selling the cows over the years.

He smiled, not a pleasant smile. Tilden didn't know that he owned land up on the Gunnison, up near Blue Mesa. Owned it under the name of Matthew Harrison. Everybody around here knew him as Clint Harris. He'd changed his name as a snot-nosed boy, when he'd run off from his home down in Texas, after he'd shot his abusive stepfather. Clint never knew whether he'd killed the man, or not. He'd just taken off.

And that was what he was going to do now. Just take off.

The foreman—no! he corrected that—ex-foreman . . . had not had a good night's sleep since that . . . awfulness with Velvet Colby. He sat down at his rough-hewn desk and slowly wrote out instructions on a piece of paper. Finished with the letter, he walked to the door and opened it, calling for a puncher to get over there.

"Billy, can you read and write?"

"Yes, sir, Mister Clint," the cowboy said. "I finished sixth grade."

"Fine. Come on in." With the cowboy inside Clint's quarters, Clint pointed to the letter. "Sign your name where it says Witness."

"Yes, sir, Mister Clint." The cowboy did not read the letter; that wasn't none of his business. He signed his name. "You want me to date this, Mister Clint?"

"Yes. Good thought, Billy."

After Billy had gone, Clint looked around his spartan living quarters. Looked around for one last time. He could see nothing left that he wished to take. Outside, he rigged the pack horse and swung onto his own horse. Looking around, he spotted several punchers just down from the high country. They walked over to him.

"Where you goin', Mister Clint?" a puncher called Rosie asked.

"Haulin' my ashes, Rosie. And if you got any sense about you, you will too." He looked at the others. "All of you."

"You got a new job, Mister Clint?" a cowboy named Austin asked.

"Yeah, I do, Austin. And I'm hirin' punchers. I'm payin' forty a month and found. You interested?"

They all were.

Clint figured he could run his place with four hands, including himself. At least for a time.

"Pack your warbags, boys. And do it quiet-like. Meet me just north of Big Rock, south of Slumgullion Pass."

He swung his horse's head and moved out.

The punchers moved quietly to the bunkhouse and packed their meager possessions. One by one, they moved out, about thirty minutes behind Clint. None of them knew why the foreman was pullin' out. But with Clint gone, damned if they was gonna stay around with all these lazy-assed, overpaid gunhands.

As they rode over and out of TF range, they met other TF punchers—not hired guns, cowboys. The punchers looked at those leaving, put it all together, and one by one, silently at first, made their plans to pull out.

"I ain't seen my momma in nigh on three years," one said. "I reckon it's time to head south."

"I got me a pard works over on the Saguache," another said. "Ain't seen him in two, three years. It's time to move on anyway."

"I know me a widder woman who owns a right-nice little farm up near Georgetown," yet another cowboy said. "I'm tared of lookin' at the ass end of cows. I think I'll just head up thataway."

"I ain't never seed the ocean," another cowboy lamented. "I think I'll head west."

Clint rode into Big Rock and tied his horses at the post outside the Big Rock Saloon. As he was stepping up onto the still-raw-smelling boardwalk, he saw Johnny North and that Belle Colby woman coming out of the general store. They stopped to chat with Lawyer Hunt Brook.

Clint removed his gunbelt and walked slowly over to them. Johnny saw the man coming at him and instinctively slipped the thongs off the hammers of his Colts.

Then he noticed that Clint was not armed. His eyes found the pack horse.

"What the hell . . ." he muttered.

Clint had some papers in his right hand.

Clint stopped about twenty-five feet from the trio. "I'm friendly," he said.

"Come on," Johnny said.

Clint held the papers out to Belle. Slowly, she took them. Clint said, "It won't make up for what was done to your daughter and your husband, but it's something I'd like to do." He turned and walked back to his horses.

Belle, Johnny, and Hunt watched him swing into the saddle and ride out of their lives.

"Let me see those papers, Belle," Hunt said. The lawyer quickly scanned first one paper, then the others—older, slightly yellowing around the edges. He began to smile.

"What is it, Mister Brook?" Belle asked.

"Why, Belle . . . you own ten percent of the TF Ranch. I think you have just become a very wealthy woman."

Tilden called for his houseboy.

"Yes, sir?"

"Get Clint for me, boy."

"Yes, sir."

The houseboy returned a few minutes later. "Sir? Mister Clint is gone."

"Gone . . . where, damnit?"

"He packed up and rode out. His quarters is empty, and so is the bunkhouse. Old Ramon at the stable says all the punchers packed up and left. Following Mister Clint."

"Get out!" Tilden said, real menace in his voice.

"Yes, sir," the houseboy said. "I most certainly will do that, Mister Tilden."

Thirty minutes later, the servant had packed his kit and was walking toward Fontana.

In his study, Tilden called for his houseboy. "Bring me a cup of coffee, boy!"

The big house creaked in empty silence.

"Boy!" Tilden roared. "You bring me a cup of coffee or I'll take a whip to your lazy greaser ass!"

Silence. And Tilden Franklin, the man who would be king, knew he was alone in his large, fine home.

He walked to a large window and looked out. His thoughts were savage. "I'm gonna kill you, Jensen. I'm gonna bring Fontana to its knees first. Then I'm gonna burn your goddamn Big Rock to the ground. Then I'm gonna kill you and have your woman."

He walked to a rack and took down his gunbelt, buckling it around his hips. He put his hat on his head and walked outside.

"Ramon?" he yelled.

"*Si, señor?*" the old man called.

"Bring me my horse. Then you find your mule and get Luis for me."

"*Si, señor.*" Son of a bitch! he silently added.

8

The houseboy heard the thundering of hooves long before he saw them. He did not know what they meant, other than a lot of riders were in a big hurry. He shifted his heavy satchel to his other hand and trudged on, walking along the side of the rutted dirt road. As the thunder grew louder, he turned around, fear and panic on his face.

"Ride the insubordinate bastard down!" he heard Tilden Franklin scream, his voice just carrying over the steel-shod thunder.

The houseboy tried to run. He dropped his belongings and leaped to one side. He was too slow.

The rushing shoulder of a horse hit him in the back, tossing him to the road. Pain filled him as he heard his bones break. He looked up in time to see Tilden's crazed face and his stallion rear up, the hooves flashing in the hard sunlight.

The houseboy screamed.

His screaming was cut off as the steel hooves came down on his face, crushing his skull. The riders galloped on, leaving the houseboy lying in the road, his blood staining and dampening the dust.

They were fifty-odd strong, drunk not with alcohol, but with the power given them by Tilden Franklin. Raw, unbridled, killing power. He was paying them good money, and offering them immunity and total impunity.

From the law. None of them was taking Smoke Jensen into consideration as any form of punishment. They should have.

One deputy saw them coming hard and ran for his horse. He hauled his ashes, leaving everything he owned behind him in Fontana. If it ever calmed down, he might be back. If not, to hell with it!

Yet another deputy, nicknamed Stonewall, saw the riders coming and ran across the street to the sheriff's office. "Monte!" he hollered, jumping into the office and running to the shotgun rack. "Tilden and his gun-hawks comin' fast. Get ready."

A third deputy ran inside the office-jail just as gunfire ripped the street. Like Monte and Stonewall, he grabbed a Greener from off the rack and stuffed his pockets full of shells

"Take the back, Dave," Monte said, his voice calm. "Where are the others?"

"I seen Slim haulin' his ashes outta here," Dave told him. "I think Joel is out in the county somewheres servin' a notice from Judge Proctor."

"Stay calm," Monte told his men. "We got some food, and we got a pump for water. Tilden wanted this place built of stone for strength, so that's gonna work agin him. It'd take a cannon to bring these walls down."

"Hey!" a miner back in lockup hollered. "What about me?"

"Turn him loose and give him a shotgun," Monte ordered. "If he tried to get of here, those gunnies would cut him to rags."

The miner looked out at the angry group of heavily armed riders. "Who the hell is all them people?"

"That's your buddy, Tilden Franklin, and his gun-hands," Stonewall told him. "Would you like to go out and kiss him hello?"

"Would you like to kiss another part of me?" the miner challenged.

Stonewall laughed and handed the man a sawed-off shotgun and a sack of shells.

Monte called out through an open but barred window "As Sheriff I am ordering you to break this up and leave this town or you'll all be under arrest."

"That's gonna be a good trick," Dave muttered.

A TF gunhand made the mistake of firing into the jail. Monte lifted his express gun and blew the rider clear out of the saddle.

The street erupted in gunfire, the hard exchange returned from those in the fortlike jail.

Blood dropped onto the dusty street as the shotguns cleared half a dozen saddles of living flesh, depositing dead, dying, and badly wounded men into the dirt.

Monte reloaded his express gun and lined up a gunhand he knew only as Blackie. He gave Blackie both barrels full of buckshot. The double charge lifted the gunhand out of the saddle, a hole in his chest so large it would take a hat to cover it.

The screaming of frightened and bucking horses filled the gunsmoke air. The riders were hard pressed to control their mounts, much less do any fighting.

Louis Longmont stepped out of his gaming tent, a Colt in each hand. As calmly as in a seconded duel, Louis lifted first one Colt and then the other, firing coolly and with much deliberation. He emptied two saddles and then paused, not wanting to shoot a horse.

The man who owned and cooked at the Good Eats Cafe stepped out of his place with a Sharps .50. The man, a Civil War veteran with four hard years of fighting as a Union cavalryman, lifted the Sharps and emptied yet another saddle.

Big Mamma ran out of her place and literally jerked one gunhand off his horse. She began smashing his face with big, hard fists, beating the man into bloody unconsciousness.

Billy, up in the loft of the stable with his newly bought .22 caliber rifle, grinned as he took careful aim at the big man on the big horse. Gently he squeezed the trigger.

And shot Tilden Franklin smack in one cheek of his ass.

With a roar of rage, Tilden wheeled his horse around and took off at a gallop, out of town, the gunhands following closely.

Nobody treed a Western town in the 1870s. Nobody. Nearly every man in every town was a combat veteran of some war, whether it be against Indians, outlaws, the Union Blue, or the Rebel Gray. But nobody treed a Western town.

Two years prior to the formation of Fontana, back in September of 1876, Jesse James and his outlaw gang had tried to collar Northfield, Minnesota. They were shot to rags by the townspeople.

The dust settled slowly, and a quiet settled over Fontana. Only the moaning of the badly wounded TF gunslicks could be heard. Doctor Spalding came wheeling up in his buggy, sliding to a halt in the street. His unbelieving eyes took in the carnage before him. He began counting. He stopped at ten, knowing there were several more scattered about in the dirt and dust.

Monte and his deputies stepped out of the jail building. "Get 'em patched up, Doc," he said. "Them that is able, bunk 'em in yonder." He jerked his thumb toward the jail. "You!" His eyes found a man lounging about. "Git the undertaker on down here."

The photographer was coming at an awkward run, his tripod-and-hood camera-and-flash container a cumbersome burden. He set up and began taking pictures.

"Sheriff!" Doc Spalding called. "Most of these men are dead. Several more are not going to make it much longer."

"Good," Monte said. "Saves the town the expense of a trial."

Tilden Franklin lay on his belly, in bed, while the old camp cook probed and poked at his buttock, finally cutting out the small .22 slug. He dropped the bloody pellet into a pan.

"Somebody was a-funnin' you with that thing," the cook observed.

Tilden swore, loud and long.

News of the attempted collaring of Fontana was quick to reach Big Rock and the small spreads scattered out from it. When Smoke took the news to Ralph, the minister sat down on a log he was hewing and laughed.

"Billy shot Tilden Franklin in the ass!" he hollered, then started laughing again.

Bountiful came on the run, sure something was wrong with her husband. Sally was with her. The ladies had been working, making a list of prospective members for the Big Rock Women for Equal Rights Club.

"What's wrong?" Bountiful asked.

"Billy shot Tilden Franklin in his big ass!" Ralph again hollered, then bent over with laughter.

The laughter was infectious; soon they were all howling and wiping their eyes.

Judge Proctor was furious. Since he had begun his program of alcohol abstention, he had realized he was supposed to help maintain law and order, not make a mockery of it by drunken antics.

The judge signed arrest warrants for Tilden Franklin and as many of the TF gunslicks that people on the street could recall being present during the shooting spree.

Louis Longmont put up five thousand dollars reward for the arrest and conviction of Tilden Franklin, and the judge had Haywood's printing press cranking out wanted posters for Tilden Franklin. He then had them posted throughout the county.

Louis thought it all hysterically amusing.

Now everybody, or most everybody, knew that no one was really going to try to arrest Tilden Franklin. Or, for that matter, any of the TF gunhawks. But it did keep them out of Fontana and Big Rock and, for the most part, confined to the TF ranges. Punching cattle. Which pissed off the gunslicks mightily.

"You got no choice," Tilden said to his new foreman, Luis Chamba. Tilden was unshaven, and sitting on a pillow. "Not if you want to stay alive. All them damned old gunslingers have ringed my range. They're just waiting for you or me or some of the others to step off of this range. Anyway, what are you boys bitching about? You're all drawing top wages for sitting around really doing nothing." Tilden did manage a rueful smile. "Except herdin' beeves, that is."

Luis did not see the humor in it. He stalked out of the great house. But Luis was no fool. He knew that, for the time being, he was stuck. Herding cattle.

And then two things happened that would forever alter the histories of Fontana and Big Rock and the lives of most of those who called them home.

Belle Colby, accompanied by Johnny North and Lawyer Hunt Brook, claimed her ten percent of the TF.

And Utah Slim finally made his move, setting out to do what he had been paid to do.

Kill Smoke Jensen.

9

"Riders coming, Boss!" Luis Chamba hollered through an open window of the large home.

"Who are they?" Tilden shouted returning the holler. He was sitting in his study, drinking whiskey. The interior of the home was as nasty as Tilden Franklin's unwashed body and unshaven face.

"Can't tell yet," the gunslinger called. "But there's a woman in a buckboard, I can tell that much."

Tilden heaved himself up and out of his chair. For a moment, the big man swayed unsteadily on his booted feet. He stumbled to a water basin and washed his face. Lifting his dripping face, he stared into a mirror. He was shocked at his appearance. A very prideful man, Tilden had always been a neat dresser and almost fastidious when it came to washing his body.

He could smell his own body odors wafting up to assail his nostrils. With a grimace, he called to Luis.

"Tell them I'll be out in fifteen minutes, Luis."

"*Sí*, Boss."

Hurriedly, Tilden washed himself best he could out back of the great house and toweled himself dry. He had water on the stove heating for shaving. He shaved, very carefully, noting his shaking hands. Somehow, he managed not to nick his face.

For some reason, his crazed mind felt that the woman in the buckboard was Sally Jensen, coming to see him.

Tilden splashed Bay Rum on his face and sprinkled some on his body, then dressed in clean clothes. He was shocked when he stepped out onto the porch and saw it was not Sally Jensen.

The woman was Belle Colby. With her was Johnny North, the lawyer Hunt Brook, Sheriff Monte Carson, and someone Tilden had never seen before. A man dressed in a dark suit, white shirt, and string tie. His face was tanned and his eyes were hard. A drooping moustache.

He cleared up who he was in a hurry. "My name is Mitchell," he said. "United States Marshal. I don't know who started the war in this part of the country, Franklin, and I don't much care. But I'm delivering two messages today. One to you, another to Smoke Jensen. The war is over. If I have to come back in here, I'll bring the Army with me and declare a state of martial law. You understand all that?"

"Yes . . . sir," Tilden said, the words bitter on his tongue. He glared at Carson.

"Fine," Mitchell said. "Now then, Lawyer Brook is here representing Mrs. Colby. Me and Sheriff Carson will just sit here and see that the lady gets her due."

"Her . . . *due*?" Tilden questioned.

Briefly, Hunt Brook explained. He further explained that the papers given Belle Colby were now part of court records.

"I want to see your books, Mister Franklin," Hunt told Tilden. "When that is done, I shall determine how much is owed Mrs. Colby. She has confided in me that she is willing to sell her ten percent back to you. Once a fair price is determined. By me. Shall we get to it, Mister Franklin?"

Speaking through an almost blind rage, Tilden started to choke out his reply. Then some small bit of reason crept into his mind. He did not want these people inside his smelly house. That would not look good, and the word would get around.

"I'll get my books. We'll go over them on the porch. All right?"

"Fine, Mister Franklin," the lawyer said.

Luis Chamba had discreetly disappeared into the bunk house. He had known who Mitchell was at first sighting. And while the Mexican gunfighter felt he could best him, no one in their right mind killed a federal marshal. He told his men to stay low and out of sight.

Chamba felt, along with many of the other gunhands, that Tilden Franklin had just about come to the end of his string. But as long as he could pay the money, they would stay. Anyways, Luis wanted his chance at Smoke Jensen. Now that the elusive gunfighter had finally surfaced, a lot of gunslicks wanted to try their skills against his.

Tilden was seething as the lawyer went over his books. As far as the money went, the money to buy out Belle Colby, Tilden had that much in his safe inside the house. It wasn't the money. It was the fact that Clint had given his percentage to this trashy nester woman. Husband not even cold in the grave and she was probably hunchin' and bumpin' the gunslinger Johnny North. Trash, that's all she was.

Tilden listened as the lawyer quoted an absurdly high figure. But Tilden wasn't going to quibble about it. He just wanted his holdings intact, and this hard-eyed U.S. marshal out of the area. Mitchell was damn sure wrong on one count, though: the war was not over. Not by a long shot.

"All right," Tilden said, agreeing to the figure.

The lawyer reached into his case and handed Tilden what the man knew was a binding note. He signed it,

Belle signed it, and then Mitchell and North both witnessed it. Belle Colby was now a woman of some means.

Tilden Franklin sat in a chair and watched them leave. Slowly, the gunfighters began to once more gather around the porch.

"Play it close to the vest for a time," Tilden said. "Let that damned marshal get clear of this area. Then you'll all start earning your wages. I don't care who you have to kill in order to get to him, but I want Smoke Jensen dead. Dead, goddamnit . . . *dead!*"

U.S. Marshal Mitchell looked at the legendary gunfighter Smoke Jensen. He was even younger than Mitchell had been led to believe. The man was still a ways from thirty.

"If I tried real hard, Jensen, I probably could come up with half a dozen arrest warrants for you. You know that, don't you?"

Smoke grinned boyishly. "But findin' people to stand up in court, look me in the eyes, and testify against me might give you some problems."

Smart too, Mitchell thought. The marshal returned Smoke's smile. "There is always that to consider, yes."

"The war is not over, Marshal. You must know that."

"I mean what I say, Jensen. If I have to, I'll bring the Army in here. The Governor of the State of Colorado is tired of hearing about this place. In terms of blood."

"Tilden Franklin is a crazy man, Marshal. I don't know why he hates me, but he does. He will never rest until one of us is dead."

"I know that," Mitchell said. "But don't sell him short, Jensen. Not even Luis Chamba is as fast as Tilden Franklin. He's poison with a short gun."

"He thought he was poison with his fists too," Smoke replied, again with that boyish grin.

"So I heard." The marshal's reply was very dry. "That beating you gave him didn't help matters very much."

"It gave me a great deal of satisfaction."

"I really hope I never see you again, Jensen. But somehow I feel I will."

"I didn't start this, Marshal. But if it comes down to it, I'll damn sure finish it."

The marshal looked at Smoke for a moment. "Other than Tilden Franklin, you know anyone else who might pay a lot of money to have you killed?"

Smoke thought about that for a moment. Then he shook his head. "No, not right off hand."

Time took him winging back more than three years, back to the ghost town of Slate, where Smoke had met the men who had killed his brother and his father, then raped and killed his wife Nicole, and then killed Nicole and Smoke's son Arthur.

Mitchell, as if sensing what was taking place in Smoke's mind, stood motionless, waiting.

"Them old mountain men is pushin' us toward Slate," a gunhand said.

The one of the Big Three who had ordered all the killing, Richards, smiled at Smoke's choice of a showdown spot. A lot of us are going to be ghosts in a very short time, he thought.

As the old ghost town loomed up stark and foreboding on the horizon, located on the flats between the Lemhi River and the Beaverhead Range, a gunslick reined up and pointed. "The goddamn place is full of people."

"Miners," another of the nineteen men who rode to kill Smoke said. "Just like it was over at the camp on the Uncompahgre."

The men checked their weapons and stuffed their pockets full of extra shells and cartridges.

They moved out in a line toward the ghost town and toward the young gunfighter named Smoke.

"There he is," Britt said, looking up the hill toward a falling-down store.

Smoke stood alone on the old curled-up and rotted boardwalk. The men could just see the twin .44s belted around his waist. He held a Henry repeating rifle in his right hand, a double-barreled express gun in his left hand. Suddenly, Smoke ducked into the building, leaving only a slight bit of dust to signal where he once stood.

"Two groups of six," Richards said. "One group of three, one group of four. Move out."

Smoke had removed his spurs, hanging them on the saddlehorn of Drifter. As soon as he'd ducked out of sight, he had run from the store down the hill, staying in the alley. He stashed the express gun on one side of the street in an old store, his rifle across the weed-grown street.

He met the gunslick called Skinny Davis in the gloom of what had once been a saloon.

"Draw!" Skinny hissed.

Smoke put two holes in his chest before Davis could cock his .44s.

"In the saloon!" someone yelled.

Williams jumped through an open, glassless window of the saloon. Just as his boots hit the old warped boards, Smoke shot him, the .44 slug stopping him and twisting the gunhawk back out the window to the boardwalk. Williams was hurt, but not out of it. He crawled along the side of the building, one arm broken and dangling, useless.

"Smoke Jensen!" the gunnie called Cross called. "You ain't got the sand to face me."

"That's one way of putting it," Smoke muttered. He took careful aim and shot the man in the stomach, doubling him over and dropping him to the dirty street.

The miners had hightailed it to the ridges surrounding the old town. There they sat, drinking and betting and cheering. The old Mountain Men, Preacher among them, watched expressionless.

The young man called Smoke, far too young to have been one of that rare and select breed of adventuring pioneers called Mountain Men, had, nonetheless, been raised, at least in part, by Preacher, so that made Smoke one of them. Indeed, the last of the Mountain Men.

A bullet dug a trench along the old, rotting wood, sending splinters flying, a few of them striking Smoke in the face, stinging and bringing a few drops of blood.

Smoke ran out the back, coming face to face with Simpson, the outlaw gunfighter having both his dirty hands filled with .44s.

Smoke pulled the trigger on his own .44s, the double hammer-blows of lead taking Simpson in the lower chest, knocking him dying to the ground.

Smoke reloaded, then grabbed up Simpson's guns and tucked them behind his belt. He ran down the alley. A gunslick stepped out of a gaping doorway just as Smoke cut to his right, jumping through a windowless opening. A bullet burned his shoulder. Spinning, he fired both Colts, one slug taking Martin in the throat, the second striking the outlaw just above the nose, almost removing the upper part of the man's face.

Smoke caught a glimpse of someone running. He dropped to one knee and fired. His slug shattered the hip of Rogers, sending the big man sprawling in the dirt, howling and cussing. Another gunslick spurred his horse and charged the building where Smoke was crouched. He smashed his horse's shoulder against the old door and came thundering inside. The animal, wild-eyed and scared, lost its footing and fell, pinning the outlaw to the floor, crushing the man's stomach and chest. The outlaw, Reese, cried in agony as blood filled his mouth and darkness clouded his eyes.

Smoke slipped out the side door.

"Get him, Turkel!" a hired gun yelled.

Smoke glanced up roof-level high; he ducked as a rifle bullet flattened against the building. Smoke snapped off a shot and got lucky, the slug hitting Turkel in the chest. He crashed through an awning, bringing down the rotting awning. The hired gun did not move.

A bullet removed a small part of Smoke's right ear; blood poured down the side of his face. He ran to where he had stashed the shotgun, grabbing it up and cocking it, leveling the barrels just as the doorway filled with gunslicks.

Smoke pulled both triggers, fighting the recoil of the 12-gauge. The blast cleared the doorway of all living things.

"Goddamn you, Jensen," a hired gun yelled, his voice filled with rage and frustration. He stepped out into the street.

Smoke dropped the shotgun and picked up a rifle, shooting the gunhand in the gut.

It was white-hot heat and gunsmoke for the next few minutes. Smoke was hit in the side, twisting him into the open doorway of a rotting building where a dead man lay. Smoke picked up the man's bloody shotgun and stumbled into the darkness of the building just as spurs jingled in the alley. Smoke jacked back both hammers and waited.

The spurs came closer. Smoke could hear the man's heavy breathing. He lifted the shotgun and pulled both triggers, blowing a bullet-sized hole in the rotting pine wall.

The gunslick stumbled backward, and slammed into an outhouse. The outhouse collapsed, dumping the dying gunhand into the shit-pit.

Smoke checked his wounds. He would live. He reloaded his own Colts and the guns taken from the dead gunnie. He listened as Fenerty called for his buddies.

There was no response.

Fenerty was the last gunslick left.

He called again and Smoke pinpointed his voice. Picking up a Henry, Smoke emptied the rifle into the storefront. Fenerty came staggering out, stumbled on the rotting steps, and pitched face-forward into the street. There, he died.

Smoke laid down the challenge to Richards, Potter, and Stratton. "All right, you bastards!" he yelled. "Face me in the street if you've got the balls!"

The sharp odor of sweat mingled with blood and gunsmoke filled the summer air as four men stepped out into the death-street.

Richards, Potter, and Stratton stood at one end of the block. A tall, bloody figure stood at the other. All guns were in leather.

"You son of a bitch!" Stratton lost his cool and screamed, his voice as high-pitched as an hysterical girl's. "You ruined it all!" He clawed for his .44.

Smoke drew, cocked, and fired before Stratton's pistol could clear leather.

Screaming his outrage, Potter jerked out his pistol. Smoke shot him dead with his left-hand Colt. Holstering both Colts, Smoke faced Richards and waited.

Richards had not moved. He stood with a faint smile on his lips, staring at Smoke.

"You ready to die?" Smoke asked him.

"As ready as I'll ever be." There was no fear in his voice that Smoke could detect. Richards was good with a short gun, and Smoke kept that in mind. Richards's hands were steady. "Janey gone?"

"Took your money and pulled out."

Richards laughed. "Well, it's been a long run, hasn't it Smoke?"

"It's just about over."

"What happens to all our—" He looked down at his dead partners. "—*my* holdings?"

"I don't care what happens to the mines. The miners

can have them. I'm giving all your stock to decent honest punchers and homesteaders."

A puzzled look crawled over Richards's face. "I don't understand. You mean, you did all . . . *this*!" He waved his left hand. "For nothing?"

Someone moaned, the sound painfully inching up the bloody, dusty, gunsmoke-filled street.

"I did it for my pa, my brother, my wife, and my baby son. You, or your hired guns, killed them all."

"But it won't bring them back!"

"Yeah, I know."

"I wish I had never heard the name of Jensen."

"After this day, Richards, you'll never hear it again."

"One way to find out," he replied with a smile, and went for his Colt. He cleared leather fast and fired. He was snake-quick, but he hurried his shot, the lead digging up dirt at Smoke's feet.

Smoke shot him in the right shoulder, spinning the man around. Richards drew his left-hand gun and Smoke fired again, the slug striking the man in the left side of his chest. He struggled to bring up his Colt. He managed to cock it before Smoke's third shot struck him in the belly. Richards sat down in the street, the pistol slipping from suddenly numbed fingers.

He opened his mouth to speak, and tasted blood on his tongue. The light began to fade around him. "You'll . . . meet . . ."

Smoke never found out, that day, who he was supposed to meet. Richards toppled over on his side and died.

Smoke looked up at the ridge where the Mountain Men had gathered.

They were gone, leaving as silently as the wind.

And to this day, he had never seen or heard from any of them again.

* * *

"You been gone a time, boy," Marshal Mitchell said.

Smoke sighed. "Just a few years. Bloody ones, though."

He told the marshal about that day in the ghost town.

"I never knew the straight of it, Smoke. But you did play hell back then. That person Richards told you you'd meet?"

"Yeah?"

"He was talkin' about the man who will be faster than you. We who live by the gun all have them in our future."

Smoke nodded his head. "Yeah, I know. And yeah, I know who would pay to see me dead."

"Oh?"

"My sister. Janey."

10

"Your own sister would pay to have you killed!" Bountiful said, appalled at just the thought. "How dreadful. What kind of person is she?"

Ralph and Bountiful were having supper with Smoke and Sally. "She must have a lot of hate in her heart," Ralph said.

"I reckon," Smoke said. "Well, I'll just have to be more careful and keep looking over my shoulder from now on." He smiled. "That's something I'm used to doing."

Then he remembered Utah Slim. The man had aligned with no side in the mountain country war. No, Smoke thought, he didn't have to. He already had a job.

U.S. Marshal Mitchell had told Smoke that his office had received word that a gunslick had been paid to kill Jensen. But none of their usual sources could, or would, shed any light on who that gunslick might be.

Or why.

Smoke felt he knew the answer to both questions.

Utah Slim.

"You've got a funny look in your eyes, Smoke," Sally said, looking at her husband.

"I'm not going to sit around and wait for a bullet, Sally. I just made up my mind on that."

"I felt that was coming too."

"What are you two talking about?" Bountiful asked.

"A showdown," Smoke told her, buttering a biscuit. He chewed slowly, then said, "Might as well brace him in the morning and get it over with."

Ralph and Bountiful stopped eating and sat staring at the young gunfighter. Ralph said, "You're discussing this with no more emotion than if you were talking about planting beets!"

"No point in gettin' all worked up about it, Ralph. If I try to avoid it, it just prolongs the matter, and maybe some innocent person gets caught up in it and gets hurt. I told you and your friends a time back that we do things differently out here. And I'm not so sure that it isn't the best way."

"In the morning?"

"In the morning."

"I'll go in with you," the minister-turned farmer said. His tone indicated the matter was not up for debate.

"All right, Ralph."

Ralph was a surprisingly good horseman, and Smoke said as much.

"I was raised on a farm," he said. "And I'm also a very good rifle shot."

"I noticed you putting the Henry in the boot this morning."

The morning was very clear and very bright as the two men rode toward Fontana. As they worked their way out of the mountains and toward the long valley where Fontana was located, the temperature grew warmer.

"Ever shot a man, Ralph?"

"No."

"Could you?"

"Don't ever doubt it."

Smoke smiled faintly. He didn't doubt it for a minute.

The town of Fontana seemed to both men to be a bit smaller. Ralph commented on that.

"The easy pickings have been found and taken out, Ralph. For however long this vein will last, it's going to be hard work, dirty work, and dangerous work. Look yonder. One whole section of Fontana is gone. Half a dozen bars have pulled out."

"Why . . ." Ralph's eyes swept the visibly shrinking town that lay below them. "At this rate, there will be nothing left of Fontana by the end of summer."

"If that long," Smoke said, a note of satisfaction in his statement. "If we all can just settle the matter of Tilden Franklin, then we can all get on with the business of living."

"And it will have to be settled by guns." Ralph's remark was not put in question form. The man was rapidly learning about the unwritten code of the West.

"Yes."

Smoke reined up in front of Sheriff Monte Carson's office. The men dismounted and walked toward the bullet-scarred stone building. As they entered, Monte smiled and greeted them.

His smile faded as he noted the hard look in Smoke's eyes.

"I've had that same look a few times myself, Smoke," Monte said. "Gonna be a shootin'?"

"Looks that way, Monte. I'd rather not have it in town if I can help it."

"I'd appreciate that, Smoke. But sometimes it can't be helped. I got to thinkin' after talkin' with that marshal. It's Utah Slim, ain't it?"

"Yeah." Smoke poured a tin cup of coffee and sat down. "I got a strong hunch my sister hired him to gun me."

"Your . . . *sister*?"

Smoke told him the story of Janey. Or at least as much as he knew about her life since she'd taken off from that hard-scrabble, rocky, worthless farm in the hills of Missouri. Back when Smoke was just a boy, after their ma had died, when their pa was off fighting in the War Between the States. And Smoke had had to shoulder the responsibilities of a boy forced into early manhood.

It was a story all too common among those who drifted West.

It sounded all too painfully familiar to Monte Carson, almost paralleling his own life.

"I seen Utah early this mornin', sittin' on the hotel porch." He smiled. "The only hotel we got left here in Fontana, that is."

"Won't be long now," Smoke told him. "How many businesses are you losing a day?"

"Half a dozen. As you know, up there in Big Rock, the stage is runnin' twice a day now, carryin' people out of here."

"Seen some TF riders in town as we rode in," Smoke said. "And didn't see any of those flyers the Judge had printed up. What happened?"

"Some state man was on the stage three, four days ago, from the governor's office. He looked at the charges I had agin Tilden and his men and told me to take them dodgers down. They wasn't legal." He shrugged. "I took 'em down."

Smoke grinned. "It was fun while it lasted, though, wasn't it?"

"Damn shore was."

Conversation became a bit forced, as both Monte and Smoke, both gunfighters, knew the clock was ticking toward a showdown in the streets of Fontana. Stonewall and Joel came into the office.

"Git the people off the boardwalks," Monte told his deputies. "And have either of you seen Utah Slim?"

"He's standin' down by the corral, leanin' up agin a post," Joel said. "He's got a half dozen of them punk gunslingers with him. They lookin' at Utah like he's some sort of god."

"Run 'em off," Monte ordered. "I'll not have no mismatched gunfight in this town."

The deputies left, both carrying sawed-off express guns.

Monte looked at Smoke after the office door had closed. "Utah is fast, Smoke. He's damn good. I'd rate him with the best."

"Better than Valentine?"

"He don't blow his first shot like Valentine, but he's just as fast."

Ralph looked out a barred window. "Streets are clear," he announced. "Nobody moving on the boardwalks."

Smoke stood up. "It's time." He slipped the leather thongs from the hammers of his Colts and put his hat on his head. "I'd like to talk to Utah first, find out something about my sister. Hell, I don't even know if she's the one behind this. I'll give it a try."

Smoke walked out onto the shaded boardwalks outside the sheriff's office. He pulled his hat lower over his eyes and eased his Colts half out of leather a few times, letting them fall back naturally into the oiled leather. He stepped out into the street and turned toward the corral.

As he walked down the center of the street, his spurs jingling and his boots kicking up little pockets of dust, he was conscious of many unseen eyes on him, and even a few he could associate with a body.

Stonewall and Joel were on the opposite sides of the broad street, both still carrying shotguns. The duded-up dandies who fancied themselves gunslingers had gathered as close to the corral as the deputies would allow them. Smoke saw the young punk Luke had made eat crow that day. Lester Morgan, Sundance. He had himself some new Colts. And that kid who called himself The Silver Dollar Kid was there, along with a few other no-names who wanted to be gunfighters.

Smoke wondered how they got along; where did they get eating money? Petty thievery, probably.

Louis Longmont had stepped out of his gaming tent. "How many you facing, Smoke?" he asked, as Smoke walked by.

"Just one that I know of. Utah Slim. I think my sis, Janey, sent him after me."

Louis paced Smoke, but stayed on the boardwalk. "Yes, it would be like her."

"Where is she, Louis?"

"Tombstone, last I heard. Runnin' a red-light place. She's worth a lot of money. Richards's money, I presume."

"Yeah. Richards ain't got no use for it. I never heard of no Wells Fargo armored stage followin' no hearse."

Louis laughed quietly. "I'll watch your back, Smoke."

"Thanks."

Smoke kept on walking. He knew Louis had fallen back slightly, to keep an eye on Smoke's back trail.

Then the corral loomed up, Utah Slim standing by the corral. Smoke's eyes flicked upward to the loft of the barn. Billy was staring wide-eyed out of the loft door.

"Billy!" Smoke raised his voice. "You get your butt outta that loft and across the street. Right now, boy— move!"

"Yes, sir!" Billy hollered, and slipped down the hay rope to the street. He darted across the expanse and got behind a water trough.

"That there's a good kid," Utah said. "Funny the other week when he shot Tilden in the ass."

"Yeah, I'd like to have seen that myself."

"I ain't got nothin' personal agin you, Jensen. I want you to know that."

"Just another job, right, Utah?"

"That's the way it is," the killer said brightly.

"My sister hire you?"

"Damned if'n I know. Some woman named Janey, down in Tombstone paid me a lot of money, up front."

He squinted at Smoke. "Come to think of it, y'all do favor some."

"That's my darlin' sister."

"Makes me proud I ain't got no sister."

"Why don't you just get on your horse and ride on out, Utah. I don't want to have to kill you."

The killer looked startled. "Why, boy! You ain't gonna kill me."

"You want to wager on that?" Louis called.

"Yeah." Utah smiled. "I'll bet a hundred."

"Taken," Louis told him.

"How much did she pay you, Utah?" Smoke asked the man.

"Several big ones, boy." He grinned nastily. "She's a whoor, you know."

"So I heard." Smoke knew the killer was trying to anger him, throw him off, make him lose his composure.

"Yeah, she is," Utah said, still grinning. "I tole her, as part of the payment, I'd have to have me a taste of it."

"Is that right?"

"Shore is. Right good, too."

"I hope you enjoyed it."

"I did for a fact." This wasn't working out the way Utah had planned it. "Why do you ask?"

Smoke drew, cocked, and fired twice. Once with his right-hand Colt, that slug taking Utah in the chest and staggering him backward. The second slug coming from his left-hand gun and striking the gunslick in the stomach, dropping the killer to his knees, his left arm looped around the center railing of the corral.

Smoke holstered his left-hand Colt and waited for Utah. The killer managed to drag his Colt out of leather and cock it. That seemed to take all his strength. He pulled the trigger. The slug tore up the dirt at his knees.

Utah dropped the Colt. He lifted his eyes to Smoke. Just as the darkness began to fade his world, he managed to gasp, "How come you axed me if I enjoyed it?"

"'Cause you damn sure ain't gonna get no more, Utah."

Utah died hanging onto the corral railing. He died with his eyes open, staring at emptiness.

Smoke holstered his pistol and walked away.

11

The undertaker's hack rumbled past Louis Longmont's tent just as the gambler and the gunfighter were pouring tumblers of scotch.

Louis lifted his glass. "May I pay you a compliment, Smoke Jensen?"

"I reckon so, Louis."

"I have seen them all, Smoke. All the so-called great gunfighters. Clay Allison, John Wesley Hardin, Bill Longley, Jim Miller. I've drank with Wild Bill Hickok and Jim, Ed, and Bat Masterson. I've gambled with Doc Holliday and Wyatt Earp. I've seen them all in action. But you are the fastest gun I have ever seen in my life."

The men clinked glasses and drank of the Glenlivet.

"Thank you, Louis. But I'll tell you a secret."

Louis smiled. "I'll bet you a double eagle I already know what it is."

"No bets, Louis, for I imagine you do."

"You wish you were not the faster gun."

"You got that right."

The men finished their drinks and stepped out onto the boardwalk. The photographer had set up his equipment at the corral and was taking his shots of Utah Slim. The duded-up dandies had gathered around, managing to get themselves in almost every shot the man took.

"Fools!" Smoke muttered.

"Look at them with their hands on the butts of their guns," Louis pointed out. "They'll be bragging about that picture for the rest of their lives."

"However short they may be," Smoke added.

"Yes."

Ralph walked up, joining the gambler and the gun-fighter. Louis smiled at him.

"I would offer you a drink, Mister Morrow, but I'm afraid I might offend you."

"I'm not adverse to a cool beer, Mister Longmont."

Louis was more than slightly taken aback. "Well, I'll just be damned!" he blurted.

"Oh, I think not, sir," Ralph replied. He met the man's cool eyes. "How is your orphanage up in Boulder doing? Or that free hospital out in San Francisco?"

Louis smiled. "For a man of the cloth, you do get around, don't you, Ralph?"

"But I wasn't always a preacher, Mister Longmont," he reminded the gambler.

"Tell me more," Smoke said with a grin, looking at Louis.

"Don't let the news of my . . . philanthropic urges get out," the gambler said. "It might destroy my reputation."

Smoke looked at him and blinked. "Hell, Louis! I don't even know what that means!"

Laughing, the men entered the gaming tent for a cool one.

And the photographer's flash pan popped again.

And Utah Slim still clung to the corral railing.

The town of Fontana had begun to die, slowly at first, and then more rapidly as the gold vein began to peter out. More businesses shut down, packed up, and pulled out. The rip-roaring boom town was not yet busted, but a hole had been pierced in the balloon.

Those who elected to stay until the very end of the

vein had been found were slowly shifting their trading to the new town of Big Rock. But since the Mayor of Big Rock, Wilbur Mason, refused to allow gaming and hurdy-gurdy girls in, the town of Fontana soon became known as the pleasure palace of the high country.

But that was both a blessing and a curse for Sheriff Monte Carson and his three remaining deputies. A curse because it kept them on the run at all hours; a blessing because it kept them all in steady work, and doubly so for Monte, because it gave him a new direction in life to pursue. One that he found, much to his surprise, he enjoyed very much.

Louis had, of course, noticed the change in Monte, and in his quiet way tried to help the man, as did Judge Proctor, Louis helping the man with his reading and Proctor loaning him books on the law.

And Tilden Franklin maintained a very low profile, as did most of his gunslicks. Tilden wanted the area to settle down, stop attracting the governor's attention. More importantly, he wanted that damned hard-eyed U.S. marshal to stay out of the high country.

But both Tilden and Smoke knew that the undeclared war in the high country was not over, that the uneasy truce was apt to break apart at any time. And when it did, the high lonesome was going to run red with blood.

Someone was going to come out on top, and Tilden was making plans for that someone to be named Tilden Franklin. And he had not given up on his plans to possess Sally Jensen. Not at all. They had just been shelved for a time. But not forgotten.

The festering blot on the face of the high country began to leak its corruption when Paul Jackson rode into Fontana after a lonely six weeks in the mountains. Paul had heard talk of the new town of Big Rock, but had never seen it. He had heard talk of Fontana slowly dying, but had given it little thought. Paul had been busy digging gold. Lots of gold. More gold than even he had ever imagined he would ever find. His saddlebags were stuffed with the precious dust. His packhorses were loaded down.

He rode slowly into Fontana and could not believe his eyes. He had remembered a town, just six weeks past, full of people.

Place looked dead.

No, he corrected that. Just dying.

And where had the good people gone? Place looked to be full of whores and gamblers and pimps and ne'er-do-wells.

Made Paul feel kind of uncomfortable.

He reined up in front of the bank. But the damn bank was closed. He saw a deputy and hailed him.

Stonewall ambled over. "Something wrong, Paul?"

"Where's the bank?"

"Ain't got no bank no more, Paul," the deputy informed him. "It shut down when the gold began to peter out."

Paul, not a bright person to begin with, had to think about that for a minute or so.

"The gold is petering out?"

Now Stonewall never figured himself to be no genius, but even he was a shining light compared to this yoyo sitting his horse in front of the empty bank building.

"Yeah, Paul. The vein is about gone. If you got gold, we can store it at the jail until you can figure out what to do with it."

"I plan on taking my woman and my gold out of here," Paul said. "We are going to San Francisco and becoming man and wife."

"Your . . . woman?"

"Yes. I should like to see Bountiful now. So if you'll excuse me . . ."

"The minister's wife . . . Bountiful?" Stonewall asked.

"Yes."

"Paul . . . they don't live here in Fontana no more. The

preacher quit his church and took to farmin'. He bought hisself some land up near the Sugarloaf. He preaches ever' Sunday morning at the new church up in Big Rock."

"Bountiful?"

Stonewall was rapidly losing patience with this big dumbbell. "Why, hell, man! She's with her husband."

"Not when she sees me," Paul said, then swung his horses and rode slowly out of town, toward the high lonesome and the town of Big Rock.

And Bountiful.

"What the hell was all that about?" Monte asked, walking up to his deputy.

Stonewall took off his hat and scratched his head. "Sheriff, I don't rightly know. That Paul Jackson never was too bright, but I think the time up in the mountains has flipped him over the edge."

He told Monte the gist of the conversation.

"Strange," Monte agreed. "But Paul is gonna be in for a surprise if he tries to mess with Ralph's wife. That preacher'll whip his butt up one mountain and down the other."

"Surely Paul ain't *that* dumb!"

"Don't bet on it. Did he really have them horses loaded with gold?"

"Said he did."

"Outlaws workin' the high country; he'll be lucky if he makes it to Big Rock."

"Bountiful," Paul said, sitting his horse in front of the Morrow cabin. "I've come for you."

Bountiful blinked her baby blues. "You've . . . *come* for me?"

"Yes. Now get your things. I'm a rich man, Bountiful. We can have a beautiful life together. I'll buy you everything you ever dreamed of."

"Paul, everything I have ever dreamed of is right

here." She waved her hand. "What you see is what I want. I have it all."

"But . . . I don't understand, Bountiful. The way you looked at me . . . I mean . . . I was sure about your feelings."

It had been that way all her life; men were constantly misreading her. Mistaking friendliness for passion. It was very difficult for a beautiful woman to have men friends.

"Paul, I like you. You're a good man. And I'm happy that you found gold. I hope it brings you a lot of happiness. And you'll find a nice lady. I just know it. Now you'd better leave."

Smoke and Ralph rode into the yard. Sally stepped out of the cabin where she had been helping Bountiful make curtains.

"Hello, Paul," Ralph said. "How have you been?"

"Very well, thank you, Ralph. I've come for your wife." Ralph blinked. "I beg your pardon?"

Bountiful looked at Sally and shook her head. Sally knew the story; Bountiful had told her that Paul was infatuated with her.

"Leave, Paul," Sally told the man. "You've got everything all mixed up in your mind. It isn't the way you think it is."

"Is too!"

"Now Paul," Ralph said soothingly. "You don't want to make trouble for us. Why don't you just leave?"

Paul shook his head and dismounted. With a knife, he cut open one saddlebag, the yellow dust pouring out onto the ground.

"See, Bountiful?" Paul cried. "See? It's all for you. I did it for you. You can have it all."

"I don't want it, Paul," Bountiful said softly. "It's yours. You keep it."

Paul stood like a big, dumb ox, slowly shaking his head. It was all so confusing. He had thought he had it all worked out in his mind, but something was wrong.

Then he thought he knew what would bring Bountiful

to him. "I know," he said. "You're afraid to leave because of Tilden Franklin. I can fix that for you, Bountiful. I really can."

"What do you mean, Paul?" Smoke asked.

Paul turned mean eyes toward Smoke. "You stay out of this. You're one of the reasons Bountiful won't go with me."

Smoke blinked. "Huh?"

"I can use a gun too," Paul said, once more looking at Bountiful. "I'll show you. I'll show you all."

Smoke looked at Paul's pistol. It was in a flap-type holster, the flap secured. Smoke figured he could punch Paul out before any real damage was done—if he went for his gun.

"I'll come back a hero, Bountiful," Paul said. "I'll be the hero of the valley, Bountiful." He cut the saddlebags loose and let them fall to the ground. He tossed the reins of the packhorses to the ground. "You keep this for me, Bountiful. Play with it. It's not as pretty as you. But it's pretty. I'll be back, Bountiful. You go on and pack your things. Wait for me."

Paul swung awkwardly into the saddle and rode off.

"Paul is not very bright," Ralph said. "What in the world do you suppose he's going to do?"

No one would even venture a guess.

Smoke squatted down and fingered the dust and the nuggets. He looked at them closely. Then he stood up with a sad smile on his face.

"It's all fool's gold."

"If it wasn't so pitiful, it would be funny," Ralph said. "But Paul really believes, after he does whatever in the world he plans to do, that Bountiful is going with him. I wonder what he has in mind."

"What was that about Tilden Franklin?" Sally asked.

"He said I was afraid to leave because of Tilden Franklin," Bountiful said. "But that's silly. Why should I be afraid of that man?"

No one could answer that.

And in a few hours, it wouldn't matter to Paul either.

12

"Rider comin', Boss," Valentine called to Tilden.

Tilden stepped out onto the porch and squinted his eyes against the sun. It was that fool shopkeeper's brother, Paul Jackson. "What in the hell does he want?"

"That one ain't playin' with a full deck," Slim said. "That's the one used to foller the preacher's wife around with his tongue a-hangin' out like a big ugly hound dog."

"He looks like a hound dog," Donnie observed. "A goofy one."

The gunfighters had a good laugh at that remark; even Tilden laughed. But for some reason he could not explain, the big man slipped the thongs off his six-guns.

Luis Chamba noticed the movement. "What's wrong, Boss?"

"I don't know. Just something about the way he's riding that bothers me."

"You want me to kill him?" Donnie asked.

Tilden waved that off. "No. Let's see what he's got on his mind."

Paul rode up to the house and sat his weary horse. "May I dismount?"

"Ain't he po-lite?" a gunfighter said, laughing.

"Sure, Jackson," Tilden said. "Climb down. What can I

do for you?" Tilden noticed that the flap on the military-type holster was missing. Looked like it'd been freshly cut off. Paul's gun was riding loose.

"I've come to meet you man to man, Mister Franklin," Paul said.

"Well, Jackson, here I am. Speak your piece and then carry your ass off my range."

"I've come to kill you," Paul stated flatly.

"Is that so? Why?"

"Personal reasons."

"Don't I deserve better than that?" Tilden asked. This stupid sod was beginning to irritate him.

Several of the gunhands were beginning to giggle and titter and circle in the area of their temples with their forefingers.

Paul looked at the giggling gunslicks. "You men seem to find this amusing. Why?"

That brought them all down laughing. Tilden joined in the laughter. "Get off my range, you silly bastard!"

"Draw, goddamn you!" Paul shouted, and began fumbling for his gun.

Tilden drew, cocked, and fired with one blindingly fast motion. His slug hit Paul in the right shoulder, knocking the man to the dirt.

"You stupid son of a bitch!" Tilden snarled at the man, cocking the .44.

As Paul struggled to get to his feet, Tilden shot him again, this time the slug hitting the man in the right leg. Paul's feet flew out from under him and he landed hard in the dirt.

Screaming his rage at the rancher, Paul tried to claw his pistol out of leather. Tilden shot him in the other shoulder, rendering the man helpless.

Laughing, Tilden cocked and fired, the bullet striking Paul in the stomach.

"Tie him on his goddamned old nag and send him on

his way," Tilden ordered, punching out the empties and reloading.

The gunslicks tied Paul upright in his saddle and slapped the already spooked horse on the rump. Paul went bouncing and swaying down the road, unconscious.

It was almost breaking dawn when Charlie Starr knocked on Smoke's cabin door. "Charlie Starr, Smoke. Got news for you."

In his longhandles, a Colt in his right hand, Smoke lifted the latch and peered out. "Mornin', Charlie. Come on in. I'll make us some coffee."

"Put your pants on first," Charlie said drily. "You ain't no sight to see first thing in the mornin'."

Smoke put on coffee to boil, visited the outhouse, then sat down at the kitchen table. "What's wrong, Charlie?"

"Paul Jackson was found late yesterday afternoon by some miners. He was tied to his horse. Somebody had a good time putting a lot of unnecessary lead in the fool. He's alive, but just barely. He told Doc Spalding he braced Tilden Franklin out at the TF ranch house. Then he went into a coma. Doc says he probably won't come out of it. My question is, why'd he do it?"

Sipping coffee, Smoke told Charlie about Paul's visit the day before.

"But there ain't nothin' between Bountiful and Paul Jackson. Is there?"

"No. It was all in Paul's mind."

"Fool's gold," Charlie muttered. "Finding that and thinkin' it was real might have been what pushed him over the edge."

"Probably was. How many times was he shot, Charlie?"

"Both shoulders, leg, and stomach. Me and Monte been up all night talkin' about it. He admitted goin' out there and bracin' Tilden. Tilden had a right to protect hisself. But tyin' the man on that horse was cruel. Still, the judge says there ain't no laws to cover that."

"How's Ed taking it?"

"Harder than he'll let on. Monte said the man was cryin' last night after leavin' the Doc's office. He's tore up pretty bad. And . . . he's talkin' about goin' out there and seein' Tilden."

"That wouldn't be smart on his part."

"He's a growed-up man, Smoke. I sure can't stop him if that's what he wants to do."

"And he thought Tilden hung the stars and the moon."

"Lots of folks seein' the light about that crazy bastard. Monte told me to tell you something else too."

Smoke lifted his eyes.

"Tilden's replaced all them gunhawks that was shot in town. But he's scrapin' the bottom of the slime pit doin' it. He's hirin' the real hardcases. Cold-blooded killers. Range-war types. He's hiring some of them that was vigilantes down on the Oklahoma-Texas border. He's hirin' thugs, punks, cattle thieves, horse thieves . . . anybody who can pack a gun and even just brag about usin' one. Them dandies in town, The Silver Dollar Kid and Sundance and them other punks? Tilden hired them too."

"I guess we'd all better get ready for the balloon to bust, Charlie. I don't see any other way out of it."

Sally entered the kitchen and poured coffee. She set a plate of doughnuts on the table between the two men. Charlie grinned and helped himself.

"You heard?" Smoke asked his wife.

"I heard. I feel sorry for Paul. He wasn't quite right in the head."

Speaking around a mouthful of bearsign, Charlie said, "Out here, ma'am, man straps on a six-shooter, that gun makes him ten feet tall. Out here, they's a sayin'. God didn't make man equal. Colonel Colt did."

* * *

Paul Jackson died mid-morning, the day after he was shot. And once more, the undertaker's hack rumbled through the streets of Fontana. The streets were far less busy than they had been just a week before. The one remaining hotel had already announced plans to close.

Several TF riders had come to town, and the story of what had happened at the TF ranch was beginning to spread throughout the rapidly shrinking town. The TF gunhawks were drinking and laughing in the Blue Dog Saloon, telling the story of how Paul Jackson braced Tilden Franklin and how Paul had flopped around on the ground like a headless chicken after Tilden started putting lead into the man.

Stonewall stepped into the saloon just in time to hear the story being told for the umpteenth time. Each time it had been told with a bit more embellishment. Stonewall had not really cared much for Paul Jackson, but Jackson had been a decent sort of fellow . . . if a bit off in the head. But he had been no thief or footpad, just a hardworking guy who deserved a better death than the one he'd received.

The deputy said as much to the gunhands.

The saloon suddenly became very quiet as the TF gunslicks set their shot glasses and beer mugs on the bar and turned to face Stonewall.

"You makin' light of Mister Franklin, Deputy?" a gunslinger asked.

Stonewall thought about that for a few seconds. "Yeah," he said. "I reckon I am. A fair shootin' is one thing. Torturin' a man for sport is another thing."

"Well, Mister Franklin ain't here to defend hisself."

"You here," Stonewall said softly.

Monte took that time to step onto the boardwalk.

The TF gunhawks jerked iron and Stonewall matched their draw. The Blue Dog started yelping and barking with gunfire. Monte stepped through the batwing doors, his hands full of Colts. Stonewall was leaning against the bar, hard hit, but he had managed to drop two of the TF gunslingers. The front of Stonewall's shirt was stained with blood.

Monte's Colts started belching smoke and fire and lead. Two more TF riders went down, but not before Monte was hit twice, in the side and upper chest.

Stonewall died on his feet, his gun still clutched in his fingers. Monte was knocked back against a wall, losing one Colt on the way. He lifted his second Colt and got lead into the last remaining TF gunslick before he slid into darkness.

The wounded TF rider stumbled outside and made it to his horse, galloping out of town, holding onto the saddle horn with bloody fingers. Joel ran out of the sheriff's office and lifted his rifle. The TF rider twisted in the saddle and shot the deputy through the head before he could get off a shot.

Dave jumped into the saddle and took off after the TF gunslick. He ran slap into a dozen TF riders, on their way into town, the wounded TF rider in the middle of the pack. Dave was literally shot out of the saddle, a dozen holes in him.

Slim turned in his saddle and said, "Singer, take him back to the ranch with you." He indicated the wounded gunhawk. "And tell Mister Franklin that Fontana is ours!"

Dave was left where he had fallen, the deputy's horse standing over its master, nudging at Dave with its nose.

Bob Colby reined up in Smoke's yard in a cloud of dust. "Mister Smoke!" he hollered.

Smoke and Sally both ran from the cabin. "What's the matter, Bob?"

"Mister Luke tole me to tell you to come quick. Tilden Franklin's men done took over Fontana and this time they done 'er good. Sheriff Carson is hard hit, and all his deputies is dead!"

"Where's Johnny?"

"He took Ma over to a neighbor's house, then said he would meet you at Big Rock."

"I'm on my way, Bob."

Smoke instructed some of the old gunfighters to stay at the ranch in case any TF riders might choose to attack either the ranch or Ralph's new cabin, and told Ralph to keep his butt close by, and to carry his rifle wherever he went.

Smoke and the old gunslingers lit out for Big Rock.

"'Bout time," Pistol Le Roux muttered. "I was beginnin' to think we wasn't never gonna see no action."

In the town of Fontana, the bully-boys who made up Tilden Franklin's army were having a fine ol' time exercising their muscle on the citizens.

The Silver Dollar Kid and the punk who called himself Sundance were strutting up and down the boardwalk, shooting at signs and anything else they took a mind to fire at.

Big Mamma lay on the floor of her pleasure palace, her head split open from a rifle butt. A few of the TF riders were busying themselves with her stable of red-light girls. Free of charge.

At Beeker's store, the shopkeeper and his wife had barricaded themselves in a sturdy storeroom. They huddled together, listening to the rampaging TF gunslicks loot their store.

Billy lay in the loft of the stable, watching it all, his .22 rifle at the ready, in case any of the TF riders tried to hurt him.

Louis Longmont sat in his gaming room, rifling a deck of cards. His Colts were belted around his lean waist. A rifle and double-barreled shotgun lay on a table. Mike sat across the room, armed with two pistols and a rifle. Louis was not worried about any TF riders attempting to storm his place. They knew better.

Colton and Mona Spalding and Haywood and Dana Arden sat in the newspaper office, listening to the occasional bursts of gunfire from the town.

All had made up their mind they were leaving Fontana at the first chance. Perhaps to Big Rock, perhaps clear out of the state.

And at his general store, Ed Jackson and his wife were being terrorized.

13

"How in the hell did they manage to tree the town?" Smoke asked.

"I reckon the townspeople—them that's left—was in shock over the sheriff and his deputies bein' gunned down the way they was," Luke said. "And Tilden's bunch just overpowered them that stood to fight."

"How many men are we looking at?" Silver Jim asked.

"I'd say over a hundred," Charlie replied. "But Beaconfield sent word in about two hours ago that Tilden left a good-sized bunch at the ranch. I'd say he's got a good hundred and twenty-five to a hundred and fifty men under his command."

"You got any ideas, Smoke?"

"Where is Monte?"

"At the Doc's clinic. He's hanging on, so I was told."

"Judge Proctor?"

"Out of town. Denver, I think," Luke said.

Smoke paced the street in front of the large general store of Big Rock. "It would be foolish for us to try to retake the town. If we leave here, Tilden would probably send his men from the ranch to take this place, burn it probably. And any ranch or farm up here he could find."

"You're right," Hunt Brook said.

"Damn!" Charlie said. "I hate to just sit here and do nothing, but I don't know what else we can do."

"I just wish I knew what was going on down at Fontana," Wilbur said.

Smoke grimaced. "I got a pretty good idea."

Smoke was silent for a moment. "I hope Billy is all right. I should have got that kid out of there before this."

The men fell silent, all looking in the direction of Fontana.

A group of TF riders had stripped Peg Jackson naked and were raping her, enjoying her screaming. Ed Jackson had been trussed up like a hog and tossed to the floor, forced to watch his wife being violated.

"You don't understand," Ed kept saying. "I like and respect Mister Franklin. We're friends."

One TF rider named Belton got tired of listening to Ed and kicked him in the mouth, then in the stomach. Ed lay on the floor, vomiting up blood and bits of teeth and the ham and eggs he'd had for breakfast.

Peg continued screaming as yet another TF gunhand took her.

In Louis's gaming tent, the gambler looked at his bouncer. "Mike, go get our horses and bring them around to the back. And if you find that boy, Billy, bring him along. I'm thinking that at full dark, when those rowdies get enough booze in them, they'll rush us. I'd like to get that boy out of this place."

"Yes, sir, Mister Longmont," Mike said, and was gone into the night.

Louis looked at the roulette wheels, the faro cue boxes, the card presses, the keno gooses . . . all the other paraphernalia of gambling.

"I shall not be needing any of it," Louis muttered.

"When I again gamble, it will be in the company of ladies and gentlemen . . . with champagne and manners and breeding."

He rose from his chair, picked up his weapons, and walked into the back of the tent.

Mike returned in less than fifteen minutes, with saddled horses and Billy in tow.

"Any trouble?" Louis asked.

"One TF rowdy braced me," the huge bouncer replied. "I broke his neck."

The men and the boy mounted up. Andre said, "I will not miss this miserable place."

"Nor will I, Andre," Louis said. He pointed his horse's nose toward the high lonesome. "Quiet now," he cautioned. "Ride light until we're clear of the town."

"Boss?" Mike said. "Them thugs is rapin' the shopkeeper's woman. I could hear her screamin'."

Louis' face was tight as he said, "If she's lucky, that's all they'll do."

They cleared the town and then rode hard for the town of Big Rock.

"Grim," was Louis's one-word reply to Smoke's asking about Fontana.

"Can't we ride for the Army?" Hunt asked.

"Nearest Army post is four days away," Smoke explained. "And the next stage isn't due for twenty-four hours. If then." He looked at the old gunfighter called Buttermilk. "Think you boys could handle those gunhawks left at the TF ranch?"

Buttermilk smiled his reply.

"All right. Leave Dad Weaver and three others at the Sugarloaf. One in the barn with a rifle and lots of shells. Let me have Crooked John and Bull, and the rest of you take off to the TF. Pin 'em down and wear 'em down with rifle fire, then cut 'em down when they get enough and try to pull out."

Buttermilk nodded and turned to his compadres. "Let's ride, boys!"

Louis smiled. "Those old boys will lay up on the ridges around the TF spread and put so much lead in that house those gunhawks will be crying to get out."

"Those old men will allow their adversaries to surrender, won't they?" Hunt asked.

Louis cut his eyes to the lawyer. "You just have to be joking!"

Crooked John and Bull rode with Louis, Smoke, and Johnny North. Pearlie stayed behind with Luke and Charlie. The men rode slowly, sparing their horses, and making plans as they rode.

"I think we should let them get good and drunk," Louis remarked. "A full twenty-five percent of them will be passed out by night. That will make our work easier."

"Good idea," Johnny said. "And we need to get Monte outta there. Come night, I'll slip in from the blind side, through all them shacks that was left behind, and get to the Doc's place. We can hitch up the horses, put some hay in the back to keep Monte comfortable, and point the pilgrims on the way to Big Rock."

Smoke nodded his approval. "All right. While you're doing that, I'll ease in and see about Ed and his wife. Johnny, let's make it a mite easier for us. Bull, you and Crooked John create a diversion on this end of town. At full dark. You can leave your horses in that dry run behind the stable. Louis, how about you?"

Louis smiled. "I'll be doing some head-hunting on my own."

What they were going to do firmly implanted in their minds, the men urged their horses into a trot and began putting the miles behind them.

It was full dark when they pulled up, the lights of Fontana below them. They could hear an occasional gunshot and a faint, drunken whoop.

"I wonder where Tilden is," Smoke said expressing his thought aloud. "If I could get lead in him, this would be over."

"Well protected, wherever he is," Louis said. "But what puzzles me is this: why is he letting his men do this?"

"He's gone over the edge," Smoke said. "He's a crazy man, drunk with power. He's made no telling how many thousand of dollars on gold shares with the miners and doesn't care how much of it he spends. And he hates me," Smoke added.

None of the men needed to add that Tilden Franklin also wanted Sally Jensen.

"Let's go, boys," Smoke said. "And good luck."

The men separated, Smoke turning his horse's head toward the right, Johnny moving out to the left. Bull and Crooked John headed straight in toward the lights of Fontana, and Louis Longmont moved out alone into the night.

Each man stashed his horse in the safest place he could find and slipped into the town to perform his assigned job.

The diversion that Crooked John and Bull made was a simple one. They set several buildings blazing, lighting up one end of the town.

Smoke slipped to the rear of Jackson's general store and eased up onto the loading dock. His spurs were left hanging on his saddle horn and he made no noise as he pushed open the back door and entered the storeroom area of the building. Listening, he could hear the faint sobbing of Peg Jackson and the drunken grunting of men.

He wondered what had happened to Ed.

Smoke heard the excited shouting out in the street and wondered what kind of diversion the gunslingers had set. He glanced behind him, out the open back door of the store, and saw the reflection of the dancing, leaping flames reddening the night sky.

Grinning, he slipped closer to the cracked-open door that would lead into the store. He peeked through the crack and silently cursed under his breath.

He could see Ed, trussed up like a hog, on the floor of the store. The man's face appeared to be badly swollen. There was blood and puke on his shirt front.

Lifting his eyes, searching, he saw Peg. The woman had been badly used and appeared to be just conscious enough to sob. A TF gunhawk, his pants down around his boots, his back to Smoke, was having his way with the woman. Several TF riders were sprawled on the floor and on the counters. They seemed to be dead drunk and out of it.

Two TF gunslicks were leaning against a counter, drinking whiskey straight out of the bottle, an amused look on their faces as they watched the rape of Peg Jackson.

Those men seemed to be the only ones still conscious enough to give Smoke any cause for worry.

The sounds of gunfire came hard through the night air. It was followed by a choking scream. The two TF men looked at each other.

"Let's check that out," one said.

The other man nodded and they both walked out onto the boardwalk in front of the general store.

Smoke slipped into the large area of the store. Looking down, he saw that Ed was awake and staring at him through wide and very frightened eyes. Smoke nodded his head at the man and put a finger to his lips, urging Ed to keep silent. Ed nodded his head.

Picking up an axe handle, Smoke slipped up behind the rapist, busy at his ugly work. Smoke hit him on the side of the head with the axe handle. The man's skull popped under the impact and he fell to one side, dying as he was falling. Smoke glanced at him for a second. The man's head was split open, his brains exposed.

Smoke jerked Peg to her unsteady feet and handed her a blanket. She looked at the blanket through dull and uncomprehending eyes. Glancing toward the open front door, Smoke could not see the two TF gunnies who had stepped outside. Walking swiftly to the counter, he picked up one half-empty bottle of whisky and returned to Peg. He tilted her head back and poured the raw booze down her throat. She coughed and gagged and gasped as her eyes cleared a bit.

She pulled the blanket over her nakedness and slowly nodded her head in understanding.

"Get to the back of the store," Smoke whispered. "And wait there for us."

She walked slowly, painfully, toward the rear of the store.

Smoke didn't bother cutting Ed's bonds. He just picked the man up and slung him over his shoulder. He walked swiftly out of the show and business area of the store, joining Peg on the loading dock. There, he dumped Ed on the dock and cut his bonds.

"Hitch up your team, Ed," he spoke softly. "And do it very quietly and very quickly. Take the old road that circles the town and head for Big Rock. A couple of miles out of town, pull up and wait for Spalding and Arden."

"My store!" the man protested.

Smoke almost hit the man. He controlled his temper at the last second and said, "Get your goddamned ass moving, Ed. Or I'll turn you back over to those TF riders. How do you want it?"

Shocked at the cold threat in Smoke's voice, Ed moved quickly to his barn, Peg walking slowly behind him, the blanket clutched tightly around her.

Smoke walked back into the store just as more gunfire erupted throughout the town. Smoke entered the store just as the two TF gunslicks walked back in through the front door.

They all saw each other and jerked iron at the same time. Smoke's Colts roared and bucked in his hands. The TF men were thrown to the floor as the .44 slugs from Smoke's guns hit big bones and vital organs. Smoke's draw was so fast, his aim so true, the men were unable to get off a single shot before death took them into its cold arms.

Smoke quickly reloaded and holstered his .44s. He walked to the gun rack and took down a sawed-off shotgun, breaking it down and loading it with buckshot, then stuffing his pockets full of shells. He took two new .44 pistols from the arms showcase, checked the action, and loaded them full, tucking them behind his gunbelt. Shotgun in hand, Smoke stepped out onto the boardwalk and prepared to lessen the odds just a tad.

The passed-out gunslicks in the store snored on, probably saving their lives . . . for the time being.

A TF gunslick made the mistake of riding up just at that moment. Lifting the Greener, Smoke literally blew the man out of the saddle, dumping him, now a bloody mass, onto the dusty ground.

He looked around him, his eyes picking up the black-dressed figure of Louis Longmont, standing on the boardwalk across the street. Louis had a Colt in each hand, the hammers back.

"Where's Johnny?" Smoke called.

"Right up there," Louis said returning the call, pointing with a Colt.

Smoke looked through the smoky night air and spotted Johnny North, about a half a block away.

"I got the pilgrims on the way!" Johnny called. "Looks like Monte's gonna make it if he can stand the trip."

Reloading the Greener, Smoke called, "Let's do some damage and then get the hell out of here!"

One of the duded-up dandies who had been strutting

about picked that time to brace Johnny North. "Draw, North!" he called, standing in the dusty street.

Johnny put two holes in the punk before the would-be gunhand could blink. The dandy died on his back in the dirt, his guns still in leather.

Two gunhawks came running up the street, on Louis's side. The gambler dropped them both, his guns roaring and belching gray smoke and fire.

Smoke heard a noise to his left and spun around, dropped to one knee and lifting the shotgun. As he dropped, lead whistled over his head. He pulled both triggers on the Greener, the buckshot spreading a TF rider all over a storefront and the boardwalk.

At the far end of town, Bull Flager was holding his own and then some, the old gunfighter Crooked John Simmons by his side, both gnarled hands full of Colts. Bull's shotgun roared and Crooked John's pistols belched death with each cocking and firing.

"Let's go!" Smoke shouted, and began falling back. He stepped into Ed's store just as one of the drunken TF riders reared up, a pistol in his hand.

Smoke shot him in the chest with the sawed-off and the gunnie died amid the corsets and the bloomers.

Running out the back, Smoke got his horse and swung into the saddle. He cut into an alley and came out just on the far edge of Fontana. With the reins in his teeth, both hands full of guns, Smoke galloped straight up the last few blocks of the boom town now going bust. Johnny North was right behind him and Louis Longmont just behind Johnny. Bull and Crooked John were waiting at the end of town, rifles in their hands, and their aim was deadly.

The five gunfighters took a fearful toll on Tilden Franklin's gunhands those last few blocks.

Most of the gunnies were busy with a bucket-line, trying to keep the raging fires contained at one end of town. Smoke, Johnny, and Louis rode right through the bucket-brigade, guns sparking the fiery night, adding death and confusion to the already chaotic scene.

Louis, Johnny, and Smoke sent the gunhands-turned-firemen running and diving and sprawling for their lives. Most made it; a few did not.

Louis knocked a leg from under a TF gunnie and the man fell backward, into the raging inferno. His screams were hideous in the fiery, smoky, gunshot-filled night.

Tilden Franklin stood in the best suite of the hotel and watched it all, his hate-filled eyes as hot as the flames that threatened to consume the town. He turned to the small woman who had been the sole property of Big Mamma and, in his rage, broke the woman's neck with his powerful hands.

He screamed his hate and rage and picked up the naked, ravaged woman and threw her body out the second floor window.

The young woman lay dead on the street.

Then, with slobber wetting his lips and chin, Tilden Franklin emptied his guns into the battered body.

"I'll kill you, Jensen!" the man howled. "I'm gonna burn your goddamned town to the ground and have your woman . . . right in front of your eyes!"

14

The old gunfighters who had ridden to the TF ranch house lay on the ridges that surrounded the huge home and made life miserable for those TF gunhawks who had survived the initial attack.

The moon was full and golden in the starry night skies, the illumination highlighting the bodies of those gunnies who now lay sprawled in death on the grounds surrounding the bunkhouse and the main ranch house.

Those trapped in the bunkhouse and in the main house were not at all happy about their situation. Several had thought the night would cover them as they tried to escape. Those with that thought now lay dead.

"What are we gonna do?" a TF gunslick, who felt more sick than slick, asked.

"Hold out 'til the boss gets back," was the reply. "There ain't that many of 'em up there on the ridges."

"Yeah, but I got me a peek at who they is," another paid gunhand said. "That's them old gunfighters. And I think I seen The Apache Kid 'mong 'em."

Nobody said anything for a long time. Nobody had to. They were all thinking the same thing. Toot Tooner and Red Shingletown had already been spotted, briefly. Now the Apache Kid. They all knew what that meant: these hard ol' boys didn't take prisoners. Never had. They expected no quarter, and they gave none.

"I ain't goin' out there, boys," a gunman said. "No way."

"I wish to hell someone had told me this Jensen feller was raised up by Preacher. I'd have kept my butt up in Montana."

"He ain't so good," another said.

Nobody paid any attention to him. The man was speaking without any knowledge of the subject. He was too young to have any real awareness of the legendary Mountain Man known as Preacher. If he had, he'd have kept his mouth shut.

"So we wait, is that it?" The question was thrown out of the darkened room.

"You got any better ideas?"

Silence, and more silence.

Even with only the sounds of their breathing to be heard, none of the TF gunhands could hear the moccasined feet of The Apache Kid as he slipped through the kitchen and into the large dining area. Sutter Cordova was right behind him. There had been a guard at the back door. He now lay on the porch, his throat cut, his blood staining the ground.

Both men had their hands full of pistols, the hammers jacked back.

"Something is wrong!" a TF gunslick suddenly said, his voice sharp in the darkened house.

"What?"

"I don't know. But there ain't a shot fired in more 'un fifteen, twenty minutes."

"Maybe they pulled out?"

"Sure they did, and a hog is gonna fly any day now."

Apache and Sutter stepped into the room and started letting the lead fly. They were grateful to Smoke Jensen for giving them this opportunity to go out as gunfighters should. They had all outlived their time, and they all knew it. They had no one to live for, and no one to grieve for them when they died.

They were a part of the West's rapidly vanishing past. So they would go out as they lived.

The room filled with gray smoke, the booming of Colts and Remingtons deafening.

The Apache Kid died with his back to a wall, his hands full of guns. But the old man had taken a dreadful toll while he had lived this night.

Sutter Cordova went into that long sleep with a faint smile on his lips. His guns empty, the gunfighter buried his knife into the chest of a TF gunhawk and rode him down to the floor.

When the booming of the gunfire had faded away into the night, the other aging gunfighters walked slowly down to the big house. They checked out the bunkhouse and found no life there.

Carefully, they went into the house and lighted a lamp. They found one TF rider alive, but not for long.

"You old . . . bastards played . . . hell!" he managed to gasp.

"You got a name, boy?" Dan Greentree asked, squatting down beside the young man.

"It . . . don't matter." He closed his eyes and died.

"Funny goddamn name," Red Shingletown said.

"We'll bury them in the morning," Smoke said. "I'll come back into town and bring the minister with me."

"What'd y'all do with the dead TF gunnies?" Luke asked.

"Left 'em where they lay," Red replied. "Let somebody else worry with them."

"'Pache and Sutter both tole me they was a-goin' out this run," Luke Nations said. "'Pache had a bad ticker and Sutter was havin' a hard time passin' his water. It's good they went out this way. I'm right happy for 'em."

"You're happy your friends died?" Hunt asked, his robe pulled tightly around him against the night chill.

"Shore. That's the way they wanted it."

The lawyer walked away, back to his cabin. He was thinking that he would never understand the Western way of doing things.

"Peg Jackson?" Louis asked.

"Physically, not hurt too badly," Belle Colby said. "But like my Velvet, she's not good in the head. She said they did terrible things to her."

Belle walked back into the store where they had set up a hospital.

"Monte?" Bull asked.

"He's in rough shape, but the Doc says he thinks he's gonna pull through."

"How about Ed?" somebody finally asked, although few if any among them really gave a damn how Ed was.

"He's all right," Haywood said, joining the group. "He's bitching about losing his store. It's just his way, gentlemen. And he'll never change. He's already talking of pulling out."

"He don't belong here," Charlie Starr said, lighting a tightly rolled cigarette. "This country's still got some rough and woolly years ahead of it. And it's gonna take some tough-minded men and women to see it through."

"What's the plan, Smoke?" Louis asked. "I know you've got one. You've been thinking hard for about an hour now."

"I'm gonna get a few hours sleep and then get the preacher. After the services, I'm riding into Fontana and get this matter settled, one way or the other. Anybody who wants to come along is welcome to ride."

They left the graveyard at nine o'clock the next morning. They had said their goodbyes to The Apache Kid and Sutter Cordova, and then those that had family to worry about them said their goodbyes to womenfolk and kids and swung into the saddle.

They left behind them some heavily armed hands who worked for Beaconfield and Mike Garrett, but who were hands, not gunhands, and half a dozen teenagers who were excellent shots with a rifle. In addition, Hunt, Colton, and Haywood were armed with rifles and shotguns. All the Western women could shoot rifles and shotguns as well as, and sometimes better than, the men. Mike, the big bouncer, was there, as well as Wilbur Mason, Dad Weaver, and Billy. The general store had been turned into a fort in case of attack.

Twenty-eight men rode toward the town of Fontana. They had guns in leather, guns tucked behind gunbelts, guns stashed in their saddlebags, and rifles and shotguns in saddleboots.

Smoke had warned them all that even though the previous night's raid into Fontana had taken some TF riders out, they were probably facing four- or five-to-one odds, and anyone who wanted out had damn well better speak up now.

His words had been met with a stony silence.

Smoke had nodded his head and pulled his hat brim down low, securing the chin strap, "Let's ride."

There had been no stopping Ralph Morrow. He had stuck out his chin, picked up his Henry rifle, and stuffed his pockets full of cartridges. "I'm going," he had said. "And that's final."

The men trotted their horses for a time, and then walked them, alternating back and forth, eating up the miles.

Then they looked down on the town of Fontana . . . and stared at the long line of wagons that were pulling out.

Smoke looked at Silver Jim. "Find out about that, will you, Jim?"

Silver Jim rode down to the lead wagon, talked for a

moment, then rode back to where Smoke sat his horse with the others.

"Big Mamma's dead," Silver Jim said. "She stormed into a saloon last night, after she learned that Tilden Franklin had raped and killed her . . . wife. Tilden ordered her hanged. They hung her slow. That feller I talked to said it took a long time for her to die. One of Big Mamma's girls tried to run away last night. Tilden's gunslicks caught her and . . . well, done some per-verted things to her, then they dragged her and set her on far. Tilden personal kilt Beeker at the store. Then his boys had they way with his wife. She set up such a squall, they shot her."

"Dear Jesus Christ!" Ralph muttered.

"Them people down there," Silver Jim said, pointing to the line of wagons, "is near-bouts all that's left of any decent folks, and some of them would steal the pennies off a dead man's eyes. That's how bad it's got down in town."

"So Tilden and his men are waiting for us?" Smoke asked.

"Dug in tight."

"Proctor didn't come back, did he?"

"They didn't say and I didn't think to ask."

Smoke stepped down from the saddle and said, "Let's talk about this some."

Dismounted, the men sipped water from canteens and ate a few biscuits and some beef packed for them before they pulled out.

"If we go in there," Smoke said, "we're going to have to take the place building by building, and like Silver Jim said, they're dug in and waiting. The cost, for us, will be too high."

"What choice do we have?" Luke said.

"Well, let's talk about that," Mike Garrett said. "We could wait them out while someone rides for the Army."

"No!" Ralph said, considerable heat in his voice.

"You want to explain that, Ralph?" Johnny said.

"Maybe I wasn't cut out to be a minister," the man said. "There is violence and hate in my heart. Anyway, it is my belief that people like Tilden Franklin should not be allowed to live. Back East—and I know, that's where I'm from—lawyers are already using the insanity pleas to get killers off scot free. And it's going to get worse. Let's not start a precedent out here."

"A what?" Johnny asked.

"Let's not let Tilden Franklin go free," Ralph said.

All present loudly and profanely agreed with that.

"There is another way," Smoke said.

"And that is?" Louis asked, knowing full well what was coming.

"I challenge Tilden Franklin. Best man with a gun wins."

"No," Louis said. "No. Tilden Franklin is a man totally without honor. Basically, he is a coward, a backshooter. He'd set you up, Smoke. No to your plan."

And all agreed with Louis on that.

"Well," Moody said. "We could burn the bastards out."

"How many days since we've had rain?" Smoke asked. "Too long. That's why Tilden ordered his men to put out the fire last night instead of concentrating on us. We can't risk a grass fire. Feel this hot wind? It would spread faster than anyone could contain it."

Charlie Starr grinned. "Besides, ol' tight-fisted Ed Jackson would probably sue us all for destroying his goods."

All the men enjoyed a tension-relieving laugh at that.

"Well, boys," Pistol Le Roux said, "that don't leave us with too gawddamned many options, do it?"

The men turned to tightening saddle cinches. They knew the discussion was over.

Hardrock swung into the saddle and looked at his friends. "You know what my momma wanted me to be?" he asked.

They stared at him.

"An apothecary, that's what."

Toot Tooner climbed into the saddle. "Shit, I wouldn't let you fix up nuttin' for me. You'd probably mix up something so's I couldn't get a boner up."

Sunset laughed. "Hell, you ain't had one in so long it'd probably scare you to death!"

The men swung their horses toward Fontana, lying hot under the sun and wind.

15

Hardrock, Moody, and Sunset were sent around to the far end of town, stationed there with rifles to pick off any TF gunhand who might try to slip out, either to run off or try and angle around behind Smoke and his party for a box-in.

The others split up into groups of twos and threes and rode hunched over, low in the saddle, to present a smaller target for the riflemen they had spotted lying in wait on the rooftops in Fontana. And they rode in a zig-zagging fashion, making themselves or their horses even harder to hit. But even with that precaution, two men were hit before they reached the town limits. Beacon-field was knocked from the saddle by rifle fire. The one-time Tilden Franklin supporter wrapped a bandana around a bloody arm, climbed back in the saddle, and, cursing, continued onward. Hurt, but a hell of a long way from being out.

The old gunfighter Linch was hit just as he reached the town. A rifle bullet hit him in the stomach and slapped him out of the saddle. The aging gunhand, pistols in his hands, crawled to the edge of a building and began laying down a withering line of fire, directed at the rooftops. He managed to knock out three snipers before a second bullet ended his life.

Leo Wood, seeing his long-time buddy die, screamed his outrage and stepped into what had once been a dress shop, pulled out both Remington Frontier .44s, and let 'em bang.

Leo cleared the dress shop of all TF riders before a single shot from a Peacemaker .45 ended his long and violent life.

Pearlie settled down by the corner of a building and with his Winchester .44-40 began picking his shots. At ranges up to two hundred yards, the .44-40 could punch right through the walls of the deserted buildings of Fontana. Pearlie killed half a dozen TF gunhawks without even seeing his targets.

A few of Tilden's hired guns, less hardy than they thought, tried to slip out the rear of the town. They went down under the rifle fire of Moody, Hardrock, and Sunset.

Bill Foley, throwing caution to the wind, like most of his friends having absolutely no desire to spend his twilight years in any old folks' home, stepped into an alley where he knew half a dozen TF gunnies were waiting and opened fire. Laughing, the old gunfighter took his time and picked his shots while his body was soaking up lead from the badly shaken TF men. Foley's old body had soaked up a lot of lead in its time, and he knew he could take three or four shots and still stay upright in his boots. Bill Foley, who had helped tame more towns than most people had ever been in, died with his boots on, his back to a wall, and his guns spitting out death. He killed all six of the TF gunslicks.

Toot Tooner, his hands full of Colts, calmly walked into what was left of the Blue Dog Saloon, through the back door, and said, "I declare this here game of poker open. Call or fold, boys."

Then he opened fire.

His first shots ended the brief but bloody careers of two cattle rustlers from New Mexico who had signed on with the TF spread in search of what Tilden had promised would be easy money. They died without having the opportunity to fire a shot.

Toot took a .45 slug in the side and it spun him around. Lifting his pistol, he shot the man who had shot him between the eyes just as he felt a hammer-blow in his back, left side. The gunshot knocked him to his knees and he tasted blood in his mouth.

Toot dropped his empty Colts and pulled out two Remington .44s from behind his gunbelt. Hard hit, dying; Toot laughed at death and began cocking and firing as the light before his eyes began to fade.

"Somebody kill the old son of a bitch!" a TF gunhand shouted.

Toot laughed at the dim figure and swung his guns. A slug took him in the gut and set him back on his butt. But Toot's last shots cleared the Blue Dog of hired guns. He died with a very faint smile on his face.

Louis Longmont met several TF gunhands in an alley. The gambler never stopped walking as his Colts spat and sang a death song. Reloading, he stepped over the sprawled bloody bodies and walked on up the alley. A bullet tugged at the sleeve of his coat and the gambler dropped to one knee, raised both guns, and shot the rifleman off the roof of the bank building. A bullet knocked Louis to one side and his left arm grew numb. Hooking the thumb of his left hand behind his gunbelt, the gambler rose and triggered off a round, sending another one of Tilden Franklin's gunslicks to hell.

Louis then removed a white linen handkerchief from an inside breast pocket of his tailored jacket. He plugged the hole in his shoulder and continued on his hunt.

The Reverend Ralph Morrow stepped into what had been the saloon of Big Mamma and the bidding place of her soiled doves and began working the lever on his

Henry .44. The boxer-turned-preacher-turned-farmer-turned-gunfighter muttered a short prayer for God to forgive him and began blasting the hell out of any TF gunhand he could find.

His Henry empty, Ralph jerked out a pair of .45s and began smoking. A lousy pistol shot, and that is being kind, Ralph succeeded in filling the beery air with a lot of hot lead. He didn't hit a damn thing with the pistols, but he did manage to scare the hell out of those gunhands left standing after his good shooting with the rifle. They ran out the front of the saloon and directly into the guns of Pistol Le Roux and Dan Greentree.

Ralph reloaded his rifle and stepped to the front of the building. "Exhilarating!" he exclaimed. Then he hit the floor as a hard burst of gunfire from a rooftop across the street tore through the canvas and wood of the deserted whorehouse.

"Shithead!" Ralph muttered, lifting his rifle and sighting the gunman in. Ralph pulled the trigger and knocked the TF gunman off the roof.

Steve Matlock, Ray Johnson, Nolan, Mike Garrett, and Beaconfield were keeping a dozen or more TF gunslicks pinned down in Beeker's general store.

Charlie Starr had cleared a small saloon of half a dozen hired guns and now sat at a table, having a bottle of sweetened soda water. He would have much preferred a glass of beer, but the sweet water beat nothing. Seeing a flash of movement across the street, Charlie put down the bottle and picked up a cocked .45 from the table. He sighted the TF gunhand in and pulled the trigger. The slug struck the man in the shoulder and spun him around. Charlie shot him again in the belly and that ended it.

"Now leave me alone and let me finish my sodie water," Charlie muttered.

The Silver Dollar Kid came face to face with Silver Jim.

The old gunfighter grinned at the punk. Both men had their guns in leather.

"All right, kid," Silver Jim said. "You been lookin' for a rep. Here's your chance."

The Silver Dollar Kid grabbed for his guns.

He never cleared leather. Silver Jim's guns roared and bucked in his callused hands. The Kid felt twin hammer blows in his stomach. He sat down in the alley and began hollering for his mother.

Silver Jim stepped around the punk and continued his prowling. The Kid's hollering faded as life ebbed from him.

Smoke met Luis Chamba behind the stable. The Mexican gunfighter grinned at him. "Now, Smoke, we see just how good you really are."

Smoke lifted his sawed-off shotgun and almost blew the gunfighter in two. "I already know how good I am," Smoke said. "I don't give a damn how good you . . . were."

Smoke reloaded the 10-gauge sawed-off and stepped into the stable. He heard a rustling above him and lifted the twin muzzles. Pulling the triggers, blowing a hole the size of a bucket in the boards, Smoke watched as a man, or what was left of a man, hurled out the loft door to come splatting onto the shit-littered ground.

Smoke let the shotgun fall to the straw as the gunfighter Valentine faced him.

"I'm better," Valentine said, his hands over the butts of his guns.

"I doubt it," Smoke said, then shot the famed gunfighter twice in the belly and chest.

With blood streaking his mouth, Valentine looked up from the floor at Smoke. "I . . . didn't even clear leather."

"You sure didn't," the young man said. "We all got to meet him, Valentine, and you just did."

"I reckon." Then he died.

Listening, Smoke cocked his head. Something was very wrong. Then it came to him. No gunfire.

Cautiously, Smoke stepped to the stable door and looked out. Gunsmoke lay over the town like a shroud. The dusty streets were littered with bodies, not all of them TF gunhands.

Smoke was conscious of his friends looking at him, standing silently.

Louis pointed with the muzzle of his pistol.

Smoke looked far up the street. He could make out the shape of Tilden Franklin. Smoke stepped out into the street and faced the man.

Tilden began walking toward him. As the man came closer, Smoke said, "It's over, Tilden."

"Not yet," the big man said. "I gotta kill you, then it's over."

"Make your play," Smoke said.

Tilden grabbed for his guns. Both men fired at almost the same time. Smoke felt a shock in his left side. He kept earing back the hammers and pulling the triggers. Dust flew from Tilden's chest as the slugs slammed into his body. The big man took another step, staggered, and then slumped to his knees in the center of the street.

Blood leaking from his wounded side, Smoke walked up to the man who would be king.

"You had everything a man could ask for, Tilden. Why weren't you satisfied?"

Tilden tried to reply. But blood filled his mouth. He looked at Smoke, and still the hate was in his eyes. He fell forward on his face, in the dust, his guns slipping from his dead fingers.

It was over.

Almost.

16

They all heard the single shot and whirled around. Luke Nations lay crumpled on the boardwalk, a large hole in the center of his back.

Lester Morgan, a.k.a. Sundance, stepped out of a building, a pistol in his hand. He looked up and grinned.

"I did it!" he hollered. "Me. Sundance. I kilt Luke Nations!"

"You goddamned backshootin' punk!" Charlie Starr said, lifting his pistol.

"No!" Smoke's voice stopped him. "Don't, Charlie." Smoke walked over to Lester, one hand holding his bleeding side. He backhanded the dandy, knocking him sprawling. Lester-Sundance landed on his butt in the street. His mouth was busted, blood leaking from one corner. He looked up at Smoke, raw fear in his wide eyes.

"You gonna kill me, ain't you?" he hissed.

The smile on Smoke's lips was not pleasant. "What's your name, punk?"

"Les . . . Sundance. That's me, Sundance!"

"Well, *Sundance.*" Smoke put enough dirt on the name to make it very ugly. "You wanna live, do you?"

"Yeah!"

"And you wanna be known as a top gunhand, right, Sundance?"

"Yeah!"

Smoke kicked Lester in the mouth. The punk rolled on the ground, moaning.

"What's your last name, craphead?"

"M . . . Morgan!"

"All right Les Sundance Morgan. I'll let you live. And Les, I'm going to have your name spread all over the West. Les Sundance Morgan. The man with one ear. He's the man who killed the famed gunfighter Luke Nations."

"I got both ears!"

Before his words could fade from sound, Smoke had drawn and fired, the bullet clipping off Lester's left ear. The action forever branded the dandy.

Lester rolled on the dirt, screaming and hollering.

"Top gun, huh, punk?" Smoke said. "Right, that's you, Sundance." He looked toward Johnny North. "Get some whiskey and fix his ear, will you, Johnny?"

Lester really started hollering when the raw booze hit where his ear had been. He passed out from the pain. Ralph took that time to bandage the ugly wound.

Then Smoke kicked him awake. Lester lay on the blood- and whiskey-soaked ground, looking up at Smoke.

"What for you do this to me?" he croaked.

"So everybody, no matter where you go, can know who you are, punk. The man who killed Luke Nations. Now, you listen to me, you son of a bitch! You want to know how it feels to be top gun? Well, just look around you, ask anybody."

Lester's eyes found Charlie Starr. "You're Charlie Starr. You're more famouser than Luke Nations. But I'm gonna be famous too, ain't I?"

Charlie rolled a cigarette and stuck it between Lester's

lips. He held the match while Lester puffed. Charlie straightened up and smiled sadly at Lester.

"How is it, punk? Oh, well, it's a real grand time, punk. You can't sit with your back to no empty space, always to a wall. Lots of backshooters out there. You don't never make your fire, cook, and then sleep in the same spot. You always move before you bed down, 'cause somebody is always lookin' to gun you down . . . for a reputation.

"You ain't never gonna marry, punk. 'Cause if you do, it won't last. You got to stay on the move, all the time. 'Cause you're the man who kilt Luke Nations, punk. And there's gonna be a thousand punks just like you lookin' for you.

"You drift, boy. You drift all the time, and you might near always ride alone, lessen you can find a pard that you know you can trust not to shoot you when you're in your blankets.

"And a lot of towns won't want you, punk. The marshal and the townspeople will meet you with rifles and shotguns and point you the way out. 'Cause they don't want no gunfighter in their town.

"And after a time, if you live, you'll do damn near anything so's people won't know who you are. But they always seem to find out. Then you'll change your name agin. And agin. Just lookin' for a little peace and quiet.

"But you ain't never gonna find it.

"You might git good enough to live for a long time, punk. I hope you do. I hope you ride ten thousand lonely miles, you backshootin' bastard. Ten thousand miles of lookin' over your back. Ten thousand towns that you'll ride in and out of in the dead of night. Eatin' your meals just at closin' time . . . you can find a eatin' place that'll serve you.

"A million hours that you'll wish you could somehow change your life . . . but you cain't, punk. You cain't change, 'cause *they* won't let you.

"Only job you'll be able to find is one with the gun,

punk. 'Cause you're the man who kilt Luke Nations. You got your rep, punk. You wanted it so damned bad, you got 'er." He glanced at Johnny North.

Johnny said, "I had me a good woman one time. We married and I hung up my guns, sonny-boy. Some god-damned bounty-hunters shot into my cabin one night. Killed my wife. I'd never broke no law until then. But I tracked them so-called lawmen down and hung 'em, one by one. I was on the hoot-owl trail for years after that. I had both the law and the reputation-hunters after me. Sounds like a real fine life, don't it, punk? I hope you enjoy it."

Smoke kicked Lester Sundance Morgan to his boots. "Get your horse and ride, punk! 'Fore one of us here takes a notion to brace the man who killed Luke Nations."

Crying, Lester stumbled from the street and found his horse, back of the building that once housed a gun shop.

"It ain't like that!" the gunfighters, the gambler, the ranchers, and the minister heard Lester holler as he rode off. "It ain't none at all like what you say it was. I'll have wimmin a-throwin' themselves at me. I'll have money and I'll have . . ."

His horse's hooves drummed out the rest of what Lester Sundance Morgan thought his reputation would bring him.

"Poor, sad, silly son of a bitch," Ralph Morrow said.

Charlie Starr looked at the minister. "I couldn't have said 'er no better myself, preacher."

The bodies of the gunfighters and Tilden Franklin were dragged to a lone building just at the edge of what was left of the boom town named Fontana. The building was doused with kerosene and torched just as a very gentle rain began falling.

"Lots of folks comin', Smoke," Charlie said, pointing toward the road leading to the high lonesome.

It was Sally and Belle and Bountiful and nearly all of those the men had left behind.

Sally embraced and kissed her man, getting blood all over her blouse as she did so. "How'd you folks know it was done with?" Smoke asked her.

"Hook Nose's people set up relay points with runners," she said. "They were watching from the hills over there." She pointed.

"What a story this will make," Haywood Arden said, his eyes wide as he looked at the bullet-pocked buildings and empty shell-casings on the ground.

"Yeah," Smoke said wearily. "You be sure and write it, Haywood. And be sure you spell one name right."

"Who is that?" the newspaperman asked.

"Lester Morgan, known as Sundance."

"What'd he do?" Haywood was writing on a tablet as fast as he could write.

Smoke described Lester, ending with, "And he ain't got but one ear. That'll make him easy to spot."

"But what did this Lester Sundance Morgan *do*?"

"Why . . . he's the gunfighter who killed Luke Nations."

17

Ed Jackson and his wife went back East . . . anywhere east of the Mississippi River. They did not say goodbye to anybody, just loaded their wagon and pulled out early one morning.

Louis Longmont, Mike, and Andre left the town of Big Rock. Louis thought he'd retire for a time. But Smoke knew he would not . . . not for long. The raw and woolly West had not seen the last of Louis Longmont.

Word drifted back that Lester Sundance Morgan had been braced by a couple of young duded-up dandies looking for a reputation down in New Mexico Territory. Sundance had managed to drop them both and was now riding low, keeping out of sight. The report that Smoke received said that Lester was not a very happy young man.

Monte Carson recovered from his wounds and became the sheriff of Big Rock, Colorado. He married himself a grass widow and settled down.

The aging gunfighters pulled out of the area, riding out in small groups of twos and threes . . . or alone. Alone. As they had lived.

Charlie Starr shook hands with Smoke and swung into the saddle. With a smile and a small salute, he rode out of Big Rock and into the annals of Western history. Smoke would see the famed gunslinger again . . . but that's another story.

The *Fontana Sunburst* became the *Big Rock Guardian*. And it would remain so until the town changed its name just before the turn of the century.

Colton Spalding remained the town's doctor until his death in the 1920s.

Sally and Mona and Bountiful and Dana and Willow would live to "see the vote." But, there again, that's another story.

Judge Proctor returned and was named district judge. He lived in the area until his death in 1896.

The gold vein ran dry and all the miners left as peace finally settled over the High Lonesome.

The gold still lies in the ground on Smoke and Sally's Sugarloaf. They never touched it.

The last store in Fontana closed its doors in 1880. The lonely winds hummed and sang their quiet Western songs throughout the empty buildings and ragged bits of tent canvas for many years; the songs sang of love and hate and violence and bloody gunfights until the last building collapsed in the 1940s. Now, nothing is left.

Danner and Signal Hill died out near the turn of the century, but the town that was once called Big Rock remains, and the descendants of Smoke and Sally Jensen, Johnny and Belle North, Pearlie, and all the others still live there . . . finally in peace.

But peace was a long time coming to that part of Colorado, for not all the gunslicks were killed that bloody day in Fontana. Those few that managed to escape swore they'd come back and have their revenge.

They would try.

It would be many more years before Smoke Jensen could hang up his guns for good. Many years before Smoke and Sally Jensen's sons and daughters could live in peace. For Smoke Jensen was the West's most famous gunfighter. And for years to come, there would be those who sought a reputation.

But before that, on a bright, sunny, warm, late-summer morning, Velvet Colby called out for her mother and for Johnny.

The newly wed man and woman ran to Velvet's bedroom. Johnny North, one of the West's most feared gunfighters, knelt and took the girl's hands in his hard and calloused hands.

"Yes, baby?" he said, his voice gentle.

Velvet smiled. Her voice, husky from lack of use, was a lovely thing to hear. She had not spoken in months. "Can I go outside?" she asked. "It looks like such a beautiful day."

And a gentle, peaceful breeze stirred the branches and the flowers and the tall lush grass of the High Lonesome . . .

. . . along the trail of the last Mountain Man.

REVENGE OF THE
MOUNTAIN MAN

This book is pure Western fiction. Any resemblance to actual persons, living or dead, is purely coincidental. To the best of my knowledge, there are no towns in Colorado named Big Rock or Dead River.

I am the wound and the knife!
I am the blow and the cheek!
I am the limbs and the wheel
—the victim and the executioner.

Baudelaire

1

They had struck as cowards usually do, in a pack and at night. And when the man of the house was not at home. They had come skulking like thieving foot-padders; but instead of robbery on their minds, their thoughts were of a much darker nature.

Murder.

And they had tried to kill Smoke Jensen's wife, Sally. When Smoke and Sally had married, just after Smoke almost totally wiped out the small town of Bury, Idaho, Smoke had used another name; but later, during the valley war around Big Rock and Fontana, he had once more picked up his real name, and be damned to all who didn't like the fact that he had once been a gunfighter.

It had never been a reputation that he had sought out; rather, it had seemed to seek him out. Left alone as a boy, raised by an old mountain man called Preacher, the young man had become one of the most feared and legended gunslingers in all the West. Some say he was the fastest gun alive. Some say that Smoke Jensen had killed fifty, one hundred, two hundred men.

No one really knew for certain.

All anyone really knew was that Smoke had never been

an outlaw, never ridden the hoot-owl trail, had no warrants out on him, and was a quiet sort of man. Now married, for several years he had been a farmer/rancher/horse breeder. A peaceful man who got along well with his neighbors and wished only to be left alone.

The night riders had shattered all that.

Smoke had been a hundred miles away, buying cattle, just starting the drive back to his ranch, called the Sugarloaf, when he heard the news. He had cut two horses out of his remuda and tossed a saddle on one. He would ride one, change saddles, and ride the other. They were mountain horses, tough as leather, and they stood up to the hard test.

Smoke did not ruin his horses on the long lonely ride back to the Sugarloaf, did not destroy them as some men might. But he rode steadily. He was torn inside, but above it all Smoke remained a realist, as old Preacher had taught him to be. He knew he would either make it in time, or he would not.

When he saw the snug little cabin in the valley of the high lonesome, the vastness of the high mountains all around it, Smoke knew, somehow, he had made it in time.

Smoke was just swinging down from the saddle when Dr. Colton Spalding stepped out of the cabin, smiling broadly when he spied Smoke. The doctor stopped the gunfighter before Smoke could push open the cabin door.

"She's going to make it, Smoke. But it was a close thing. If Bountiful had not awakened when she did and convinced Ralph that something was the matter . . ." The doctor shrugged his shoulders. "Well, it would have been all over here."

"I'm in their debt. But Sally is going to make it?"

"Yes. I have her sedated heavily with laudanum, to help her cope with the pain."

"Is she awake?"

"No. Smoke, they shot her three times. Shoulder, chest, and side. They left her for dead. She was not raped."

"Why did they do it? And who were they?"

"No one knows, except possibly Sally. And so far, the sheriff has not been able to question her about it."

"Bounty hunters, maybe. But there is no bounty on my head. I'm not wanted anywhere that I'm aware of."

"Nevertheless, Sheriff Carson believes it was bounty hunters. Someone paid to kill you. Or to draw you out, to come after them. The sheriff is with the posse now, trying to track the men."

"I'll just look in on her, Colton."

The doctor nodded and pushed open the cabin door. Smoke stepped past him.

The doctor's wife, Mona, a nurse, was sitting with several other women in the big main room of the cabin. They smiled at Smoke as he removed his hat and hung it on a peg by the door. He took off his gunbelt and hung it on another peg.

"Doc said it was all right for me to look in on her."

Mona nodded her head.

Smoke pushed open the bedroom door and stepped quietly inside, his spurs jingling faintly with each step. A big man, with a massive barrel chest and arms and shoulders packed with muscle, he could move as silently as his nickname implied.

Smoke felt a dozen different emotions as he looked at the pale face of his wife. Her dark hair seemed to make her face look paler. In his mind, there was love and hate and fury and black-tinged thoughts of revenge, all intermingled with sorrow and compassion. Darker emotions filled the tall young man as he sat down in a chair beside the bed and gently placed one big rough hand on his wife's smaller and softer hand.

Did she stir slightly under his touch? Smoke could not

be sure. But he was sure that somehow, in her pain-filled mind, Sally knew that he was there, beside her.

Now, alone, Smoke could allow emotions to change his usually stoic expression. His eyes mirrored his emotions. He wished he could somehow take her pain and let it fill his own body. He took the damp cloth from her head, refreshed it with water, wrung it out, and softly replaced it on her brow.

All through the rest of that day and the long, lonely night that followed, the young man sat by his wife's bed. Mona Spalding would enter hourly, sometimes shooing Smoke out of the room, tending to Sally's needs. Doc Spalding slept in a chair, the two other women, Belle North and Bountiful Morrow, Smoke and Sally's closest neighbors, slept in the spare bedroom.

Outside, the foreman, Pearlie, and the other hands had gathered, war talk on their lips and in the way they stood. Bothering a woman, good or bad, in this time in the West, was a hangin' matter . . . or just an outright killin'.

Little Billy, Smoke and Sally's adopted son, sat on a bench outside the house.

Just as the dawn was breaking golden over the high mountains around the Sugarloaf, Sally opened her eyes and smiled at her husband.

"You look tired," she said. "Have you had anything to eat?"

"No."

"Have you been here long?"

"Stop worrying about me. How do you feel?"

"Washed out."

He smiled at her. "I don't know what I'm going to do with you," he said gently. "I go off for a time and you get into a gunfight. That isn't very ladylike, you know? What would your folks back east think?"

She winked at him.

"Doc says you're going to be all right, Sally, But you're going to need lots of rest."

"Three of them," she whispered. "I heard them talking. I guess they thought I was dead. One was called Dagget . . ."

"Hush now."

"No. Let me say it while I still remember it. I heard one call another Lapeer. He said that if this doesn't bring you out, nothing will."

She closed her eyes. Smoke waited while she gathered strength.

Doc Spalding had entered the room, standing in the doorway, listening.

He met Smoke's eyes and inwardly cringed at the raw savagery he witnessed in the young man's cold gaze. Spalding had seen firsthand the lightning speed of Smoke's draw. Had witnessed the coldness of the man when angered. Fresh from the ordered world back east, the doctor was still somewhat appalled at the swiftness of frontier justice. But deep inside him, he would reluctantly agree that it was oftentimes better than the ponderousness of lawyers jabbering and arguing.

Sally said. "The third one was called Moore. Glen Moore. South Colorado, I think. I'm tired, honey."

Spalding stepped forward. "That's all, Smoke. Let her sleep. I want to show you something out in the living room."

In the big room that served as kitchen, dining, and sitting area, the doctor dropped three slugs into Smoke's callused palm.

He had dug enough lead out of men since his arrival to be able to tell one slug from another. ".44s, aren't they?"

"Two of them," Smoke said, fingering the off-slug. "This is a .44-40, I believe."

"The one that isn't mangled up?"

"Yes."

"That's the one I dug out of her chest. It came close to killing her, Smoke." He opened his mouth to say something, sighed, and then obviously thought better of it.

"You got something else to say, Doc?"

He shook his head. "Later. Perhaps Sally will tell you herself; that would be better, I'm thinking. And no, she isn't going to die. Smoke, you haven't eaten and you need rest. Mona agrees. She's fixing you something now. Please. You've got to eat."

"You will eat, and then you will rest," Belle said, a note of command in her voice. "Johnny is with the posse, Smoke. Velvet is looking after the kids. You'll eat, and then sleep. So come sit down at the table, Smoke Jensen."

"Yes, ma'am," Smoke said with a smile.

"I was waiting to be certain," Sally told him the next morning. "Dr. Spalding confirmed it the day before those men came. I'm pregnant, Smoke."

A smile creased his lips. He waited, knowing, sensing there was more to come.

Sally's eyes were serious. "Colton is leaving it all up to me, isn't he?"

"I reckon, Sally. I don't know. I do know that your voice is much stronger."

"I feel much better."

Smoke waited.

"You're not going to like what I have to say, Smoke. Not . . . in one way, that is."

"No way of knowing that, Sally. Not until you say what's on your mind."

She sighed, and the movement hurt her; pain crossed her face. "I'm probably going to have to go back east, Smoke."

Smoke's expression did not change. "I think that might be best, Sally. For a time."

She visibly relaxed. She did not ask why he had said that. She knew. He was going after the men who attacked her. She expected that of him. "You're not even going to ask why I might have to go back east?"

"I would think it's because the doctor told you to. But you won't be going anywhere for weeks. You were hard hit." He smiled. "I've been there, too." He kissed her mouth. "Now, you rest."

Mona and Belle stayed for three days; Bountiful lived just over the hill and could come and go with ease. On the morning of the fourth day, Sally was sitting up in bed, her color back. She was still in some pain and very weak, and would be for several more weeks.

Smoke finally brought up the subject. "The Doc is sure that you're with child?"

"Both of us are," she smiled with her reply. "I knew before the doctor."

Discussion of women's inner workings embarrassed Smoke. He dropped that part of it. "Now tell me why you think you might have to go back east."

"I have several pieces of lead in me, Smoke. Colton could not get them all. And he does not have the expertise nor the facilities to perform the next operation. And also, I have a small pelvis; the birth might be a difficult one. There is a new—well, a more highly refined procedure that is being used back east. I won't go into detail about that."

"Thank you," Smoke said dryly. "'Cause so far I don't have much idea of what you're talking about."

She laughed softly at her husband. A loving laugh and a knowing laugh. Smoke knew perfectly well what she was saying. He was, for the most part, until they had married, a self-taught man. And over the past few years, she had been tutoring him. He was widely read, and to her delight and surprise, although few others knew it, Smoke was a very good actor, with a surprising range of voices and inflections. She was continually drawing out that side of him.

"Mona's from back east, isn't she?"

"I'm way ahead of you, Smoke. Yes, she is. And if I have to go—and I'm thinking it might be best, and you know why, and it doesn't have anything to do with the baby or the operation—Mona will make all the arrangements and travel most of the way with me."

"That'll be good, Sally. Yes. I think you should plan on traveling east." She knew the set of that chin. Her leaving was settled; her husband had things to do. "You haven't seen your folks in almost five years. It's time to visit. Tell you what I'll do. I'll come out for you when it's time for you and the baby to return."

This time her laugh was hearty, despite her injuries. "Smoke, do you know the furor your presence would arouse in Keene, New Hampshire?"

"If *fu-ror* means what I think it does, why should people get all in a sweat about me coming east?"

"For sure, bands would play, you would be a celebrity, and the police would be upset."

"Why? I ain't wanted back there, or anywhere else for that matter."

She could but smile at him. If he knew, he had dismissed the fact that he was the most famous gunfighter in all of the West; that books—penny dreadfuls—had been and still were being written about his exploits— some of them fact, many of them fiction. That he had been written up in tabloids all over the world, and not just in the English-speaking countries. Her mother and father had sent Sally articles about her husband from all over the world. To say that they had been a little concerned about her safety—for a while—would be putting it mildly.

"People don't really believe all that crap that's been written about me, do they? Hell, Sally, I've been reported at fourteen different places at once, according to those stories."

"If they just believed the real things you've done, Smoke, that is enough to make people very afraid of you."

"That's silly! I never hurt anybody who wasn't trying to hurt me. People don't have any reason to be afraid of me."

"Well, I'm not afraid of you, Smoke. You're sort of special to me."

He smiled. "Oh, yeah? Well, I'd have to give it a lot of thought if someone was to offer to trade me a spotted pony for you, Sally."

2

Smoke Jensen and Sally Reynolds, gunfighter and schoolteacher, had met several years back, in Idaho. Just before Smoke had very nearly wiped out a town and all the people in it for killing his first wife and their child, Nicole and Baby Arthur; the boy named after Smoke's friend and mentor, the old mountain man, Preacher.

Smoke and Sally had married, living in peace for several years in the high lonesome, vast and beautiful mountains of Colorado. Then a man named Tilden Franklin had wanted to be king of the entire valley . . . and he had coveted Smoke's wife, making it public news.

Gold had been discovered in the valley, and a bitter, bloody war had ensued.

And in the end, all Tilden Franklin got was a half-a-dozen slugs in the belly, from the guns of Smoke Jensen, and six feet of hard cold ground.

That had been almost two years back; two years of peace in the valley and in Smoke and Sally's high-up ranch called the Sugarloaf.

Now that had been shattered.

On the morning of the first full week after the assault on Sally, Smoke sat on the bench outside the snug cabin and sipped his coffee.

Late spring in the mountains.

1880, and the West was slowly changing. There would be another full decade of lawlessness, of wild and woolly days and nights; but the law was making its mark felt all over the area. And Smoke, like so many other western men, knew that was both good and bad. For years, a commonsense type of justice had prevailed, for the most part, in the West, and usually—not always, but usually— it worked. Swiftly and oftentimes brutally, but it worked. Now, things were changing. Lawyers with big words and fancy tongues were twisting facts, hiding the guilt to win a case. And Smoke, like most thinking people, thought that to be wrong.

The coming of courts and laws and lawyers would prove to be both a blessing and a curse.

Smoke, like most western men, just figured that if someone tried to do you a harm or a meanness, just shoot the son of a bitch and have done with it. 'Cause odds were, the guilty party wasn't worth a damn to begin with. And damn few were ever going to miss them.

Smoke, like so many western men, judged other men by what they gave to society as opposed to what they took away from it. If your neighbor's house or barn burned down or was blown down in a storm, you helped him re- build. If his crops were bad or his herd destroyed, you helped him out until next season or loaned him some cows and a few bulls. If he and his family were hungry through no fault of their own, you helped out with food and clothing.

And so on down the line of doing things right.

And if a man wouldn't help out, chances were he was trash, and the sooner you got rid of him, the better.

Western justice and common sense.

And if people back east couldn't see that—well, Smoke thought . . . Well, he really didn't know what to think about people like that. He'd reserve judgment until he got to know a few of them.

He sipped his coffee and let his eyes drift over that part of his land that he could see from his front yard. And that was a lot of land, but just a small portion of all that he and Sally owned . . . free and clear.

There was a lot to do before Smoke put Sally on the steam trains and saw her off to the East—and before he started after those who had attacked her like rabid human beasts in the night.

And there was only one thing you could do with a rabid beast.

Kill it.

Billy stepped out of the house and took a seat on the bench beside his adopted father. The boy had been legally adopted by the Jensens; Judge Proctor had seen to that. Billy was pushing hard at his teen years, soon turning thirteen. Already he was a top hand and, even though Smoke discouraged it, a good hand with a gun. Uncommon quick. Smoke and Sally had adopted the boy shortly after the shoot-out in Fontana, and now Billy pulled his weight and then some around the Sugarloaf.

"You and Miss Sally both gonna go away?" Billy asked, his voice full of gloom.

"For a time, Billy. Sally thought about taking you back east with her, but you're in school here, and doing well. So Reverend Ralph and Bountiful are going to look after you. You'll stay here at the ranch with Pearlie and the hands. We might be gone for the better part of a year, Billy, so it's going to be up to you to be the man around the place."

Pearlie was leaning up against a hitch rail and Smoke winked at his friend and foreman.

"If I hadn't a-been out with the hands the other night . . ." Billy said.

Smoke cut him off. "And if your aunt had wheels, she'd have been a tea cart, Billy. You and the hands were doing what I asked you to do—pushing cattle up to the high grass. Can't any of you blame yourselves for what happened."

"I don't think my aunt had no wheels, Smoke," Billy said solemnly. Then he realized that Smoke was funning with him and he smiled. "That would be a sight to see though, wouldn't it?"

Pearlie walked up to the man and boy. "We'll be all right here, Billy. I don't know what I'd do without you. You're a top hand."

Billy grinned at the high compliment.

When the foreman and the boy had walked away, Smoke stepped back into the house and fixed breakfast for Sally, taking it to her on a tray. He positioned pillows behind her shoulders and gently eased her to an upright position in the bed.

He sat by the bed and watched her eat; slowly she was regaining her strength and appetite. But she was still very weak and had to be handled with caution.

She would eat a few bites and then rest for a moment, gathering strength.

"I'm getting better, Smoke," she told him with a smile. "And the food is beginning to taste good."

"I can tell. At first I thought it was my cooking," he kidded her. "Your color is almost back to normal. Feel like telling me more about what happened?"

She ate a few more bites and then pushed the tray from her. "It's all come back to me. The doctor said it would. He said that sometimes severe traumas can produce temporary memory loss."

Colton had told Smoke the same thing.

She looked at him. "It was close, wasn't it?"

"You almost died, honey."

She closed her eyes for a moment and then opened them, saying, "I remember the time. Nine o'clock. I was just getting ready for bed. I remember glancing at the clock. I was in my gown." Her brow furrowed in painful remembrance, physically and mentally. "I heard a noise outside, or so I thought. But when it wasn't repeated, I ignored it. I walked in here, to the bedroom, and then I heard the noise again. I remember feeling a bit frightened. . . ."

"Why?" he interrupted. He was curious, for Sally was not the spooky or flighty kind. She had used a rifle and pistol several times since settling here, and had killed or wounded several outlaws.

"Because it was not a natural sound. It was raining, and I had asked Billy, when he came in to get lunch packets for the crew, to move the horses into the barn, to their stalls for the night. Bad move, I guess. If Seven or Drifter had been in the corral, they would have warned me."

"I would have done the same thing, Sally. Stop blaming yourself. Too much of that going on around here. It was nobody's fault. It happened, it's over, and it's not going to happen again. Believe me, I will see to that."

And she knew he would.

"When the noise came again, it was much closer, like someone brushing up against the side of the house. I was just reaching for a pistol when the front door burst open. Three men; at least three men. I got the impression there was more, but I saw only three. I heard three names. I did tell you the names, didn't I? That part is hazy."

"Yes."

"Dagget, Lapeer, and Moore. Yes. Now I remember telling you. The one called Dagget smiled at me. Then he said"—she struggled to remember—"'Too bad we don't have more time. I'd like to see what's under that gown.' Then he lifted his pistol and shot me. No warning. No time at all to do anything. He just lifted his gun and shot me. As I was falling, the other two shot me."

Smoke waited, his face expressionless. But his inner thoughts were murderous.

Sally closed her eyes, resting for a moment before

once more reliving the horrible night. "Just as I was falling into darkness, losing consciousness, I heard one say, 'Now the son of a bitch has us all to deal with.'"

And I will deal with you, Smoke thought. One by one, on a very personal basis. I will be the judge, the jury, and the executioner.

Smoke started to roll and light one of his rare cigarettes, then thought better of it. The smoke might cause Sally to cough and he knew that would be harmful.

"Do you know any of the men I mentioned, Smoke?"

"No. I can't say that I've even heard of them." There was a deep and dangerous anger within him. But he kept his voice and his emotions well in check. He hated night riders, of any kind. He knew those types of people were, basically, cowards.

He kept his face bland. He did not want Sally to get alarmed, although he knew that she knew exactly what he was going to do once she was safely on the train heading east. He also knew that when she did mention it—probably only one time—she would not attempt to stop him.

That was not her way. She had known the kind of man he was when she married him.

He met her eyes, conscious of her staring at him, and smiled at her. She held out a hand and Smoke took it, holding it gently.

"It's a mystery to me, honey," she said. "I just don't understand it. The valley has been so peaceful for so many months. Not a shot fired in anger. Now this."

Smoke hushed her, taking the lap tray. He had never even heard of a lap tray until Sally had sent off for one from somewhere back east. "You rest now. Sleep. You want some more laudanum?"

She minutely shook her head. "No. Not now. The pain's not too bad. That stuff makes my head feel funny."

She was sleeping even before Smoke had closed the door.

He scraped the dishes and washed them in hot water taken from the stove, then pumped a pot full of fresh water and put that on the stove, checking the wood level that heated the back plate and checking the draft. He peeled potatoes for lunch and dropped them into cold water. Then he swept the floor and tidied up the main room, opening all the windows to let the house cool.

Then the most famous and feared gunfighter in all the west washed clothes, wrung them out, and hung them up to dry on the clothesline out back, the slight breeze and the warm sun freshening them naturally.

He walked around to the front of the cabin and sat beside the bedroom window, open just a crack, so he could hear Sally if she needed anything.

Lapeer, Moore, and Dagget. He rolled those names around in his mind as his fingers skillfully rolled a cigarette. He had never heard of any of them. But he knew one thing for certain.

They were damn sure going to hear from him.

3

Smoke did not leave the Sugarloaf range for weeks. If supplies were needed, one of the hands went into town for them. Smoke did not want to stray very far from Sally's side.

The days passed slowly, each one bringing another hint of the summer that lay lazily before them. And Sally grew stronger. Two weeks after the shooting, she was able to walk outside, with help, and sit for a time, taking the sun, taking it easy, growing stronger each day.

Smoke had spoken with Sheriff Monte Carson several times since the posse's return from a frustrating and fruitless pursuit. But Monte was just as baffled as Smoke as to the why of Sally's attack and the identity of the attackers.

Judge Proctor had been queried, as well as most of the other people around the valley. No one had ever heard of the men.

It was baffling and irritating.

Not even the legended Smoke could fight an enemy he could not name and did not know and could not find.

Yet.

But he was going to find them, and when he did, he was going to make some sense out of this.

Then he would kill them.

It was midsummer before Dr. Colton Spalding finally gave Sally the okay to travel. During that time, he had wired the hospital in Boston several times, setting up Sally's operation. The doctor would use a rather risky procedure called a caesarean to take the baby—if it came to that. But the Boston doctor wanted to examine Sally himself before he elected to use that drastic a procedure. And according to Dr. Spalding, the Boston doctor was convinced a caesarean was necessary.

"What's this operation all about?" Smoke asked Dr. Spalding.

"It's a surgical procedure used to take the baby if the mother can't delivery normally."

"I don't understand, but I'll take your word for it. Is it dangerous?"

Colton hesitated. With Smoke, it was hard to tell exactly what he knew about any given topic. When they had first met, the doctor thought the young man to be no more than an ignorant brute, a cold-blooded killer. It didn't take Colton long to realize that while Smoke had little formal education, he was widely read and quite knowledgeable.

And Colton also knew that Smoke was one of those rare individuals one simply could not lie to. Smoke's unblinking eyes never left the face of the person who was speaking. Until you grew accustomed to it, it was quite unnerving.

Before Colton could speak, Smoke said, "Caesar's mother died from this sort of thing, didn't she?"

The doctor smiled, shaking his head. Many of the men of the West were fascinating with what they knew and how they had learned it. It never ceased to amaze the man to see some down-at-the-heels puncher, standing up in a barroom quoting Shakespeare or dissertating on some subject as outrageous as astrology.

And knowing what he was talking about!

"Yes, it is dangerous, Smoke. But not nearly so dangerous as when Caesar was born."

"Let's hope not. What happens if Sally decides not to have this operation?"

"One of two things, Smoke. You will decide whether you want Sally saved, or the baby."

"I won't be there, Doc. So I'm telling you now—save my wife. You pass the word along to this doctor friend of yours in Boston town. Save Sally at all costs. You'll do that, right?"

"You know I will. I'll wire him first thing in the morning."

"Thank you."

Colton watched as Smoke helped Sally back to bed. He had not fully leveled with the young man about the surgical procedure. Colton knew that sometimes the attending physician had very little choice as to who would be saved. And sometimes, mother and child both died.

He sighed. They had come so far in medicine, soaring as high as eagles in such a short time. But doctors still knew so very little . . . and were expected to perform miracles at all times.

"Would that it were so," Colton muttered, getting into his buggy and clucking at the mare.

As the weather grew warmer and the days grew longer, Sally grew stronger . . . and was beginning to show her pregnancy. Several of the women who lived nearby would come over almost daily, to sew and talk and giggle about the damndest things.

Smoke left the scene when all that gabble commenced.

And he was still no closer to finding out anything about the men who attacked his wife.

Leaving Sally and the women, with two hands always on guard near the cabin, Smoke saddled the midnight-black horse with the cold, killer eyes, and he and Drifter went to town.

The town of Fontana, once called No Name, which had been Tilden Franklin's town, was dying just as surely as Tilden had died under Smoke's guns. Only a few stores remained open, and they did very little business.

It was to the town of Big Rock that Smoke rode, his .44s belted around his lean waist and tied down, the Henry rifle in his saddle boot.

Big Rock was growing as Fontana was dying. A couple of nice cafés, a small hotel, one saloon, with no games and no hurdy-gurdy girls. There was a lawyer, Hunt Brook, and his wife, Willow, and a newspaper, the *Big Rock Guardian,* run by Haywood and Dana Arden. Judge Proctor, the reformed wino, was the district judge and he made his home in Big Rock, taking his supper at the hotel every evening he was in town. Big Rock had a church and a schoolhouse.

It was a nice quiet little town; but as some men who had tried to tree it found out, Big Rock was best left alone.

Johnny North, who had married the widow Belle Colby after her husband's death, was—or had been—one of the West's more feared and notorious gunfighters. A farmer/rancher now, Johnny would, if the situation called for it, strap on and tie down his guns and step back into his gunfighter's boots. Sheriff Monte Carson, another ex-gunfighter, was yet another gunhawk to marry a grass widow and settle in Big Rock. Pearlie, Smoke's foreman, had married and settled down; but Pearlie had also been, at one point in his young life, a much-feared and re-spected fast gun. The minister, Ralph Morrow, was an ex-prizefighter from back east, having entered the ministry after killing a man with his fists. Ralph preached on Sun-days and farmed and ranched during the week. Ralph would also pick up a gun and fight, although most would rather he wouldn't. Ralph couldn't shoot a short gun worth a damn!

Big Rock and the area surrounding it was filled with men and women who would fight for their families, their homes, and their lands.

The dozen or so outlaws who rode into town with the thought of taking over and having their way with the women some months back soon found that they had made a horrible and deadly mistake. At least half of them died in their saddles, their guns in their hands. Two more were shot down in the street. Two died in the town's small clinic. The rest were hanged.

The word soon went out along the hoot-owl trail: Stay away from Big Rock. The town is pure poison. Folks there will shoot you quicker than a cat can scat.

Smoke caught up with Johnny North, who was in town for supplies. The two of them found Sheriff Carson and went to the Big Rock saloon for a couple of beers and some conversation. The men sipped their beers in silence for a time. Finally, after their mugs had been refilled, Johnny broke the silence.

"I been thinkin' on it some, Smoke. I knew I'd heard that name Dagget somewheres before, but I couldn't drag it out of my head and catch no handle on it. It come to me last night. I come up on that name down near the Sangre de Cristo range a few years back. It might not be the same fellow, but I'm bettin' it is. Sally's description of him fits what I heard. If it is, he's a bad one. Bounty hunter and bodyguard to somebody. I don't know who. I ain't never heard of the two other men with him."

"I ain't never heard of any of them," Monte said sourly. "And I thought I knew every gunslick west of the Big Muddy. That was any good, that is."

"Dagget don't ride the rim much," Johnny explained. "And he only takes jobs his boss wants him to take. If this is the same fellow, he's from back east somewheres.

Came out here about ten years ago. Supposed to be from a real good family back there. Got in trouble with the law and had to run. But his family seen to it that he had plenty of money. What he done, so I'm told, is link up with some other fellow and set them up an outlaw stronghold; sort of like the Hole-In-The-Wall. All this is just talk; I ain't never been there."

Smoke nodded his head. Something else had jumped into his mind; something the old mountain man, Preacher, had said one time. Something about the time he'd had to put lead into a fellow who lived down near the Sangre de Cristo range. But what was the man's name? Was it Davidson? Yes. Rex Davidson.

"Rex Davidson," Smoke said it aloud.

Both Monte and Johnny stiffened at the name, both men turning their heads to look at Smoke.

When Johnny spoke, his voice was soft. "What'd you say, Smoke?"

Smoke repeated the name.

Monte whistled softly. "I really hope he ain't got nothing to do with the attack agin Sally."

Smoke looked at him. "Why?"

Monte finished his beer and motioned the two men outside, to the boardwalk. He looked up and down the street and then sat down on the wooden bench in front of the saloon, off to the side from the batwing entrance. Johnny and Smoke joined him.

"That name you just mentioned, Smoke . . . what do you know about him?"

"Absolutely nothing. I heard Preacher mention it one time, and one time only. That was years back, when I was just a kid. The name is all I know except that Preacher told me he had to put lead into him one time."

Monte nodded his head. "So that's it. Well, that clears it up right smart. Finishes the tale I been hearin' for years. I'll just be damned, boys!"

The men waited until Monte had rolled and licked a cigarette into shape and lighted it.

"Must have been . . . oh, at least twenty years back, so the story goes. Rex Davidson was about twenty, I guess. Might have been a year or two younger than that. I don't know the whole story; just bits and pieces. But this Davidson had just come into the area from somewheres. California, I think it was. And he though he was castin' a mighty big shadow wherever it was he walked. He was good with a gun, and a mighty handsome man, too. I seen him once, and he is a lady killer. What's the word I'm lookin' for? Vain, that's it. Pretties himself up all the time.

"There was a tradin' post down on the Purgatoire called Slim's. Run by a Frenchman. It's still there, and the same guy runs it. Only now it's a general store. It sits east and some north of Trinidad, where the Francisco branches off from the Purgatoire.

"This Davidson was there, braggin' about how he was gettin' rich diggin' gold and running cattle up between the Isabel and the Sangre de Cristos. Said he was gonna build hisself a town. Done it, too."

Monte dragged on his cigarette and Johnny said, "Dead River."

"You got it."

"Damn good place to stay shut of."

"Sure is," Monte ground out his smoke under the heel of his boot. "Whole damn town is owned by this Davidson and maybe by this Dagget, too. Anyways, this was back . . . oh, 'bout '60, I reckon, and this mountain man come into the tradin' post with some pelts he'd taken up near the Apishapa and the Arkansas. Him and Slim was jawin' over the price when this Rex Davidson decided he'd stick his nose into the affair. He made some crack about the mountain man's weapons and the way he was talkin'. This mountain man wasn't no big fellow; but size don't amount to a hill of beans when you start gettin' smart-lipped with them people—as you well know, Smoke."

Smoke nodded his head. He knew all too well the truth in that statement. Mountain men, for the most part, stayed away from people and civilization, keeping mostly to themselves, but God have mercy on your soul if you started trouble with them.

Oh, yes, Smoke knew. He had been raised up during his formative years by the most legended of all mountain men—old Preacher.

"Well, that mountain man's name was Preacher," Monte continued. "Slim told me that Preacher didn't say nothin' to Davidson; just ignored him. And that made Davidson hot under the collar. He called out, "Hey, you greasy old bastard. I'm talking to you, old man!'"

"He shouldn't have done that," Smoke said softly.

And in his mind's eye, as Monte told his tale, Smoke could see what had happened. Smoke smiled as he visualized the long-ago day. . . .

Preacher turned slowly, looking at the young man with the twin Colt Navy .36s belted around his waist and tied down low. The fast draw was new to the West, and some that thought they were fast weren't. The mountain man, slim and lean-waisted, had a faint smile on his lips.

"What'd you want, Tadpole?"

"Davidson flushed red, hot and unreasonable anger flashing in his eyes.

The kid is crazy, Preacher guessed accurately. And he's a killer.

"The name is Rex Davidson, old man."

"Do tell? Is that 'pposed to mean something to me, Tadpole?"

"Yeah. I'm a gunfighter."

"Is that right?" Preacher drawled. "Well, now, how come it is I ain't never seen none of your graveyards, Tadpole?"

"Well, old man, maybe you just haven't been in the right

towns, standing in the right boot hill. I got 'em scattered around, here and there."

"My, my! I 'spect I should be im-pressed." He smiled. "But I ain't," he added softly.

"I thought you mountain men was supposed to be so damn tough!" Rex sneered. "You sound like you're scared to visit a graveyard."

"Oh . . . well, now, I tend to shy away from graveyards, Tadpole. They can be mighty spooky places. Some Injuns believe a man can lose his soul by wanderin' around in a graveyard. Mayhaps that's what happened to you, Tadpole."

"What the hell are you babbling about, you old bastard? I think you're silly!"

"Tadpole, I think you've prowled around so many old bone-yards, lookin' up names on markers so's you could lie about how bad you want people to think you is . . . why, hell, Tadpole, I think you lost your soul."

"You calling me a liar, old man?" Rex fairly screamed the question, his hands dropping to his sides to hover over the butts of his Navy Colts.

"Could be, Tadpole," Preacher spoke softly. "But if I was you, I wouldn't take no of-fense. Not if you want to go on livin' healthy."

Slim Dugas got the hell out of the line of fire. He didn't know this punk-faced kid from Adam's Off Ox, but he sure as hell knew all about Preacher and that wild breed of men called mountain men. There just wasn't no back-up in a mountain man. Not none at all.

"No man calls me a liar and lives, you greasy old fart!" Rex screamed.

"Well, now, Tadpole. It shore 'ppears like I done it, though, don't it?"

"Damn your eyes! Draw!" Davidson shouted, his palms slapping the butts of his guns.

Preacher lifted his Sharps and pulled the trigger. He had cocked it while Davidson was running off at the mouth about how bad he was. The .52 slug struck the young man in the side, *exactly where Preacher intended it to go; he didn't want to kill the punk. But in later years he would realize that he should have. The force of the slug turned Davidson around and spun him like a top, knocking him against a wall and to the floor. He had not even cleared leather.*

Monte chuckled and that brought Smoke back from years past in his mind.

"Slim told me that Preacher collected his money for his pelts, picked up his bacon and beans, and walked out the door; didn't even look at Davidson. There was four or five others in the room, drinking rotgut, and they spread the story around about Davidson. Smoke, Davidson has hated Preacher and anyone connected with him for years. And one more thing: All them men in that room, they was all back-shot, one at a time over the years. Only one left alive was Slim."

"That tells me that this Davidson is crazy as a bessie-bug."

"Damn shore is," Johnny agreed. "What kind of man would hate like that, and for so long? It ain't as if Smoke was any actual kin of Preacher's. Why wait this long to do something about it?"

"You askin' me questions I ain't got no answers for," Monte replied.

Smoke stood up. "Well, you can all bet one thing. I'm damn sure going to find out!"

4

Smoke could tell that Sally was getting anxious to travel east and see her folks. She tried to hide her growing excitement, but finally she gave in and admitted she was ready to go.

Some men—perhaps many men—would have been reluctant to let their wives travel so far away from the hearth of home, especially when taking into consideration the often terrible hardships that the women of the West had to endure when compared with the lifestyle of women comfortably back east, with their orderly, structured society and policemen walking the beat.

Why, Sally had even told of indoor plumbing, complete with relief stations, not just bathing tubs. Smoke couldn't even imagine how something like that might work. He reckoned it would take a hell of a lot of digging, but it sure would be smelly if the pipes were to clog.

"You real sure you're up to this thing?" Smoke asked her.

"I feel fine, honey. And the doctor says I'm one hundred percent healed."

He patted her swelling belly and grinned. "Getting a little chubby, though."

She playfully slapped at his hand. "What are you going to do if it's twins?"

He put a fake serious look on his face. "Well, I might just take off for the mountains!"

She put her arms around him. "Mona says all the travel arrangements are complete. She says we'll be leaving the last part of next week."

"She told me. The Doc and me will ride down to Denver with you and see you both off."

"I'll like that. And then, Smoke? . . ."

"You know what I have to do, Sally. And it isn't a question of wanting to do it. It's something I have to do."

She lay her head on his chest. "I know. When will they ever leave us alone?"

"Maybe never, honey. Accept that. Not as long as there is some punk kid who fancies himself a gunslick and is looking to make a rep for himself. Not as long as there are bounty hunters who work for jackasses like this Rex Davidson and his kind. And not as long as there are Rex Davidsons in the world."

"It's all so simple for you, isn't it, Smoke?"

He knew what she was talking about. "Yes. If we could get rid of the scum of the earth, it would be such a very nice place to live."

With her arms still around him, feeling the awesome physical strength of the man, she said, "Didn't you tell me that this Dagget person came from back east?"

"Yeah. That's what Johnny told me and the sheriff. Came out here about ten years ago. Are you thinking that you know this fellow?"

"It might be the same person. Maybe. It was a long time ago, Smoke. And not an experience that I wanted to remember. I've tried very hard to put it out of my mind."

"Put what out of your mind?"

She pulled away from him and walked to the open window, the curtains ruffling with the slight breeze. "It

was a long time ago. I was . . . oh, I guess nine or ten."
She paused for a time, Smoke waiting patiently. "I finally
forced myself to remember something else Dagget said
that night. He said that he . . . had wanted to see me
naked for a long time. Then he grinned. Nasty. Evil. Per-
verted. Then I recalled that . . . experience so long ago."

She turned to face him.

"I was . . . molested as a child. I was not raped, but molested. By a man whom I believe to be this Dagget
person. I screamed and it frightened him away. But
before he left me, he slapped me and told me that if I
ever told, he would kill my parents." She shrugged her
shoulders. "I never told anyone before this."

"And you believe this Dagget is the same man?"

"I'm sure of it now. Shortly after my . . . incident, the
man was forced to leave town; he killed a man in a
lover's quarrel."

"All the more reason to kill the man."

"I was not the only little girl he molested. Some were
actually raped. It's the same man," she said flatly. "That
is not something a woman ever forgets."

"They still have warrants out for him in New Hampshire, you reckon?"

"I'm sure they do. Why do you ask?"

"Maybe I'll bring his head back in a bag. Give it to the
police."

She shuddered. "Smoke, you don't do things like that
in New Hampshire."

"Why? He's worse than a rabid beast. What's the
matter with the people back east?"

"It's called civilization, honey."

"Is that right? Sounds to me like they got a yellow
streak running up their backs."

She shook her head and fought to hide a smile.

"If I take him alive, you want me to wrap him up in a
fresh deer hide and stake him out in the sun?"

Sally sighed and looked at her man. "Smoke . . . no! How gruesome! What would that accomplish?"

"Pay back, Sally. Sun dries the hide around them; kills them slow. Helps to tie a fresh cut strip of green rawhide around their heads. That really lets them know they've done wrong; that someone is right displeased with them."

She shuddered. "I think they would get that message, all right."

"Almost always, Sally. Your folks back east, Sally, they've got this notion about treating bad men humanely. That's what I've been reading. But the bad men don't treat their victims humanely. Seems like to me, your folks got things all screwed up in their heads. You won't have crime, Sally, if you don't have criminals."

She sighed, knowing there was really no argument against what he was saying. It was a hard land, this frontier, and it took a hard breed to survive. They were good to good people. Terribly brutal to those who sought the evil way.

And who was to say that the hard way was not the right way?

She smiled at her man. "I guess that's why I love you so much, Smoke. You are so direct and straightforward in your thinking. I think you are going to be a most refreshing cool breeze to my family and friends back in New Hampshire."

"Maybe."

"Smoke, I am going to say this once, and I will not bring it up again. I married you, knowing full well what kind of man you are. And you are a good man, but hard. I have never tried to change you. I don't believe that is what marriage is all about."

"And I thank you for that, Sally."

"I know you are going man-hunting, Smoke. And I know, like you, that it is something you have to do. I don't always understand; but in this case, I do. My parents and brothers and sisters will not. Nor will my friends. But I do."

"And you're going to tell them what I'm doing?"

"Certainly. And you'll probably be written up in the local newspaper."

"Seems to me they ought to have more important things to write about than that."

Sally laughed at his expression. How could she explain to him that the people back in Keene didn't carry guns; that most had never seen a fast draw; that many of them didn't believe high noon shoot-outs ever occurred?

He probably wouldn't believe her. He'd have to see for himself.

"Smoke, I know that you take chances that many other men would not take. You're a special breed. I learned early on why many people call you the last mountain man. Perhaps that is yet another of the many reasons I love you like I do. So do this for me: When you put me on that train and see me off, put me out of your mind. Concentrate solely on the job facing you. I know you have that quality about you; you do it. I will leave messages at the wire offices for you, telling you how I am and where I can be reached at all times. You try to do the same for me, whenever you can."

"I will, Sally. And that's a promise. But I'm going to be out-of-pocket for a couple of months, maybe longer."

"I know. That's all I ask, Smoke. We'll say no more about it." She came to him and pulled his head down, kissing him.

"I have an idea, Sally."

"What?"

"All the hands are gone. The place is all ours. But it might hurt the baby."

"I bet it won't." She smiled impishly at him.

She was right.

* * *

Smoke stood watching until the caboose was out of sight. Dr. Spalding had walked back into the station house. Spalding and his wife, Mona, along with Sally, had ridden the stage into Denver. Smoke had ridden Drifter. He had not brought a pack animal; he'd buy one in the city.

There were already laws in parts of Denver about carrying guns, so Smoke had left his twin Colts back in the hotel room. He carried a short-barreled Colt, tucked behind his belt, covered by his coat.

Smoke turned away from the now-silent twin ribbons of steel that linked the nation. "See you soon, Sally," he muttered. He walked back into the station house.

"Are you going to stay in town for a time and see some of the shows?" Colton asked.

Smoke shook his head. "No. I'm going to gear up and pull out." He held out his right hand and Colton shook it. "You'll stay in touch with the doctors in Boston?"

"Yes. I'll have progress reports for you whenever you wire Big Rock."

"Check on Billy every now and then."

Colton nodded. "Don't worry about him. He'll be fine. You take care, Smoke."

"I'll be in touch." Smoke turned and walked away.

He bought three hundred rounds of .44s. The ammo was interchangeable between rifle and pistols. He bought a tent and a ground sheet, a coffee pot and a skillet. Coffee and beans and flour and a small jug of lard. Bacon. He walked around the store, carefully selecting his articles, choosing ones he felt a back-east dandy come west might pick up to take on his first excursion into the wilds.

He bought lace-up boots and a cap, not a hat. He bought a shoulder holster for his short-barreled Colt. He bought a sawed-off 12-gauge shotgun and several boxes of buckshot shells.

"Have this gear out back on the loading dock in two hours," Smoke instructed the clerk. "That's when I'll be coming for it. And I'll pay you then."

"Yes, sir. That will be satisfactory. I shall see you in two hours."

"Fine."

Smoke inspected several packhorses and chose one that seemed to have a lot of bottom. Then he took a hansom to a fancy art-house and bought a dozen sketch pads and several boxes of charcoal pencils.

He had not shaved that morning at the hotel and did not plan on doing anything other than trimming his beard for a long time to come.

At a hardware store, he picked up a pair of scissors to keep his beard neat. An artist's beard. He would cut off his beard when it came time to reveal his true identity.

When it came time for the killing.

Smoke had a natural talent for drawing, although he had never done much with it. Now, he thought with a smile, it was going to come in handy.

At the art store, the clerk was a dandy if Smoke had ever seen one, prissing around like a peacock, fussing about this and that and prancing up one aisle and down the other.

Smoke told him what he wanted and let the prissy little feller fill the bill.

Smoke studied the way the clerk walked. Wasn't no damn way in hell he was gonna try to walk like that. Some bear might think he was in heat.

He went to a barbershop and told the barber he wanted his hair cut just like the dandies back east were wearing theirs. Just like he'd seen in a magazine. Parted down the middle and greased back. The barber looked at him like he thought Smoke had lost his mind, but other than to give him a queer look, he made no comment. Just commenced to whacking and shaping.

Smoke did feel rather like a fop when he left the barber chair, and he hoped that he would not run into anyone he knew until his beard grew out. But in a big city like Denver—must have been four or five thousand people in the city—that was unlikely.

Smoke checked out of the hotel and got Drifter and his packhorse from the stable, riding around to the rear of the store, picking up and lashing down his supplies. His guns were rolled up and stored in a spare blanket, along with the sawed-off express gun.

He was ready.

But he waited until he got outside of the city before he stuck that damn cap on his head.

He rode southeast out of Denver, taking his time, seeing the country—again. He and old Preacher had ridden these trails, back when Smoke was just a boy. There were mighty few trails and places in Colorado that Smoke had not been; but oddly enough, down south of Canon City, down between the Isabels and the Sangre de Cristo range, was one area where Preacher had not taken him.

And now Smoke knew why that was. The old man had been protecting him.

But why so much hate on the part of this Rex Davidson? And was Sally right? Was this Dagget the same man who had molested her as a child? And how were he and Davidson connected—and why?

He didn't know.

But he was sure going to find out.

And then he would kill them.

Smoke spent a week camped along the West Bijou, letting his beard grow out and sketching various scenes, improving upon his natural talent. He still didn't like the silly cap he was wearing, but he stuck with it, getting used to the damned thing. And each day he combed and brushed his hair, slicking it down with goop, retraining it.

Damned if he really wasn't beginning to look like a dandy. Except for his eyes; those cold, expressionless, and emotionless eyes. And there wasn't a damn thing he could do about that.

Or was there? he pondered, smiling.

Oh, yes, there was.

Allowing himself a chuckle, he swiftly broke camp and packed it all up, carefully dousing his fire and then scattering the ashes and dousing them again. He mounted up and swung Drifter's head toward the south and slightly west. If he couldn't find what he was looking for in Colorado City, he'd head on down to Jim Beckworth's town of Pueblo—although some folks tended to spell it Beckwourth.

Smoke stopped in at the fanciest store in town and browsed some, feeling silly and foppish in his high-top lace-up boots and his city britches tucked into the tops like some of them explorer people he'd seen pictures of. But if he was gonna act and look like a sissy, he might as well learn the part—except for the walk—cause he damn sure was gonna look mighty funny if he could find him a pair of those tinted eyeglasses.

He found several pairs—one blue-tinted, one yellow-tinted, and one rose-tinted.

"Oh, what the hell," he muttered.

He bought all three pairs and a little hard case to hold them in, to keep them from getting broken.

Smoke put on his red-tinted eyeglasses and walked outside, thinking that they sure gave a fellow a different outlook on things.

"Well, well," a cowboy said, stepping back and eyeballing Smoke and his fancy getup. "If you jist ain't the purtiest thing I ever did see." Then he started laughing.

Smoke gritted his teeth and started to brush past the half-drunk puncher.

The puncher grabbed Smoke by the upper arm and spun him around, a startled look on his face as his fingers gripped the thick, powerful muscles of Smoke's upper arm.

Smoke shook his arm loose. Remembering all the grammar lessons Sally had given him, and the lessons that the urbane and highly educated gambler, Louis Longmont, had taught him, Smoke said, "I say, my good fellow, unhand me, please!"

The cowboy wasn't quite sure just exactly what he'd grabbed hold of. That arm felt like it was made of pure oak, but the speech sounded plumb goofy.

"What the hell is you, anyways?"

Smoke drew himself erect and looked down at the smaller man. "I, my good man, am an ar-tist!"

"Ar-tist? You paint pitchers?"

"I sketch pic-tures!" Smoke said haughtily.

"Do tell? How much you charge for one of them sketchies?"

"Of whom?"

"Huh?"

Smoke sighed. "Whom do you wish me to sketch?"

"Why, hell . . . me, o' course!"

"I'm really in a hurry, my good fellow. Perhaps some other time."

"I'll give you twenty dollars."

That brought Smoke up short. Twenty dollars was just about two thirds of what the average puncher made a month, and it was hard-earned wages. Smoke stepped back, taking a closer look at the man. This was no puncher. His boots were too fancy and too highly shined. His dress was too neat and too expensive. And his guns—two of them, worn low and tied down—marked him.

"Well . . . I might be persuaded to do a quick sketch.

But not here in the middle of the street, for goodness sake!"

"Which way you headin', pardner?"

Smoke gestured with his arm, taking in the entire expanse. "I am but a free spirit, a wanderer, traveling where the wind takes me, enjoying the blessing of this wild and magnificent land."

Preacher, Smoke thought, wherever you are, you are probably rolling on the ground, cackling at this performance.

Smoke had no idea if Preacher were dead or alive; but he preferred to believe him alive, although he would be a very old man by now. But still? . . .

The gunfighter looked at Smoke, squinting his eyes. "You shore do talk funny. I'm camped on the edge of town. You kin sketch me there."

"Certainly, my good man. Let us be off."

Before leaving town, Smoke bought a jug of whiskey and gave it to the man, explaining, "Sometimes subjects tend to get a bit stiff and they appear unnatural on the paper. For the money, I want to do this right."

The man was falling-down drunk by the time they got to his campsite.

Smoke helped him off his horse and propped him up against a tree. Then he began to sketch and chat as he worked.

"I am very interested in the range of mountains known as the Sangre de Cristos. Are you familiar with them?"

"Damn sure am. What you wanna know about them? You just ax me and I'll tell you."

"I am told there is a plethora of unsurpassed beauty in the range."

"Huh?"

"Lots of pretty sights."

"Oh. Why didn't you say so in the first place? Damn shore is that."

"My cousin came through here several years ago, on his way to California. Maurice DeBeers. Perhaps you've heard of him?"

"Cain't say as I have, pardner."

"He stopped by a quaint little place for a moment or two. In the Sangre de Cristos. He didn't stay, but he said it was . . . well, odd."

"A town?"

"That's what he said."

"There ain't no towns in there."

"Oh, but I beg to differ. My cousin wrote me about it. Oh . . . pity! What was the name? Dead something-or-the-other."

The man looked at him, an odd shift to his eyes. "Dead River?"

"Yes! That's it! Thank you!"

Drunk as he was, the man was quick in snaking out a pistol. He eased back the hammer and pointed the muzzle at Smoke's belly.

5

Smoke dropped his sketch pad and threw his hands into the air. He started running around and around in a little circle. "Oh, my heavens!" he screamed, putting as much fright in his voice as he could. Then he started making little whimpering sounds.

The outlaw—and Smoke was now sure that he was—smiled and lowered his gun, easing down the hammer. "All right, all right! Calm down 'fore you have a heart attack, pilgrim. Hell, I ain't gonna shoot you."

Smoke kept his hands high in the air and forced his knees to shake. He felt like a total fool but knew his life depended on his making the act real. And so far, it was working.

"Take all my possessions! Take all my meager earnings! But please don't shoot me, mister. Please. I simply abhor guns and violence."

The outlaw blinked. "You does what to 'em?"

"I hate them!"

"Why didn't you just say that? Well, hell, relax. Don't pee your fancy britches, sissy-boy. I ain't gonna shoot you. I just had to check you out, that's all."

"I'm terribly sorry, but I don't understand. May I please lower my hands?"

"Yeah, yeah. Don't start beggin'. You really is who you say you is, ain't you?" His brow furrowed in whiskey-soaked rumination. "Come to think of it, just who in the hell is you, anyways?"

"I am an artist."

"Not that! What's your name, sissy-britches?" He lifted the jug and took a long, deep pull, then opened his throat to swallow.

"Shirley DeBeers," Smoke said.

The outlaw spat out the rotgut and coughed for several minutes. He pounded his chest and lifted red-rimmed eyes, disbelieving eyes to Smoke.

"Shirley! That there ain't no real man's name!"

Smoke managed to look offended. What he really wanted to do was take the jerk's guns away from him and shove both of them down his throat. Or into another part of the outlaw's anatomy.

"I will have you know, sir, that Shirley is really a very distinguished name."

"I'll take your word for that. Get to sketching, Shirley."

"Oh, I simply couldn't!" Smoke fanned his face with both hands. "I feel flushed. I'm so distraught!"

"Shore named you right," the outlaw muttered. "All right, Shirley. If you ain't gonna draw my pitcher, sit down and lets us palaver."

Smoke sat down. "I've never played palaver; you'll have to teach me."

The outlaw put his forehead into a hand and muttered under his breath for a moment. "It means we'll talk, Shirley."

"Very well. What do you wish to talk about?"

"You. I can't figure you. You big as a house and strong as a mule. But if you're a pansy, you keep your hands to yourself, you understand that?"

"Unwashed boorish types have never appealed to me," Smoke said stiffly.

"Whatever that means," the gunhawk said. "My name's Cahoon."

"Pleased, I'm sure."

"What's your interest in Dead River, Shirley?"

"I really have no interest there, as I told you, other than to sketch the scenery, which I was told was simply breathtakingly lovely."

Cahoon stared at him. "You got to be tellin' the truth. You the goofiest-lookin' and the silliest-talkin' person I ever did see. What I can't figure out is how you got this far west without somebody pluggin' you full of holes."

"Why should they do that? I hold no malice toward anyone who treats me with any respect at all."

"You been lucky, boy, I shore tell you that. You been lucky. Now then, you over the vapors yet?"

"I am calmed somewhat, yes."

"Git to sketchin', Shirley."

When Smoke tossed off his blankets the next morning, the outlaw, Cahoon, was gone. Smoke had pretended sleep during the night as the outlaw had swiftly gone through his pack, finding nothing that seemed to interest him. Cahoon had searched one side of the pack carefully, then only glanced at the other side, which held supplies. Had he searched a bit closer and longer, he would have found Smoke's twin Colts and the shotgun.

Smoke felt he had passed inspection. At least for this time. But he was going to have to come up with some plan for stashing his weapons close to Dead River.

And so far, he hadn't worked that out.

Cahoon had left the coffee pot on the blackened stones around the fire and Smoke poured a cup. He was careful in his movements, not knowing how far Cahoon might have gone; he might well be laying out a few hundred yards, watching to see what Smoke did next.

Smoke cut strips of bacon from the slab and peeled

and cut up a large potato, dropping the slices into the bacon grease as it fried. He cut off several slices of bread from the thick loaf and then settled down to eat.

He cut his eyes to a large stone and saw his sketch pad, a double eagle on the top page, shining in the rays of the early morning sun.

Cahoon had printed him a note: YOU DO FARLY GOOD DRAWINS. I PASS THE WORD THAT YOU OK. MAYBE SEE YOU IN DEAD RIVER. KEEP THIS NOTE TO HEP YOU GIT IN. CAHOON.

Smoke smiled. Yes, he thought, he had indeed passed the first hurdle.

Smoke drifted south, taking his time and riding easy. He had stopped at a general store and bought a bonnet for Drifter and the packhorse. The packhorse didn't seem to mind. Drifter didn't like it worth a damn. The big yellow-eyed devil horse finally accepted the bonnet, but only after biting Smoke twice and kicking him once. Hard.

Smoke's beard was now fully grown out, carefully trimmed into a fuller Vandyke but not as pointed. The beard had completely altered his appearance. And the news was spreading throughout the region about the goofy-talking and sissy-acting fellow who rode a horse with a bonnet and drew pictures. The rider, not the horse. The word was, so Smoke had overheard, that Shirley DeBeers was sorta silly, but harmless. And done right good drawin's, too.

And Cahoon, so Smoke had learned by listening and mostly keeping his mouth shut, was an outlaw of the worst kind. He fronted a gang that would do anything, including murder for hire and kidnapping—mostly women, to sell to whoremongers.

And they lived in Dead River, paying a man called Rex Davidson for security and sanctuary. And he learned that a man named Danvers was the Sheriff of Dead River. Smoke had heard of Danvers, but their trails had never crossed. The title of Sheriff was a figurehead title, for outside of Dead River he had no authority and would have been arrested on the spot.

Or shot.

And if Smoke had his way, it was going to be the latter.

Smoke and Drifter went from town to town, community to community, always drifting south toward the southernmost bend of the Purgatoire.

Smoke continued to play his part as the city fop, getting it down so well it now was second nature for him to act the fool.

At a general store not far from Quarreling Creek—so named because a band of Cheyenne had quarreled violently over the election of a new chief—Smoke picked up a few dollars by sketching a man and his wife and child, also picking up yet more information about Dead River and its outlaw inhabitants.

"Outlaws hit the stage outside Walensburg last week," he heard the rancher say to the clerk. "Beat it back past Old Tom's place and then cut up into the Sangre de Cristos."

The clerk looked up. There was no malice in his voice when he said, "And the posse stopped right there, hey?"

"Shore did. I reckon it's gonna take the Army to clean out that den of outlaws at Dead River. The law just don't wanna head up in there. Not that I blame them a bit for that," he was quick to add.

"Nobody wants to die," the clerk said, in a matter of agreeing.

"I have heard so much about this Dead River place," Smoke said, handing the finished sketch to the woman, who looked at it and smiled.

"You do very nice work, young man," she complimented him

"Thank you. And I have also heard that around Dead

River is some of the most beautiful scenery to be found anywhere."

The rancher put a couple of dollars into Smoke's hand and said, "You stay out of that place, mister. It just ain't no place for any decent person. And you seem to be a nice sort of person."

"Surely they wouldn't harm an unarmed man?" Smoke asked, holding on to his act. He managed to look offended at the thought. "I am an artist, not a trouble-maker."

The clerk and the rancher exchanged knowing glances and smiles, the clerk saying, "Mister, them are bad apples in that place. They'd as soon shoot you as look at you. And that's just if you're lucky. I'd tell you more, but not in front of the woman and child."

"Mabel" the rancher spoke to his wife. "You take Jenny and wait outside on the boardwalk. We got some man-talking to do." He glanced at Smoke. "Well . . . some talk-ing to do, at least."

Smoke contained his smile. He could just imagine Sally's reaction if he were to tell her to leave the room so the men could talk. A lady through and through, she would have nevertheless told Smoke where to put his suggestion.

Sideways.

The woman and child waiting on the boardwalk of the store, under the awning, the rancher looked at Smoke and shook his head in disbelief. Smoke was wearing a ruffle-front shirt, pink in color, tight-fitting lavender britches—he had paid a rancher's wife to make him sev-eral pairs in various colors—tucked into the tops of his lace-up hiking boots, tinted eyeglasses, and that silly cap on his head.

Foppish was not the word.

"Mr. DeBeers," the rancher said, "Dead River is the dumping grounds for all the scum and trash and bad hombres in the West. Some of the best and the bravest lawmen anywhere won't go in there, no matter how big the posse. And for good reason. The town of Dead River sits in a valley between two of the biggest mountains in the range. Only one way in and one way out."

The clerk said, "And the east pass—the only way in— is always guarded. Three men with rifles and plenty of ammunition could stand off any army forever."

Smoke knew that one-way-in and one-way-out business was nonsense. If he could find some Indians, he'd discover a dozen ways in and out. When he got close to the range of mountains, he'd seek out some band and talk with them.

The rancher said, "There've been reports of them outlaws gettin' all drunked up and draggin' people to death just for the fun of doin' it, up and down the main street. Some men from the Pinkerton agency, I think it was, got in there a couple of years ago, disguised as outlaws. When it was discovered what they really was, the outlaws stripped 'em nekkid and nailed 'em up on crosses, left the men there to die, and they died hard."

"Sometimes," the clerk added, "they'll hang people up on meathooks and leave them to die slow. Takes 'em days. And it just ain't fittin' to speak aloud what they do to women they kidnap and haul in there. Makes me sick to just think about it."

"Barbaric!" Smoke said.

"So you just stay out of that place, mister," the rancher said.

"But Mr. Cahoon said I would be welcome," Smoke dropped that in.

"You know Cahoon?" The clerk was bug-eyed.

"I sketched him once."

"You must have done it right. Cause if you hadn't, Cahoon would have sure killed you. He's one of the worst. Likes to torture people—especially Indians and women; he ain't got no use for neither of them."

"Well, why doesn't someone do something about it?"

Smoke demanded. "They sound like perfectly horrid people to me."

"It'd take the Army to get them out," the rancher explained. "At least five hundred men—maybe more than that; probably more than that. But here's the rub, mister: No one has ever come out of there to file no complaints. When a prisoner goes in there, he or she is dead. And dead people don't file no legal complaints. So look, buddy . . . eh, fellow, whatever, the day'll come when the Army goes in. But that day ain't here yet. So you best keep your butt outta there."

Smoke drifted on, and his reputation as a good artist went before him. He cut east, until he found a town with a telegraph office and sent a wire to Boston. He and Sally had worked out a code. He was S.B. and she was S.J. He waited in the town for a night and a day before receiving a reply.

Sally was fine. The doctors had removed the lead from her and her doctor in Boston did not think an operation would be necessary for child-birthing.

Smoke drifted on, crossing the Timpas and then following the Purgatoire down to Slim's General Store. A little settlement had been built around the old trading post, but it was fast dying, with only a few ramshackle buildings remaining. Smoke stabled his horses and stepped into the old store.

An old man sat on a stool behind the article-littered counter. He lifted his eyes as Smoke walked in.

"I ain't real sure just perxactly what you might be, son," the old man said, taking in Smoke's wild get-up. "But if you got any fresh news worth talkin' 'bout, you shore welcome, whether you buy anything or not."

Smoke looked around him. The store was empty of customers. Silent, except for what must have been years of memories, crouching in every corner. "Your name Slim?"

"Has been for nigh on seventy years. Kinda late to be changin' it now. What can I do you out of, stranger?"

Smoke bought some supplies, chatting with Slim while he shopped. He then sat down at the offer of a cup of coffee.

"I am an artist," he announced. "I have traveled all the way from New York City, wandering the West, recreating famous gunfights on paper. For posterity. I intend to become quite famous through my sketchings."

Slim looked at the outfit that Smoke had selected for that morning. It was all the old man could do to keep a straight face. Purple britches and flame-red silk shirt and colored glasses.

"Is that right?" Slim asked.

"It certainly is. And I would just imagine that you are a veritable well of knowledge concerning famous gunfighters and mountain men, are you not?"

Slim nodded his head. "I ain't real sure what it is you just said, partner. Are you askin' me if I knowed any gunfighters or mountain men?"

"That is quite correct, Mr. Slim."

"And your name be? . . ."

"Shirley DeBeers."

"Lord have mercy. Well, Shirley, yeah, I've seen my share of gunfights. I personal planted six or eight right back yonder." He pointed. "What is it you want to know about, pilgrim?"

Smoke got the impression that he wasn't fooling this old man, not one little bit. And he was curious as to the why of that.

"I have come from New York," he said. "In search of any information about the most famous mountain man of all time. And I was told in Denver that you, and you alone, could give me some information about him. Can you?"

Slim looked at Smoke, then his eyes began to twinkle. "Boy, I come out here in '35, and I knowed 'em all. Little Kit Carson—you know he wasn't much over five feet tall—Fremont, Smith, Big Jim, Caleb Greenwood, John Jacobs; hell, son, you just name some and I bet I knew 'em and traded with 'em."

"But from what I have learned, you did not name the most famous of them all!"

Slim smiled. "Yeah, that's right. I sure didn't—Mr. Smoke Jensen."

6

Over a lunch of beef and beans and canned peaches, Smoke and Slim sat and talked.

"How'd you know me, Slim? I've never laid eyes on you in my life."

"Just a guess. I'd heard people describe you 'fore. And I knowed what went on up on the Sugarloaf, with them gunnies and your wife; I figured you'd be comin' on along 'fore long. But what give you away was your accent. I've had folks from New York town in here 'fore. Your accent is all wrong."

"Then I guess I'd better start working on that, right?"

"Wrong. What you'd better do is shift locations. You ain't never gonna talk like them folks. You best say you're from Pennsylvannie. From a little farm outside Pittsburgh on the river. That ought to do it. If you're just bounded and swore to go off and get shot full of holes."

Smoke let that last bit slide. "How's Preacher?" He dropped that in without warning.

Slim studied him for a moment, then nodded his head. "Gettin' on in years. But he's all right, last I heard. He's livin' with some half-breed kids of hisn up in Wyoming. Up close to the Montanie line."

"It's good to know that he's still alive. But I can't figure why he won't come live with me and Sally up on the Sugarloaf."

"That ain't his way, Smoke, and you know it. He's happy, boy. That's what's important. Why, hell, Smoke!" he grinned, exposing nearly toothless gums. "They's a whole passel of them ol' boys up yonder. They's Phew, Lobo, Audie, Nighthawk, Dupre, Greybull—two/three more. Couple of 'em has died since they hepped you out three/four years back."

Smoke remembered them all and smiled with that re-membrance.

"Yeah," Slim said. "I'm thinkin' hard on sellin' out and headin' up that way to join them. Gettin' on in years myself. I'd like to have me a woman to rub my back ever now and then. But," he sighed, "I prob'ly won't do that. Stay right here until I keel over daid. But Preacher and them? They happy, boy. They got their memories and they got each other. And when it's time for them to go, they'll turn their faces to the sky and sing their death songs. Don't worry none 'bout Preacher, Smoke. He raised you better than that."

"You're right, Slim." Smoke grinned. "As much as I'd like to see him, I'm glad he can't see me in this get-up today."

Slim laughed and slapped his knee. "He'd prob'ly laugh so hard he'd have a heart attack, for sure. I got to tell you, Smoke, you do look . . . well . . . odd!"

"But it's working."

"So far, I reckon it is. Let's talk about that. You got a plan, Smoke?"

"About getting into Dead River?" Slim nodded. "No. Not really. But for sure, I'm going in like this."

Smoke did not hesitate about talking about his plans to Slim. He could be trusted. Preacher had told him that.

"Might work," Slim said.

"The outlaws think they've got everybody convinced there is only one way in and one way out. I don't be-lieve that."

"That's a pile of buffalo chips! You get on with the Utes, don't you?"

"Stayed with them many times."

"White Wolf and a bunch of his people is camped over just west of Cordova Pass. The word is, from old-timers that I talked to, White Wolf's braves make a game out of slippin' in and out of Dead River. White Wolf ain't got no use for none of them people in there. They been hard on Injuns. You talk to White Wolf. He's an old friend and enemy of Preacher."

Smoke knew what he meant. You might spend a summer with the Indians and the winter fighting them. That's just the way it was. Nearly anyone could ride into an Indian camp and eat and spend the night and not be bothered. 'Course they might kill you when you tried to leave. But at least you'd die after a good night's sleep and a full stomach.

Indians were notional folks.

"I did meet and sketch and convince some outlaw name of Cahoon." He showed Slim the note.

The old man whistled. "He's a bad one; 'bout half crazy. Hates Injuns and women; ain't got but one use for a woman and you know what that is. Then he tortures them to death. How'd you meet him?"

Smoke told him, leaving nothing out. Slim laughed and wiped his eyes.

"Well, you can bet that Cahoon has told his buddies 'bout you plannin' on comin' in. And you can bet somebody is right now checkin' on your back trail. And they'll be here 'fore long. So you best draw me two or three of them pitchers of yourn and I'll stick 'em up on the wall."

Smoke spent several days at Slim's, relaxing and learning all that the old man knew about Dead River, Rex Davidson, and the man who called himself Dagget.

And Slim knew plenty.

They were the scum of the earth, Slim said, reinforcing what Smoke had already guessed. There was nothing they would not do for money, or had not already done. Every man in Dead River had at least one murder warrant out on his head.

That was going to make Smoke's job a lot easier.

"Smoke, if you do get inside that outlaw stronghold," Slim warned him, "don't you for one second ever drop that act of yourn. 'Cause ifn you do, sure as hell, someone'll pick up on it and you'll be a long time dyin'.

"Now, listen to me, boy: Don't trust nobody in there. Not one solitary soul. You cain't afford to do that.

"Now personal, Smoke, I think you're a damn fool for tryin' this. But I can see Preacher's invisible hand writ all over you. He'd do the same thing." He eyeballed Smoke's foppish get-up and grinned. "Well, he'd go in there; let's put it that way! I ain't gonna try to turn you around. You a growed-up man."

"But they have people being held as slaves in there, or so I'm told."

"Yeah, that's right. But some of them would just as soon turn you in as look at you, for favor's sake. You know what I mean?"

Smoke knew. It sickened him, but he knew. "How many you figure are in there, Slim? Or do you have any way of knowing that?"

"Ain't no way of really tellin' 'til you git in there," Slim said. "Them outlaws come and go so much. Might be as many as three hundred. Might be as low as fifty. But that's just the real bad ones, Smoke. That ain't countin' the shop owners and clerks and whores and sich. Like the minister."

"Minister! Wait a minute. We'll get back to him. What about the clerks and shop owners and those types of people?"

"What about them? Oh, I get you. Don't concern yourself with them. They're just as bad, in their own way, as them that ride out, robbin' and killin'. The clerks and shopkeepers are all on the run for crimes they done. There ain't no decent people in that town. Let me tell you something, boy: When a baby is borned to them shady gals in there, they either kill it outright or tote it into the closest town and toss it in the street."

Smoke grimaced in disgust. "I can't understand why this town hasn't attracted more attention."

"It has, boy! But lak I done tole you, can't no legal thing be done 'cause no decent person that goes in there ever comes out. Now, I hear tell there's a federal marshal over to Trinidad that might be convinced to git a posse together if somebody would go in and clear a path for them. His name's Wilde."

Smoke made a mental note of that. "Tell me about this so-called minister in Dead River."

"Name is Tustin. And he's a real college-educated minister, too. Got him a church and all that goes with it."

"But you said there wasn't any decent people in the town!"

"There ain't, boy. Tustin is on the run jist lak all the rest. Killed his wife and kids back east somewheres. He's also a horse thief, a bank robber, and a whoremonger. But he still claims to be a Christian. Damndest thing I ever did hear of."

"And he has a church and preaches?"

"Damn shore does. And don't go to sleep durin' his sermons, neither. If you do, he'll shoot you!"

Smoke leaned back in his chair and stared at Slim. "You're really serious!"

"You bet your boots I am. You git in that place, Smoke, and you're gonna see sights like the which you ain't never seen."

"And you've never been in there?"

"Hell, no!"

Smoke rose from his chair to walk around the table a

few times, stretching his legs. "It's time to put an end to Dead River."

"Way past time, boy."

"You think my wife was attacked just because of a twenty-year-old hate this Davidson has for Preacher?"

"I'd bet on it. Davidson lay right over there in that corner," he pointed, "and swore he'd get Preacher and anyone else who was a friend of hisn. That's why them outlaws is so hard on Injuns. 'Specially the Utes. Preacher was adopted into the Ute tribe, you know."

Smoke nodded. "Yeah. So was I."

"All the more reason for him to hate you. Law and order is closin' in on the West, Smoke. And," he sighed, "I reckon, for the most part, that's a good thing. Them lak that scum that's over to Dead River don't have that many more places to run to . . . and it's time to wipe that rattler's nest out. Sam Bass was killed 'bout two years ago. Billy the Kid's 'bout run out his string, so I hear. John Wesley Hardin is in jail down in Texas. The law is hot on the trail of the James gang. Bill Longley was hanged a couple of years back. The list is just gettin' longer and longer of so-called bad men that finally got they due. You know what I mean, Smoke?"

"Yes. And I can add some to the list you just named. You heard about Clay Allison?"

"Different stories about how he died. You know the truth of it?"

"Louis Longmont told me that Clay got drunk and fell out of his wagon back in '77. A wheel ran over his head and killed him."

Slim laughed and refilled their coffee cups. "I hear Curly Bill is goin' 'round talkin' bad about the Earp boys. He don't close that mouth, he's gonna join that list, too, and you can believe that."

Smoke sipped his coffee. "Three hundred bad ones," he said softly. "Looks like I just may have bitten off more than I can chew up and spit out."

"That's one of the few things you've said about this adventure of yourn that makes any sense, boy."

Smoke smiled at the old man. "But don't mean I'm gonna give it up, Slim."

"I's afeared you'd say that. Boy, I don't lak that grin on your face. Now, what the hell have you got up that sleeve of yourn?"

"Where is the nearest wire office, Slim?"

"Trinidad. It's a real big city. Near'bouts three thousand people in there. All jammed up lak apples in a crate. Gives me the willies."

"That U.S. Marshal might be in town."

"Could be. I know he comes and goes out of there a whole lot. What's on your mind, boy?"

Smoke just grinned at him. "Can you get a message to Preacher?"

"Shore. Good God, boy! You ain't figurin' on dealing Preacher in on this, are you?"

"Oh, no. Just tell him I'm all right and I'm glad to hear that he's doing okay."

"I'll do it. You keep in touch, boy."

Smoke rose to leave. "See you around, Slim."

"Luck to you, boy."

After the U.S. Marshal got over his initial shock of seeing the red and lavender-clad Shirley DeBeers introduce himself, he looked at the young man as if he had taken leave of his senses.

He finally said, "Have you got a death wish, boy? Or are you as goofy as you look?"

"My name is not really Shirley DeBeers, Marshal."

"That's a relief. I think. What is your handle—Sue?"

"Smoke Jensen."

The U.S. Marshal fell out of his chair.

7

"The reason I wanted us to talk out here," Marshal Jim Wilde said, standing with Smoke in the livery stable, "is 'cause I don't trust nobody when it comes to that lousy damn bunch of crud over at Dead River."

Smoke nodded his agreement. "You don't suspect the sheriff of this county of being in cahoots with them, do you?"

"Oh, no. Not at all. He's a good man. We've been working together, trying to come up with a plan to clean out that mess for months. It's just that you never really know who might be listening. Are you really Smoke Jensen?" He looked at Smoke's outfit and shuddered.

Smoke assured him that he was, despite the way he was dressed.

"And you want to be a U.S. Marshal?"

"Yes. To protect myself legally."

"That's good thinkin'. But this plan of yours ain't too bright, the way I see it. Let me get this straight. You're goin' to act as point man for a posse to clean up Dead River?"

"That is my intention. At my signal, the posse will come in."

"Uh-huh."

"You, of course, will lead the posse."

"Uh-huh." The marshal's expression was hound-dog mournful. "I was just afraid you was gonna say something 'bout like that."

U.S. Marshal Wilde checked his dodgers to see if there were any wanted flyers out on Smoke. There were not. Then he sent some wires out to get approval on Smoke's federal commission. Smoke lounged around the town, waiting for the marshal's reply wires.

Trinidad was built at the foot of Raton Pass, on a foothill chain of the Culebra Range. The streets of the town twisted and turned deviously, giving it a curiously foreign look. The Purgatoire River separated the residential area from the business district.

Trinidad was known as a tough place, full of rowdies, and due to its relative closeness to Dead River, Smoke kept a close eye on his back trail.

On his third day in town, sensing someone was following him, he picked up his pursuers. They were three rough-looking men. Inwardly, he sighed, wanting nothing so much as to shed his role as Shirley DeBeers, foppish artist, and strap on his guns.

But he knew he had to endure what he'd started for a while longer.

He had deliberately avoided any contact with any lawmen, especially Jim Wilde. He had spent his time sketching various buildings of the town and some of the more colorfully dressed Mexicans.

But the three hard-looking gunhawks who were always following him began to get on his nerves. He decided to bring it to a head, but to do it in such a way as to reinforce his sissy, foppish act.

With his sketch pad in hand, Smoke turned to face the three men, who were standing across a plaza from him. He began sketching them.

And he could tell very quickly that his actions were not being received good-naturedly. One of the men made that perfectly clear in a hurry.

The man, wearing his guns low and tied down, walked across the plaza and jerked the sketch pad out of Smoke's hands, throwing it to the street.

"Jist what in the hell do you think you're doin', boy?"

Smoke put a frightened look on his face. "I was sketching you and your friends. I didn't think you would mind. I'm sorry if I offended you."

Smoke was conscious of the sheriff of the county and of Jim Wilde watching from across the plaza, standing under the awning of a cantina.

The outlaw—Smoke assumed he was an outlaw—pointed to the sketch pad on the ground and grinned at Smoke. "Well, you shored did o-fend me, sissy-pants. Now pick that there pitcher book up offen the ground and gimme that drawin' you just done of us."

Smoke drew himself up. "I most certainly will do no such thing . . . you ruffian."

The man slapped him.

It was all Smoke could do to contain his wild urge to tear the man's head off and hand it to him.

Smoke fought back his urge and put a hand to his reddened cheek. "You struck me!" he cried. "How dare you strike me, you—you animal!"

The man laughed as his friends walked across the plaza to join him. "What you got here, Jake?" one of them asked. "Looks to me like you done treed a girl dressed up in britches."

"I don't know what the hell it is, Red. But he shore talks funny."

"Le's see if he'll fight, Shorty," Jake said.

The three of them began pushing Smoke back and forth between them, roughing him up but doing no real physical damage; just bruising his dignity some. A crowd had gathered around, most of the men drinking, and they were getting a big laugh out of the sissy being shoved back and forth.

"Now, you all stop this immediately!" Smoke protested, putting a high note of fear into his voice. "I want you to stop this now . . . you hooligans!"

"Oh, my!" the outlaw called Red said, prancing around, one hand on his hip. "We hooligans, boys!"

Shorty reached out and, with a hard jerk, sent Smoke's trousers down around his ankles. Red shoved Smoke, who hit the ground hard and stayed there.

"I guess Cahoon was right, Shorty," Red said. "He ain't got a bit of sand in him." Then he turned and gave Smoke a vicious kick in the side, bringing a grunt of pain from him.

Forcing himself to do it, Smoke rolled himself up in a ball and hid his face in his hands. "Oh, don't hurt me anymore. I can't stand pain."

The crowd laughed. "Hell, Jake," Red said. "We wastin' our time. Sissy-boy ain't gonna fight."

Not yet, Smoke thought.

"Le's make him eat some horseshit!" Shorty suggested.

"Naw, I got a better idee. 'Sides, there ain't fresh piles around. We done found out what we come to find out: He's yeller."

"That shore was funny the time we made that drummer eat a pile of it, though!"

Shorty then unbuttoned his pants and urinated on Smoke's legs. The crowd fell silent; only Jake and Red thought that was funny.

Smoke's thoughts were savage.

The three hardcases then left and the crowd broke up, with no one offering to help Smoke to his feet.

Smoke hauled up his britches, found his sketch pad, and brushed himself off, then, with as much dignity as he could muster, he walked across the plaza. As he passed by the sheriff and the U.S. Marshal, Smoke whispered, "I think I'm in."

He stopped to brush dirt off his shirt.

"Picked a hard way to do it," the sheriff said. "I'd a never been able to lay there and take that."

"Let's just say it's going to be interesting when I come out of this costume," Smoke whispered.

"We'll be there," Wilde whispered. "There is a packet for you in your room. Good luck."

The packet contained a U.S. Marshal's badge, his written federal commission, and a letter.

On the night of Smoke's seventh day in Trinidad, two hours after dusk, unless Smoke could get a signal out to tell them differently, the U.S. Marshals, and various sheriffs and deputies from a four-county area, beefed up with volunteers from throughout the area, would strike at Dead River. They would begin getting into position just at dusk. It would be up to Smoke to take out the guards at the pass. Do it any way he saw fit.

And to Smoke's surprise, the marshal had a plant inside Dead River, one that had been there for about six months.

A woman. Hope Farris.

It would be up to Smoke to contact her. The marshal had no way of knowing whether she was dead or alive; they had received no word from her in several months.

They feared she might have been taken prisoner. Or worse.

Good luck.

"Yeah," Smoke muttered, burning the note in the cut-off tin can that served as an ashtray. "I am sure going to need that."

He pulled out of Trinidad before dawn the next morning, after resupplying the night before. He headed west, avoiding the tiny settlements for the most part. But a threatening storm forced him to pull up and seek shelter in the small town of Stonewall.

And Stonewall was not a place Smoke cared to linger long. The town and the area around it was torn in a bitter war between cattlemen and the lumber industry on one side and the homesteaders on the other side, over grazing and lumber interests.

Smoke knew he would have to be very careful which saloon he entered that night, if any, for each side would have their own watering holes in this war. Finally he said to hell with having a drink and sketching anyone. He got him a room and stayed put.

He pulled out before daylight, before the café even opened, and made his way to Lost Lake. There he caught some trout for breakfast, broiling them. Looking around, far above the timberline, Smoke could see the tough and hardy alpine vegetation: kinnikinnick, creeping phlox, and stunted grass.

After a tasty breakfast and several cups of strong hot coffee, Smoke bathed quickly—very quickly—in the cold blue waters of Lost Lake.

Shivering, even though it was the middle of summer, he dressed and had one more cup of coffee. He was still a good three days hard ride from the outlaw town, but he wanted to sort out all his options, and considering where he was going, they were damn few.

And once again, the question entered his mind: Was he being a fool for doing this?

And the answer was still the same: yes, he was. But if he didn't settle it now, it would just happen again and again, and with a child coming, Smoke did not want to run the risk of losing another family.

So it had to be settled now; there was no question about that.

And, if the truth be told—and Smoke was a truthful man—there was yet another reason for his challenging the seemingly impossible. He wanted to do it.

* * *

He followed an old Indian trail that cut between Cordova Pass to the east and Cucharas Pass to the west. He found what he hoped was White Wolf's Ute camp and approached it cautiously. They seemed curious about this big strong-looking white man who dressed and behaved like a fool.

Smoke asked them if they would like to share his food in return for his spending the night. They agreed, and over the meal, he explained where he was going but not why.

The Ute chief, White Wolf, told him he was a silly man to even consider going into the outlaw town.

And Smoke could not understand the twinkle in the chief's eyes.

He asked them what they could tell him about the town called Dead River.

Smoke was stunned when White Wolf said, "What does the adopted son of my brother Preacher wish to know about that evil place?"

When he again found his voice, Smoke said, "For one thing, how did you know I was not who I claimed to be, White Wolf?"

Dark eyes twinkling, the chief of the small band of Utes said, "Many things give you away, to us, but probably not to the white man. The white man looks at many things but sees little. Your hands are as hard as stones. And while you draw well, that is not what you are."

Smoke did not offer to sketch the Indians, for many tribes believe it is not good medicine to have their pictures taken or their images recreated.

Smoke told them of his true plans.

They told him he was a very brave man, like Preacher.

"Few are as brave and noble as Preacher."

"That is true," White Wolf agreed. "And is my brother well?"

"Slim Dugas just told me that Preacher and a few other mountain men are well and living up near Montana."

"Thank you. That is also truth. Preacher is living with the children of my sister, Woman-Who-Speaks-With-Soft-Voice. Because she married Preacher, the children are recognized as pure and are not called Apples."

Red on the outside, white on the inside. Indians practiced their own form of discrimination.

"It is good to know they are true Human Beings."

"As you are, Smoke Jensen."

"Thank you. I have a joke for you."

"A good laugh makes a good meal even better."

"I was told that most people believe there is but one way in and one way out of Dead River."

The Indians, including the squaws, all found that richly amusing. After the laughter, White Wolf said, "There are many ways in and out of that evil place. There are ways in and out that the white man have not now and never will know, not in our lifetime."

Smoke agreed and finished his meal, belching loudly and patting his full belly. The Indians all belched loudly and smiled, the sign of a good meal. And the squaws were very pleased.

Smoke passed around several tobacco sacks, and the Indians packed small clay pipes and smoked in contentment. Smoke rolled a cigarette and joined them.

"You still have not told me how you knew I was the adopted son of Preacher, White Wolf."

The chief thought on that for a moment. "If I told you that, Smoke, then you would know as much as I know, and I think that would not be a good thing for one as young as you."

"It is true that too much knowledge, learned before one is ready, is not a good thing."

White Wolf smiled and agreed.

Smoke waited. The chief would get to the matter of Dead River when he was damn good and ready.

White Wolf smoked his pipe down to coals and carefully tapped out the ashes, then handed the pipe to his woman. "It has been a fine game for us to slip up on the outlaw town and watch them. All without their knowing, of course," he added proudly.

"Of course," Smoke agreed. "Anyone who does not know the Ute is as brave as the bear, cunning as the wolf, and sharp-eyed as the eagle is ignorant."

The braves all nodded their heads in agreement. This white man was no fool. But they all wished he would do something about his manner of dress.

"A plan has come to me, White Wolf. But it is a very dangerous plan, if you and your braves agree to it."

"I am listening, Smoke."

"I met with a man in Trinidad. I believe he can be trusted. He is a government man. His name is Jim Wilde."

"I know this man Wilde," White Wolf said. "He carries Indian blood in his veins. Co-manche from Texas place. He is to be trusted."

"I think so, too. Could you get a message to him?"

"Does the wind sigh?"

Smoke smiled. Getting his sketch pad, he sketched the campfire scene, leaving the faces of the Utes blank but drawing himself whole. On the bottom of the sketch, he wrote a note to Wilde.

"If you agree to my plan, have this delivered to Wilde, White Wolf."

"If we agree, it will be done. What is this thing that you have planned?"

"Times have not been good for you and your people."

"They have been both good and bad."

"Winter is not that far away."

"It is closer tonight than it was last night, but not as close as it will be in the morning."

"There are guns and much food and clothing and warm blankets in the outlaw town."

"But not as many as in the town of Trinidad."

"But the people of Trinidad are better than the people in Dead River."

"A matter of opinion. But I see your point. I think that I also see what you have in mind."

"If you agree, some of your people will surely die, White Wolf."

"Far better to die fighting like a man than to grovel and beg for scraps of food from a nonperson."

Only the Indians felt they were real people. Most whites had no soul. That is the best way they could find to explain it.

"I know some of how you feel. I do not think you want the buildings of the town."

White Wolf made an obscene gesture. "I spit on the buildings of the outlaw town."

"When the battle is over, you may do with them as you see fit."

"Wait by the fire," Smoke was told. "I will talk this over with my people."

Smoke sat alone for more than an hour. Then White Wolf returned with his braves and they took their places.

"We have agreed to your plan, Smoke."

They shook hands solemnly.

"Now it depends on the government man, Jim Wilde."

"I will send a brave to see him at first light. Once he has agreed, then we will make our final plans."

"Agreed."

They once more stuffed their pipes and smoked, with no one talking.

White Wolf finally said, "There is a young squaw, Rising Star. She does not have a man. She is very hard to please. I have thought of beating her for her stubbornness. Do you want her to share your robes this night?"

"I am honored, White Wolf, but I have a woman and I am faithful to her only."

"That is good. You are an honorable man."

"I'll pull out at first light. I'll be camped at the head of Sangre de Cristo creek, waiting to hear from you."

White Wolf smiled. "It will be interesting to see if the white men at the outlaw town die well."

"I think they will not."

"I think you are right," White Wolf agreed.

8

Smoke angled down the slopes and onto the flats, then cut northwest, reaching his campsite by late afternoon. He made his camp and waited.

And waited.

It was three full days before a brave from White Wolf's band made an appearance.

He handed Smoke a note, on U.S. Marshal's stationery. Jim Wilde had agreed to the plan and complimented Smoke on enlisting the Utes.

He told the brave what the scratchings on the paper meant.

"Yes," the brave said. "The Co-manche lawman told me the same thing. All the rest of your plan is to remain the same. Now I must return and tell him when you plan to enter the outlaw town."

Smoke had calculated the distance; about a day and a half of riding over rough country. "Tell Wilde I will enter the town day after tomorrow, at late afternoon. Do you know a place near the town where you could hide some guns for me?"

The brave thought for a moment, and then smiled. "Yes. Behind the saloon with an ugly picture of a bucket on the front of it. The bucket is filled with what I think is supposed to be blood."

"The bloody bucket?" Smoke guessed.

"Yes! Behind the little building where the men go to relieve themselves there is a rotting pile of lumber. I will put them under the lumber."

"Good. What is your name?"

"Lone Eagle."

"Be very careful, Lone Eagle. If you're caught, you will die hard."

The Ute nodded. "I know. The Co-manche lawman says that two hours after dark, on the seventh day of your entering the outlaw place, we shall attack. And White Wolf says that you need not worry about the guards. Concern yourself only with the town. It might take the main body of men an hour to fight their way to your location."

"Tell White Wolf thank you. It will be a good coup for you all."

The brave nodded. "The outlaws in the town have not been kind to my people. They have seized and raped some of our young girls. Twice, they have taken young braves and have been cruel beyond any reason. One they cut off his feet and left him to die, slowly. They called it sport. On the night of the seventh day, we shall have our sport with the outlaws."

Smoke nodded, repeating what he had said to the chief, "They shall not die well, I am thinking."

The Ute smiled, very unpleasantly. "We are counting on that."

Then he was gone, back to his pony hidden in the deep timber.

The outlaws of Dead River had had their way for years, torturing, raping, robbing and looting, enslaving the innocent and ravaging the unsuspecting for several hundred miles, or more, in any direction. Now they were about to have the tables turned on them. And Smoke knew the more fortunate ones would die under his guns or the guns of the posse.

It would be very unpleasant for those taken alive by the Utes.

For the Utes knew ways of torture that would make the Spanish Inquisitioners green with envy. Dying well was an honor for the Indians, and if a prisoner died well, enduring hours and sometimes days of torture, they would sing songs about that person for years, praising his courage. That person who died well would not be forgotten.

The Indians had nothing but contempt for a man who begged and cried and died in dishonor.

They had their own code of honor and justice, and the whites had theirs. There were those who said the red man was nothing but a barbaric savage. But he had learned to scalp from the European white man. The Indians were different; but they would not steal from within their own tribe. The white man could not say that. War was a game to the Indians—until the white man entered the picture and began killing in war. For the Indians, for centuries, counting coup by striking with a club or stick was preferable to killing.

So it is very questionable who was the savage and who was the instructor in barbarism.

Smoke had lived with the Indians and, in many ways, preferred their lifestyle to the white ways. Smoke, as did nearly anyone who learned their ways, found the Indians to be honest, extremely gentle, and patient with their children or any captured children, of any color. The Indians lived a hard life in a hard land, so it was foolish to think their ways to be barbaric. They were, Smoke felt, just different.

Smoke felt nothing for the outlaws in the town. He knew the truth in the statement that whatever befalls a man, that man usually brought the bad onto himself. Every person comes, eventually, to a fork in the road.

The direction that person takes comes from within, not from without, as many uninformed choose to believe when slavering pity on some criminal. The outlaw trail is one that a person can leave at any time; they are not chained to it.

An outlaw is, in many ways, like an ignorant person, who knows he is ignorant and is proud of it, enjoying wallowing in blind unenlightenment, knowing that he is is wrong but too lazy to climb the ladder of knowledge. Too inwardly slovenly to make the effort of reaching out and working to better himself.

To hell with them!

"It's a different world for me," Sally said, sitting in her parents' fine home in New Hampshire. "And a world, I fear, that I no longer belong in."

"What an odd thing to say, dear," her mother said, looking up from her knitting.

Sally smiled, glancing at her. She shifted her gaze to her brothers and sisters and father, all of them seated in the elegant sitting room of the mansion. And all of them, including her father, not quite sure they believed anything Sally had told them about her husband, this seemingly wild man called Smoke.

"Odd, Mother? Oh, I think not. It's just what a person wants; what that person becomes accustomed to, that's all. You would consider our life hard; we just consider it living free."

"Dear," her father spoke, "I am sure you find it quite amusing to entertain us with your wild stories about the West and this . . . person you married. But really now, Sally, don't you think it a bit much to ask us to believe all these wild yarns?"

"Wild yarns, Father?"

Jordan, Sally's oldest brother, and a bore and stuffed shirt if there ever were one, took some snuff gentlemanly and said, "All that dribble-drabble about the wild West is just a bunch of flapdoodle as far as I'm concerned."

Sally laughed at him. She had not, as yet, shown her family the many newspapers she had brought back to New Hampshire with her; but that time was not far off.

"Oh, Jordan! You'll never change. And don't ever come west to where I live. You wouldn't last fifteen minutes before someone would slap you flat on your backside."

Jordan scowled at her but kept his mouth closed.

For a change.

Sally said, "You're all so safe and secure and comfortable here in Keene, in all your nice homes. If you had trouble, you'd shout for a constable to handle it. There must be more than a dozen police officers here in this town alone. Where I live in Colorado, there aren't a dozen deputies within a two-thousand-square-mile radius."

"I will accept that, Sally," her father, John, said. "I have heard the horror stories about law and order in the West. But what amazes me is how you handle the business of law and order."

"We handle it, Father, usually ourselves."

"I don't understand, Sally," her sister Penny said. "Do you mean that where you live women are allowed to sit on juries?"

Sally laughed merrily. "No, you silly goose!" She kidded her sister. "Most of the time there isn't even any trial."

Her mother, Abigal, put her knitting aside and looked at her daughter. "Dear, now I'm confused. All civilized places have due process. Don't you have due process where you live?"

"We damn sure do!" Sally shocked them all into silence with the cuss word.

Her mother began fanning herself vigorously. Her sisters

momentarily swooned. Her brothers looked shocked, as did her brothers-in-law, Chris and Robert. Her father frowned.

"Whatever in the world do you mean, dear?" Abigal asked.

"Most of the time it's from a Henry," Sally attempted to explain, but only added to the confusion.

"Ah-hah!" John exclaimed. "Now we're getting to it. This Henry person—he's a judge, I gather."

"No, a Henry is a rifle. Why, last year, when those TF riders roped and dragged Pearlie and then attacked the house, I knocked two of them out of the saddle from the front window of the house."

"You struck two men?" Betsy asked, shocked. "While they were stealing your pearls?"

Sally sighed. "Pearlie is our foreman at the ranch. Some TF riders slung a loop on him and tried to drag him to death. And, hell, no, I didn't strike them. When they attacked the house, I shot them!"

"Good Lord," Chris blurted. "Where was your husband while this tragedy was unfolding?"

Sally thought about that. "Well, I think he was in Fontana, in the middle of a gunfight. I believe that's where he was."

They all looked at her as if she had suddenly grown horns and a tail.

Smiling, Sally reached into her bag and brought out a newspaper, a copy of Haywood's paper, which detailed the incident at the Sugarloaf, where she and young Bob Colby had fought off the attackers.

"Incredible!" her father muttered. "My own daughter in a gunfight. And at the trial, dear, you were, of course, acquitted, were you not?"

Sally laughed and shook her head. They still did not understand. "Father, there was no trial."

"An inquest, then?" John asked hopefully, leaning forward in his chair.

Sally shook her head. "No, we just hauled off the bodies and buried them on the range."

John blinked. He was speechless. And for an attorney, as he and his sons were, that was tantamount to a phenomenon.

"Hauled off the . . . bodies," Robert spoke slowly. "How utterly grotesque."

"What would you have us do?" Sally asked him. "Leave them in the front yard? They would have attracted coyotes and wolves and buzzards. And smelled bad, too." Might as well have a little fun with them, she concluded.

Robert turned an ill-looking shade of green.

And Sally was shocked to find herself thinking: what a lily-livered bunch of pansies.

Abigal covered her mouth with a handkerchief.

"Did the sheriff even come out to the house?" Walter inquired.

"No. If he had, we'd have shot him. At that time, he was in Tilden Franklin's pocket."

John sighed with a parent's patience.

Penny was reading another copy of Haywood's newspaper. "My God!" she suddenly shrieked in horror. "According to this account, there were ten people shot down in the streets of Fontana in one week."

"Yes, Sister. Fontana was rather a rowdy place until Smoke and the gunfighters cleaned it up. You've heard of Louis Longmont, Father?"

He nodded numbly, not trusting his voice to speak. He wondered if, twenty-odd years ago, the doctor had handed him the wrong baby. Sally had always been a bit . . . well, free-spirited.

"Louis was there, his hands full of Colts."

Sally's nieces and nephews were standing in the archway, listening, their mouths open in fascination. This was stuff you only read about in the dime novels. But Aunt Sally—and this was the first time most of them could remember seeing her—had actually lived it! This was exciting stuff.

Sally grinned, knowing she had a captive audience. "There was Charlie Starr, Luke Nations, Dan Greentree, Leo Wood, Cary Webb, Pistol LeRoux, Bill Foley, Sunset Hatfield, Toot Tooner, Sutter Cordova, Red Shingletown, Bill Flagler, Ol' Buttermilk, Jay Church, The Apache Kid, Silver Jim, Dad Weaver, Hardrock, Linch— they all stayed at our ranch, the Sugarloaf. They were really very nice gentlemen. Courtly in manner."

"But those men you just named!" Jordan said, his voice filled with shock and indignation. "I've read about them all. They're killers!"

"No, Jordan," Sally tried to patiently explain, all the while knowing that he, and the rest of her family, would never truly understand. "They're gunfighters. Like my Smoke. A gunfighter. They have killed, yes; but always because they were pushed into it, or they killed for right and reason and law and order."

"Killed for right and reason," John muttered. His attorney's mind was having a most difficult time comprehending that last bit.

Abigal looked like she might, at any moment, fall over from a case of the vapors. "And . . . your husband, this Smoke person, he's killed men?"

"Oh, yes. About a hundred or so. That's not counting Indians on the warpath. But not very many of them. You see, Smoke was raised by the mountain man, Preacher. And we get along well with the Indians."

"Preacher," John murmured. "The most famous, or infamous, mountain man of the West."

"That's him!" Sally said cheerfully. "And," she pulled an old wanted poster out of her bag and passed it over to her father, "that's my Smoke. Handsome, isn't he?"

Under the drawing of Smoke's likeness, was the lettering:

WANTED
DEAD OR ALIVE
THE OUTLAW AND MURDERER
SMOKE JENSEN
$10,000.00 REWARD

"Ye, Gods!" her father yelled, "the man is wanted by the authorities!"

Sally laughed at his expression. "No, Father, That was a put-up job. Smoke is not wanted by the law. He never has been on the dodge."

"Thank God for small favors." John wiped his sweaty face with a handkerchief.

Walter said, "And your husband has killed a hundred men, you say?"

"Well, thereabouts, yes. But they were all fair fights."

The kids slipped away into the foyer and silently opened the front door, stepping out onto the large porch. Then they were racing away to tell all their friends that their uncle, Smoke Jensen, the most famous gunfighter in all the world, was coming to Keene for a visit.

Really!

Sally passed around the newspapers she had saved over the months, from both Fontana and Big Rock. The family read them, disbelief in their eyes.

"Monte Carson is your sheriff?" John questioned. "But I have seen legal papers that stated he was a notorious gunfighter."

"He was. But he wasn't an outlaw. And Johnny North is now a farmer/rancher and one of our neighbors and close friends."

They had all heard of Johnny North. He was almost as famous as Smoke Jensen.

"Louis Longmont is a man of great wealth," Jordan muttered, reading a paper. "His holdings are quite vast.

Newspaper, hotels, a casino in Europe, and a major stockholder in a railroad."

"He's also a famous gunfighter and gambler," Sally informed them all. "And a highly educated man and quite the gentleman."

Shaking his head, John laid the paper aside. "When is your husband coming out for a visit, Sally?"

"As soon as he finishes with his work."

"His work being with his guns." It was not put as a question.

"That is correct. Why do you ask, Father?"

"I'm just wondering if I should alert the governor so he can call out the militia!"

9

On the morning he set out for Dead River, Smoke dressed in his most outlandish clothing. He even found a long hawk feather and stuck that in his silly cap. He knew he would probably be searched once inside, or maybe outside the outlaw town, and what to do with his short-barreled .44 worried him. He finally decided to roll it up in some dirty longhandles and stick it in his dirty clothes bag, storing it in his pack. He was reasonably sure it would go undetected there. It was the best idea he could come up with.

He adjusted the bonnets on Drifter and his packhorse, with Drifter giving him a look that promised trouble if this crap went on much longer. Smoke swung into the saddle, pointing Drifter's nose north. A few more miles and he would cut west, into the Sangre de Cristo range and into the unknown.

About two hours later, he sensed unfriendly eyes watching him as he rode. He made no effort to search out his watchers, for a foppish gent from back east would not have developed that sixth sense. But White Wolf had told him that there were guards all along the trail, long before one ever reached the road that would take him to Dead River.

Smoke rode on, singing at the top of his lungs, stopping occasionally to admire the beautiful scenery and to make a quick sketch. To ooh and aah at some spectacular wonder of nature. He was just about oohed and aahed out, and Drifter looked like he was about ready to throw Smoke and stomp on him, when he came to a road. He had no idea what to expect, but this startled him with its openness.

A sign with an arrow pointing west, and under the arrow: DEAD RIVER. Under that: IF YOU DON'T HAVE BUSINESS IN DEAD RIVER, STAY OUT!

Smoke dismounted and looked around him. There was no sign of life. Raising his voice, he called, "I say! Yoo, hoo! Oh, yoo hoo! Is anyone there who might possibly assist me?"

Drifter swung his big bonneted head around and looked at Smoke through those cold yellow eyes. Eyes that seemed to say: Have you lost your damn mind!

"Just bear with me, boy," Smoke muttered. "It won't be long now. I promise you."

Drifter tried to step on his foot.

Smoke mounted up and rode on. He had huge mountains on either side of him. To the north, one reared up over fourteen thousand feet. To the south, the towering peaks rammed into the sky more than thirteen thousand feet, snow-capped year-round.

The road he was on twisted and climbed and narrowed dramatically.

The road was just wide enough for a wagon and maybe a horse to meet it, coming from the other direction. Another wagon, and somebody would have to give. But where? Then Smoke began to notice yellow flags every few hundred yards. A signal for wagon masters, he supposed, but whether they meant stop or go, he had no idea.

He had ridden a couple of miles, always west and always climbing, when a voice stopped him.

"Just hold it right there, fancy-pants. And keep your hands where I can see them. You get itchy, and I'll blow your butt out of the saddle."

Smoke reined up. Putting fear into his voice, he called, "I mean you no harm. I am Shirley DeBeers, the artist."

"What you gonna be is dead if you don't shut that god-damn mouth."

Smoke shut up.

The faint sounds of mumbling voices reached him, but he could not make out the words.

"All right, fancy-britches," the same voice called out. "Git off that horse and stand still."

Smoke dismounted and stood in the roadway. Then he heard the sounds of bootsteps all around him: There was Hart, the backshooter; Gridley, who murdered his best friend and partner, and then raped and killed the man's wife; Nappy, a killer for hire. There were others, but Smoke did not immediately recognize them, except for the fact that they were hardcases.

"Take off that coat," he was ordered, "and toss it to me. Frisk 'im, Nappy."

Smoke was searched and searched professionally; even his boots were removed and inspected. His pack ropes were untied and his belongings dumped in the middle of the road.

"Oh, I say now! Is that necessary, gentlemen?"

"Shut up!"

Smoke shut up.

His belongings were inspected, but his bag of dirty underwear was tossed to one side after only a glance. Luckily the bag landed on a pile of clean clothes and the weight of the .44 did not make a sound.

So far, so good, Smoke thought.

Finally, the search was over and the men stared at him for a moment. One said, "I reckon Cahoon and them others was right. He ain't got nothing but a pocket knife. And it's dull."

"Is my good friend Cahoon in town? Oh, I hope so. He's such a nice man."

"Shut your mouth!"

"What about it, Hart?"

"I reckon some of us can take silly-boy on in."

"I say," Smoke looked around him at the mess in the road. "Are some of you good fellows going to help me gather up and repack my possessions?"

The outlaws thought that was very funny. They told him in very blunt language that they were not. And to make their point better understood, one of them kicked Smoke in the butt. Smoke yelled and fell to the ground. Drifter swung his head and his yellow eyes were killer-cold. Smoke quickly crawled to the horse and grabbed a stirrup, using that to help pull himself up, all the while murmuring to Drifter, calming him.

Rubbing his butt, Smoke faced the outlaws. "You don't have to be so rough!"

"Oh, my goodness!" Gridley cried, prancing about to the laughter of the others. "We hurt his feelin's, boys. We got to stop bein' so rough!"

And right then and there, Smoke began to wonder if he would be able to last a week.

He calmed himself and waved his hand at his pile of belongings. "I say, as you men can see from your trashing of my possessions, I am low on supplies. Might I be allowed to continue on to Dead River and resupply?" He had left most of his supplies at the head of the Sangre de Cristo creek.

"Cahoon was supposed to have given you a note," a man said. A hardcase Smoke did not know. "Lemme see the note, sissy-pants."

"I am not a sissy! I am merely a man of great sensibilities."

"Gimme the goddamn note!"

The note was handed over and passed around.

"That's Cahoon's writin' all right. What about it, Hart, it's up to you?"

"Yeah, let him go on in. He can draw us all, and then we'll have some fun with him."

Smoke caught the wink.

"Yeah. That's a good idee. And I know just the person to give him to."

"Who?" Nappy asked.

"Brute!"

That drew quite a laugh and narrowed Smoke's eyes. He had heard of Brute Pitman. A huge man, three hundred pounds or more of savage perversions. He was wanted all over the eastern half of the nation for the most disgusting crimes against humanity. But oddly enough, Smoke had never heard of a warrant against him west of the Mississippi River. Bounty hunters had tried to take him, but Brute was hard to kill.

It was rumored that Brute had preyed on the miners in the gold camps for years, stashing away a fortune. And he had lived in Dead River for a long time, keeping mostly to himself.

But, Smoke thought, if these cruds think Brute is going to have his way with me, I'll start this dance with or without the rest of the band.

Smoke looked from outlaw to outlaw. "This Brute fellow sounds absolutely fascinating!"

The outlaws laughed.

"Oh, he is, sweetie," Hart told him. "You two gonna get along just fine, I'm thinkin'."

Uh-huh, Smoke thought. We'll get along until I stick a .44 down his throat and doctor his innards with lead.

"Oh, I'm so excited!" Smoke cried. "May we proceed onward?"

"Son of a bitch shore talks funny!" Gridley grumbled.

Smoke had killed his first man back on the plains, back when he was fifteen or sixteen; he wasn't quite sure. And he had killed many times since then. But as accustomed as he was to the sights of brutality, he had to struggle to keep his lunch down when they passed by a line of poles and platforms and wooden crosses sunk into the ground. Men and women in various stages of death and dying were nailed to the crosses; some were hung from chains by their ankles and left to rot; some had been horse-whipped until their flesh hung in strips, and they had been left to slowly die under the sun.

Smoke had never seen anything like it in his life. He did not have to force the gasp of horror that escaped from his lips. He turned his face away from the sight.

The outlaws thought it was funny, Hart saying, "That's what happens to people who try to cross the boss, Shirley. Or to people who come in here pretendin' to be something they ain't."

Gridley pointed to a woman, blackened in rotting death, hanging by chains. "She was a slave who tried to escape. Keep that in mind, sissy-boy."

"How hideous!" Smoke found his voice. "What kind of place is this?"

"He really don't know," Nappy said with a laugh. "The silly sod really don't know. Boy, are we gonna have some fun with this dude."

"I don't wish to stay here!" Smoke said, putting fear and panic in his voice. "This place is disgusting!" He tried to turn Drifter.

The outlaws escorting him boxed him in, none of them noticing the firm grip Smoke held on Drifter's reins, steadying the killer horse, preventing him from rearing up and crushing a skull or breaking a back with his steel-shod hooves.

The bonnet had worked in disguising Drifter for what he really was. Worked, so far.

"You just hold on, fancy-pants," Hart told him. "You wanted to come in here, remember?"

"But now I want to leave! I want to leave right this instant!"

"Sorry, sweets. You're here to stay."

* * *

Jim Wilde looked at the late afternoon sunlight out-side his office window. He sighed and returned to his chair. "He ought to be in there by now. God have mercy on his soul; I guess I got to say it."

"Yeah," Sheriff Mike Larsen agreed. "He's got more guts than I got, and I'll stand out in the middle of the damn street and admit that."

Jim sipped his coffee. "You told your boys not a word about this to anybody, right?"

"Damn well bet I did. I told 'em if they even thought hard on it, I'd catch the vibrations and lock 'em up."

And the marshal knew the sheriff would do just that. Mike ran a good solid straight office in a tough town.

"You got the final tally sheet of all that's goin' in, Mike?"

"Yep. The boys is gearin' up now. Quietly. Three sher-iffs, including myself. Twenty regular deputies. Twenty volunteers—all of them top riders and good with short gun and rifle—and you and ten marshals."

"The other marshals will be comin' in by train two at a time, staring tomorrow at noon. They're goin' to stay low. I just wish we had some way of findin' out how many hardcases we're gonna be up against."

"I think that's impossible, Jim. But if I had to make a guess on it . . . I'd say two hundred at the low end. We all gonna tie a white handkerchief on our left arm so's the Injuns won't mistake us for outlaws . . . that is still the plan, ain't it?"

"Yeah. Best I can come up with. I've already con-tracted for horses to be stashed along the way. So when we start ridin', we ain't gonna stop until it's over and done with. One way or the other," he added grimly.

Mike Larsen chose not to elaborate on that last bit. He would tell his wife only at the last moment, just before he stepped into the saddle. It was not a job he looked forward to doing, but he knew it was a job that had to be done. "Where you got the horses?"

"We'll switch to fresh at Spanish Peaks, then again at La Veta Pass. The last stop will be at Red Davis's place. I ain't gonna kill no good horse on that final run. Most of that is gonna be uphill."

Both men knew the fastest way to tire a horse was riding uphill.

"Red is givin' us the best of his line and wanted to go in with us. I thanked him but told him no. Told him he was doin' enough by loanin' us fresh horses."

"He's a tough old man. But you was right in refusin' him. You think he took offense?"

"No. He understands. White Wolf says he'll have at least thirty braves around that town when Jensen opens the dance. And Jensen is goin' to start the music as soon as White Wolf signals him that we've left the trail and entered the pass. White Wolf says the guards along the road will be taken care of. Them Utes ain't got no use for anybody in Dead River. And I told the boys that volunteered that the reward money will be split up amongst 'em."

"That's good, but I don't like Smoke openin' the show by hisself." Larsen frowned. "We're gonna be a good forty-five minutes of hard ridin' away from the town when he starts draggin' iron and lettin' it bang."

"I know it. But he was by hisself when he met them ol' boys up there on the Uncompahgre. And he killed ever' damn one of them."

"Yep," the sheriff agreed. "He damn shore did that, didn't he?"

"Unhand me, you beast!" Smoke shrilled his protest, struggling against the hands that held him in front of the saloon.

"My, my." A man stepped out of the Bloody Bucket

and onto the boardwalk. "What manner of creature do we have here, boys?"*

"It's that sissy-boy that draws them pitchers, Mr. Davidson. The one that Cahoon told us about."

"Where is my friend, Cahoon?" Smoke asked.

No one from the gathering crowd of thugs and hardcases replied.

"Well, well," Davidson said with a smile, his eyes taking in Smoke's outlandish dress. "So it is. And how do you like our little town, Mr. DeBeers?"

"I think it is appalling and disgusting and most offensive. And I do not like being manhandled by thugs. Tell your henchmen to unhand me this instant!"

Rex Davidson stepped from the boardwalk, faced Smoke and then backhanded him viciously across the face. He slapped him again. Smoke allowed his knees to buckle and he slumped to the ground, whimpering.

"You, silly boy," Rex said, standing over Smoke, "do not give me orders. Around here, I give the orders, and you obey. I say who lives and dies, and who comes and goes. Do you understand that, Shirley?"

"Yes, sir," Smoke gasped. The blows from Davidson had hurt. The man was no lightweight; he was big and muscled. Smoke decided to remain on the ground, on his hands and knees, until ordered to rise.

"Here, silly-boy," Rex continued, "I am king. You are nothing. However, if I decide you may live—and that is a big if—I might elect to make you my court jester. Would you like that, silly-boy?"

"Yes, sir." Until I shed this costume and put lead in you, you overbearing jackass!

King Rex kicked Smoke in the belly, knocking him flat on the ground. "When you address me, silly-boy, you will address me as Your Majesty. Now, say it, you foppish-looking fool!"

"Yes, Your Majesty." and Smoke knew it was going to

take a miracle for him to last out the entire seven days. Maybe two or three miracles.

"That's better, Jester. Some of you men get this fool on his feet and drag him inside the saloon. I wish to talk with him about doing my portrait."

Smoke started to tell him that he didn't do portraits, then decided it would be best if he'd just keep his mouth shut for the moment. He let the hardcases drag him to his feet and shove him up the steps, onto the boardwalk, and through the batwings. And it was all done with a lot of unnecessary roughness and very crude language.

What the hell did you expect, Jensen? Smoke silently questioned. *A tea party?*

The saloon—and from what Smoke had been able to glean, the only one in town—was a huge affair, capable of seating several hundred people. There was a large stage on one end of the building. The stage had red velvet curtains. Smoke wondered who did the acting and singing.

He was shoved roughly into a chair and then, looking up, got his first good look at Rex Davidson.

The man was a handsome rascal, no doubt about that. And a big man, in his mid-forties, Smoke guessed, solid, with heavily muscled arms and shoulders, thick wrists. Big hands. His eyes were cruel but not tinged with any sign of madness that Smoke could readily detect.

Rex leaned against the polished bar and smiled at Smoke; but the smile did not reach the man's eyes. "Talk to me, Jester."

"About what, Your Majesty?" Smoke promptly responded as instructed.

"Good, good!" Rex shouted to the hardcases gathered in the saloon. "You all see how quickly he learns? I think this one will do just fine. Oh, my, yes. Where are you from, Jester?"

"I am originally from Pennsylvania, Your Majesty."

"What city?"

"I am not from a city, Your Majesty."

"Oh? You certainly don't speak like a hick."

"Thank you, Your Majesty." You royal pain in the ass! "I was born on a small farm. Both my mother and father were highly educated people. They taught us at home." And I'm going to teach you a thing or two, King Jackass! "There were no schools nearby."

"Thank you, Jester. And where did you learn to draw, Jester?"

"I suppose I was born with the talent, Your Majesty." Just like I was born good with a gun, which you shall certainly get the chance to see . . . briefly. "My brother, Maurice, has the ability to write quite eloquently."

"Ah, yes, Maurice. Did you tell Cahoon that this Maurice person had stopped by here?"

"That is what he wrote and told me. But I have no way of knowing if he did stop or not. Maurice, ah, tends to story a bit."

"I see. In other words, he's nothing more than a goddamned liar?"

"Ah, yes, Your Majesty."

"Where is he now, Jester?"

"I have no idea, Your Majesty."

"I see. Does he look like you, Jester?"

"No, Your Majesty. Maurice was adopted, you see. While my hair is—"

Rex waved him silent as a man carrying a tray of drinks stumbled and went crashing to the floor. The glasses shattered and the smell of raw whiskey and beer filled the huge room.

"Incompetent fool!" Rex yelled at the fallen man.

"I'm sorry, sir. It was an accident."

"Your services will no longer be needed here, idiot."

The man tried to crawl to his feet just as Rex pulled out a .44. "I cannot tolerate clumsiness." He eased back the hammer and shot the man in the chest, knocking him back to the floor. The man began screaming in pain. Rex calmly shot him in the head. The screaming stopped.

Smoke watched it all, then remembered to put a shocked look on his face. Just in time, for Rex had cut his eyes and was watching Smoke carefully.

"Oh, my goodness!" Smoke gasped, putting a hand over his mouth. "That poor fellow."

"Drag him out of here and sprinkle some sawdust over the blood spots," Rex ordered. He punched out the empty brass in the cylinder and replaced the spent cartridges, then cut his eyes to Smoke. "Life is the cheapest commodity on the market around here, Jester. Bear that in mind at all times. Now then, how long were you planning on staying in my town?"

"My original plans were to spend about a week, sketching the scenery, which I was told was lovely. Then I was going to resupply and move on."

"A week, hey?"

"Yes, Your Majesty."

"Give me all your money."

"Sir?"

King Rex slapped Smoke out of the chair. And as he hit the floor, Smoke was really beginning to question his own sanity for getting himself into this snakepit. And wondering if he were going to get out of it alive.

Smoke was jerked up from the floor and slammed into his chair. The side of his face ached and he tasted blood in his mouth. And if Rex, king of Dead River, could just read Smoke's thoughts . . .

"Never, never question me, Jester," Rex told him. "You will obey instantly, or you will die. Very slowly and very painfully. Do you understand me, Jester?"

"Yes, Your Majesty. Just don't hurt me. I can't stand pain. It makes me ill."

"Stop your goddamned babblings, you fool. Give me your money!"

Smoke dug in his trousers and handed the man his slim roll of greenbacks.

Rex counted the money. "Sixty dollars. I charge ten dollars a day to stay here, Jester, unless you work for me, which you don't. What are you going to do at the end of six days, Jester?"

A woman began screaming from one of the rooms upstairs. Then the sounds of a whip striking flesh overrode the screaming. A man's ugly laughter followed the sounds of the lashing.

"A slave being punished, Jester," Rex told him. "We have many slaves in this town. Some live a long, long time. Others last only a few weeks. How long do you think you would last, Jester?"

"I don't know, Your Majesty."

"An honest answer. Now answer my original question, Jester."

"Well, I suppose after my six days are up, I'll just leave, sir." *After I kill you, Davidson.*

From the depths of the crowd, a man laughed, and it was not a very nice laugh. Smoke looked around him; all the hardcases were grinning at him.

"So you think you'll leave, hey, Jester?" Davidson smiled at him.

"Yes, sir. I hope to do that."

"Well, we'll see. If you behave yourself, I'll let you leave."

Sure you will, Smoke thought. *Right. And Drifter is going to suddenly start reciting poetry at any moment.*

Davidson shook the greenbacks at Smoke. "This money only allows you to stay in this protected town. You pay for your own food and lodgings. You may leave now, Jester."

Smoke stood up.

"Welcome to Dead River, Mr. DeBeers," Rex said with a smile.

Smoke began walking toward the batwings, half

expecting to get a bullet in his back. But it was a pleasant surprise when none came. He pushed open the batwings and stepped out onto the boardwalk. He mounted up, packhorse rope in his hand, and swung Drifter's bonneted head toward the far end of town, away from the sights and sounds and smells of the dead and slowly dying men and women at the other end of the town. He got the impression that hell must be very much like what he had witnessed coming in.

One thing for sure, he knew he would never forget that sight as long as he lived. He didn't have to sketch it to remember it; it was burned into his brain.

He wondered what had finally happened to that slave woman he had heard being beaten back at the Bloody Bucket. He thought he knew.

How in the name of God could a place like this have existed for so long, without somebody escaping and telling the horrors that were going on?

He had no answers for that question either.

But he knew that this place must be destroyed. And he also knew that when Marshal Jim Wilde and Sheriff Larsen and the posse members saw this chamber of horrors, there would never be any due process of law. No courts with judge and jury would decide the fate of the outlaws of Dead River. It would be decided on the seventh night, with gunsmoke and lead.

If the posse could help it, no outlaw would leave this valley alive.

Smoke pushed those thoughts out of his mind and concentrated on his own predicament: He did not have a cent to his name and had very few supplies left. Maybe enough to last a couple of days, if he was careful.

Smoke Jensen, the most famous and feared gunfighter in all the West, didn't know what in the hell he was going to do.

10

"So that's it." Sally's father's voice was filled with ill-disguised disgust. "What a wretched excuse for a human being."

Abigal's face mirrored her shock and horror.

Sally sat with her mother and father in the book-lined study of the mansion. Her father's room, which few of them had dared enter when they were children. But Sally had never been afraid of doing so. She used to love to sit in her father's chair and look at all the books about law and justice.

The three of them were alone; her brothers and sisters had left for the evening. And the town was fairly buzzing about the news of the famous gunfighter who was soon to be arriving.

"Why didn't you tell us when it happened, dear?" her mother asked.

"Because he told me he would kill you both. Then, after he left town, after killing that man, I just did my best to put the incident out of my mind, as much as possible. As the years went by, the memory became dimmer and dimmer. But there is no doubt in my mind that Dagget is the same man who tried to molest me years ago."

John rose from his chair to pace the room, his anger very evident. Wife and daughter watched him until he composed himself and returned to his leather chair. "The first thing in the morning, I shall inform the authorities as to this scoundrel's whereabouts. Then we shall begin extradition proceedings to have him returned to New Hampshire to stand trial."

Sally could not contain the smile that curved her lips. "Father, by the time you do all that legal mumbojumbo, the matter will most probably be taken care of—if it isn't already tended to. However, Smoke did suggest he cut off Dagget's head and bring it back here in a sack."

Abigal turned a bit green around the mouth and began fanning herself. "For heaven's sake!" she finally blurted. "He was joking, of course?"

"Oh, no, Mother. He wasn't joking a bit."

"Just exactly what is your husband doing while you are visiting here, Sally?" John asked.

Sally then explained to her parents what her husband was doing.

"Are you telling us, expecting us to believe," John said, astonishment in his voice, "that your husband . . . ah . . . Smoke, one man, is going to . . . ah . . . attack and destroy an entire town of thugs and hooligans and ne'er-do-wells—all by himself? Now, really, Sally!"

"Oh, he's found some help. And I think you will approve of his methods, Father, or what you think his methods will be—in your New England straight-by-the-book mind."

"You disapprove of law and order, Sally?"

"Of course not, Father. Your way works here; our way works for us in the West. This will not be the first time Smoke has taken on an entire town." Then she told them about the shoot-out at the silver camp and what had happened in Bury, Idaho.

Her parents sat in silence and stared at her.

"And you can believe what I say, the both of you. I was

in Bury. I saw it all. When Smoke gets his back up, you better get out of the way. 'Cause he's going to haul it out, cock it back, and let her bang."

"The finest schools in the country and Europe," John muttered. "And she hauls it out and lets her bang. Incredible."

Sally laughed openly at the expression on her father's face. "It's just a western expression, father."

"It's just that it is terribly difficult for us, here in the long-settled East, to fully understand the ways of the West, Sally," Abigal said. "But we don't doubt for a moment what you've told us. Sally, when Smoke comes out here for a visit, will he be armed?"

"If he's got his pants on."

John looked heavenward, shook his head, and sighed. "Yet another delightful colloquialism."

Sally reached into a pocket of her dress—she was getting too large to wear jeans, but she would have loved to do so, just to see the expression on her parents' faces—and took out a piece of paper. "This wire came this morning, while you both were out. It's from Smoke."

"Shall I contact the governor and have him call out the militia?" John asked his daughter, only half-joking. He wanted to meet his son-in-law, certainly; but he had absolutely no idea what to expect. And just the thought of an armed western gunfighter riding into the town made him slightly nauseous.

Sally laughed at him. "You're both thinking my husband to be some sort of savage. Well," she shrugged her shoulders, "when he has to be, he is, to your way of thinking. Yet, he is a fine artist, well-read, and highly intelligent. He knows the social graces; certainly knows what fork and spoon to use. But we don't go in for much of that where we live. In the West, eating is serious business, and not much chitchat goes on at the table. But I really think you'll like Smoke if you'll give him just half a chance."

Abigal reached over and patted Sally's hand. "I know we will, dear. And of course he'll be welcomed here. Now please tell us what is in the wire. I'm fairly bursting with excitement." She looked at her husband. "This is the most exhilarating thing that's happened in Keene in twenty years, John!"

"Not yet, dear," John said. "Smoke hasn't yet arrived in town, remember."

Sally laughed so hard she had to wipe her eyes with a handkerchief. She read from the wire. "Smoke has been appointed a deputy U.S. Marshal. This is from the marshal's office in Denver. He has entered the outlaw town in disguise. They'll wire me when the operation has been concluded."

"Well!" John said, obviously pleased. "I'm happy to hear that your husband has chosen the legal way, Sally. He'll properly arrest the criminals and bring them to trial the way it's supposed to be, according to the laws of this land."

Sally smiled. "Father, do you believe pigs can fly like birds?"

"What! Of course not."

"Father, the only law Smoke is going to hand out to those outlaws will be coming out of the muzzles of his .44s. And you can believe that."

"But he's an officer of the law!" the man protested. "More than that, he is operating under a federal badge. He must see to due process. That is his sworn duty!"

Sally's smile was grim. "Oh, he'll see that the outlaws get their due, Father. Trust me."

Smoke made his camp at the very edge of town, pitching his tent and unrolling his blankets. He gathered and stacked wood for a fire. Saving his meager supplies, he cut a pole and rigged it for fishing, walking to a little stream not far away. There he caught his supper, all the while letting his eyes stay busy, checking out the terrain. The stream had to come from somewhere; it didn't just come out of the ground here. For it was full of trout.

He had deliberately made his camp far enough away so he could not hear the terrible cries and the begging of those men and women at the far end of town, being tortured to death. He wished desperately to help, but he knew for the moment, he was powerless to do so.

Huge peaks rose stately and protectively all around the little valley that housed Dead River. Smoke wondered where and how it had gotten its name. At first glance, he could understand why a lot of people would believe the myth of one way in and one way out. But Smoke knew that was crap, and he felt that most of the outlaws knew it as well. But those who would try to seek escape, when the attack came, would be in for a very ugly surprise when they tried those secret trails. White Wolf and his braves would be in hiding, waiting for them.

As Smoke had ridden to his camp, he had seen the compound where some prisoners were being held; but mostly the town itself was a prison, and he had noticed many slaves had free access to the town.

They obviously had been convinced, probably very brutally, that there was no way out except for the road, so why lock them up? But they were probably locked up at night. The compound, then, must be for any newcomers to the town. Or perhaps those were people being punished for some infraction of the rules.

Or waiting to die.

He wondered if the marshal's plant, Hope Farris, was in the compound.

Or had she been discovered and killed?

He cleaned his fish and cooked his supper, all the while watching the comings and goings of the outlaws. So far, few had paid any attention to him.

Smoke judged the number of outlaws in the town at

right around two hundred, and that was not counting the shopkeepers and clerks and whores. Rex Davidson had himself a profitable operation going here, Smoke concluded, and he was sure King Rex got his slice of the pie from every store in town and from every whore who worked.

Not that there were that many stores; Smoke had counted six. But they were all huge stores. By far, the biggest place in town was the livery stable and barns, a half dozen of them, all connected by walkways. And during bad weather, many men, Smoke guessed, would live and sleep in those barns. He knew that this high up the winters would be brutal ones.

And so far, Smoke had not seen the man called Dagget. He felt sure he would recognize him from Sally's description. Already he had seen a dozen or more hardcases he had brushed trails with years back; but his disguise had worked. They had paid him no mind, other than a quick glance and equally quick dismissal as being nothing more than a fop and totally harmless.

He wondered if Lone Eagle had hidden his guns behind the privy yet, then decided he had not. Not enough time had gone by since Smoke had met with the brave at the head of the creek.

Smoke heard a harsh shriek of pain from a shack across the wide road. Then a man's voice begging somebody not to do something again. Wild cursing followed by more shrieks of pain.

The door to the cabin was flung open and Smoke watched as a naked man ran out into the road. He was screaming. Then the obscene bulk of Brute Pitman appeared in the door of the shack. He was shirtless, his galluses hanging down to his knees. Brute held a long-barreled pistol in his hand.

The face of the running man was a mask of terror and pain. His body bore the bruises and markings of the many beatings he had endured until he could no longer take any more of it. And because he was naked, Smoke knew that beatings were not the only thing the man had been forced to endure.

But the man's agony was about to end, Smoke noted, watching as Brute lifted the pistol and jacked the hammer back, shooting the man in the back. The naked man stumbled, screamed, and fell forward, sliding on his face in the dirt and the gravel. The bullet had gone clear through the man, tearing a hole in his chest as it exited. The man kicked once, and then was still.

"How shocking!" Smoke said.

Brute turned, looking at him. "You, come here!" he commanded.

"Not on your life, you obscene tub of lard!"

A dozen outlaws had stopped what they were doing and they were motioning for others to come join them; come listen and watch. For sure, they thought, the fop was about to get mauled.

Brute stepped away from his shack. "What'd you call me, sissy-boy?"

Smoke could see Rex Davidson and another man, dressed all in black from his boots to his hat, walking up the dirt street to join the crowd.

Dagget.

And he wore his guns as Smoke preferred to wear his: the left hand Colt high and butt-forward, using a cross draw.

It was going to be a very interesting match when it came, Smoke thought. For no man wore his guns like that and lived very long, unless he was very, very quick.

Smoke turned his attention back to Brute. The man had moved closer to him. And, Jesus God, was he big and ugly! He was so ugly he could make a buzzard puke.

"Is aid you were a fat tub of lard, blubber-butt!" Smoke shouted, his voice high-pitched.

"I'll tear your damn head off!" Brute shouted, and began lumbering toward Smoke.

"Only if you can catch me!" Smoke shouted. "Can't catch me, can't catch me!"

He began running around in circles, taunting the huge man.

The outlaws thought it funny, for few among them liked Brute and all could just barely tolerate his aberrant appetites. He lived in Dead River because there he could do as he pleased with slaves, and because he could afford the high rent, paying yearly in gold. He left the place only once a year, for one month to the day. Those who tried to follow him, to find and steal his cache of stolen gold, were never seen again.

Smoke knew that he could never hope to best Brute in any type of rough and tumble fight—not if he stayed within the limits of his foppish charade—for Brute was over three hundred pounds and about six and a half feet tall. But he was out of shape, with a huge pus-gut, and if Smoke could keep the ugly bastard running around after him for several minutes, then he might stand a chance of besting him and staying known as a sissy.

It was either that or getting killed by the huge man, and the odds of Smoke getting killed were strong enough without adding to it.

Smoke stopped and danced around, his fists held in the classic fighter's stance. He knew he looked like a fool in his fancy-colored britches and silk shirt and stupid cap with a feather stuck in it.

"I warn you!" Smoke yelled, his voice shrill. "I am an expert pugilist!"

"I'm gonna pugile you!" Brute panted, trying to grab Smoke.

"First you have to catch me!" Smoke taunted. "Can't catch me!"

The outlaws were all laughing and making bets as to how long Smoke would last when Brute got his hands on him, and some were making suggestions as to how much they would pay to see Brute do his other trick, with Smoke on the receiving end of it.

"No way, hombre!" Smoke muttered, darting around Brute. But this time he got a little too close, and Brute got a piece of Smoke's silk shirt and spun him around.

Jerking him closer, Brute grinned, exposing yellowed and rotted teeth. "Got ya!"

Smoke could smell the stink of Brute's unwashed body and the fetid animal smell of his breath.

Before Brute could better his hold on Smoke, Smoke balled his right hand into a hard fist and, with a wild yell, gave Brute five, right on his big bulbous nose.

Brute hollered and the blood dripped. Smoke tore free and once more began running around and around the man, teasing and taunting him. The crowd roared their approval, but the laughter ceased as Smoke lost his footing, slipping to the ground, and Brute was on him, his massive hands closing around Smoke's throat, clamping off his supply of air.

"I'll not kill you this way," Brute panted, slobber from his lips dripping onto Smoke's face. "I have other plans for you, pretty-boy."

Smoke twisted his head and bit Brute on the arm, bringing blood. With a roaring curse, Brute's hand left his throat and Smoke twisted from beneath him, rolling and coming to his feet. He looked wildly around him, spotting a broken two-by-four and grabbing it. The wood was old and somewhat rotten, but it would still make a dandy club.

Brute was shouting curses and advancing toward him.

Smoke tried the club, right on the side of Brute's head. The club shattered and the blood flew, but still the big man would not go down.

He shook his head and grinned at Smoke.

"All right, you nasty ne'er-do-well," Smoke trilled at him. "I hate violence, but you asked for this."

Then he hit Brute with everything he had, starting the

punch chest-high and connecting with Brute's jaw. This time when Brute hit the ground, he stayed there.

Smoke began shaking his right hand and moaning as if in pain, which he was not.

He heard Davidson say, "Doc, look at DeBeers's hand. See if it's broken. Sheriff Danvers? If DeBeers's hand is broken and he can't draw, shoot Brute."

"Yes, sir," the so-called sheriff said.

An old whiskey-breathed and unshaven man checked Smoke's hand and pronounced it unbroken.

Smoke turned to Rex Davidson. "I am sorry about this incident, sir. I came in peace. I will leave others alone if they do the same for me."

Davidson looked first at the unconscious Brute, then at Smoke. "You start drawing me first thing in the morning. Sheriff Danvers?"

"Yes, sir?"

"When Brute comes out of it, advise him I said to leave Mr. DeBeers alone. Tell him he may practice his sickening perversions on the slaves, but not on paying guests."

"Yes, sir."

He once more looked at Smoke. "Breakfast at my house. Eight o'clock in the morning. Be there."

"Yes, sir," Smoke replied, and did not add the "Majesty" bit.

"Does this place offend your delicate sensibilities, Mr. DeBeers?" Davidson asked.

"Since you inquired, yes, it does."

It was after breakfast, and Davidson was posing for the first of many drawings.

"Why, Mr. DeBeers?" For some reason, Davidson had dropped the "Jester" bit.

"Because of the barbarous way those unfortunate people at the edge of town are treated. That's the main reason."

"I see. Interesting. But in England, Mr. DeBeers, drawing and quartering people in public was only stopped a few years ago. And is not England supposed to be the bastion of civilized law and order . . . more or less?"

"Yes, sir, it is."

"Well, this is still a young country, so it's going to take us a while to catch up."

What an idiotic rationalization, Smoke thought. Louis Longmont would be appalled. "Yes, sir, I suppose you're right."

"Don't pander to me, Mr. DeBeers. You most certainly do not think I am right."

"But when I do speak my mind, I get slapped or struck down."

"Only in public, Mr. DeBeers. When we are alone, you may speak your mind."

"Thank you, sir. In that case, I find this entire community the most appalling nest of human filth I have ever had the misfortune to encounter!"

Davidson threw back his head and laughed. "Of course, you do! But after a time, one becomes accustomed to it. You'll see."

"I don't plan on staying that long, sir." Smoke looked at King Rex, checking for any signs of annoyance. He could see none.

Instead, the man only smiled. "Why would you want to leave here?"

Smoke stopped sketching for a moment, to see if the man was really serious. He was. "To continue on with my journey, sir. To visit and sketch the West."

"Ah! But you have some of the most beautiful scenery in the world right around you. Plus many of the most famous outlaws and gunfighters in the West. You could spend a lifetime here and not sketch it all, could you not?"

"That is true, but two of the people I want to meet and sketch are not here."

"Oh? And who might those be?"

"The mountain man, Preacher, and the gunfighter, Smoke Jensen."

The only sign of emotion from the man was a nervous tic under his right eye. "Then you should wait here, Mr. DeBeers, for I believe Jensen is on his way."

"Oh, really, sir! Then I certainly shall wait. Oh, I'm so excited."

"Control yourself, Shirley."

"Oh, yes, sir. Sorry. Sir?"

"Yes?"

"Getting back to this place . . . The west, from what I have been able to see, is changing almost daily. Settling. Surely this town is known for what it really is?"

Davidson met his eyes. "So?"

"Do you think this will go on forever and ever? As the town becomes known outside of this immediate area, the citizens will eventually grow weary of it and demand that the Army storm the place."

"Ummm. Yes, you're probably right. And I have given that much thought of late. But, young man,"—he smiled and held up a finger, breaking his pose—"this town has been here for twenty years and still going. How do you account for that?"

"Well, when you first came here, I suppose there were no others towns nearby. Now all that has changed. Civilization is all around you and closing in. That, sir, is why I wanted to come west now, before the wild West is finally tamed."

"Ummm. Well, you are a thinking man, Mr. DeBeers, and I like that. There is so little intellectual stimulation to be found around here." He abruptly stood up. "I am weary of posing." He walked around to look at the sketch. "Good. Very good. Excellent, as a matter of fact. I thought it would be. I have arranged for you to take your meals at the Bon Ton Café. I will want at least a hundred of your sketches of me. Some with an outside setting. When that is done, to my satisfaction, then you may leave. Good day, Mr. DeBeers."

Gathering up his pencils and sketch pads, Smoke left the house, which was situated on a flat that sat slightly above the town, allowing Rex a commanding view. As he walked back to his tent, Smoke pondered his situation. Surely, Rex Davidson was insane; but if he was, would that not make all the others in this place mad as well?

And Smoke did not believe that for a moment.

More than likely, Davidson and Dagget and all the others who voluntarily resided in Dead River were not insane. Perhaps they were just the personification of evil, and the place was a human snake pit.

He chose that explanation. Already, people who had committed the most terrible of crimes were saying they were not responsible for their actions because they had been crazy, at the time, before the time, whatever. And courts, mostly back east in the big cities, were accepting that more and more, allowing guilty people to be set free without punishment. Smoke did not doubt for one minute that there were people who were truly insane and could not help their actions.

But he also felt that those types were in the minority of cases; the rest were shamming. If a person were truly crazy, Smoke did not believe that malady could be turned off and on like a valve. If a person were truly insane, they would perform irrational acts on a steady basis, not just whenever the mood struck them.

He knew for an ironclad fact that many criminals were of a high intelligence, and that many were convincing actors and actresses. Certainly smart enough to fool this new thing he'd heard about called psychiatry. Smoke Jensen was a straight-ahead, right-was-right and wrong-was-wrong man, with damn little gray in between. You didn't lie, you didn't cheat, you didn't steal, and you treated your neighbor like you would want to be treated.

And if you didn't subscribe to that philosophy, you best get clear of men like Smoke Jensen.

As for the scum and filth and perverts in this town of Dead River, Smoke felt he had the cure for what ailed them.

The pills were made of lead.

And the doctor's name was Smoke Jensen.

11

For one hour each day, Smoke sketched Rex Davidson; the rest of the time was his to spend as he pleased.
He took his meals at the Bon Ton—the man who owned
the place was wanted for murder back in Illinois, having
killed several people by poisoning them—and spent the
rest of his time wandering the town, sketching this and
that and picking up quite a bit of money by drawing the
outlaws who came and went. He made friends with none
of them, having found no one whom he felt possessed
any qualities that he wished to share. Although he felt
sure there must be one or two in the town who could be
saved from a life of crime with just a little bit of help.

Smoke put that out of his mind and, for the most part,
kept it out. He wanted nothing on his conscience when
the lead started flying.

He was not physically bothered by any outlaw. But the
taunts and insults continued from many of the men and
from a lot of the women who chose to live in the town.
Smoke would smile and tip his cap at them, but if they
could have read his thoughts, they would have grabbed
the nearest horse and gotten the hell out of Dead River.

Brute saw Smoke several times a day but refused to

speak to him. He would only grin nastily and make the most obscene gestures.

Smoke saw the three who had shoved him around in Trinidad—Jake, Shorty, and Red—but they paid him no mind.

What did worry Smoke was that the town seemed to be filling up with outlaws. Many more were coming in, and damn few were leaving.

They were not all famous gunfighters and famous outlaws, of course. As a matter of fact, many were no more than two-bit punks who had gotten caught in the act of whatever crimes they were committing and, in a dark moment of fear and fury, had killed when surprised. But that did not make them any less guilty in Smoke's mind. And then as criminals are prone to do, they grabbed a horse or an empty boxcar and ran, eventually joining up with a gang.

It was the gang leaders and lone-wolf hired guns who worried Smoke the most. For here in Dead River were the worst of the lot of bad ones in a three state area.

LaHogue, called the Hog behind his back, and his gang of cutthroats lived in Dead River. Natick and his bunch were in town, as was the Studs Woodenhouse gang and Bill Wilson's bunch of crap. And just that morning, Paul Rycroft and Slim Bothwell and their men had ridden in.

The place was filling up with hardcases.

And to make matters worse, Smoke knew a lot of the men who were coming in. He had never ridden any hoot-owl trails with any of them, but their paths had crossed now and then. The West was a large place but relatively small in population, so people who roamed were apt to meet, now and then.

Cat Ventura and the Hog had both given Smoke some curious glances and not just one look but several, and that made Smoke uneasy. He wanted desperately to check to see if his guns were behind the privy. But he knew it would only bring unnecessary attention to himself, and that was something he could do without. He had stayed alive so far by playing the part of a foolish fop and by maintaining a very high visibility. And with only a few days to go, he did not want to break that routine. He spent the rest of the day sketching various outlaws—picking up about a hundred dollars doing so—and checking out the town of Dead River. But there was not that much more to be learned about the place. Since he was loosely watched every waking moment, Smoke had had very little opportunity to do much exploring.

He was sitting before his small fire that evening, enjoying a final cup of coffee before rolling up in his blankets, for the nights were very cool this high up in the mountains, when he heard spurs jingling, coming toward him. He waited, curious, for up to this point he had been left strictly alone.

"Hello, the fire!" the voice came out of the campfire-lit gloom.

"If you're friendly, come on in," Smoke called. "I will share my coffee with you."

"Nice of you." A young man, fresh-faced with youth, perhaps twenty years old at the most and wearing a grin, walked up and squatted down, pouring a tin cup full of dark, strong cowboy coffee. He glanced over the hat-sized fire at Smoke, his eyes twinkling with good humor.

He's out of place, Smoke accurately pegged the young cowboy. He's not an outlaw. There was just something about the young man; something clean and vital and open. That little intangible that set the innocent apart from the lawless.

"My first time to this place," the young man said. "It's quite a sight to see, ain't it?"

Smoke had noticed that the cowboy wore his six-gun low and tied down, and the gun seemed to be a living extension of the man.

He knows how to use it, Smoke thought. "It is all of that, young man, to be sure."

"Name's York."

"Shirley DeBeers."

York almost spilled his coffee down his shirtfront at that. He lifted his eyes. "You funnin' me?"

Smoke smiled at his expression. "Actually, no. It's a fine old family name. Is York your first or last name?" he inquired, knowing that it was not a question one asked in the West.

York looked at him closely. "You new out here, ain't you?"

"Why, yes, as a matter of fact, I am. How did you know that Mr. York?"

The cowboy's smile was quick. "Just a guess. And it's just York."

"Very well." Smoke noticed that the young man's eyes kept drifting to the pan of bacon and bread he had fixed for his supper. There were a few strips of bacon left, and about half a loaf of bread. "If you're hungry, please help yourself. I have eaten my fill and I hate to throw away good food."

"Thanks," York said quickly and with a grin. "That's right big of you. You don't never have to worry 'bout tossin' out no food when I'm around." He fixed a huge sandwich and then used another piece of bread to sop up the grease in the pan.

Smoke guessed he had not eaten in several days.

When York had finished and not a crumb was left, he settled back and poured another cup of coffee. Smoke tossed him a sack of tobacco and papers.

York caught the sack and rolled and lit. "Thanks. That was good grub. Hit the spot, let me tell you. Anything I can do for you, you just let me know. Most"—he cut his eyes suspiciously—"most of the hombres around here wouldn't give a man the time of day if they had a watch in every pocket. Sorry bastards."

"I agree with you. But you be careful where you say things like that, York."

York nodded his agreement. "Ain't that the truth. Say, you don't neither talk like nor look like a man that's on the dodge, DeBeers."

"On the dodge?" Smoke kept up his act. "Oh! Yes, I see what you mean now. Oh, no. I can assure you, I am not wanted by the authorities."

York studied him across the small fire, confusion on his young face. "Then . . . what in the hell are you doin' in a place like this?"

"Working. Sketching the West and some of its most infamous people. Mr. Davidson was kind enough to give me sanctuary and the run of the place."

"And you believed him?"

Smoke only smiled.

"Yeah. You might look sorta silly—and I don't mean no o-fence by that, it's just that you dress different—but I got a hunch you ain't dumb."

"Thank you." Smoke was not going to fall into any verbal traps, not knowing if York was a plant to sound him out.

The cowboy sipped his coffee and smoked for a moment. "You really come in here without havin' to, huh?"

"That is correct."

"Weird. But," he shrugged, "I reckon you have your reasons. Me, now, I didn't have no choice at all in the matter."

"We all have choices, young man. But sometimes they are disguised and hard to make."

"Whatever that means. Anyways, I'm on the hard dodge, I am."

He tried to sound proud about that statement, but to Smoke, it came across flat and with a definite note of sadness.

"I'm very sorry to hear that, York. Is it too personal to talk about?"

"Naw. I killed a man in Utah."

Smoke studied him. "You don't sound like a man who would cold-bloodedly kill another man."

"Huh? Oh, no. It wasn't nothin' like that. It was a stand-up-and-face-him-down fight. But the law didn't see it that-away. I guess near'bouts all these people in this lousy town would claim they was framed, but I really was." He poured another cup of coffee and settled back against a stump, apparently anxious to talk and have somebody hear him out. "You see, I bought a horse from this feller. It was a good horse for fifty dollars. Too good, as it turned out. I had me a bill of sale and all that. Then these folks come ridin' up to me about a week later and claimed I stole the horse. They had 'em a rope all ready to stretch my neck. I showed 'em my bill of sale and that backed 'em down some. But they was still gonna take the horse and leave me afoot in the Uintahs. Well, I told 'em that they wasn't gonna do no such a thing. I told 'em that if the horse was rightfully theirs, well, I was wrong and they was right. But let me get to a town 'fore they took the horse; don't leave me in the big middle of nowheres on foot."

He sighed and took a swallow of coffee. "They allowed as to how I could just by God walk out of there. I told them they'd better drag iron if that's what they had in mind, 'cause I damn sure wasn't gonna hoof it outta there.

"Well, they dragged iron, but I was quicker. I kilt one and put lead in the other. The third one, he turned yeller and run off.

"I got the hell outta there and drifted. Then I learned that I had a murder charge hangin' over my head. That third man who run off? He told a pack of lies about what really happened.

"Well, bounty hunters come up on me about two or three months later. I buried one of them and toted the other one into a little town to the doc's office. The marshal, he come up all blustered-up and I told him what happened and added that if he didn't like my version of it, he could just clear leather and we'd settle it that way."

He grinned boyishly. "The marshal didn't like it, and I'll admit I had my back up some. But he liked livin' moreun gunfightin'. So I drifted on and things just kept gettin' worser and worser. I couldn't get no job 'cause of them posters out on me. I heard about this place and sort of drifted in. I ain't no outlaw, but I don't know what else to do with all them charges hangin' over my head."

Smoke thought on it. He believed the young man; believed him to be leveling as to the facts of it all. "Might I make a suggestion?"

"You shore could. I'd rather live in hell with rattlesnakes than in heaven with this bunch around here."

Smoke couldn't help it. He laughed at the young man's expression. "York, why don't you just change your name and drift. And by the way, do you still have the horse in question?"

"Naw. I turned him loose and caught me up a wild horse and broke him. He's a good horse."

"Well then, York, drift. Change your name and drift. Chances are that you'll never be caught."

"I thought of that. But damn it, DeBeers, I ain't done nothin' wrong. At least, not yet. And York is my family name. By God, I'm gonna stick with it. I'm doin' some thinkin' 'bout linkin' up with Slim Bothwell's bunch. They asked me to. I guess I ain't got no choice. I don't wanna hurt nobody or steal nothin' from nobody. But, hell, I gotta eat!"

"York, you are not cut out for the outlaw life," Smoke told him.

"Don't I know it! Look, DeBeers, I listened to some of the men talk 'bout all they've done, in here and out there." He jerked his thumb. "Damn near made me puke." He sighed heavily. "I just don't know what to do."

Could this entire thing be a setup? Smoke wondered, and concluded that it certainly could be. But something about the young cowboy was awfully convincing. He decided to take a chance, but to do it without York knowing of it.

"Perhaps something will come up to change your mind, York."

The cowboy looked up across the fire, trust in his eyes. "What?"

"I really have no idea. But hope springs eternal, York. You must always keep that in mind. Where are you staying while you're here?"

"I ain't got no place. Give that Dagget feller my last fifty dollars. He told me that give me five days in here." He shook his head. "After that . . . I don't know."

"You're welcome to stay here. I don't have much, but you're welcome to share with me."

"That's mighty white of you, DeBeers. And I'll take you up on that." He grinned at Smoke. "There is them that say you're goofy. But I don't think so. I think you're just a pretty nice guy in a bad spot."

"Thank you, York. And have you ever thought that might fit you as well?"

The grin faded. "Yeah, I reckon it might. I ain't never done a dishonest thing in my life. Only difference is, you ain't got no warrants hangin' over your head. You can ride out of this hellhole anytime you take a notion. Me? I'm stuck, lookin' at the wrong side of society!"

The next morning Smoke left the still-sleeping York a full pot of coffee, then took his sketch pad and went walking, as was his custom every morning. As the saloon came into view, Smoke noticed a large crowd gathered out front, in the street. And it was far too early for that many drinkers to have gathered.

"Let's have some fun!" Smoke could hear the excited shout.

"Yeah. Let's skin the son of a bitch!"

"Naw. Let's give him to Brute."

"Brute don't want no dirty Injun."

"Not unless it's a young boy," someone shouted with hard laugh.

"Hold it down!" a man hollered. "Mr. Davidson's got a plan, and it's a good one."

Smoke stepped up to a man standing in the center of the street. "What on earth has happened here?"

The outlaw glanced at him. "The guards caught them an Injun about dawn. He was tryin' to slip out over the mountains. No one knows what he was doin' in town." The man shut up, appraising Smoke through cool eyes, aware that he might have said too much.

"He must have slipped in on the road," Smoke said quickly, noting the coolness in the man's eyes fading. "It would be impossible to come in through those terribly high mountains around the town."

The outlaw smiled. "Yeah. That's what he done, all right. And there ain't no tellin' how long he's been tryin' to get out, right?"

"Oh, absolutely. I think the savage should be hanged immediately." Smoke forced indignation into his voice.

The outlaw grinned. His teeth were blackened, rotted stubs. "You all right, Shirley. You're beginnin' to fit right in here. Yeah, the Injun's gonna die. But it's gonna be slow."

"Why?" Smoke asked innocently.

"Why, hell's fire, Shirley! So's we can all have some fun, that's why."

"Oh. Of course."

A man ran past Smoke and the outlaw, running in that

odd bowlegged manner of one who has spent all his life on a horse.

"What's happenin', Jeff?" the outlaw asked.

"Mr. Davidson tole me to get the kid, York. Says we gotta test him. You know why?"

"Yeah."

Neither man would elaborate.

Smoke felt he knew what the test was going to involve, and he also felt that York would not pass it. There was a sick feeling in the pit of his stomach. Smoke wandered on down to the large crowd gathered in front of the saloon and tried to blend in.

The crowd of hardcases and thugs and guns-for-hire ignored him, but Smoke was very conscious of Rex Davidson's eyes on him. He met the man's steady gaze and smiled at him.

Davidson waved the crowd silent. "I have decided on a better plan," he said as the crowd fell quiet. "Forget York; we know he's a wanted man. There are some of you who claim that our artist friend is not what he professes to be. Well, let's settle that issue right now. Bring that damned Indian out here."

Smoke felt sure it would be Lone Eagle, and it was. He was dragged out of the saloon and onto the boardwalk. He had been badly beaten, his nose and mouth dripping blood. But his face remained impassive and he deliberately did not look at Smoke.

"Drag that damned savage to the shooting post," Davidson ordered. He looked at Smoke and smiled, an evil curving of the lips. "And you, Mr. Artist, you come along, too."

"Do I have to? I hate violence. It makes me ill. I'd be upset for days."

"Yes, damn it, you have to. Now get moving."

Smoke allowed himself to be pushed and shoved along, not putting up any resistance. He wondered if any

Indians were watching from the cliffs that surrounded the outlaw town and concluded they probably were.

And he also had a pretty good hunch what the test was going to entail.

The crowd stopped in a large clearing. In the center of the clearing, a bullet-scarred and blood-stained post was set into the ground.

Lone Eagle turned to face the crowd, and when he spoke, his voice was strong. "I do not need to be tied like a coward. I face death with a strong heart, and I shall die well. I will show the white man how to die with honor. Which is something that few of you know anything about."

The crowd of hardcases booed him.

Lone Eagle spat at them in contempt.

He had not as yet looked at Smoke.

Smoke was shoved to the front of the crowd and a pistol placed into his hand.

"What am I supposed to do with this weapon, Mr. Davidson?"

"Kill the Indian," Rex told him.

"Oh, I say now!" Smoke protested shrilly. "I haven't fired a gun in years. I detest guns. I'm afraid of them. I won't be able to hit the savage."

Lone Eagle laughed at Smoke, looking at him. "The white man is a woman!" Lone Eagle shouted. And Smoke knew he was deliberately goading him. Lone Eagle knew he was going to die and preferred his death to be quick rather than slow torture, torture for the amusement of the white men gathered around. He might have chosen the slow way had he been captured by another tribe, for to die slowly and with much pain was an honor—if at the hands of other Indians. But not at the hands of the white men. "The silly-looking white man is a coward."

"You gonna take that from a damned Injun, Shirley?" a man shouted.

"What am I supposed to do?"

"Hell, sissy-boy. Kill the bastard!"

Smoke lifted the pistol and pretended to have trouble cocking it. He deliberately let it fire, the slug almost hitting an outlaw in the foot. Smoke shrieked as if in fright and the outlaw cussed him.

The others thought it wildly funny.

"Watch it there, Black!" an outlaw yelled. "He lift that muzzle up some you liable to be ridin' side-saddle!"

The man whose foot was just missed by the slug stepped back into the crowd and gave Smoke some dirty looks.

"Shoot the goddamn Indian, DeBeers!" Davidson ordered.

Smoke lifted the pistol and cocked it, taking careful aim and pulling the trigger. The slug missed Lone Eagle by several yards, digging up dirt. The outlaws hooted and laughed and began making bets as to how many rounds it would take for Smoke to hit his target.

"Try again, Shirley," Davidson told him, disgust in his voice.

"What a silly, silly man you are!" Lone Eagle shouted. "If you had two pistols and a rifle and shotgun beside you, you still would not be able to hit me. It is good they are out of your sight. You might hurt yourself, foolish man."

Lone Eagle was telling Smoke that his weapons had been hidden as planned.

"Shoot the damned Injun, Shirley!" Dagget hollered in Smoke's ear.

"All right! All right!" Smoke put a hurt expression on his face. "You don't have to be so ugly about it!"

Smoke fired again. The slug missed Lone Eagle by a good two feet.

"Jesus Christ, DeBeers!" Dagget said, scorn thick in his voice.

"The pistol was fully loaded, Shirley," Davidson told him. "You have four rounds left."

Lone Eagle turned his back to Smoke and hiked up his loincloth, exposing his bare buttocks; the height of insult to a man.

Facing the crowd, Lone Eagle shouted, "There are little girls in my village who are better shots than the white man. Your shots are nothing more than farts in the wind."

"If you don't kill him," Davidson warned, "you shall be the one to gouge out his eyes. And if you refuse, I'll personally kill you. After I let Brute have his way with you."

Smoke cocked the pistol.

Lone Eagle began chanting, and Smoke knew he was singing his death song.

He fired again. This time, the slug came much closer. Lone Eagle's words changed slightly. Smoke listened while he fumbled with the gun. Lone Eagle was telling him to miss him again, and then he would charge and make the outlaws kill him; it was too much to ask a friend to do so. He told him that his death could not be avoided, that it was necessary for the plan to work. That for years it would be sung around the campfires about how well Lone Eagle had died, charging the many white men with only his bare hands for a weapon.

And it was a good way to die. The Gods had allowed a beautiful day, warm and pleasant.

Smoke cocked the pistol and lifted it, taking aim.

Lone Eagle sang of his own death, then abruptly he screamed and charged the line of outlaws and gunslingers. Using the scream as a ruse to miss him, Smoke emptied the pistol and fell to the ground just as Lone Eagle, with a final scream, jumped at the line and a dozen guns barked and roared, stopping him in midair, flinging him to the ground, bloody and dead.

Rex helped Smoke up. "You'll never change, Shirley," he said disgustedly. "Do us all a favor and don't ever carry a gun. You'd be too dangerous. Hell, you might accidentally hit something!"

Smoke fanned himself. "I feel faint!"

"If you pass out, DeBeers," Dagget told him, contempt in his eyes and his voice, "you'll damn well lie where you fall."

"I can probably make it back to the camp before I collapse," Smoke trilled.

"Stand aside, boys!" an outlaw said with a laugh. "Shirley's got the vapors!"

"Come on, boys! The drinks are on me."

As they passed by him, several hardcases jokingly complimented Smoke on his fine shooting.

Smoke looked first at Davidson and Dagget, standing by his side, and then at the bullet-riddled and bloody body of Lone Eagle. "Isn't anyone going to bury the savage?"

Dagget laughed, cutting his eyes to Davidson. "I think that'd be a fine job for Shirley, don't you, Rex?"

"Yes." That was said with a laugh. "I do. There is a shovel right over there, DeBeers." He pointed. "Now get to it."

It took Smoke more than a hour to dig out a hole in the rocky soil, even though he dug it shallow, knowing the chief would take the body from the ground and give it a proper Indian burial.

When he got back to his camp, York was laying on his blankets, looking at him, disgust in his eyes.

Smoke flopped down on his own blankets. "What a horrible experience."

"They wasn't no call to kill that Injun. He wasn't even armed and probably was lookin' for food. You was missin' him deliberate, wasn't you?"

Smoke made up his mind and took the chance. "Yes, York, I was."

"I figured as much. Can't nobody shoot that bad. 'Specially a man who was raised up on a farm the way you claim to be. You puttin' on some sort of act, DeBeers. But you best be damn careful around here. This is a hell-hole, and they ain't nothin' but scum livin' here."

"I know. Davidson at first said if I didn't kill the Indian, he was going to give me to Brute Pitman and then have me gouge out the Indian's eyes." Smoke let the mention of his putting on an act fade away into nothing, hoping York would not bring it up again.

York lay on the ground and gazed at him. "I heard of Brute; seen him around a couple of times. He's a bad one. If they'd a tried that, I'd have been forced to deal myself in and help you out."

"You'd have gotten yourself killed."

"You befriended me. Man don't stand by his friends when they in trouble ain't much of a man or a friend. That's just the way I am."

And Smoke felt the young cowboy was sincere when he said it. "I agree with you. You know, at first, they were going to make you kill the Indian."

"I'd a not done it," he said flatly. "My ma was part Nez Percé. And I'm damn proud of that blood in my veins. And I don't make no effort to hide that fact, neither."

And judging by the scars on his flat-knuckled hands, York had been battling over that very fact most of his life, Smoke noted.

York followed Smoke's eyes. "Yeah. I'm just as quick with my fists as I am with my guns." His eyes dropped to Smoke's big hands. "And you ain't no pilgrim, neither, Mr. Shirley DeBeers. Or whatever the hell your name might be."

"Let's just leave it DeBeers for the time being, shall we?"

"'Kay." York took off his battered hat and ran fingers through his tousled hair. "DeBeers?"

"Yes, York?"

"Let's you and me get the hell gone from this damn place!"

12

There was no doubt in Smoke's mind that York was serious and was no part of Davidson's scheme of things in or around Dead River. The young cowboy was no outlaw and had made up his mind never to become one. But Smoke had three days to go before the deadline was up and the posse would strike. He had a hunch that would be the longest three days of his life. He looked at York for a moment before replying.

"I'm just about through sketching Davidson. He has indicated that he would allow me to leave after that."

"Like I said before—and you believed him?"

"I have no choice in the matter."

"I guess not. But I still think you're draggin' your boots for some reason. But I'll stick around just to see what you're up to. Don't worry, DeBeers. I'll keep my suspicions to myself."

Again, Smoke had nothing to say on that subject. "What are you going to do on the outside, York?"

York shook his head. "I don't know. Drift, I reckon. I just ain't cut out for this kind of life. I think I knowed that all along. But I think I owe it to you for pointin' it out."

"Stay out of sight, York." Smoke picked up his sketch

pad. "I have to go sketch Davidson. Even though I certainly don't feel up to it."

"What if Davidson won't let you leave here like he says he will?"

"I don't know. Let's cross that bridge when we come to it."

"Bridges don't worry me," York said glumly. "It's that damn guarded pass that's got me concerned."

The next two days passed without incident. York stayed at Smoke's camp—and stayed close. Smoke continued his sketching of Rex Davidson, and his opinion that the man was a conceited and arrogant tyrant was confirmed. The man remained friendly enough—as friendly as he had ever been to Smoke—but Smoke could detect a change in him. He appeared tense and sometimes nervous. And there was distance between them now, a distance that had not been there before. Smoke knew that Davidson had never really intended to let him leave. He did not think that Rex suspected he was anything except the part he was playing, what he claimed to be. It was, Smoke felt, that Rex had been playing a game with him all along; a cat with a cornered mouse. A little torture before the death bite.

"I'm becoming a bit weary of all this," Davidson suddenly announced, breaking his pose. The afternoon of the sixth day.

"Of what, sir?" Smoke lifted his eyes, meeting the hard gaze of the man.

"Of posing, fool!" Davidson said sharply. "I have enough pictures. But as for you, I don't know what to do about you."

"Whatever in the world are you talking about, Mr. Davidson?"

Rex stared at him for a long moment. Then, rising from the stool where he'd been sitting, posing, he walked to a window and looked out, staring down at his outlaw town. He turned and said, "I first thought it was you; that you were the front man, the spy sent in here. Then I realized that no one except a professional actor could play the part of a fool as convincingly as you've done . . . and no actor has that much courage. Not to come in here and lay his life on the line. So you are what you claim to be. A silly fop. But I still don't know what to do with you. I do know that you are beginning to bore me. It was the Indian. Had to be. The marshals hired the Indian to come in here and check on us."

"Sir, I have no idea what you're talking about." But Smoke knew. Somewhere in the ranks of the marshals or the sheriffs or the deputies, there was a turncoat. Now he had to find out just how much Rex Davidson knew about the plan just twenty-four hours away from bloody reality.

And stay alive long enough to do something about it, if he could.

"That damn woman almost had me fooled," Davidson said, more to himself than to Smoke. He had turned his back again, not paying any attention to Smoke. "It was good fun torturing her, DeBeers; I wish you had been here to see it. Yes, indeed. I outdid myself with inventiveness. I kept her alive for a long time. I finally broke her, of course. But by the time I did, she was no more than a broken, babbling idiot. The only thing we learned was that the marshals were planning on coming in here at some time or the other. She didn't know when."

"Sir, I—"

Davidson whirled around, his face hard with anger. "Shut your goddamn mouth, DeBeers!" He shouted. "And never interrupt me when I'm speaking."

"Yes, sir."

"Of course, she was raped—among other things. The men enjoyed taking their perversions upon her." He was pacing the room. "Repeatedly. I enjoyed listening to her beg for mercy. Dagget can be quite inventive, too. But finally I wearied of it, just as I am rapidly wearying of you, DeBeers. You're really a Milquetoast, Shirley. I think I'll put you in a dress and parade you around. Yes. That is a thought."

Smoke kept his mouth shut.

Davidson turned back to the window, gazing out over his town of scum and filth and perversion. "I have not left this place in years. I stay aware of what is going on outside, of course. But I have not left this valley in years. It's mine, and no one is going to take it from me. I will not permit it. I know an attack is coming. But I don't know when."

Smoke knew then why the sudden influx of outlaws. Somehow, probably through outriders, Davidson had gotten the word out to them: If you want to save your refuge, you'd better be prepared to fight for it.

Or something like that.

With King Rex, however, it had probably been put in a much more flowery way.

"Ah, sir, Your Majesty?" Smoke verbally groveled, something he was getting weary of.

"What do you want, Shirley?"

"May I take my leave now, Your Magesty?"

"Yes, you silly twit!" Davidson did not turn from the window. "And stay out of my sight, goofy. I haven't made up my mind exactly what I'm going to do with you. Get out, fool!"

I've made up my mind what to do with you, King Rex, Smoke thought, on his way out. And about this time tomorrow, you're going to be in for a very large surprise. One that I'm going to enjoy handing you.

He gently closed the door behind him. He was smiling as he walked down the hill from the King's house. He had to work to get the smile off his lips before he entered the long main street of Dead River.

In twenty-four hours, he would finally and forever shed his foppish costume and strap on his guns.

And then Dr. Jenson would begin administering to a very sick town.

With gunsmoke and lead.

Smoke was conscious of York staring at him. He had been sliding furtive glances his way for several hours now, and Smoke knew the reason for the looks. He could feel the change coming over him. He would have to be very careful the remainder of this day, for he was in no mood to continue much longer with his Shirley DeBeers act.

York had just returned from town and had been unusually quiet since getting back. He finally broke his silence.

"DeBeers?"

"Yes, York?"

"I gotta tell you. The word is out that come the morning, you're gonna be tossed to the wolves. Davidson is gonna declare you fair game for anybody. And you know what that means."

Mid-afternoon of the seventh day.

"Brute Pitman."

"Among other things," York said.

"What size boots do you wear, York?"

"Huh! Man, didn't you hear me? We got to get the hell gone from this place. And I mean we got to plan on how to do it right now!"

"I heard you, York. Just relax. What size boots do you wear?"

The cowboy signed. "Ten."

"That's my size. How about that?" Smoke grinned at him.

"Wonderful!" The comment was dryly given. "You

lookin' at gettin' kilt, and you all het up about us wearin' the same size boots. You weird, DeBeers."

With a laugh, Smoke handed York some money. "Go to the store and buy me a good pair of boots. Black. Get me some spurs. Small stars, not the big California rowels. Don't say a word about who you're buying them for. We'll let that come as a surprise for them. Think you can do that for me, York?"

"Why, hell, yes, I can! What do you think I am, some sort of dummy? Boots? 'Kay. But I best get you some walkin' heels."

"Riding heels, York," Smoke corrected, enjoying the look of bewilderment on his new friend's face. "And how many boxes of shells do you have?"

"One and what's in my belt. Now why in the hell are you askin' that?"

"Buy at least three more boxes. When you get back, I'll explain. Now then, what else have you heard about me, York?"

"You ain't gonna like it."

"Oh, I don't know. It might give me more incentive to better do the job that faces me."

York shook his head. "Weird, DeBeers. That's you. Well, that Jake feller? He's been makin' his brags about how he's gonna make you hunker down in the street and eat a pile of horse-droppin's."

"Oh, is he now?"

"Yeah. He likes to be-little folks. That Jake, he's cruel mean, DeBeers. That one and them that run with him is just plain no-good. He makes ever' slave that comes in here do that. I've had half a dozen or more men tell me that. All the men here, they think it's funny watchin' Jake force folks to eat that mess."

"I wonder how Jake would like to eat a poke of it himself?"

York grinned. "Now that'd be a sight to see!"

"Don't give up hope, York. Would you please go get my stuff for me?"

"Sure." He turned, then stopped and whirled around to face Smoke. "I can't figure you, DeBeers. You've changed. I noticed that this morning."

"We'll talk when you get back, York. Be careful down in town. I think things are getting a bit tense."

"That ain't exactly the way I'd put it, but whatever you say." He walked off toward town, mumbling to himself and shaking his head. Smoke smiled at the young man and then set about preparing himself mentally for what the night held in store.

And he knew only too well what lay before him when the dusk settled into darkness in the outlaw town.

There was no fear in Smoke; no sweaty palms or pounding heart. He was deathly calm, inside and out. And he did not know if that was an asset or liability. He knew caution, for no man lived by the gun without knowing what was about him at all times. But Smoke, since age sixteen, had seldom if ever at all experienced anything even remotely akin to fear.

He sat down on his ground sheet and blankets and calmly set about making a pot of coffee. He looked up at the sound of boots striking the gravel. Brute Pitman stopped a few yards away, grinning at him.

"Go away, Bruce. The smell of you would stop a buzzard in flight."

Brute cussed him.

Smoke smiled at him.

"I'm gonna enjoy hearin' you holler, pretty-boy," Brute told him, slobber leaking past his fat lips. "With you, I'm gonna make it las' a long time."

Smoke made no reply, just sat on the ground and stared at the hulking mass of perversion. He allowed his eyes to do the talking, and they silently spoke volumes to the big slob.

Brute met the gaze and Smoke's smile was wider still

as something shifted in the hulk's eyes. Was it fear touching Brute's dark eyes? Smoke felt sure that it was, and that thought amused him. Brute Pitman was like so many men his size, a bully from boyhood. He had bulled and heavy-shouldered his way through life, knowing his sheer size would keep most from fighting back. But like most bullies, Brute was a coward at heart.

"Something the matter, Brute?"

That took him by surprise. "Huh! Naw, they ain't nothin' the matter with me, sissy-boy. Nothin'," he added, "that come night won't clear."

"You best watch the night, Brute," Smoke cautioned. "Night is a time when death lays close to a man."

"Huh! Whatda you talkin' 'bout now, pretty boy. I don't think you even know. I think you so scared you peein' your drawers."

Smoke laughed at him. Now he didn't care. It was too close to the deadline to matter. By now, the men from the posse would be approaching the ranch and would be changing horses for the last time before entering the mountain pass. Already, the Utes would be slipping into place, waiting for the guards to change.

Everything was in motion; it could not be stopped now.

"Get out of my sight, Brute. You sickin' me."

Brute hesitated, then mumbled something obscene under his breath and walked down the small hill. Twice he stopped and looked back at Smoke. Smoke gave him the finger, jabbing the air with his middle finger.

"Crazy!" Brute said. "The bassard's crazy! Done took leave of his senses."

Smoke heard the comment and smiled.

Brute met Cat Ventura on his way down. The men did not speak to each other. Cat stood over Smoke, staring down at him.

"I would wish you a good afternoon," Smoke told him, "but with you here, it is anything but that."

Cat stared at him, ignoring the remark; Smoke was not sure the man even knew what he meant by it. "I seen you somewheres before, artist," the gunfighter, outlaw, and murderer said. "And you wasn't drawin' no pitchers on paper, neither."

"Perhaps if you dwell on it long enough, it will come to you in time, Mister-whatever-your-name is. Not that I particularly care at this juncture."

"Huh! Boy, you got a damn smart mouth on you, ain't you? I'm Cat Ventura."

"Not a pleasure, I'm sure. Very well, Mr. Meow. If you came up here to ask me to sketch you, my studio is closed for the time being. Perhaps some other time; like in the next century."

"You piss-headed smart ass! When the time comes, I think I'll jist stomp your guts out; see what color they is. How 'bout that, sissy-pants?"

"Oh, I don't think so, Mr. Purr. I really have my doubts about you doin' that."

Before he turned away to walk back down the hill, Cat said, "I know you from somewheres. It'll come to me. I'll be back."

"I'll certainly be here."

Smoke lay on his ground sheet and watched a passing parade of outlaws visit him during the next few minutes. Some walked up and stared at him. A few made open threats on his life.

He would have liked to ask why the sudden shift in their attitude toward him, but he really wasn't all that interested in the why of it.

Smoke checked the mountain sky. About three hours until dusk. He rose from the ground and got his fishing pole, checking the line and hook. Jake and Shorty and Red had been watching him, hunkered down at the base of the hill. Out of the corner of his eyes, Smoke saw them all relax and reach for the makings, rolling and lighting cigarettes. He stepped back into the timber behind his camp, as if heading for the little creek to fish and catch his supper. Smoke assumed his line of credit at the Bon Ton Café had been cut off. The food hadn't been all that good anyway.

Out of sight of the trio of outlaws, Smoke dropped his pole and walked toward the center of town, staying inside the thin timber line until he was opposite the privy and the pile of lumber behind the saloon. He quickly stepped to the lumber, moved a couple of boards, and spotted the rolled-up packet.

The back door to the saloon opened, a man stepping out. "What you doin', boy? Sneakin' around here. You tryin' to slip out, pretty-pants?"

Smoke looked up as the man closed the door behind him and walked toward him. His hand closed around a sturdy two-by-four, about three feet long and solid. "Just borrowing a few boards, sir. I thought I might build a board floor for my tent. Is that all right with you?"

The outlaw stepped closer, Smoke recognizing him as a wanted murderer. "No, it ain't all right with me. You jist git your butt on out of here."

Smoke could smell the odor of rotting human flesh from those unfortunates hanging from the meat hooks at the edge of town. Those few still alive were moaning and crying out in pain.

Smoke looked around him. They were alone. He smiled at the outlaw. "Playtime is all over, you bastard."

"What'd you say to me, fancy-pants?" The man stepped closer, almost within swinging distance. Just a few feet more and Smoke would turn out the man's lights. Forever.

"I said you stink like sheep-shit and look like the ass end of a donkey."

Cursing, growling deep in his throat, the outlaw charged Smoke. Smoke jerked up the two-by-four and laid the lumber up against the man's head. The outlaw stopped, as if he had run into a stone wall. His skull popped under the impact. He dropped to the earth, dying, blood leaking from his ears and nose and mouth.

Smoke dropped the two-by-four and quickly dragged the man behind the privy, stretching him out full length behind the two-holer. He could only be seen from the timber.

Smoke took the man's two .44s and punched out the shells from the loops of his belt. He grabbed up his own guns and walked back into the timber, heading for his campsite.

He was smiling, humming softly.

They had said their good-byes to their wives and kids and girlfriends and swung into the saddle, pointing the noses of their horses north, toward the outlaw town.

One deputy from an adjoining county had been caught trying to make it alone to Dead River. He had been brought back to face Jim Wilde. It turned out his brother was one of the outlaws living in Dead River. The deputy was now locked down hard in his own jail, under heavy guard.

The members of the posse were, to a man, hard-faced and grim. All knew that some of them would not live through the night that lay before them. And while none of them wanted to die, they knew that what lay ahead of them was something that had to be done, should have been done a long time back. The outlaw town had been a blight on society for years, and the time had come to destroy it and all who chose to reside within its confines.

The riders each carried at least two pistols belted around their waists. Most had two more six-guns, either tucked behind their belts or carried in holsters, tied to their saddles. All carried a rifle in the boot; some had added a shotgun, the express guns loaded with buckshot. The men had stuffed their pockets full of .44s, .45s, and shotgun shells.

The posse rode at a steady, distance-covering gait; already they had changed horses and were now approaching Red Davis's place. While the hands switched saddles, the men of the posse grabbed and wolfed down a sandwich and coffee, then refilled canteens. All checked their guns, wiping them free of dust and checking the action.

"Wish I was goin' with you," Davis said. "I'd give a thousand dollars to see that damn town burned slap to the ground."

Wilde nodded his head. "Red, there'll be doctors and the like comin' out here and settin' up shop 'bout dark. Some of us are gonna be hard-hit and the slaves in that town are gonna be in bad shape. You got your wagon ready to meet us at the mouth of the pass?"

"All hitched up." He spat on the ground. "And me and my boys will take care of any stragglers that happen to wander out when the shootin' starts."

Jim Wilde smiled grimly. Between the Utes and Red Davis's hard-bitten hands, any outlaws who happened to escape were going to be in for a very rough time of it. Red's ranch had been the first in the area, and the old man was as tough as leather—and so were his hands.

Red clasped Jim on the shoulder. "Luck to you, boy. And I wanna meet this Smoke Jensen. That there is my kind of man."

Jim nodded and turned, facing the sixty-odd men of the posse. The U.S. Marshal wore twin .44s, tied down. He carried another .44 in his shoulder holster and a rifle and a shotgun in the boots, on his horse. "All right, boys. This is the last jumpin'-off place. From here on in, they's no turnin' back. You gotta go to the outhouse, get it done now. When we get back into the saddle, we ain't stoppin' until we're inside Dead River." He glanced at the sinking sun. "Smoke's gonna open up the dance in about an hour—if he's still alive," he added grimly. "And knowin' him he is. Anybody wanna back out of this?"

No one did.
"Let's ride!"

The guards along the pass road had just changed, the new guards settling in for a long and boring watch. Nothing ever happened; a lot of the time many of them dozed off. They would all sleep this dusky evening. Forever.

One guard listened for a few seconds. Was that a noise behind him? He thought it was. He turned, brought his rifle up, and came face to face with a war-painted Indian. He froze, opening his mouth to yell a warning. The shout was forever locked in his throat as an axe split his skull. The Ute caught the bloody body before it could fall to the ground and lowered it to the earth. The body would never be found; time and wind and rain and the elements and animals would dispose of the flesh and scatter the bones. A hundred years later, small boys playing would discover the gold coins the outlaw had had in his pockets and would wonder how the money came to be in this lonely spot.

His job done, for the moment, the brave slipped back into the timber and waited.

Up and down the heavily guarded narrow road, the guards were meeting an end just as violent as the life they had chosen to live. And they had chosen it; no one had forced them into it. One outlaw guard, who enjoyed torturing Indians, especially children, and raping squaws, was taken deep into the timber, gagged, stripped, and staked out. Then he was skinned—alive.

Their first job done, the Indians quietly slipped back and took their positions around the outlaw town of Dead River. With the patience bred into them, they waited and watched, expressionless.

York looked up and blinked, at first not recognizing the tall muscular man who was walking toward him, out of the timber. Then he recognized him.

"Damn, DeBeers. I didn't know you at first. How come you shaved off your beard?"

"It was time. And my name is not DeBeers."

"Yeah. I kinda figured it was a phony. And I didn't believe that Shirley bit, neither."

"That's right. You get my boots and spurs?"

York pointed to a bag on the ground. He had never seen such a change in any man. The man standing in front of him looked . . . awesome!

Smoke was dressed all in black, from his boots to his shirt. His belt was black with inlaid silver that caught the last glows of the setting sun. He wore a red bandana around his neck. He had buckled on twin .44s, the left handgun worn butt-forward, cross-draw style. He had shoved two more .44s behind his belt.

"Ah . . . man, you best be careful with them guns," York cautioned. "You packin' enough for an army. Are you fixin' to start a war around here?"

"That is my hope, York."

"Yeah?" Somehow, that did not come as any surprise to York. There was something about this tall man that was just . . . well, unsettling. He poured a cup of coffee and sipped it, hot, strong, and black. He looked at the tall man. Naw, he thought, it couldn't be. But he sure looked like all the descriptions York had ever heard about the gunfighter. "Who are you, man?"

Smoke pulled a badge from his pocket and pinned it to his shirt. "I'm a United States Deputy Marshal. And as far as I'm concerned, York, all those warrants against you are not valid. And when we get out of here, I'll see that they are recalled. How does that sound to you?"

York took a sip of coffee. Oddly, to Smoke, he had shown no surprise. "Sounds good to me, Marshal." He stood up and pulled a gold badge out of his pocket and pinned it on his shirt. "Buddy York is the name. Arizona Rangers. I was wonderin' if you plan on corralin' this town all by your lonesome."

"That's a good cover story of yours, Ranger," Smoke complimented him.

"Well, took us six months to set it up. The dodgers that are out are real. Had to be that way."

"I gather you have warrants for some people in here?"

"A whole passel of them, including some on Dagget."

"There is a large posse on the way in. They'll be here just at dusk. The Utes have taken care of the guards along the road."

York looked up at the sky. "That's a good hour and a half away, Marshal." He was grinning broadly.

"That's the way I got it figured, Ranger. Of course, you do know that you have no jurisdiction in this area?"

"I'll worry about that later."

"Consider yourself deputized with full government authority."

"I do thank you, Marshal."

"You ready to open this dance, Ranger?" Smoke sat down on a log and buckled on his spurs. He looked up as York opened another bag and tossed him a black hat, low crowned and flat brimmed. "Thanks. I am ever so glad to be rid of that damned silly cap." He tried the hat. A perfect fit.

"You did look a tad goofy. But I got to hand it to you. You're one hell of a fine actor."

Both men stuffed their pockets full of shells.

Rifle in hand, York said, "What is your handle, anyways?"

"Smoke Jensen," the tall, heavily muscled man said with a smile.

York's knees seemed to buckle and he sat down heavily on a log. When he found his voice, he said, "Holy jumpin' Jesus Christ!"

"I'm new to the marshaling business, Ranger. I just took this on a temporary basis." Then he explained what had happened at his ranch, to his wife.

"Takes a low-life SOB to attack a lone woman. I gather

you want Davidson and Dagget and them others all to yourself, right?"

"I would appreciate it, Ranger."

"They're all yours."

Smoke checked his guns, slipping them both in and out of leather a few times. He filled both cylinders and every loop on his gunbelt, then checked the short-barreled pistol he carried in his shoulder holster. Breaking open the sawed-off shotgun, he filled both barrels with buckshot loads. Smoke looked on with approval as the ranger pulled two spare .44s out of his warbag and loaded them full. He tucked them behind his belt and picked up a Henry repeating rifle, loading it full and levering in a round, then replacing that round in the magazine.

"I'll tell you how I see this thing, Ranger. You don't have to play this way, but I'm going to."

"I'm listenin', Smoke."

"I'm not taking any prisoners."

"I hadn't planned on it myself."

The men smiled at each other, knowing then exactly where the other stood.

Their pockets bulging with extra cartridges, York carrying a Henry and Smoke carrying the sawed-off express gun, they looked at each other.

"You ready to strike up the band, Ranger?"

"Damn right!" York said with a grin.

"Let's do it!"

13

Marshal Jim Wilde's posse had an hour to go before reaching Dead River when Smoke and York stepped into the back of the saloon. Inside, the piano player was banging out and singing a bawdy song.

"How do we do this?" York asked.

"We walk in together," Smoke whispered.

The men slipped the thongs off their six-guns and eased them out of leather a time or two, making certain the oiled interiors of the holsters were free.

York eased back the hammer on his Henry and Smoke jacked back the hammers on the express gun.

They stepped inside the noisy and beer-stinking saloon. The piano player noticed them first. He stopped playing and singing and stared at them, his face chalk-white. Then he scrambled under the lip of the piano.

"Well, well!" an outlaw said, laughing. "Would you boys just take a look at Shirley. He's done shaven offen his beard and taken to packin' iron. Boy, you bes' git shut of them guns, 'fore you hurt yourself."

Gridley stood up from a table where he'd been drinking and playing poker—and losing. "Or I decide to take 'em off you and shove 'em up your butt, lead and all, pretty-boy. Matter of fact, I think I'll jist do that, right now."

Smoke and York had surveyed the scene as they had stepped in. The barroom was not nearly filled to capacity . . . but it was full enough.

"The name isn't pretty-boy, Gridley," Smoke informed him.

"Oh, yeah? Well, mayhaps you right. I'll jist call you shit! How about that?"

"Why don't you call him by his real name?" York said, a smile on his lips.

"And what might that be, punk?" Gridley sneered the question. "Alice?"

"First off," York said. "I'll tell you I'm an Arizona Ranger. Note the badges we're wearing? And his name, you blow-holes, is Smoke Jensen!"

The name was dropped like a bomb. The outlaws in the room sat stunned, their eyes finally observing the gold badges on the chests of the men.

Smoke and York both knew one thing for an ironclad fact: The men in the room might all be scoundrels and thieves and murderers, and some might be bullies and cowards, but when it came down to it, they were going to fight.

"Then draw, you son of a bitch!" Gridley hollered, his hands dropping to his guns.

Smoke pulled the trigger on the express gun. From a distance of no more than twenty feet, the buckshot almost tore the outlaw in two.

York leveled the Henry and dusted an outlaw from side to side. Dropping to one knee, he levered the empty out and a fresh round in and shot a fat punk in the belly.

Shifting the sawed-off shotgun, Smoke blew the head off another outlaw. The force of the buckshot lifted the headless outlaw out of one boot and flung him to the sawdust-covered floor.

York and his Henry had put half a dozen outlaws on the floor, dead, dying, or badly hurt.

The huge saloon was filled with gunsmoke, the crying and moaning of the wounded, and the stink or relaxed bladders from the dead. Dark gray smoke from the black powder cartridges stung the eyes and obscured the vision of all in the room.

The outlaws had recovered from their initial shock and had overturned tables, crouching behind them, returning the deadly hail of fire from Smoke and Arizona Ranger York.

Smoke had slipped to the end of the bar closest to the batwing doors, and York had worked his way to the side of the big stage, crouching behind a second piano in the small orchestra pit. Between the two of them, Smoke and York were laying down a deadly field of fire. Both men had grabbed up the guns of the dead and dying men as they slipped to their new positions and they now had a pile of .44s, .45s, and several shotguns and rifles in front of them.

A half-dozen outlaws tried to rush the batwings in a frantic attempt to escape and were met by a half-dozen other outlaws attempting to enter the saloon from the outside. It created a massive pileup at the batwings, a pileup that was too good for Smoke to resist.

Slipping to the very end of the long bar, Smoke emptied a pair of .45s taken from a dead man into the panicked knot of outlaws. Screaming from the men as the hot slugs tore into their flesh added to the earsplitting cacophony of confusion in the saloon.

Smoke grabbed up an armload of weapons and ran to the end of the bar closest to the rear of the saloon. He caught York's attention and motioned to the storeroom where they had entered. York nodded and left his position at a run. The men ran through the darkened storeroom to the back door.

Just as they reached the back door it opened and two

outlaws stepped inside, guns drawn. Smoke and York fired simultaneously, their guns booming and crashing in the darkness, lancing smoke and fire, splitting the heavy gloom of the storeroom. The outlaws were flung backward, outside. They lay on the ground, on their backs, dying from wounds to the chest and belly.

"York, you take the north end of town," Smoke said. "I'll take the south end." He was speaking as he was stripping the weapons from the dead men.

York nodded his agreement and tossed Smoke one of two cloth sacks he'd picked up in the storeroom. The men began dumping in the many guns they'd picked up along the way.

"Find and destroy the heathens!" a man's strong voice cut the night. "The Philistines are upon us!"

"Who the hell is that?" York whispered.

"That's Tustin, the preacher. Has to be."

"A preacher? Here?" The ranger's voice was filled with disbelief.

The gunfire had almost ceased, as the outlaws in the saloon could not find Smoke or York.

"Oh, Lord!" Tustin's voice filled the night. "Take these poor unfortunate bastards into the gates of Heaven and give us the strength and the wherewithal to find and shoot the piss outta them that's attackin' us!"

"I ain't believin' this," York muttered.

Smoke smiled, his strong white teeth flashing in the night. "Good luck, York."

"Same to you, partner."

Carrying their heavy sacks of weapons and cartridge-filled belts, the men parted, one heading north, the other heading south.

York and Smoke both held to the edge of the timber as they made their way north and south. The town's inhabitants had adopted a panicked siege mentality, with outlaws filling the streets, running in every direction. No one among them knew how many men were attacking

the town. Both York and Smoke had heard the shouts
that hundreds of lawmen were attacking.

Just before Smoke slipped past the point where he
could look up and see the fine home of Davidson, he saw
the lamps in the house being turned off, the home on
the hill growing dark.

And Smoke would have made a bet that Davidson and
Dagget had a rabbit hole out of Dead River, and that
both of them, and probably a dozen or more of their
most trusted henchmen, were busy packing up and getting out.

Just for a moment, Smoke studied the darkened out-
line of the home on the hill. And then it came to him.
A cave. He would be a hundred dollars that King Rex
had built his home in front of a cave, a cave that wound
through the mountain and exited out in the timbered
range behind Dead River. And he would also bet that
White Wolf and his braves knew nothing of it. It might
exit out into a little valley where horses and gear could
be stored.

Cursing in disgust for not thinking of that sooner,
Smoke slipped on into the night, seeking a good spot
to set up a defensive position.

He paused for a moment, until York had opened fire,
showing Smoke where the ranger had chosen to make
his stand. And it was a good one, high up on the right
side of the ridge overlooking the town, as Smoke stood
looking north. With a smile, Smoke chose his position
on the opposite side of the street, above the first store
one encountered upon entering the outlaw town.

Below him, the outlaws had settled down, taking up
positions around the town. Smoke could see several
bodies sprawled in the street, evidence of York's marksmanship with his Henry.

A handful of outlaws tried to rush the ranger's position. Hard gunfire broke out on either side and above
York's position. White Wolf's Utes were making their

presence known in a very lethal manner. For years, the outlaws had made life miserable for the Utes, and now it was payback time. With a vengeance.

A horseman came galloping up the street, toward the curve that exited the town. The man was riding low in the saddle, the reins in his teeth and both hands full of six-guns. Smoke took careful aim with a rifle he'd picked up in the saloon and knocked the man out of the saddle. The rider hit the ground hard and rolled, coming up on his feet. A dozen rifles spat lead. The man was hit a dozen times, shot to bloody rags. He dropped to the roadway, his blood leaking into the dirt.

The horse, reins trailing, trotted off into an alley.

Smoke hit the ground, behind a series of boulders, as his position was found and rifles began barking and spitting in the night, the lead ricocheting and whining off the huge rocks, spinning into the night.

A Ute came rolling down the hill crashing against the boulder behind which Smoke was hiding. Smoke rolled the brave over and checked his wound—a nasty wound in the brave's side. Smoke plugged it with moss and stretched the Indian out, safe from fire. The Ute's dark eyes had never left Smoke's face, and he endured the pain without a sound.

Smoke made the sign for brother and the Indian, flat on his back returned the gesture. Gunfighter and Indian smiled at each other in the gunfire-filled night above the outlaw town.

Smoke picked up his rifle as the Indian, who had never let go of his rifle, crawled to a position on the other end of the line of boulders. Smoke tossed him a bag of cartridges and the men began lacing the town with .44 rifle fire. The .44s, which could punch through a good three inches of pine, began bringing shouts and yells of panic from the outlaws in the town below.

Several tried to run; they were knocked down in the

street. One outlaw, his leg twisted grotesquely, tried to crawl to safety. A slug to the head stopped his strugglings.

Smoke spoke to the Ute in his own language. "If they ever discover how few we are up here, we're in trouble, brother."

The Ute laughed in the night and said, "My people have always fought outnumbered, gunfighter. It is nothing new to us."

Smoke returned the laugh and began working the lever on his Henry, laying a line of lead into a building below their position. The sudden hard fire brought several screams of pain from inside the building. One man fell through a shattered window to hang there, half in and half out of the building.

The Ute shouted a warning as a dozen outlaws charged their position, the men slipping from tree to tree, rock to rock, working closer.

Smoke quickly reloaded the Henry and laid two .44s on the ground beside him, one by each leg. There was no doubt in his mind that the outlaws would certainly breach their position, and then the fighting would be hand to hand.

Smoke heard the ugly sound of a bullet striking flesh and bone, and turning his head, he saw the Ute fall backward, a blue-tinged hole in the center of his forehead. With his right hand, Smoke made the Indian sign for peaceful journey and then returned to the fight.

He took out one outlaw who made the mistake of exposing too much of his body, knocking the man spinning from behind a tree; a second slug from Smoke's rifle forever stilled the man.

Then there was no time for anything except survival, as the outlaws charged Smoke's position.

Smoke fought savagely, his guns sending several outlaws into that long darkness. Then his position was overrun. Something slammed into the side of his head, and Smoke was dropped into darkness.

14

He was out for no more than a few seconds, never really losing full consciousness. He felt blood dripping down the side of his face. He was still holding onto his guns, and he remembered they were full. Lifting them, as a dozen shapes began materializing around him in the night, Smoke began cocking and pulling the triggers.

Hoarse screams filled the air around him as the slugs from his pistols struck their mark at point-blank range. Unwashed bodies thudded to the ground all around him, the dead and dying flesh unwittingly building a fort around his position, protecting him from the returning fire of the outlaws.

Then, half-naked shapes filtered silently and swiftly out of the timber, firing rifles and pistols. By now, the remaining outlaws were too confused and frightened to understand how a man whom they believed to be dead from a head wound had managed to inflict so hideous a toll on them.

And then the Utes came out of the timber, and in a matter of seconds, what had been twenty outlaws were no more than dying, cooling flesh in the still-warm mountain air slightly above Dead River.

The Utes vanished back into the timber, as swiftly and as silently as they had come.

Smoke reloaded his guns, pistols, and rifles, and slung the rifles across his shoulders. He wrapped his bandana around his head and tied it, after inspecting his head-wound with his fingers and finding it not serious; he knew that a head wound can bleed hard and fast for a few moments, and then, in many cases, stop.

He loaded his pistols, then loaded the sawed-off shotgun. Then he began making his way down the hill, back into the town of Dead River. He was going to take the fight to the outlaws.

He stopped once to tie a white handkerchief around his arm, so not only the Indians would know who he was but so the posse members would not mistakenly shoot him.

He slipped down to the building where the outlaw was still hanging half out of the window and quietly checked out the interior. The building was void of life. Looking up the street, he could see where he, York, and the Utes had taken a terrible toll on the population of the outlaw town. The street, the alleys, and the boardwalks were littered with bodies. Most were not moving.

He did not know how much time had transpired since he and Ranger had opened the dance. But he was sure it was a good half hour or forty-five minutes.

He slipped to the south a few yards and found a good defensible position behind a stone wall that somebody had built around a small garden. Smoke pulled a ripe tomato off the vine, brushed the dust off it, and ate it while his eyes surveyed the street, picking out likely targets.

He unslung the rifles, laid his sack of guns and cartridges by one side, the express guns by his other side, and then picked up and checked out a Henry.

He had found a man stationed on top of a building. Sighting him in, Smoke let the other outlaws know he was still in the game by knocking the man off the roof with one well-placed shot to his belly. The sniper fell screaming to the street below. His howling stopped as he impacted with earth.

Putting his hand to the ground, Smoke thought he could detect a trembling. Bending over, being careful not to expose his butt to the guns of the outlaws, he pressed his ear to the ground and picked up the sound of faint rumblings. The posse was no more than a mile away.

"York!" he yelled.

"Yo, Smoke!" came the call.

"Here they come, Ranger! Shovel the coals to it!"

Smoke began levering and pulling the trigger, laying down a blistering line of fire into the buildings of the town. From his position at the other end, York did the same. The Utes opened up from both sides of the town, and the night rocked with gunfire.

"For the love of God!" Sheriff Larsen cried out, reining up by the lines of tortured men and women on the outskirts of town. His eyes were utterly disbelieving as they touched each tortured man and woman.

"Help us!" came the anguished cry of one of the few still alive. "Have mercy on us, please. We were taken against our will and brought here."

The posse of hardened western men, accustomed to savage sights, had never seen anything like this. All had seen Indian torture; but that was to be expected from ignorant savages. But fellow white men had done this.

Several of the posse leaned out of their saddles and puked on the ground.

"Three or four men stay here and cut these poor wretches down," Jim Wilde ordered, his voice strong over the sound of gunfire. "Do what you can for them."

"Jim!" Smoke called. "It's Jensen. Hold your fire, I'm coming over."

Smoke zigzagged over to the posse, catching the reins

of a horse as the man discounted. "Your horses look in good shape."

"We rested them about a mile back. Let them blow good and gave them half a hatful of water. How's your head?"

"My Sally has hit me harder," Smoke grinned, swinging into the saddle. He patted the roan's neck and rubbed his head, letting the animal know he was friendly.

"You comin' in with us?" the marshal asked.

"I got personal business to tend to. There's an Arizona Ranger named York up yonder." He pointed. "I forgot to tell him to tie something about his arm. He's a damn good man. Good luck to you boys."

Smoke swung the horse's head, and with a screaming yell from the throats of sixty men, the posse hit the main street hard. The reins in their teeth, the posse members had their hands full of .44s and .45s, and they were filling anybody they saw with lead.

Smoke rode behind the buildings of the town and dismounted, ground-reining the horse. He eased the hammers back on the express gun and began walking, deliberately letting his spurs jingle.

"Jensen!" a voice shouted from the forward darkness. "Smoke Jensen!"

Stepping behind a corner of a building, Smoke said, "Yeah, that's me."

"Cat Ventura here. You played hell, Jensen."

"That's what I came here to do, Ventura."

Step out and face an ambush, you mean, Smoke thought. "No, thanks, Ventura. I don't trust you."

As soon as he said it, Smoke dropped to the ground. A half-dozen guns roared and sparked, the lead punching holes in the corner of the building where he'd been standing.

Smoke came up on one knee and let the hammers fall on both barrels of the sawed-off shotgun. He almost lost the weapon as both barrels fired, the gun recoiling in his strong hands.

The screaming of the wounded men was horrible in the night. Smoke thought of those poor people at the end of town and could not dredge up one ounce of sympathy for the outlaws he'd just blasted.

He reloaded the shotgun just as Cat called out, "Goddamn you, Jensen."

Smoke fired at the sound of the voice. A gurbling sound reached his ears. Then silence, except for the heavy pounding of gunfire in the street.

He slipped out of the alley and looked down at what was left of Cat Ventura. The full load of buckshot had taken him in the chest and throat. It was not pretty, but then, Cat hadn't been very pretty when he was alive.

Smoke stepped over the gore and continued his walking up the back alley. The posse had dismounted and were taking the town building by building. But the outlaws remaining were showing no inclination to give up the fight. The firing was not as intense as a few moments past, but it was steady.

Smoke caught a glimpse of several men slipping up the alley toward him. He eased back the hammers of the express gun and stepped deeper into the shadows, a privy to his left.

Smoke recognized the lead man as an outlaw called Brawley, a man who had been in trouble with the law and society in general since practically the moment of birth. There were so many wanted posters out on Brawley that the man had been forced to drop out of sight a couple of years back. Now Smoke knew where he'd been hiding.

Smoke stepped out of the shadows and pulled both triggers. The sawed-off shotgun spewed its cargo of ball bearings, nails, and assorted bits of metal. Brawley took one load directly in the chest, lifting the murderer off his feet and sending him sprawling. The man to Brawley's right caught part of a load in the face.

Smoke recalled that the man had thought himself to be handsome.

That was no longer the case.

The third man had escaped most of the charge and had thrown himself to the ground. He pulled himself up to his knees, his hands full of .44s. Holding the shotgun in his left hand, Smoke palmed his .44 and saved the public the expense of a trial.

"The goddamn Injuns got Cahoon!" a hoarse yell sprang out of the night.

Smoke turned, reloading the sawed-off, trying to determine how close the man was.

"Hell with Cahoon!" another yelled. Very close to Smoke. "It's ever' man for hisself now."

Smoke pulled the triggers and fire shot out of the twin barrels, seeming to push the lethal loads of metal. Horrible screaming was heard for a moment, and then the sounds of bootheels drumming the ground in death.

Smoke reloaded and walked on.

At a gap between buildings, Smoke could see York, still in position, still spitting out lead from his Henry. The bodies in the street paid mute testimony to the ranger's dead aim.

A man wearing a white armband ducked into the gap and spotted Smoke.

"Easy," Smoke called. "Jensen here."

Smoke could see the badge on his chest, marking him as a U.S. Marhsal.

"Windin' down," the man said. "Thought I'd take me a breather. You and that Arizona Ranger played hell, Smoke."

"That was our intention. You got the makin's? I lost my sack."

The man tossed Smoke a bag of tobacco and papers. Squatting down, out of the line of fire, Smoke and the marshal rolled, licked, and lit.

Smoke could see the lawman had been hit a couple of

times, neither of the wounds serious enough to take him out of a fight.

"I figure the big boys got loose free," Smoke spoke over a sudden hard burst of gunfire. He jerked his head. "That's Davidson's big house up yonder on the ridge. . . ."

Jim Wilde almost got himself plugged as he darted into the alley and slid to a halt, catching his breath.

"I dearly wish you would announce your intentions, ol' hoss," the marshal said to him. "You near'bouts got drilled."

"Gimme the makin's, Glen, I lost my pouch. " Jim holstered his guns.

While Jim rolled a cigarette, Smoke elaborated on his theory of the kingpins escaping.

"Well, let us rest for a minute and then we'll take us a hike up yonder to the house. Check it out." He puffed for a moment. "I've arranged for a judge to be here at first light," he said. "The hands from Red Davis's place is gonna act as jury. Red'll be jury foreman. Soon as we clean out the general store, I got some boys ready to start workin' on ropes."

"Hezekiah Jones the judge?" Glen asked.

"Yep."

"Gonna be some short trials."

"Yep."

"And they's gonna be a bunch of newspaper folks and photographers here, too."

"Yep."

An outlaw tried to make a break for it, whipping his horse up the street toward the edge of town. A dozen guns barked, slamming the outlaw out of the saddle. He rolled on the street and was still.

Glen looked at the body of the outlaw. "I'm thinkin' there might not be all that many to be tried."

Jim Wilde ground out the butt of his smoke under his heel and stood up. "Yep," he said.

Jim was known to be a spare man with words.

15

The battle for the outlaw town of Dead River was winding down sharply as Smoke and the marshals made their way up the hill to Rex Davidson's fine home. They passed a half-dozen bodies on the curving path, all outlaws. All three men were conscious of eyes on them as they walked up the stone path. . . . Utes, waiting in the darkness, watching.

Somewhere back in the timber, a man screamed in agony.

"Cahoon," Smoke told the men.

Glen replied, "Whatever he gets, he earned."

That pretty well summed up the feelings of all three men. Jim pulled out his watch and checked the time. Smoke was surprised to learn it was nearly ten o'clock. He stopped and listened for a moment. Something was wrong.

Then it came to him: The gunfire had ceased.

"Yeah," Jim remarked. "I noticed it too. Eerie, ain't it?"

The men walked on, stepping onto the porch of the house. Motioning the lawmen away from the front door in case it was booby-trapped, Smoke stepped to one side and eased it open. The door opened silently on well-oiled hinges.

Smoke was the first in, the express gun ready. Jim and Glen came in behind him, their hands full of pistols. But the caution had been unnecessary; the room was void of human life.

The men split up, each taking a room. They found nothing. The big house was empty. But everywhere there were signs of hurried packing. The door to the big safe was open, the safe empty of cash. Jim began going through the ledgers and other papers, handing a pile to Glen while Smoke prowled the house. At the rear of the house he found the rabbit hole, and he had been correct in his thinking. The home had been built in front of a cave opening. He called for Jim and Glen.

"You was right," Jim acknowledged. "We'll inspect it in the morning. I'll post guards here tonight." He held out the papers taken from the safe. "Interestin' readin' in here, Smoke. All kinds of wanted posters and other information on the men who lived here. What we've done—it was mostly you and York—is clean out a nest of snakes. We've made this part of the country a hell of a lot safer."

On the way back to the town, Smoke spotted the Ute chief, White Wolf. The men stopped, Jim saying, "We're goin' to try them that's still alive, White Wolf. Do that in the mornin'. We should be out of the town by late tomorrow afternoon. When we pull out, the town and everything in it is yours."

"I thank you," the chief said gravely. "My people will not be cold or hungry this winter." He turned to Smoke and smiled. "My brother, Preacher, would be proud of you. I will see that he hears of this fight, young warrior."

"Thank you, Chief. Give him my best."

White Wolf nodded, shook hands with the men, and then was gone.

Cahoon was still screaming.

* * *

It was a sullen lot that were rounded up and herded into the compound for safekeeping. A head count showed fifty hardcases had elected to surrender or were taken by force, usually the latter.

But, as Smoke had feared, many of the worst ones had slipped out. Shorty, Red, and Jake were gone. Bill Wilson's body had been found, but Studs Woodenhouse, Tie Medley, Paul Rycroft, and Slim Bothwell were gone. Hart and Ayers were dead, riddled with bullets. But Natick, Nappy, LaHogue, and Brute Pitman had managed to escape. Tustin could not be found among the dead, so all had to assume the so-called minister had made it out alive. Sheriff Danvers had been taken prisoner, and Sheriff Larsen had told him he was going to personally tie the noose for him. Dagget, Glen Moore, Lapeer and, of course, Rex Davidson were gone.

Smoke knew he would have them to deal with—sooner or later, and probably sooner.

Smoke bathed in the creek behind the campsite, and he and York caught a few hours sleep before the judge and his jury showed up. They were to be in Dead River at dawn.

As had been predicted, there were several newspaper men with the judge, as well as several photographers. The bodies of the outlaws still lay in the street at dawn, when the judge, jury, reporters, and photographers showed up. Two of the half-dozen reporters were from New York City and Boston, on a tour of the wild West, and they were appalled at the sight that greeted them.

Old Red Davis, obviously enjoying putting the needle to the Easterners, showed them around the town, pointing out any sight they might have missed.

"See that fellow over yonder?" he pointed. The reporters and a photographer looked. "The man with a gold badge on his chest? That's the most famous gunfighter in all the

West. He's kilt two/three hundred men. Not countin' Injuns. That's Smoke Jensen, boys!"

The Easterners gaped, one finally saying, "But why is the man wearing a badge? He's an outlaw!"

"He ain't no such thing," Red corrected. "He's just fast with a gun, that's all. The fastest man alive. Been all sorts of books writ about Smoke. Want to meet him?"

Foolish question.

Luckily for Smoke, Jim Wilde intercepted the group and took them aside. "You boys from back east walk light around the men in this town. This ain't Boston or New York. And while Smoke is a right nice fellow, with a fine ranch up north of here, he can be a mite touchy at times." Then the marshal brought the men up to date on what Smoke had done in Dead River.

The photographer set up his awkward equipment and began taking pictures of Smoke and the Arizona Ranger, York. Both men endured it, Smoke saying to York, "You got any warrants on any of them that cut and run?"

"Shore do. What you got in mind?"

The camera popped and puffed smoke into the air.

"I think Sally told me she was going to give birth about October. I plan on bein' there when she does. That gives us a few months to prowl. Tell your bosses back in Arizona not to worry about the expenses; it's on me."

The camera snapped and clicked, and smoke went into the air as the chemical dust was ignited.

And Marshal Jim Wilde, unintentionally, gave the newspaper reporters the fuel that would, in time, ignite the biggest gunfight, western-style, in Keene, New Hampshire history.

"Smoke's wife is back in New Hampshire. He'll be going back there when she gives birth to their child. Now come on, I'll introduce you gentlemen to Smoke Jensen."

* * *

Judge Hezekiah Jones had set up his bench, so to speak, outside the saloon, with the jury seated to his left, on the boardwalk. Already, a gallows had been knocked together and ropes noosed and knotted. They could hang three at a time.

The trial of the first three took two and a half minutes. A minute and a half later, they were swinging.

"Absolutely the most barbaric proceedings I have ever witnessed," the Boston man sniffed, scribbling in his journal.

"Frontier justice certainly does leave a great deal to be desired," the New York City man agreed.

"I think I'm going to be ill," the photographer said, a tad green around the mouth.

"Hang 'em!" Judge Jones hit the table with his gavel, and three more were led off to meet their maker.

Sheriff Danvers stood before the bench, his hands tied behind his back. "I have a statement to make, Your Honor," he said.

Hezekiah glared at him. "Oh, all right. Make your god-damn statement and then plead guilty, you heathen!"

"I ain't guilty!" Danvers shouted.

The judge turned to face the men of the jury. "How do you find?"

"Guilty!" Red called.

"Hang the son of a bitch!" Hezekiah ordered.

And so it went.

The hurdy-gurdy ladies and shopkeepers were hauled off in wagons. Smoke didn't ask where they were being taken because he really didn't care. The bodies of the outlaws were tossed into a huge pit and dirt and gravel shoveled over them. "I'd like to keep my federal commission, Jim," Smoke said. "I got a hunch this mess isn't over."

"Keep it as long as you like. You're makin' thirty a

month and expenses." He grinned and shook Smoke's hand, then shook the hand of the ranger. "I'll ride any trail with you boys any time."

He wheeled his horse and was gone.

The wind sighed lonely over the deserted town as Smoke and York sat their horses on the hill overlooking the town. White Wolf and his people were moving into the town. The judge had ordered whatever money was left in the town to remain there. Let the Indians have it for their help in bringing justice to the godforsaken place, he had said.

Smoke waved at White Wolf and the chief returned the gesture. Smoke and York turned their horses and put their backs to Dead River.

"What is this?" York asked. "July, August . . . what? I done flat lost all track of the months."

"I think it's September. I think Sally told me the first month she felt she was with child was March. So if she's going to have the baby the last part of October . . ."

York counted on his fingers, then stopped and looked at Smoke. "Do you want March as one?"

"Damned if I know!"

"We'll say you do." He once more began counting. "Yep. But that'd be eight months. So this might be August."

Smoke looked at him. "York . . . what in the hell are you talking about?"

York confessed that what he knew about the process of babies growing before the birth was rather limited.

"I think I better wire Sally and ask her," Smoke suggested.

"I think that'd be the wise thing to do."

Jim Wilde had told Smoke he would send a wire to Sally, telling her the operation was over and Smoke was all right. And he would do the same for York, advising the Arizona Ranger headquarters that York was in pursuit of those who had escaped.

Smoke and York cut across the Sangre de Cristo range, in search of the cave Davidson and his men had used to escape.

Sally got the wire one day before the Boston and New York newspapers ran the front-page story of the incident, calling it: JUSTICE AT DEAD RIVER. The pictures would follow in later editions.

John read the stories, now carried in nearly all papers in the East, and shook his head in disbelief, saying to his daughter, "Almost fifty men were hanged in one morning. Their trials took an average of three minutes per man. For God's sake, Sally, surely you don't agree with these kangaroo proceedings?"

"Father," the daughter said, knowing that the man would never understand, "it's a hard land. We don't have time for all the niceties you people take for granted back here."

"It doesn't bother you that your husband, Smoke, is credited—if that's the right choice of words—with killing some thirty or forty men?"

Sally shook her head. "No. I don't see why it should. You see, Father, you've taken a defense attorney's position already. And you immediately condemned Smoke and the other lawmen and posse members, without ever saying a word about those poor people who were kidnapped, enslaved, and then hung up on hooks to die by slow torture. You haven't said a word about the people those outlaws abused, robbed, murdered, raped, tortured, and then ran back to Dead River to hide and spend their ill-gotten gain. Even those papers there," she pointed, "admit that every man who was hanged was a confessed murderer, many of them multiple killers. They got whatever they deserved, Father. No more, and no less."

The father sighed and looked at his daughter. "The West has changed you, Sally. I don't know you anymore."

"Yes, I've changed, Father," she admitted. "For the better." She smiled. "It's going to be interesting when you and Smoke meet."

"Yes," John agreed. "Quite."

It took Smoke and York three days after crossing the high range to find the cave opening and the little valley beneath it.

"Slick," York said. "If they hadn't a knocked down the bushes growin' in front of the mouth of that cave, we'd have had the devil's own hard time findin' it."

The men entered the cave opening, which was barely large enough to accommodate a standing man. And they knew from the smell that greeted them what they would find.

They looked down at the bloated and maggot-covered bodies on the cave floor.

"You know them?" Smoke asked.

"I seen 'em in town. But I never knowed their names. And I don't feel like goin' through their pockets to find out who they was, do you?"

Smoke shook his head. Both men stepped back outside, grateful to once more be out in the cool, fresh air. They breathed deeply, clearing their nostrils of the foul odor of death.

"Let's see if we can pick up a trail," Smoke suggested.

Old Preacher had schooled Smoke well. The man could track a snake across a flat rock. Smoke circled a couple of times, then called for York to join him.

"North." He pointed. "I didn't think they'd risk getting out into the sand dunes. They'll probably follow the timber line until they get close to the San Luis, then they'll ride the river, trying to hide their tracks. I'll make a bet they'll cut through Poncha Pass, then head east to the railroad town. They might stop at the hot springs first. You game?"

"Let's do it."

They picked up and lost the tracks a dozen times, but it soon became apparent that Smoke had pegged their direction accurately. At a village called Poncha Springs, past the San Luis Valley, Smoke and York stopped and re-supplied and bathed in the hot waters.

Yes, about a dozen hard-looking men had been through. Oh, five or six days back. They left here ridin' toward Salida. They weren't real friendly folks, neither. Looked like hardcases.

Smoke and York pulled out the next morning.

At Salida, they learned that Davidson and his men had stopped, bought supplies and ammunition, and left the same day they'd come.

But one man didn't ride out with the others.

"He still in town?" Smoke asked.

"Shore is. Made his camp up by the Arkansas. 'Bout three miles out of town. But he's over to the saloon now."

Salida was new and raw, a railroad town built by the Denver and Rio Grande railroad. Salida was the division point of the main line and the narrow-gauge lines over what is called Marshall Pass.

"What's this ol' boy look like?" York asked.

The man described him.

"Nappy," Smoke said. "You got papers on him?"

"'Deed I do," York said, slipping the hammer thong off his .44.

"I'll back you up. Let's go."

"You look familiar, partner," the citizen said to Smoke. "What might be your name?"

"Smoke Jensen."

As soon as the lawmen had left, the man hauled his ashes up and down the muddy streets, telling everyone he could find that Smoke was in town.

"I know Nappy is wanted for rape and murder," Smoke said. "What else did he do?"

"Killed my older brother down between the Mogollon Plateau and the Little Colorado. Jimmy was a lawman, workin' out of Tucson. Nappy had killed an old couple just outside of town and Jimmy had tracked him north." York talked as they walked. "Nappy ambushed him. Gutshot my brother and left him to die. But Jimmy wasn't about to die 'fore he told who done him in. He crawled for miles until some punchers found him and he could tell them what happened, then he died. I was fifteen at the time. I joined the Rangers when I was eighteen. That was six years ago."

"I figured you for some younger than that."

"It's all the clean livin' I done," York said with a straight face.

Then they stepped into the saloon.

And Nappy wasn't alone.

The short, barrel-chested, and extremely ugly outlaw stood at the far end of the bar, his hands at his sides. Across the room were two more hardcases, also standing, each wearing two guns tied down low. To Smoke's extreme right, almost in the shadows, was another man, also standing.

"Napoleon Whitman?" York spoke to the stocky outlaw.

"That's me, punk."

"I'm an Arizona Ranger. It is my duty to inform you that you are under arrest for the murder of Tucson deputy sheriff Jimmy York."

"Do tell? Well, Ranger, this is Colorado. You ain't jackshit up here."

"I have also been appointed a deputy U.S. Marshal, Nappy. Now how is it gonna be?"

"Well," Nappy drawled, as the men at the tables drifted back, out of the line of fire. And since Nappy had men posted all around the room, that meant getting clear outside, which is what most did. "I think I'm gonna finish my drink, Ranger. That's what I think I'm gonna do. And since both you squirts is about to die, why don't y'all order yourselves a shot?"

Then he arrogantly turned his left side to the man and faced the bar. But both Smoke and York knew he was watching them in the mirror.

"He's all yours," Smoke murmured, just loud enough for York to hear. "Don't worry about the others."

York nodded. "I don't drink with scum," he told the ugly outlaw.

Nappy had lifted the shot glass to his mouth with his left hand. With that slur, he set the glass down on the bar and turned, facing the younger man. "What'd you say to me, punk?" The outlaw was not accustomed to be talked to in such a manner. After all, he was a famous and feared gunfighter, and punk kids respected him. They sure didn't talk smart to him.

"I said you're scum, Nappy. You're what's found at the bottom of an outhouse pit."

All were conscious of many faces peering inside the dark barroom; many men pressed up against the glass from the boardwalk.

"You can't talk to me lak 'at!" Nappy almost screamed the words, and he could not understand the strange sensation that suddenly filled him.

It was fear.

Fear! The word clutched at Nappy's innards. Fear! Afraid of this snot-nosed pup with a tin star? He tried to shrug it off but found he could not.

"I just did, Nappy," York said. He smiled at the man; he could practically smell the fear-stink of the outlaw.

Nappy stepped away from the bar to stand wide-legged, facing York. "Then fill your hand, you son of a bitch!"

16

Smoke had been standing, half turned away from York, about three feet between them, his arms folded across his lower chest. When Nappy grabbed for iron, Smoke went into a low crouch and cross-drew, cocking and firing with one blindingly fast motion. First he shot the man in the shadows with his right-hand .44, then took out the closest of the two men to Nappy's immediate left.

Nappy had beaten York to the draw, but as so often happens, his first slug tore up the floor in front of York's boots. York had not missed a shot, but the stocky outlaw was soaking up the lead as fast as York could pump it into him and was still standing on his feet, tossing lead in return. He was holding onto the bar with his left hand and firing at York.

Smoke rolled across the floor and came up on his knees, both .44s hammering lead into the one man he faced who was still standing. The .44 slugs drew the life from the man and Smoke turned on one knee, splinters from the rough wood floor digging into his knee with the move. The man in the shadows was leaning against a wall, blood all over his shirt front, trying to level his .45.

Smoke shot him in the face, and the man slid down the wall to rest on his butt, dead.

As the roaring left his ears and Smoke could once more see, Nappy was still standing, even though York had emptied his .44 into the man's chest and belly.

But Smoke could see he was not going to be standing much longer. The man's eyes were glazing over, and blood was pouring out of his mouth. His guns were laying on the floor beside his scuffed and dirty boots.

Nappy cut his eyes to Smoke. "That you, Jensen?" he managed to say.

"It's me, Nappy." Smoke stood up and walked toward the dying outlaw.

"Come closer, Jensen. I cain't see you. Dark in here, ain't it?"

Death's hand was slowly closing in on Nappy.

"What do you want, Nappy?"

"They'll get you, Jensen. They're gonna have their way with your uppity wife in front of your eyes, then they're gonna kill you slow. You ain't gonna find them, Jensen. They're dug in deep. But they'll find you. And that's a promise, Jensen. That's . . ."

His knees buckled and his eyes rolled back into his head until only the whites were showing. Nappy crashed to the barroom floor and died.

Both lawmen punched out empties and reloaded. York said, "I'll send a wire to the Tucson office and tell them to recall the dodgers on Nappy. You hit anywhere?"

"'Bout a dozen splinters in my knee is all."

"I'll be back, and then we'll have us a drink."

"Sounds good. I'll have one while I'm waiting. Hurry up, I hate to drink alone."

Smoke lost the trail. It wasn't the first time it had happened in his life, but it irked him even more this time. Smoke and York had trailed the outlaws to just outside of Crested Butte, and there they seemed to just drop off the face of the earth.

The lawmen backtracked and circled, but it was no use; the trail was lost.

After five more days of fruitless and frustrating looking, they decided to give it up.

They were camped near the banks of Roaring Fork, cooking some fish they'd caught for supper, both their mouths salivating at the good smells, when Drifter's head and ears came up.

"We got company," Smoke said softly.

"So I noticed. Injuns, you reckon?"

"I don't think so. Drifter acts different when it's Indians."

"Hallo, the fire!" a voice called.

"If you're friendly," Smoke returned the shout, "come on in. We caught plenty of fish and the coffee's hot."

"Music to my ears, boys." A man stepped into camp, leading his horses, a saddle mount and a packhorse. "Name's McGraw, but I'm called Chaw."

"That's Buddy York and I'm Smoke Jensen."

Chaw McGraw damn near swallered his chaw when he heard the name Smoke Jensen. He coughed and spat a couple of times, and then dug in his kit for a battered tin cup. He poured a cup of coffee and sat down, looking at Smoke.

"Damned if it ain't you! I figured you for some older. But there you sit, bigger 'en life. I just read about you in a paper a travelin' drummer gimme. Lemme git it for you; it ain't but a week old. Outta Denver."

The paper told the story of the big shoot-out and the hangings and the final destruction of the outlaw town of Dead River. It told all about Smoke and York and then, with a sinking feeling in the pit of his stomach, Smoke read about Sally being back in Keene, New Hampshire, awaiting the birth of their first child.

"What's wrong, partner?" York asked, looking at the strange expression on Smoke's face.

Not wanting to take any chances on what he said being repeated by Chaw, Smoke minutely shook his head and handed the paper to York. "Nothing."

York read the long article and lifted his eyes to Smoke. The men exchanged knowing glances across the fire and the broiling fish.

"Help yourself, Chaw," Smoke offered. "We have plenty."

"I wanna wash my hands 'fore I partake," Chaw said. "Be right back. Damn, boys, but that do smell good!"

Chaw out of earshot, Smoke said, "You ever been east of the Big Muddy, York?"

"Never had no desire to go." Then he added, "Until now, that is."

"Davidson is crazy, but like a fox. We destroyed his little kingdom, brought his evil down on his head. And now he hates you as much as he does me. And I would just imagine this story is all over the West." He tapped the newspaper. "It would be like King Rex to gather up as many hardcases as he could buy—and he's got the money to buy a trainload of them—and head east. What do you think?"

"I think you've pegged it. Remember what Nappy said back in the bar, just before he died?"

"Yes. But I'm betting he wants the child to be born before he does anything. It would be like him. What do you think?"

"That you're right, all the way down the line. Dagget was one of the men who shot your wife, right?"

"Yes."

"But she wasn't showin' with child then, right?"

"Yes."

"Well, Rex can count. He'll time it so's the baby will be born, I'm thinkin'."

"I think you're right. And I'm thinking none of them would want to get back east too soon. Dagget is wanted back there, remember? You with me, York?"

"All the way, Smoke."

"We'll pull out in the morning. Here comes Chaw. We'd better fix some more fish. He looks like he could eat a skunk, and probably has."

They said their good-byes to Chaw and headed east, taking their time, heading for Leadville, once called Magic City and Cloud City, for it lies just below timberline, almost two miles above sea level. Some have described the climate as ten months winter and two months damn late in the fall. Smoke and York followed old Indian trails, trails that took Smoke back in time, when he and Preacher roamed wild and free across the land, with Preacher teaching first the boy and then the man called Smoke. It brought back memories to Smoke, memories that unashamedly wet his eyes. If York noticed—and Smoke was sure he did—the ranger said nothing about it.

Located in the valley of the Arkansas, Leadville was once the state's second largest city. It was first a roaring gold town, then a fabulous silver boom town, and then once more a gold-rush town. When Smoke and York rode into Leadville late one afternoon, the town was still roaring.

Smoke and York had experienced no trouble on their way into the boom town, unlike so many other not-so-lucky travelers. Roving gangs of thugs and outlaws had erected toll booths on several of the most important roads leading into the town, and those who refused to pay were robbed at gunpoint; many were killed. Robberies, rapes, assaults, and wild shoot-outs were almost an hourly occurrence within the town's limits.

When Smoke and York rode into the busy city, Leadville's population was hovering between fifty thousand and sixty thousand—no one ever really knew for sure. It was the wildest place in the state, for a time. The town's only hospital was guarded by a hundred men, day and night, to keep it from being torn down by thugs. Churches were forced to hire armed guards to work around the clock. The handful of police officers were virtually powerless to keep any semblance of order, so that fell to various vigilante groups. It was a town where you took your life in your hands just by getting out of bed in the morning.

"I ain't too thrilled about no hotel, Smoke," York commented on the way in.

"There wouldn't be a room anyway. We'll stable the horses, pick up some supplies, and hit the saloons. We might be able to hear something. Let's take off these badges."

The only "hotel" in town that might have had empty beds was the Mammoth Palace, a huge shed with double bunks that could easily sleep five hundred. A guest paid a dollar for an eight-hour sleeping turn.

And in the midst of it all, churches were flourishing. If not spiritually, then financially. One member suggested that he buy a chandelier for the church. Another member asked, "Why? None of us knows how to play it!"

Smoke and York turned their horses onto State Street, where several famous New York chefs operated fancy eating places. Oxtail soup cost five cents a bowl at Smoothey's, and it was famous from the Coast to the Rockies.

Smoke waved at a ragged newsboy and bought a local newspaper, *The Chronicle.* They rode on and found a stable that had stalls to spare.

"We'll sleep with our horses," Smoke told the livery man.

"That'll be a dollar extra, boys. Apiece."

York started to protest, then noted the look on Smoke's face and held his peace.

"Give them a bait of corn and all the hay they can

handle," Smoke told the man. "And do it now. If you go into Drifter's stall after I'm gone, he'll kill you."

"Son of a bitch tries to stomp on me," the livery blustered, "I'll take a rifle to him."

"Then I'll kill you," Smoke said softly, but with steel in his voice.

The man looked into those cold, hard eyes. He swallowed hard. "I was jokin', mister."

"I wasn't."

The liveryman gulped, his Adam's apple bobbing up and down. "Yes, sir. I'll take the best of care of your horses. Whatever you say mister . . . ah? . . ."

Smoke smiled and thought, To hell with trying to disguise who we are. "Smoke Jensen."

The liveryman backed up against a stall. "Yes, sir, Mr. Jensen, I mean, whatever you say, sir."

Smoke patted the man on the shoulder. "We'll get along fine, I'm sure."

"Yes, sir. You can bet I'll do my damndest!"

Smoke and York stepped out into the hustle and confusion of the boom town. Both knew that within the hour, every resident of the town would know that Smoke Jensen had arrived.

They stepped into a general store, checked the prices of goods, and decided they'd resupply further on.

"Legal stealin'," York said, looking at the price of a pair of jeans. He put the jeans back on the table.

They walked back outside.

"We can cover more ground if we split up," the Arizona Ranger suggested. "I'll take the other side of the street. What say we meet back at the stable in a couple of hours?"

"Sounds good to me. Watch your back, York."

"I hear you." York checked the busy street, found his chance, and darted across. As it was, he almost got run over by a freighter. The freighter cursed him, and rumbled and rattled on.

Smoke walked on. There was something about the tall man with the two guns, in cross-draw style, that made most men hurry to step out of his way. If someone had told Smoke that he looked menacing, he would not have believed it. He could never see the savage look that was locked into his eyes.

Smoke turned a corner and found himself on Harrison Avenue, a busy business thoroughfare. He strolled the avenue, left it, and turned several corners, cutting down to hit State and Main.

Then he saw Natick, stepping out of a brothel. Smoke stopped and half turned, blending in better with the crowd. He backed against a building and began reading the paper he'd bought, still keeping a good eye on Natick. He hoped the outlaw might lead him to Davidson and Dagget.

But Natick stepped out into the street and walked toward a saloon. Smoke turned away and walked in the opposite direction, not wanting to stare too long at the man, knowing how that can attract someone's attention.

Smoke lounged around a bit, buying a cup of coffee and a sandwich at prices that would make a Scotsman squall in outrage. The coffee was weak and the sandwich uneatable. Smoke gave both to a ragged man who seemed down on his luck, and then he waited.

Soon he saw York walking up the street and turning into the saloon. Smoke hurriedly crossed the street and stepped into the crowded saloon, elbowing and shouldering his way through the crowd. Several turned to protest, looked into the unforgiving eyes of the tall stranger with the two six-guns, and closed their months much faster than they opened them.

York was facing Natick and two other hard-looking men that Smoke did not know and did not remember seeing in Dead River.

And the crowd was rapidly moving back and away, out of the line of fire.

It was almost a repeat performance of Nappy and his crew. Except that this time a photographer was there and had his equipment set up, and he was ready to start popping whenever the action began.

The town marshal, a notorious bully and killer, was leaning up against the bar watching it all, a faint smile on his face. He was not going to interfere on behalf of either side.

"Mort!" Smoke called.

The marshal turned and faced Smoke, and his face went a shade paler.

"Jensen," he whispered.

"Either choose a side or get out," Smoke warned him, clear menace in his voice.

It was a warning and a challenge that rankled the town marshal, but not one he wanted to pick up. Quick with his guns and his fists, boasting that he had killed seven men, Mort's reputation was merely a dark smudge on the ground when compared to Smoke's giant shadow.

The marshal nodded and walked outside, turning and going swiftly up the street.

"All right, boys," York said. "You all know Smoke Jensen. Make your play."

The three outlaws drew together. One did not even clear leather before Smoke's guns belched fire and smoke, the slug striking the outlaw in the center of the chest. The second outlaw that Smoke faced managed to get the muzzle free of leather before twin death-blows of lead hammered at his belly and chest.

York's guns had roared and bucked and slammed Natick against a rear wall of the saloon, down but not quite dead.

Smoke walked to him. "Natick?"

"What do you want, Jensen?" the outlaw gasped.

"I know why you broke with Davidson and the others."

"Yeah? Why?"

"Because you may be a lot of bad things, but you're no baby killer."

Natick nodded his bloody head. "Yeah. I couldn't go along with that. I'm glad it was you boys who done me in. Pull my boots off for me, Jensen?"

Smoke tugged off the man's boots. One big toe was sticking through a hole in his sock.

"Ain't that pitiful?" Natick observed. "I've stole thousands and thousands of dollars and cain't even afford to buy a pair of socks." He cut his eyes to Smoke. "Rex and Dagget's got some bad ones with them, Jensen. Lapeer, Moore, The Hog, Tustin, Shorty, Red, and Jake. Studs Woodenhouse, Tie Medley, Paul Rycroft, Slim Bothwell, and Brute Pitman. I don't know where they're hidin', Jensen, and that's the truth. But Davidson plans on rapin' your woman and then killin' your kid."

Natick was whispering low, so only Smoke and York could hear his dying words. The photographer was taking pictures as fast as he could jerk plates and load his dust.

Smoke bent his head to hear Natick's words, but the outlaw would speak no more. He was dead.

Smoke dug in his own pocket and handed some money to a man standing close by. "You'll see that he gets a proper burial?"

"I shore will, Mr. Jensen. And it was a plumb honor to see you in action."

The photographer fired again.

The batwings snapped open and a dirty man charged into the bar, holding twin leather bags. "She's pure, boys. Assayed out high as a cat's back. The drinks is on me! Git them damn stiffs outta the way!"

17

John and his sons and daughters and their families looked at the pictures John had sent in from New York, looked at them in horror.

Bodies were sprawling in the street, on the boardwalks, hanging half in and half out of broken windows. One was facedown in a horse trough, another was sprawled in stiffened death beside the watering trough.

And John's son-in-law, Smoke Jensen, handsome devil that he was, was standing on the boardwalk, calmly rolling a cigarette.

"That's my Smoke!" Sally said, pointing.

Smoke was wearing his guns cross-draw, and he had another one tucked behind his gunbelt. In another picture, the long-bladed Bowie knife he carried behind one gun could be clearly seen. In still another picture, Smoke was sitting on the edge of the boardwalk, eating an apple. In the left side of the picture, bodies could be seen hanging from the gallows.

John's stomach felt queasy. He laid the pictures aside and stifled a burp when Sally grabbed them up and began glancing at them.

"There's a bandage on Smoke's head," she noted. "But I can't see that he was shot anywhere else."

"Who is that handsome man standing beside him?" Walter's sister-in-law asked. "He's so . . . rugged-looking!"

"Lord, Martha!" her sister exclaimed. "He's savage-looking!"

"He's some sort of law enforcement officer," Walter explained, examining the picture. But his badge is somewhat different from . . . ah . . . Smoke's. Excuse my hesitation, Sister, but I never heard of a man being called Smoke."

"Get used to it, Walt," Sally said, a testy note to her statement. After being in the West, with its mostly honest and open and non-pompous people, the East was beginning to grate on her more and more.

Her father picked up on her testiness. "Sally, dearest, it'll soon be 1882. No one carries a gun around here except the law officers, and many times they don't even carry a gun, only a club. There hasn't been an Indian attack in this area in anyone's memory! We are a quiet community, with plans underway to have a college here; a branch of the state university. We are a community of laws, darling. We don't have gunfights in the streets. Keene was settled almost a hundred and fifty years ago. . . ."

"Yes, Father," Sally said impatiently. "I know. 1736, as a matter of fact. It's a nice, quiet, stable, pleasant little community. But I've grown away from it. Father, Mother, all of you . . . have you ever stood on the Great Divide? Have you ever ridden up in the High Lonesome, where you knew you could look for a hundred miles and there would be no other human being? Have any of you ever watched eagles soar and play in the skies, and knew yours were the only eyes on them? No, no you haven't. None of you. You don't even have a loaded gun in this house. None of you women would know what to do if you were attacked. You haven't any idea how to fire a gun. All you ladies know how to do is sit around looking pretty and attend your goddamn teas!"

John wore a pained expression on his face. Abigail

started fanning herself furiously. Sally's brothers wore frowns on their faces. Her sisters and sisters-in-law looked shocked.

Martha laughed out loud. "I have my teacher's certificate, Sally. Do you suppose there might be a position for me out where you live?"

"Martha!" her older sister hissed. "You can't be serious. There are . . . savages out there!"

"Oh . . . piddly-poo!" Martha said. She would have liked to have the nerve to say something stronger, like Sally, but didn't want to be marked as a scarlet woman in this circle.

"We're looking for a schoolteacher right this moment, Martha," Sally told her. "And I think you'd be perfect. When Smoke gets here, we'll ask him. If he says you're the choice, then you can start packing."

Martha began clapping her hands in excitement.

"Smoke is a one-man committee on the hiring of teachers?" Jordan sniffed disdainfully.

"Would you want to buck him on anything, Brother?"

Jordan stroked his beard and remained silent. Unusually so for a lawyer.

Smoke and York left Leadville the next morning, riding out just at dawn. They rode north, past Fremont Pass, then cut east toward Breckenridge. No sign of Davidson or Dagget or any of the others with them. They rode on, with Bald Mountain to the south of them, following old trails. They kept Mount Evans to their north and gradually began the winding down toward the town of Denver.

"We gonna spend some time in Denver City?" York asked.

"Few days. Maybe a week. We both need to get groomed and curried and bathed, and our clothes are kind of shabby-looking."

"My jeans is so thin my drawers is showin'," York agreed. "If we goin' east, I reckon we're gonna have to get all duded up like dandies, huh?"

"No way," Smoke's reply was grim. "I'm tired of pretending to be something I'm not. We'll just dress like what we are. Westerners."

York sighed. "That's a relief. I just cain't see myself in one of them goofy caps like you wore back in Dead River."

Smoke laughed at just the thought. "And while we're here, I've got to send some wires. Find out how Sally is doing and find out what's happened up on the Sugarloaf."

"Pretty place you got, Smoke?"

"Beautiful. And there's room for more. Lots of room. You ever think about getting out of law work, York?"

"More and more lately. I'd like to have me a little place. Nothin' fancy; nothin' so big me and a couple more people couldn't handle it. I just might drift up that way once this is all over."

"You got a girl?"

"Naw. I ain't had the time. Captain's been sendin' me all over the territory ever since I started with the Rangers. I reckon it's time for me to start thinking about settlin' down."

"You might meet you an eastern gal, York." Smoke was grinning.

"Huh! What would I do with her? Them eastern gals is a different breed of cat. I read about them. All them teas and the like. I got to have me a woman that'll work right alongside me. You know what ranchin' is like. Hard damn work."

"It is that. But my Sally was born back east. Educated all over the world. She's been to Paris!"

"Texas?"

"France."

"No kiddin'! I went to Dallas once. Biggest damn

place I ever seen. Too damn many people to suit me. I felt all hemmed in."

"It isn't like that up in the High Lonesome. I think you'd like it up there, York. We need good stable people like you. Give it some thought. I'll help you get started; me and Sally."

"Right neighborly of y'all. Little tradin' post up ahead. Let's stop. I'm out of the makin's."

While York was buying tobacco, Smoke sat outside, reading a fairly recent edition of a Denver paper. The city was growing by leaps and bounds. The population was now figured at more than sixty thousand.

"Imagine that," Smoke muttered. "Just too damn many folks for me."

He read on. A new theatre had been built, the Tabor Grand Opera House. He read on, suddenly smiling. He checked the date of the paper. It was only four days old.

"You grinnin' like a cat lickin' cream, Smoke," York said, stepping out and rolling a cigarette. "What got your funny bone all quiverin'?"

"And old friend of mine is in town, York. And I just bet you he'd like to ride east with us."

"Yeah? Lawman?"

"Businessman, scholar, gambler, gunfighter."

"Yeah?" Who might that be?"

"Louis Longmont."

"By the Lord Harry!" Louis exclaimed, standing up from his table in the swanky restaurant and waving at Smoke. "Waiter! Two more places here, *s'il vous plait*."

"What the hell did he say?" York whispered.

"Don't ask me," Smoke returned the whisper.

The men all shook hands, Smoke introducing York to Louis. Smoke had not seen Louis since the big shoot-out at Fontana more than a year ago. The man had not changed. Handsome and very sure of himself. The gray just touching his hair at the temples.

Smoke also noted the carefully tailored suit, cut to accommodate a shoulder holster.

Same ol' Louis.

After the men had ordered dinner—Louis had to do it, the menu being in French—drinks were brought around and Longmont toasted them both.

"I've been reading about the exploits of you men," Louis remarked after sipping his Scotch. York noticed that all their liquor glasses had funny-looking square bits of ice in them, which did make the drink a bit easier on the tongue.

"We've been busy," Smoke agreed.

"Still pursuing the thugs?"

"You know we are, Louis. You would not have allowed your name to appear in the paper if you hadn't wanted us to find you in Denver."

York sat silent, a bit uncomfortable with the sparkling white tablecloth and all the heavy silverware—he couldn't figure out what he was supposed to do; after all, he couldn't eat but with one fork and one knife, no how. And he had never seen so many duded-up men and gussied-up women in all his life. Even with new clothes on, it made a common fella feel shabby.

"Let's just say," Louis said, "I'm a bit bored with it all."

"You've been traveling about?"

"Just returned from Paris a month ago. I'd like to get back out in the country. Eat some beans and beef and see the stars above me when I close my eyes."

"Want to throw in with us, Louis?"

Louis lifted his glass. "I thought you were never going to ask."

Smoke and York loafed around Denver for a few days, while Louis wrapped up his business and Smoke sent and received several wires. Sally was fine; the baby was due in two months—approximately.

"What does she mean by that?" York asked, reading over Smoke's shoulder.

"It means, young man," Louis said, "that babies do not always cooperate with a timetable. The child might be born within several weeks of that date, before it or after it."

Louis was dressed in boots, dark pants, gray shirt, and black leather vest. He wore two guns, both tied down and both well-used and well-taken care of, the wooden butts worn smooth with use.

York knew that Louis Longmont, self-made millionaire and world-famous gambler, was a deadly gunslinger. And a damn good man to have walkin' with you when trouble stuck its head up, especially when that trouble had a six-gun in each hand.

"Do tell," York muttered.

"What's the plan, Smoke?" Louis asked.

"You about ready to pull out?"

"Is tomorrow morning agreeable with you?"

"Fine. The sooner the better. I thought we'd take our time, ride across Kansas; maybe as far as St. Louis if time permits. We can catch a train anywhere along the way. And by riding, we just might pick up some information about Davidson and his crew."

"Sounds good. Damn a man who would even entertain the thought of harming a child!"

"We pull out at dawn."

Sally had not shown her family all the wires she'd received from Smoke. She did not wish to alarm any of them, and above all, she did not wish to alert the local police as to her husband's suspicions about Davidson and his gang traveling east after her and the baby. Her father would have things done the legal way—ponderous and, unknowing to him, very dangerous for all concerned. John had absolutely no idea of what kind of man this Rex Davidson was.

But Sally did. And Smoke could handle it, his way. And she was glad Louis and York were with him.

York just might be the ticket for Martha out of the East and into the still wild and wide-open West. He was a good-looking young man.

The servant answered the door and Martha entered the sitting room. Sally waved her to a chair with imported antimacassars on the arms and back. The day was warm, and both women fanned themselves to cool a bit.

"I was serious about going west, Sally."

"I thought as much. And now," she guessed accurately, "you want to know all about it."

"That's right."

Where to start? Sally thought. And how to really explain about the vastness and the emptiness and the magnificence of it all?

Before she could start, the door opened again, and this time the room was filled with small children: Sally's nieces and nephews and a few of their friends.

"Aunt Sally," a redheaded, freckle-faced boy said. "Will you tell us about Uncle Smoke?"

"I certainly will." She winked at Martha. "I'll tell you all about the High Lonesome and the strong men who live there."

They pulled out at first light. Three men who wore their guns as a part of their being. Three men who had faced death and beaten it so many times none of them could remember all the battles.

Louis had chosen a big buckskin-colored horse with a mean look to his eyes. The horse looked just about as mean as Smoke knew Drifter really was.

Before leaving Denver, Smoke had wired Jim Wilde

and asked for both York and Louis to be formally deputized as U.S. Marshals. The request had been honored within the day.

So they were three men who now wore official badges on their chests. One, a millionaire adventurer. One, a successful rancher. One, a young man who was only weeks away from meeting the love of his life.

They rode east, veering slightly south, these three hard-eyed and heavily armed men. They would continue a southerly line until reaching a trading post on the banks of the Big Sandy; a few more years and the trading post would become the town of Limon.

At the trading post, they would cut due east and hold to that all the way across Kansas. They would stay south of Hell Creek, but on their ride across Colorado, they would ford Sand Creek, an offshoot of the Republican River. They would ride across Spring Creek, Landsman, East Spring, and cross yet another Sand Creek before entering into Kansas.

Kansas was still woolly but nothing like it had been a few years back when the great cattle herds were being driven up from Texas, and outlaws and gunfighters were just about anywhere one wished to look.

But the three men rode with caution. The decade had rolled into the eighties, but there were still bands of Indians who left the reservation from time to time; still bands of outlaws that killed and robbed. And they were riding into an area of the country where men still killed other men over the bitterness of that recent unpleasantness called by some the Civil War and by others the War Between the States.

The days were warm and pleasant or hot and unpleasant as the men rode steadily eastward across the plains. But the plains were now being dotted and marred and scarred with wire. Wire put up by farmers to keep ranchers' cattle out. Wire put up by ranchers to keep nesters out of water holes, creeks, and rivers. Ranchers who wished to breed better cattle put up wire to keep inferior breeds from mixing in and to keep prize bulls at home.

But none of the men really liked wire, even though all could see the reasons—most of the time—behind the erecting of barbed wire fences.

They did not seek out others as they rode toward the east and faraway New Hampshire. Every third or fourth day, late in the afternoon, if a town was handy, they would check into a hotel and seek out a shave and a bath. If not, they would bathe in a handy stream and go unshaven until a town dotted the vast prairie.

"Ever been to this New Hamp-shire, Louis?" York asked the gambler.

"Never have, my friend. But it is an old and very settled state. One of the original thirteen to ratify the Constitution. The first settlement—I can't recall the name—was back in 1623. But I can assure you both, if we ride in like this, armed to the teeth and looking like buccaneers on horseback, we are," he smiled, "going to raise some eyebrows."

"How's that?" York asked. "We don't look no different than anybody else?"

Louis laughed pleasantly and knowingly. "Ah, but my young friend, we are much different from the folks you are about to meet in a few weeks. Their streets are well-lighted with gas lamps. A few might have telephones—marvelous devices. The towns you will see will be old and settled towns. No one carries a gun of any type; many villages and towns have long banned their public display except for officers of the law. And thank you, Smoke, for commissioning us; this way we can carry firearms openly.

"No, York, the world you are only days away from viewing is one that you have never seen before. Smoke, my suggestion would be that we ride the trains well into Massachusetts and then head north on horseback from our jumping-off place. I would suggest Springfield. And get ready for some very strange looks, gentlemen."

"I'm beginnin' not to like these folks and I ain't even

met none of 'em yet," York groused. "Don't tote no gun! What do they do if somebody tries to mess with 'em?"

"They are civilized people," Louis said, with more than a touch of sarcasm in his statement. "They let the law take care of it."

"Do tell," York said. "In other words, they ain't got the sand to fight their own fights?"

"That is one way of putting it, York," the gambler said with a smile. "My, but this is going to be a stimulating and informative journey."

Louis cantered on ahead.

"Smoke?" York asked.

"Huh?"

"What's a telephone?"

18

"They're in Salina," Sally read from the wire. "Smoke, York and Louis Longmont."

"The millionaire?" John sat straighter in his chair. "Mr. Longmont is coming east by horseback!"

Sally put eyes on her father. She loved him dearly, but sometimes he could be a pompous ass. "Father, Louis is an adventurer. He is also one of the most famous gunfighters in all the West. He's killed a dozen men on the Continent, in duels. With sword and pistol. He's killed—oh, I don't know, twenty or thirty or maybe fifty men out west, with guns. He's such a gentleman, so refined. I'll be glad to see him again."

John wiped his face with a handkerchief. In one breath, his daughter spoke of Louis killing fifty men. In the next breath, she spoke of him being so refined.

Not normally a profane man, John thought: What kind of goddamned people are going to be staying in my house!

Louis lay on his blankets and watched Smoke unroll a warbag from the pack animal. He laughed aloud when he saw what his friend was unpacking: a buckskin jacket, one that had been bleached a gray-white and trimmed ornately by a squaw.

"You have a touch of the theatrical in you, my friend," Louis observed.

"I got to thinking we might as well give the folks a show. I had it stored in Denver."

"Going to be interesting," Louis smiled, pouring another cup of coffee and turning the venison steaks.

York returned from his bath in the creek, his trousers on but shirtless. For the first time, Smoke and Louis noticed the old bullet scars that pocked the young man's hide.

"You've picked up a few here and there," Louis noted.

"Yeah." York slipped into his shirt. "Me and another ranger, name of McCoy, got all tangled up with some bad ones down in the Dos Cabezas mountains; I hadn't been with the Rangers long when it happened. McCoy got hit so bad he had to retire from the business. Started him up a little general store up near Prescott. But we buried them ol' boys where they fell. I was laid up for near'bouts a month. 'Nother time I was trackin' a bank robber up near Carson Mesa. He ambushed me; got lead in me. But I managed to stay in the saddle and rode on up into Utah after him. I nailed him up near Vermillion Cliffs. Picked up a few other scratches here and there."

And Louis knew then what Smoke had already learned: York was a man to ride the river with. There was no backup in the Arizona Ranger.

York looked up from the cooking steaks. "Where you plannin' on us pickin' up the steam cars, Smoke?"

"I'll wire Sally from Kansas City and see how she's doing. If she's doin' all right and doesn't feel like the baby's due any day, we'll ride on to St. Louis and catch the train there."

The three waited in Kansas City for two days. Sally felt fine and the baby was not due for a month. She urged him to take his time.

Smoke, York, and Louis rode out of Kansas City the next morning, riding into Missouri. It would be days later, when the trio rode into St. Louis and Smoke wired Keene, that he would learn Sally had been taken to the hospital the day after his wire from Kansas City. Sally and babies were doing fine.

"Babies!" Smoke shouted, almost scaring the telegraph operator out of his seat.

"Babies?" Louis exclaimed.

"More 'un one?" York asked.

"Boys," the stationmaster urged, "don't shoot no holes in the ceiling. We just got 'er fixed last month."

They arranged bookings for their horses and themselves, and chugged out of St. Louis the next morning. It was the first time Smoke or York had ever seen a sleeping car, and both were amazed at the luxury of the dining cars and at the quality of the food that was served.

When the finger bowl was brought around, Louis had to leave his seat to keep from laughing when York rolled up his sleeves and washed his elbows in it.

"Ain't you got no soap to go with this thing?" York asked the colored man.

The Negro rolled his eyes and looked heavenward, maintaining his composure despite the situation.

The train stopped in Ohio and the three got off to change trains. It was an overnighter, so they could exercise their horses, get their ground-legs back, and take a genuine bath in a proper tub. All were getting just a little bit gamey. The three big men, broad-shouldered and lean-hipped, with their boots and spurs and western hats, twin six-shooters tied down low, drew many an anxious look from a lot of men and more than curious looks from a lot of ladies.

"Shore are a lot of fine-lookin' gals around these parts," York observed. "But kinda pale, don't y'all think?"

Smoke and York stood on the shores of Lake Erie and marveled at the sight of it.

"Never seen so damn much water in all my life!" York said, undisguised awe in his voice. "And would you just look at them big boats!"

"Ships," Louis corrected. He pointed to one flying an odd-looking flag. "That one just came down the St. Lawrence. That's a German flag."

"How'd it git here?" York asked.

"Across the Atlantic Ocean."

"Lord have mercy!"

When they stomped and jingled back into the fancy hotel, a platoon of cops were waiting for them.

A captain of the police approached them, caution in his eyes and his step. "Lads, I can see that you're U.S. Marshals, but are ye after someone in our city?"

The cop was Irish through and through. "No," Smoke said. "But neither have we bothered anyone here." He looked at the mass of cops and smiled. "Kinda reminds me of that time I took on 'bout twenty-five guns at that silver camp."

"You fought twenty-five desperados all by yourself?" the captain asked.

"Yep."

"How did it turn out?"

"I killed them all."

"You . . . killed them all!"

"Yep."

Several news reporters and one photographer had gathered around, for real cowboys and western gun-slingers were rare in Cleveland.

"Might I ask your name, sir?" the captain inquired.

"Smoke Jensen."

Pandemonium set in.

* * *

Smoke, Louis, and York were given the keys to the city. All three answered an almost endless barrage of questions and endured dozens of cameras popping and clicking at them. A hasty parade was called, and the men rode up and down the city's streets in an open carriage.

"Goddamnedest thing I ever heard of," York muttered. "What the hell have we done to deserve something this grand?"

"You're an Arizona Ranger, York," Louis leaned over and told him. "And a gunfighter, just like Smoke and myself."

"If you say so," York told him. "Seems like a whole bunch to do about nothin' if you ask me."

"Shakespeare felt the same way," the gambler told him, smiling.

"No kiddin'? Seems to me I heard of him. Ain't he from down around El Paso?"

They chugged east the next morning, Smoke and York glad to be out of the hustle and bustle of it all. Louis waved good-bye to a dark-haired young woman who smiled and blushed as the train moved out of the station.

Louis settled back in his seat. "Ah, boys, the freshness and vitality of youth never ceases to amaze me."

Smoke grinned. "I noticed you left the party very early last night, Louis. She certainly is lovely."

But Louis would only smile in reply to questions.

They rolled on through the day and night, across Pennsylvania and into New York. In New York's massive and confusing station, they were met by a large contingent of New York's finest and personally escorted to the train heading to Springfield, with numerous stops along the way.

"It ain't that we don't respect fellow officers, boys," the commander of the police unit said. "It's just that your reputations precede you." He looked at Smoke. "Especially yours, son."

"Yes," a fresh-fashed cop said. "Were it up to me, I would insist you remove those guns."

Smoke stopped, halting the parade. He turned to face the helmeted cop. "And if refused? . . ."

The young cop was not in the least intimidated. "Then I would surely have to use force, laddy."

Louis and York joined Smoke in a knowing smile. Smoke said, "You have a pencil in your pocket, officer. I can see it. Would you jerk it out as quickly as you can?"

The older and more wiser of the cops—and that was just about all of them—backed up, with many of them holding their hands out from their sides, smiles on their faces. A half-dozen reporters had gathered around and were scribbling furiously. Photographers were taking pictures.

"So we're going to play games, eh, gunfighter?" the young cop asked.

"No. I'm going to show you how easy it is for a loud-mouth to get killed where I come from."

The young officer flushed, and placed his thumb and forefinger on the end of the pencil, and jerked it out.

Smoke swept back his beaded buckskin jacket, exposing his guns. He slipped the hammer-thong of his right hand .44. "Want to try it again?"

The young officer got exactly half of the pencil out of his pocket before he was looking down the muzzle of Smoke's .44.

"Do you get my point, officer?"

"Ah . . . 'deed, I do, sir! As one fellow officer to another, might I say, sir, that you are awfully quick with that weapon."

Smoke holstered. It was unlike him to play games with weapons, but he felt he might have saved the young man's life with an object lesson. He held out his hand, and the cop smiled and shook it.

The rest of the walk to their car was an easy one, with chatter among men who found they all had something in common after all.

It was growing late when they finally detrained in Springfield. They stabled their horses and found a small hotel for the night.

The weeks on the road had honed away any city fat that might have built up on Louis and had burned his already dark complexion to that of a gypsy. They were big men, all over six feet, with a natural heavy musculature; they were the kind of men that bring out the hostility in a certain type of man, usually the bully.

And with the knowledge that Sally and the babies—twins, Smoke had discovered when he wired during a train refueling stop—were now in danger, none of the men were in any mood for taking any lip from some loudmouth.

They elected to have their supper in the hotel's dining room to further avoid any trouble. As had been their custom, they wore their guns, and to hell with local laws. None of them knew when they might run into Davidson or Dagget or their ilk.

Louis had bought York a couple of suits in St. Louis, and Smoke had brought a suit with him. Longmont was never without a proper change of clothes; if he didn't have one handy, he would buy one.

When the men entered the dining room, conversation ceased and all eyes were on them as they walked to their table, led by a very nervous waiter. With their spurs jingling and their guns tied down low, all three managed to look as out of place as a saddle on a tiger.

The three of them ignored several comments from some so-called "gentlemen"—comments that might have led to a fight anywhere west of the Mississippi—and were seated without incident.

Louis frowned at the rather skimpy selections on the menu, sighed, and decided to order a steak. The others did the same.

"Sorry we don't have no buffalo here for you range-riders," a man blurted from the table next to them. His friend laughed, and the women with them, hennaed and painted up and half drunk, also thought fat boy's comments to be hysterically amusing.

Louis ignored the man, as did Smoke and York. "A drink before ordering, gentlemen?" a waiter magically appeared.

"I'm sure they'll want rye, George," the fat boy blurted. "That's what I read that all cowboys drink. Before they take their semi-yearly bath, that is."

His table erupted with laughter.

"I could move you to another table, gentlemen," the waiter suggested. "That"—he cut his eyes to the man seated with fat boy and the woman—"is Bull Everton."

"Is that supposed to mean something to us?" Smoke asked.

"He's quite the bully," the waiter whispered, leaning close. "He's never been whipped."

"That he's admitted," Louis commented dryly. "If he can't fight any better than he can choose women, he must have never fought a man."

Smoke and York both laughed at that.

"We'll have Scotch," Louis ordered.

"Yes, sir," The waiter was glad to get away from the scene of what he presumed would soon be disaster for the western men.

"You take them damn guns off," the voice rumbled to the men, "and I'll show you what a real man can do."

Smoke lifted his eyes to the source of the voice. Bull Everton. He surveyed the man. Even sitting, Smoke could see that the man was massive, with heavy shoulders and huge wrists and hands. But that old wildness sprang up within Smoke. Smoke had never liked a bully. He smiled at the scowling hulk.

"I'll take them off anytime you're ready, donkey-face," he threw down the challenge and insult.

Bull stood up and he was big. "How about right now, cowboy? Outside."

"Suits me, tub-butt." Smoke stood up and unbuckled and utied, handing his guns to a waiter.

The waiter looked as though he'd just been handed a pair of rattlesnakes.

"Where is this brief contest to take place?" Louis asked Bull.

"Brief, is right," Bull laughed. "Out back of the hotel will do."

"After you," Smoke told him.

When the back door closed and Bull turned around, Smoke hit him flush in the mouth with a hard right and followed that with a vicious left to the wind. Before Bull could gather his senses, Smoke had hit him two more times, once to the nose and another hook to the body.

With blood dripping from his lips and nose, Bull hollered and charged. Smoke tripped him and hit him once on the way down, then kicked him in the stomach while he was down.

Smoke was only dimly aware of the small crowd that had gathered, several of the spectators dressed in the blue uniform of police officers. He did not hear one of the cops say to Louis, "I've been waiting to see Everton get his due for a long time, boys. Don't worry. There will be no interference from us."

Smoke backed up and allowed Bull to crawl to his feet. There was a light of fury and panic in the man's eyes.

Bull lifted his hands in the classic boxer's stance: left fist held almost straight out, right fist close to his jaw.

Smoke whirled and kicked the bully on his knee. Bull screamed in pain and Smoke hit him a combination of blows, to the belly, the face, the kidneys. Smoke trip-hammered his fists, brutalizing the bigger man, knocking him down, hauling him back up, and knocking him down again.

Bull grabbed Smoke's knees and brought him down to the dirt of the alley. Pulling one leg free, Smoke savagely kicked the bully in the face. Teeth flew, glistening in the night.

Smoke pulled Bull to his feet and leaned him up against the rear wall, then went to work on the man's belly and sides. Only after he had felt and heard several ribs break did he let the man fall unconscious to the ground.

"Drag Bull to the paddy wagon, boys," the cop in charge ordered. "We'll take him to the hospital. I can tell by looking that his jaw is broken, and I'll wager half a dozen ribs are broken as well." He looked at Smoke. "You don't even look angry, young man."

"I'm not," Smoke told him.

"Lord suffer us all!" the officer said. "What would you have done had you been angry?"

"Killed him."

"I'd not like to get on the wrong side of the road with you, young man. But I would like to know your name."

"Smoke Jensen."

The crowd gasped and the cop smiled grimly. "Are you as good with your guns as you are with your dukes, me boy?"

"Better."

Louis handed Smoke a towel and held his coat while his friend wiped his face and hands. York had stood to one side, his coat brushed back, freeing the butts of his .44s.

And the cops had noticed that, too.

The cop looked at all three of the men. "You boys are

here for a reason. I'm not asking why, for you're officers of the law, and federal officers at that. But I'd not like to see any trouble in this town."

"There won't be," Smoke said, raising up from a rain barrel where he had washed his face and hands. "We'll be leaving at first light."

"You wouldn't mind if I stopped by the stable to see you off, would you now?"

"Not a bit," Smoke said, smiling.

The waiter stuck his head out the back door. "Gentlemen," he said, "I've freshened your drinks. The management has instructed me to tell you that your dinners are on the house this evening."

"That won't be necessary," Smoke told him. "I assure you, we have ample funds."

The waiter smiled. "Gentlemen, Bull Everton will not be returning to this establishment for quite some time, thanks to you. And," he grinned hugely, "if it isn't worth a free meal to get rid of a big pain in the ass, nothing is!"

19

The men were in the saddle and moving out before first light; they would take their breakfast at the first inn they came to once outside of Springfield. It was cold in the darkness before dawn, with more than a hint of fall in the air, and it was going to be a beautiful day for traveling.

The road followed the Connecticut River. The men stayed on the east side of the river, knowing they would have to veer off toward the northeast once inside New Hampshire.

All were taken in by the beauty of the state. Although the leaves were turning as fall approached, the lushness of nature was a beautiful thing to see. As they traveled, the road was bordered by red spruce, red oak, white pine, sugar maple, yellow birch, and white birch.

"It's shore purty," York observed, his eyes taking in the stone fences that surrounded the neat fields and farms. "I can't rightly describe the way I feel about this place. It's, well—" He paused and shook his head.

"Civilized," Louis finished it.

"I reckon that's it, Louis. The only gun I've seen all day is the ones we're totin'. Gives me sort of a funny feelin'."

"Bear in mind," Louis sobered them all, "that all that will change with the arrival of Davidson and his thugs."

By mid-afternoon, the schools out for the day, boys and girls began to appear by the fences and roadways, staring in mute fascination as the cowboys rode slowly by. Smoke and Louis and York all smiled and waved at the young people, and just to give the kids something to talk about and remember, they swept back their jackets, exposing the butts of their guns for the kids' wide eyes.

And the children loved it.

They could have easily made the distance to Keene by nightfall but decided to break it off at the inn on the New Hampshire/Massachusetts line. The innkeeper was a bit startled as the three jingled into his establishment.

"Innkeeper," Louis said, "rooms for three, if you please. And we'll stable our own horses."

"Yes . . . sir," the man said. "Right around back. You'll see the corn bin."

"And warn people to stay away from our horses," Smoke told him. "Anybody gets into Drifter's stall he'll kill them."

"Sir!"

"That's what he did to the last man who owned him."

"Yes, sir! I will so advise any locals."

The man and his wife and the girls who worked in the tavern and dining room were having a hard time keeping their eyes off the twin guns belted around each man's lean waist.

"We'll freshen up a bit and then come down for a drink at the bar," Louis told the man and woman.

Louis, York, and Smoke waited.

The man and woman and hired help contined to stare at the three tall men. No one seemed able to move.

Louis rapped gently on the desk. "The keys, please?"

The man came alive. "Oh! Yes! Here you are, gentlemen."

Smoke smiled at the lady behind the desk. "We don't bite, ma'am. I promise you we don't."

His smile broke the barriers between old, settled, and established codes and those who came from the freewheeling western part of the nation. She returned his smile and glanced down at the register.

"Enjoy your stay, Mr. Jensen! Smoke Jensen?"

And once more, pandemonium reigned.

The trio crossed into New Hampshire at first light, having paid their bill and slipped out quietly before dawn.

York was dressed in jeans, a red and white checkered shirt, and a leather waist-length jacket. Louis dressed in a dark suit, a white shirt with black string tie, highly polished black boots, and a white duster over his clothing to keep away the dust. Smoke was dressed in dark jeans, a black shirt, a red bandana, and his beaded buckskin jacket. All wore western hats. Only York and Smoke's big bowie knives could be seen; Louis's duster covered his own knife.

About ten miles inside New Hampshire, they picked up the Ashuelot River and followed that toward Keene. Some fifteen miles later, the outskirts of the town came into view.

The men reined up, dismounted, and knocked the dust from their clothing. Louis, loving every minute of it, removed his linen duster and tied it behind his saddle. A farmer came rattling along in a wagon, stopped, and sat his seat, staring at the heavily armed trio.

"The Reynolds house," Smoke said, walking to the man. "How do we find it?"

The man sat his wagon seat and stared, openmouthed.

"Sir?" Smoke asked. "Are you all right?"

"It's really you," the farmer said, awe in his voice. "I been readin' 'bout you for years. Knew you by your picture."

"Thank you. I'm glad to meet you, too. Could you direct us to the Reynolds house?"

"Oh . . . sure! That's easy. Cross the bridge and go three blocks. Turn right. Two blocks down they's a big white two-story house on the corner. You can't miss it. Wait'll I tell my wife I seen Smoke Jensen!" He clucked to his team and rattled on.

"What day is this?" York asked. "I'm havin' the damndest time keepin' track of things."

"Saturday," Louis told them. "Smoke, do we inform the local authorities as to why we are here?"

"I think not. If we did that, they'd want to handle it the legal way. With trials and lawyers and the such. We'd be tied up here for months. So let's keep it close to the vest and wait until Davidson makes his play. Then we'll handle it our way."

"Sounds good to me," York said. He swung into the saddle.

Smoke and Louis mounted up.

They cantered across the wooden bridge, three big men riding big western horses. They slowed to a walk on the other side of the street. People began coming out of houses to stand and stare at the men as they rode slowly by. Little children stood openmouthed; for all, it was the first time they had ever seen a real western cowboy, much less three real gunslingers like they'd been reading about in the penny dreadfuls and the tabloids.

Louis tipped his hat to a group of ladies, and they simpered and giggled and twirled their parasols and batted their eyes.

A little boy spotted them as they turned the street corner, and he took off like the hounds of hell were nipping at his feet.

"Aunt Sally! Aunt Sally!" he hollered. "They're here, Aunt Sally!"

He ran up the steps of the huge house and darted inside.

The front porch filled with people, all staring at the three horsemen walking their mounts slowly up the street.

"Your relatives, Smoke," Louis said. "Looks like quite a gathering."

"I am not looking forward to this, Louis," Smoke admitted. "I just want to get this over with, see Davidson and his bunch dead in the streets, and take Sally and the babies and get the hell back to the Sugarloaf."

"You'll survive it," the gambler said. "I assure you, my friend. But I feel it will be somewhat trying for the lot of us."

And then Sally stepped out onto the porch to join her family. Smoke felt he had never seen anything so beautiful in all his life. She stood by an older man that Smoke guessed was her father.

The entire neighborhood had left their houses and were standing in their front yards, gawking at the gunslingers.

"Smoke Jensen!" a teenager said, the words reaching Smoke. "He's killed a thousand men with those guns. Bet he took that coat off an Indian after he killed him."

Smoke grimaced and cut his eyes at Louis. The gambler said, "I feel awed to be in the presence of someone so famous." Then he smiled. "A thousand men, eh? My how your reputation has grown in such a short time."

Smoke shook his head and could not help but smile.

John Reynolds said, "That horse he's riding looks like it came straight out of the pits of hell!"

"That's Drifter," Sally told him. "He's a killer horse. Killed the last man who tried to own him."

John looked at his daughter. "Are you serious?"

"Oh, yes. But he's really quite gentle once he gets to know you. I was baking pies one afternoon and he stuck his head into the kitchen and ate a whole pie before I realized it. I picked up a broom and spanked him."

"You . . . spanked him," John managed to say. He

muttered under his breath and Sally laughed at his expression.

The riders turned and reined up, dismounting at the hitchrail. Sally stepped off the porch and walked toward the picket fence, a smile on her lips.

Smoke stood by the gate and stared at her, not trusting his voice to speak.

"You've lost weight," Sally said.

"I've been missing your cooking."

He opened the gate.

Her eyes sparkled with mischief. "Is that all you've been missing?" She spoke low, so her words reached only his ears.

Smoke stepped through the open gate, his spurs jingling. He stopped a few feet from her. "Well, let's see. I reckon I might have missed you just a tad."

And then she was in his arms, loving the strong feel of him. Her tears wet his face as she lifted her lips to his.

York lifted his hat and let out a war whoop.

Walter Reynolds swallowed his snuff.

20

"Should you be out of bed this soon?" Smoke asked his wife.

"Oh, the doctors tried to get me to stay in bed much longer, but since I didn't have the time to get to the city to have the babies, and they came so easily, I left the bed much earlier than most, I imagine."

"I keep forgetting how tough you are." Smoke smiled across the twin cradles at her.

"Have you thought about names, Smoke?"

"Uh . . . no, I really haven't. I figured you'd have them named by now."

"I have thought of a couple."

"Oh?"

"How about Louis Arthur and Denise Nicole?"

Louis for Louis Longmont. Arthur for Old Preacher. And Nicole for Smoke's first wife, who was murdered by outlaws, and their baby son, Arthur, who was also killed. Denise was an old family name on the Reynolds side.

"You don't object to naming the girl after Nicole?"

"No," Sally said with a smile. "You know I don't."

"Louis will be pleased."

"I thought so."

Smoke looked at the sleeping babies. "Are they ever going to wake up?"

She laughed softly. "Don't worry. You'll know when they wake. Come on. Let's go back and join the rest of the family."

Smoke looked around for Louis and York. John caught his eye. "I tried to get them to stay. I insisted, told them we had plenty of room. But Mr. Longmont said he felt it would be best if they stayed at the local hotel. Did we offend them, Son?"

Smoke shook his head as the family gathered around. "No. We're here on some business as well as to get Sally. It would be best if we split up. I'll explain."

John looked relieved. "I was so afraid we had somehow inadvertently offended Mr. Longmont."

John Reynolds stared at Smoke as his son-in-law laughed out loud. "Hell, John. Louis just wanted to find a good poker game, that's all!"

It was after lunch, and the family was sitting on the front porch. Smoke had not removed his guns and had no intention of doing so.

And it was not just the young people who stared at him with a sort of morbid fascination.

"Tell me about Dead River," Sally spoke. She glanced at her nieces and nephews. "You, scoot! There'll be a lot of times to talk to your Uncle Smoke."

The kids reluctantly left the porch.

Smoke shaped and rolled and licked and lit. He leaned back in his chair and propped his boots up on the porch railing. "Got kind of antsy there for the last day or two before we opened the dance."

"You went to a dance?" Betsy asked.

Smoke cut his eyes. "Opening the dance means I started the lead flying, Betsy."

"Oh!" Her eyes were wide.

"You mean as soon as you told the hooligans to surrender, they opened fire?" Jordan inquired.

Smoke cut his eyes to him. "No," he drawled. "It means that me and York come in the back way of the saloon, hauled iron, and put about half a dozen of them on the floor before the others knew what was happening." It wasn't really accurate, but big deal.

"We don't operate that way in the East," Walter said, a note of disdain in his voice.

"I reckon not. But the only thing Dead River was east of was Hell. And anybody who thinks they can put out the fires of Hell with kindness and conversation is a damn fool. And fools don't last long in the wilderness."

John verbally stepped in before his son found himself slapped on his butt out in the front yard. "A young lady named Martha will be along presently. She had some foolish notion of traveling back west with you and Sally. She wants to teach school out there."

"Fine with me." He looked at Sally. "Has she got the sand and the grit to make it out there?"

"Yes. I believe she does."

"Tell her to start packing."

"But don't you first have to get the permission of the school board?" Jordan asked.

"Ain't got none," Smoke slipped back into the loose speech of the western man. "Don't know what that is, anyways."

Sally laughed, knowing he was deliberately using bad grammar.

And cutting her eyes to her mother, she knew that Abigal did, too.

But her father appeared lost as a goose.

And so did her brothers.

"Well, sir," Jordan began to explain. "A school board is a body of officials who—"

"—sit around and cackle like a bunch of layin' hens

and don't accomplish a damn thing that's for the good of the kids," Smoke finished it.

Abigal smiled and minutely nodded her head in agreement.

With a sigh, Jordan shut his mouth.

Smoke looked at him. "Are you a lawyer?"

"Why, yes, I am."

"Thought so."

"Do I detect a note of disapproval in your voice, Son?" John asked.

"Might be some in there. I never found much use for lawyers. The ones I knowed, for the most part, just wasn't real nice people."

"Would you care to elaborate on that?" Walter stuck out his chin. What there was of it to stick out.

Smoke took a sip of coffee poured from the freshly made pot. Made by Sally and drinkable only by Smoke. Jordan said it was so strong it made his stomach hurt. Walter poured half a pitcher of cream in his, and John took one look at the dark brew and refused altogether.

"I reckon I might," Smoke replied. But first he rolled another cigarette. "Man chooses a life of crime, he does that deliberate. It's his choice. Hell with him. You ladies pardon my language. On the other side of the coin, a man breaks into another house and starts stealing things, the homeowner shoots him dead, and they'll be those in your profession who'll want to put the property-owner in jail. It don't make any sense. And now, so I read and hear, you folks are beginning to say that some criminals was drove to it, and the courts ought to take into consideration about how poor they was. Poor!" he laughed. "I was a man grown at thirteen; doing a man's work and going to school and looking after my sick mother, all at once. My daddy was off fighting in the war—for the gray," he added proudly. "Not that he believed in slaves, because he didn't. War wasn't fought over slaves nohow.

"We didn't have any money. Tied the soles of our shoes on with rawhide. Ate rabbit stew with wild onions for flavor. Shot them when we had the ammunition; trapped them and chunked rocks at them when we didn't.

"Or didn't eat at all," he added grimly. "But I never stole a thing in my life. Some of our neighbors had more than they needed; but I didn't envy them for it, and if I caught myself covetin' what they had, I felt ashamed.

"Y'all got a big fine house here, and I 'spect you all got lots of money. But how many times have you turned a begger-man away from your back door without givin' him a bite to eat? That don't happen often out where me and Sally live. If that man is able, we hand him an axe and tell him to chop some wood, then we'll feed him. If he ain't able, we'll feed him and see to his needs. There ain't no need to talk on it a whole lot more. Y'all know what I'm talkin' about. But if I find somebody tryin' to steal from me, I'm gonna shoot him dead."

Smoke stood up. "I'm gonna take me a ride around your pretty town." He looked down at John. "We'll talk after supper."

He stepped off the porch and around the stables, his spurs jingling.

John smiled, then he laughed. "I like your man Smoke, Sally. I didn't think I would, but I do. Even though, or perhaps because, he is a man of conviction."

"And is more than willing, just anytime at all, to back up those convictions, Father."

"Yes," John's words were dryly given. "I just bet he is."

"That's the way it shapes up, John Reynolds," Smoke finished telling his father-in-law.

The men were in the study, the door closed. Sally was the only woman present. Her brothers had not been included in the discussion. It was after dinner, and the men had smoked their cigars and had their brandy.

John looked at York; the young Arizona Ranger met his gaze without flinching. He looked at Louis Longmont; the man was handling a rare book from John's library, obviously enjoying and appreciating the feel of the fine leather. There was no doubt in John's mind that the gambler had read it.

He cut his eyes to his son-in-law. "Of course you are going to inform our local police department of this?"

"No."

"But you must!"

"No, I must not. I don't want these men tried in some damn eastern court of law and have them serve five to ten years and then walk scot-free. And you know far better than I that is exactly what would happen, John."

"Then what do you propose to do, Son?"

"I propose to notify your local police when we see them ride into town. Louis has alerted people along the way, people who work both sides of the law. Davidson is not going to ride all the way here from Colorado. Neither is Bothwell or Rycroft or Brute or any of the others. They'll be coming in on trains, one by one, and pick up horses as close to here as possible. I got a hunch they're going to try to tree this town."

"Tree?"

"Hold it hostage. You can't do that to a western town; folks there would shoot you so full of holes your mother wouldn't recognize you. But an eastern town is different. You don't have a loaded gun in this house and damn few others do, either. But I am about to correct that little problem."

"How?" John asked, seemingly stunned by the news.

"I gave York some money this afternoon. He rode over to Brattleboro and picked up some weapons."

"You are going to arm the boys and me?"

"No." Smoked dashed that. "I'm going to arm Sally." Her father looked crestfallen.

"John," Louis asked. "have you ever killed a man?"

"What? Why . . . no."

"Any of your sons ever used a gun in anger?"

"Ah . . . no."

"That's why we're not arming you, John," Smoke told him. "It isn't that we don't believe you're one hundred percent man. It's just that you'd be out of your element. You, and ninety percent of the people in this town. Oh, a lot of men in this town fought in the War Between the States and were heroes, I'm sure. But that was war, John. I'd be very surprised if one of them could ambush a man and shoot him in cold blood."

"Yes," the lawyer agreed. "So would I."

"There you have it, Mr. Reynolds," York said. "You'd be thinkin' about them bein' human bein's and all that. Well, these people ain't worth a cup of puke."

"How quaintly put," John muttered. "And you have other officers coming in to assist you, right?

"What for?" Smoke asked.

"Well, how many outlaws will there be?"

"Oh . . . probably twenty or so. We'll handle it."

John jumped up. "Are you serious?" he shouted.

"Hell, Mr. Reynolds," York said, "that ain't but six or seven apiece. I recall the time down near the Painted Rock me and two other guys fought off a hundred or more 'paches. Kilt about forty of 'em."

He turned his head and winked at Louis.

"But those were savages!" John protested, not sure whether he believed the ranger's story or not.

Louis said, "Believe you me, John, Davidson and his bunch are just as savage as any Apache that ever lived."

Then Smoke told the man about some of the methods of torture Rex and Dagget enjoyed at Dead River.

The lawyer left the room. A few seconds later, they could hear him retching in the water closet.

"I believe you finally convinced him," Sally said.

John returned to the study, his face pale. "Son," he said to Smoke, "I'll start cleaning my shotguns and my rifle."

21

The nights were cool and the days were pleasantly warm as autumn slipped into the northeast. Smoke, for the most part, stayed close to the Reynolds house; York and Louis spent their days riding around the countryside, ranging from the Vermont line to the west, up to Claremont to the north, over to Manchester to the east, and down to the state line to the south.

There was no sign of Davidson or any of his men, and Smoke began to wonder if he had figured wrong. But there was still that nagging suspicion in his gut that the outlaws were on their way and that they would make their move before the first snow. And the first possible snow, John had said, would probably come around the middle of November.

The twins were growing fast. They were fat and healthy babies, who laughed and gurgled and hollered and bawled and messed their diapers.

It was fascinating to John to watch the gunslinger with the big rough hands handle the babies with such gentleness. And the twins responded to the firm gentleness, apparently loving the touch of the big, rough-looking man who, or so it seemed to John Reynolds, never took off his guns.

The sheriff of the county and the chief of police of the town came to see Smoke, demanding to know what was going on: Why had the three come to town? What were they still doing in town?

Smoke answered that he had come to town to see his wife's family, and that he was still in town waiting for the babies to get big enough to travel.

Neither the sheriff nor the chief believed Smoke's explanation. But neither the sheriff nor the chief wanted to be the one to call him a liar.

For exercise, Smoke took a wagon out into the timber and spent the better part of several days chopping wood. He chopped enough wood to last the Reynolds family most of the winter, and he stacked it neatly.

On one cool and crisp afternoon in November, Louis rode over and chatted with Smoke, who was currying Drifter. York lounged nearby, the thongs off the hammers of his .44s. Only Smoke and Sally noticed that.

"Four of them left St. Louis a week ago," Louis said, leaning up against a stall wall. "My man was certain that one of them was Davidson. They bought tickets for Boston. Six hard-looking western men pulled out of New York City day before yesterday, after buying some fine horseflesh. Some others pulled into Pittsburgh on the river more than a month ago, bought supplies and horses, and left within a week. Still another group rode the cars from Nebraska to St. Louis, bought horses, and left weeks ago. It's taken my people some time to put all this together."

Louis's people, Smoke had learned, included not only foot-padders and whores, but paid members of the Pinkertons.

"So we can look for them by the end of the week," Smoke said, continuing to curry Drifter. "But Davidson is too smart to come riding into town in a gang, shooting the place up. From what you've said, I gather we'll be looking at twenty to twenty-five men."

"At least," the gambler agreed. "I'd guess close to thirty." Smoke was silent for a moment, trying to recall a news article he'd read several weeks back. Then it came to him.

"There was an Army depot robbed down in Maryland several weeks back. Did either of you read that article?"

Louis snapped his fingers. "Yes! I did. Uniforms and military equipment taken. Smoke, do you think—?"

"Yes. Yes, I do. That would probably be the group who left St. Louis weeks ago." He was thoughtful. "Let's play it that way. I sure wish we had Jim Wilde and a few of the boys up here with us."

"Yes. That would be nice," Louis concurred. "But it's too late to get them here. Do we still play it close to the vest?"

Smoke sighed. "Louis, I've been thinking about that. I can't put these peoples' lives in danger. They've got a right to know what and who is about to enter this area. As bad as I hate to do it, when the so-called Army patrol is sighted, I'm going to level with the sheriff and the chief of police."

"And Mr. Reynolds?" York asked.

"I'll do that as soon as he comes in from the office."

John Reynolds listened, his face impassive. When Smoke concluded, he leaned back in his chair and sighed. "I'm glad you decided to confide in me, Son. I felt that you would, after further thought, take the lives of the people of this community under deeper consideration."

"John, listen to me," Smoke urged. "Where is the nearest military unit based?"

"Why . . . New York State, I'm sure. But we have a fine militia here in New Hampshire. I'll get right on it the first thing in the morning. I'll wire the governor and he'll see to it immediately."

John did not see the look that passed between the three gunfighters.

"How long is this going to take, sir?" York was the one who asked.

"Oh, several days, I'm sure. The governor has to sign the orders mobilizing the unit, then the men have to be notified and moved into place . . ." He fell silent with a curt wave of Smoke's hand. "What is it, Son?"

"We don't have time, John. Not for all that. Can you contact the governor tonight and have him notify the Army?"

"I'm . . . why, certainly. And tell the Army what?"

"Of our suspicions."

"I'll get a wire off immediately." He shrugged into his coat and called for his buggy. He looked at Smoke. "I'll handle this part of it, Son. Be back in half an hour."

When he returned, his face was long. "The governor is taking an early Thanksgiving vacation." He grimaced. "A very early Thanksgiving vacation. I sent a wire to the commanding officer of the Army post over in New York State. He's in Washington, D.C., for some sort of hearings. Son, we appear to be hitting a stone wall every way we turn in this matter."

"I got a bad feelin' about this thing," York said. "I got a feelin' it's gonna break loose on us tomorrow."

"And those are my sentiments, as well," Louis agreed. "What is your opinion of the sheriff and the chief of police, John?"

"Oh, they're good men. But with only a small force between them."

Smoke and Louis and York had already checked on the cops in the town and county. A very small force. Five men, to be exact. But they all agreed the cops and deputies checked out to be good, stable men. But not gunfighters.

The hall clock chimed. It was growing late. "We see them first thing in the morning," Smoke said.

"I've packed my things," Louis said. "I'll stay here, with your permission, John."

"Of course, of course. I insist that the both of you stay." He glanced at York, received a nod, then looked at Smoke. "We'll see the sheriff and the chief first thing in the morning."

The sheriff was very indignant. "I don't see why you couldn't have leveled with us first thing, Marshal," he said to Smoke.

"Because by doing that, you would have alerted the militia and the Army and deputized every man in the county. And that would have scared them off."

"So? That would have been a bad thing?"

"In a way, yes. They would have just laid back and hit you when you stood the men down and sent them home. How many men can you muster? Good men, Sheriff."

"Jensen, we don't have gunfighters in this town. We have shopkeepers and schoolteachers and farmers and small businessmen. And a nice fat bank," he added grimly.

"How fat?" Louis inquired.

The sheriff hesitated. But Louis Longmont was known worldwide, not only for his talents with a gun and with cards, but also as a very rich man. "Very fat, Mr. Longmont. And need I remind you all that today is the last day of the month?"

Payday for most working people. The bank would have pulled in more money to meet the demand.

"They planned it well," Smoke said, as much to himself as to the others. "How well do the people listen to you, Sheriff?"

The question caught the lawman off guard. "Why . . . I don't know what you mean. They elected me."

"What I mean is, if you told them to stay off the streets today, would they heed your words?"

"I feel certain they would."

The door to the office burst open and a flustered-looking stationmaster stepped in.

"What's the matter, Bob?" Chief of Police Harrison asked.

"I can't get a wire out in any direction, Harrison. My unit is dead as a hammer."

Louis snapped his fingers. "They're planning on using the train to get away. Remember all the horses I was told they'd bought, Smoke? They've stashed them along the railway, and they'll ride the train north to their horses."

"Huh? Huh?" the stationmaster asked, his eyes darting from man to man.

"And the uniforms they stole were not meant to be used here," Smoke added. "They'll be used as a getaway after they've ridden the train north. And it will be north. When they get close to the Canadian line, they'll peel out of those uniforms and ride across as civilians, after splitting up."

The mayor of Keene had stepped in while Louis was talking. "What's all this?" George Mahaffery asked. "I'm trying to get a wire out to my sister in Hanover, Bob. Old Sully tells me the wires are down. What's going on here?"

Nobody paid any attention to Hizzonor.

Sheriff Poley pointed at his lone deputy on duty that day. "Peter, get the women and the kids off the streets. Arm the men."

"Oh, crap!" York muttered.

"I demand to know what is going on around here?" the mayor hollered.

Nobody paid any attention to him.

Smoke stopped the deputy. "Just hold on, partner." To Sheriff Poley: "You're gonna get a bunch of good men hurt or killed, Sheriff."

Poley stuck out his chest. "What the hell do you mean by that, Marshal?"

"This is New Hampshire, Sheriff, not Northfield, Minnesota. Parts of Minnesota is still wild and woolly. When is the last time any man in this town fired a gun in anger?"

That brought the sheriff up short.

"Goddamn!" Mayor Mahaffery hollered. "Will somebody tell me what the hell is going on around here?"

"Shut up," York said to him.

Hizzonor's mouth dropped open in shock. Nobody ever talked to him in such a manner.

"And keep it shut," York added.

"I'd guess the Civil War, Marshal," Poley finally answered Smoke's question.

"That's what I mean, Sheriff. Ten men, Sheriff. That's all I want. Ten good solid men. Outdoorsmen if possible."

The deputy named a few and the sheriff added a few more. The stationmaster named several.

"That'll do," Smoke halted the countdown. "Get them, and tell them to arm themselves as heavily as possible and be down here in one hour." He glanced at the clock. Eight-thirty. "When's the next train come in?"

"Two passengers today, Marshal," Bob told him. "Northbound's due in at eleven o'clock."

"They'll hit the bank about ten-forty-five then," Louis ventured a guess.

"That's the way I see it," Smoke's words were soft. "But when will they hit the Reynolds house? Before, or after?"

Farmer Jennings Miller and his wife had left the day before to visit their oldest daughter over in Milford. That move saved their lives, for the Miller farm was the one that had been chosen by Dagget for a hideout until it was time to strike.

The outlaws had moved in during the last two nights, riding in by ones and twos, stabling their horses in the Millers' huge barn.

The outlaws had been hitting banks on their way east

and had amassed a goodly sum of money. This was to be their last bank job before moving into Canada to lay low for as long as need be.

And Davidson was paying them all extra for this job, and paying them well. The bank was only secondary; the primary target was Sally Jensen and the babies.

Studs Woodenhouse had three men with him. Tie Medley had four from his original gang left. Paul Rycroft had brought two men with him. Slim Bothwell had three. Shorty, Jake, and Red. Brute Pitman. Tustin. La-Hogue. Glen Moore. Lapeer. Dagget. Rex Davidson.

Twenty-six men in all. Over one hundred thousand dollars in reward money lay on their heads.

All were wanted for multiple murders, at least. The outlaws had nothing at all to lose.

"Let's start gettin' the saddles on the horses," Davidson ordered. He laughed. "One damn mile from the center of town, and nobody ever thought to look here. It was a good plan, Dagget."

"All I want is a shot at that damned John Reynolds," Dagget growled. "I want to gut-shoot that fancy-talkin' lawyer so's it'll take him a long time to die."

"They any kids in the Reynolds house?" Brute asked. "Say ten or eleven years old?"

No one answered the man. He was along solely because of his ability to use a gun and his nerves of steel. Other than that, no one had any use at all for Brute Pitman.

Not even his horse liked him.

The outlaws began a final check of their guns. They were going in heavily armed, and Rex Davidson had said he wanted the streets to run red with Yankee bluenose blood: Men, women, and kids; didn't make a damn to him.

And it didn't make a damn to the outlaws. Just as long as Davidson paid in cash or gold.

They had gotten a third of the money. The other two-thirds they'd receive in Canada.

Two men eased out of the cold house and slipped to the barn to curry and then saddle their mounts.

"I sure will be glad to have me a hot cup of coffee," Tie bitched.

"You want to take a chance on smoke being seen from the chimney?" Dagget asked him.

"I ain't complainin'," Tie replied. "I just wish I had a cup of coffee, that's all."

"Coffee on the train," Rex told them all. "And probably some pretty women."

"Yeah!" several of the outlaws perked up.

"And maybe some children," Brute grinned.

The outlaw seated next to Brute got up and moved away, shaking his head.

22

Good men, Smoke thought, after looking at the men that had been chosen. Not gunfighters, but good, solid, dependable men. Their weapons were not what Smoke would have chosen for his own use, but they seemed right in the hands of local citizens. Their pistols were worn high, in flap holsters; but they wouldn't be called upon to do any fast-draw work.

Smoke looked outside. The streets of the town were empty. The storeowners had locked their doors but left the shades up, to give the impression that all was well.

"You men are going to protect the bank and other buildings along Main Street," Smoke told the locals. "When you get the bastards in gunsights, pull the damn trigger! We don't have time to be nice about it. You're all veterans of the Army. You've all seen combat. This is war, and the outlaws are the enemy. The sheriff has deputized you, and I've given you federal commissions. You're protected both ways. Now get into the positions the sheriff has assigned you and stay put. Good luck."

The men filed out and began taking up positions. Some were hidden behind barrels and packing crates in alley openings. Others were on the second floor of the buildings on both sides of the street.

The sheriff and his deputy, the chief of police and his one man on duty, armed themselves and took their positions.

Smoke, Louis, and York swung in their saddles and began a slow sweep of the town.

At the Reynolds home, the twins had been taken down into the basement, where a warm fire had been built, and they were being looked after by Abigal and her daughter-in-law.

"I say, Father," Walter asked, his hair disheveled and his face flushed with excitement, "whatever can Jordan and I do?"

"Stand aside and don't get in the way," the father ordered, picking up a double-barreled shotgun and breaking it down, loading it with buckshot. He did the same to two more shotguns and then loaded a lever-action rifle. He checked the loads in the pistols Smoke had given him and poured another cup of coffee. Cowboy coffee. John was beginning to like the stuff. Really pepped a man up!

He shoved two six-shooters in his belt, one on each side. Then he took up another notch in his belt to keep his pants from falling down.

"Who is that man running across the street?" Walter asked, peering out the window.

John looked. "This isn't a man, Son. That's Martha, in men's jeans."

"Good Lord, Father!" Jordan blurted. "That's indecent!"

John looked at the shapely figure bounding up onto the front porch. He smiled. "That's . . . not exactly the way I'd describe the lass, boy." He opened the door and let her in.

Martha carried a Smith & Wesson pocket .32 in her right hand. She grinned at John. "You know me, Mr. Reynolds. I've always been somewhat of a tomboy."

"Sally is guarding the back door, Martha. She is . . . ah . . . also in men's britches."

"Yes." Martha grinned. "We bought them at the same time." She walked back to the rear of the house.

Sally was sitting by the rear window, a rifle in her hand. She had a shotgun leaning up against the wall and wore a six-gun belt around her waist.

"Can you really shoot all those guns?" Martha asked.

"Can and have, many times. And if you're moving west, you'd better learn how."

"I think today is going to be a good day for that."

"The Indians have a saying, Martha: It's a good day to die."

"I say, Father," Jordan asked, "wherever do you want us to be posted?"

John looked at his two sons. He loved them both but knew that they were rather on the namby-pamby side. Excellent attorneys, both of them. But in a situation like the one about to face them all, about as useless as balls on a bedpost.

John laughed at his own vulgarity. "I think it would please your mother very much, boys, if you would consent to guard them in the basement."

They consented and moved out. Smartly.

Sally came in and checked on her father. She grinned at him and patted him on the shoulder. "You look tough as a gunslinger, Father."

"I feel like an idiot!" He grinned at her. "But I do think I am capable of defending this house and all in it against thugs and hooligans."

"There isn't a doubt in my mind about that, Father. Don't leave your post. I'll handle the back."

Probably with much more proficiency and deadliness than I will handle the front, he thought.

He leaned down and kissed her cheek and winked at her.

"Don't let them get on the porch, Father," she

cautioned the man. "When you get them in gunsights, let 'er bang."

He laughed. "I shall surely endeavor to do that, darling!"

Smoke rode alone to the edge of town, and the huge barn to the southeast caught his eyes. There was no smoke coming from the chimney of the house, and the day was cool enough for a fire. He wondered about that, then put it out of his mind. He turned Drifter's head and rode slowly back to town.

The town appeared deserted.

But he knew that behind the closed doors and shuttered windows of the homes, men and women and kids were waiting and watching. And the people of the town were taking the news of the outlaws' arrival calmly, obeying the sheriff's orders without question.

Smoke, York, and Louis, all in the saddle, met in the center of town.

"What's the time, Louis?" Smoke asked.

The gambler checked his gold watch. "Ten-fifteen, and not a creature is stirring," he said with a small smile.

"Unless they're hidin' awful close," York said, rolling a tight cigarette, "they're gonna have to make their first move damn quick."

Smoke looked around him at the quiet town. "They're close. Maybe no more than a mile or two outside of town. I've been thinking, boys. Jim Wilde told me that those ledger books of Davidson's showed him to be a very rich man; money in all sorts of banks . . . in different banks, under different names, Jim guessed. The assumed names weren't shown. So why would he be interested in knocking off a bank? It doesn't make any sense to me."

"You think the primary target is Sally and the babies?" Louis asked.

"Yes. And something else. John Reynolds told me that

Dagget has hated the Reynolds family for years, even before he got into trouble and had to leave."

"So John and Abigal might also be targets."

"Yes."

"This Dagget, he have any family still livin' in town?" York asked.

Smoke shook his head. "I don't know. But I'd bet he does."

"But Dagget would still know the town," Louis mused aloud.

"Yes. And he would know where the best hiding places were."

"And he just might have supporters still livin' here," York interjected.

"There is that, too."

The men sat their horses for a moment, quiet, just listening to the near silence.

"Me and Louis been talkin'. Smoke, we'll take the main street. You best head on over toward the Reynolds place."

Smoke nodded and tightened the reins. "See you boys." He rode slowly toward the Reynolds house.

York and Louis turned the other way, heading for the main street of town.

Smoke put Drifter in the stable behind the house but left the saddle on him. Pulling his rifle from the boot, he walked around the big house on the corner. The house directly across the street, on the adjacent corner, was empty. The home facing the front porch was occupied. John had said the family had taken to the basement. To the rear and the left of the Reynolds house, looking from the street, the lots were owned by John; in the summers, neat patches of flowers were grown by Abigal.

Smoke stood on the front porch, the leather hammer thongs off his .44s, the Henry repeating rifle, loaded full with one in the chamber, held in his left hand. Without turning around, he called, "What's the time, John?"

"Ten-thirty, Son," John called through the closed front door.

"They'll hit us in about ten minutes. Relax, John. Have another cup of coffee. If you don't mind, pour me one while you're at it. I'll keep an eye on the front."

The man is utterly, totally calm, John thought, walking through the house to the kitchen. Not a nerve in his entire body. He looked at his daughter. Sally was sitting in a straight-back chair by a kitchen window, her rifle lying across her lap. She looked as though she just might decide to take a nap.

"Coffee, girls?"

"Thanks, Father. Yes, if you don't mind."

Calm, John thought. But then, he suddenly realized, so am I!

Amazing.

"Why hasn't the Army been notified?" Mayor Mahaffery demanded an answer from the sheriff.

Sheriff Poley puffed on his pipe before replying. "Wire is down, George. 'Sides, Mr. Reynolds tried to get in touch with the governor last night. He's on a vacation. Tried to get in touch with the commander of that Army base over in New York State. He's in Washington, D.C. Relax, George, we'll handle it."

George pulled a Dragoon out of his belt, the barrel about as long as his arm.

Sheriff Poley looked at the weapon dubiously. "Is that thing loaded, George?"

"Certainly, it's loaded!" Hizzoner replied indignantly. "I carried it in the war!"

"What war?" Poley asked. "The French and Indian? Git away from me before you try to fire that thing, George. That thing blow up it'd tear down half the building."

Muttering under his breath, George moved to another spot in the office.

"Look at those guys," Deputy Peter Newburg said, awe in his voice.

"What guys?" Poley asked.

"Mr. Longmont and that Arizona Ranger, York. They're just standing out on the sidewalk, big as brass. Got their coats pulled back so's they can get at their guns. That York is just calm as can be rolling a cigarette."

"Hell, the gambler is reading a damn newspaper!" George spoke up. "They behave as though they're just waiting for a train!"

"In a way," Poley said, "they are."

"What time is it?" George asked.

Sheriff Poley looked at him. "About a minute later than the last time you asked."

Before George could tell the sheriff what he could do with his smart remarks, the deputy said, "The gambler just jerked up his head and tossed the paper to the street. He's lookin' up Main."

"Here they come!" a lookout shouted from atop a building. "And there's a mob of them!"

Louis and York separated, with York ducking behind a horse trough and Louis stepping back into the shallow protection of a store well. Both had drawn their guns.

Tie Medley and his bunch were leading the charge, followed by Studs Woodenhouse and his gang, then Paul Rycroft and Slim Bothwell and their followers. Bringing up the rear were Tustin, LaHogue, Shorty, Red, and Jake. Davidson, Dagget, Lapeer, Moore, and Brute were not in the bunch.

Louis yelled out, "You men on the roof, fire, goddamnit, fire your rifles!"

But they held their fire, and both Louis and York knew why: They had not been fired upon. It was the age-old myth of the fair fight; but any realist knows there is no such thing as a fair fight. There is just a winner and a loser.

Louis stepped out of the store well and took aim. His

first shot knocked a rider from the saddle. York triggered off a round and a splash of crimson appeared on an outlaw's shirtfront, but he stayed in the saddle. A hard burst of returning fire from the outlaws sent Louis back into the store well and York dropping back behind the horse trough.

The outlaws took that time to ride up to the bank and toss a giant powder bomb inside; then they charged their horses into an alley. When the bomb went off, the blast blew all the windows out of the bank front and sent the doors sailing out into the street.

Smoke and dust clouded the street. The outlaws tossed another bomb at the rear of the bank building and the concussions could be felt all over the town. The outlaws rode their horses into the back of the bombed-out bank building, and while a handful worked at the safe, the others began blasting away from the shattered front of the building.

The suddenness and viciousness of the attack seemed to stun the sheriff, the chief, and the local volunteers. From the positions chosen by the lawmen, there was nothing for them to shoot at; everything was happening on their side of the street.

Pinned down and fighting alone, Louis lost his composure and shouted, "Will you yellow-bellied sons of bitches, goddamnit, fire your weapons!"

Of course the locals were not cowardly; not at all. They just were not accustomed to this type of thing. Things like this just didn't happen in their town.

But Louis's call did get their attention, which was all he wanted.

"Call me a yellow-bellied son of a bitch, will you?" Mayor George muttered, his ears still ringing from the bomb blasts. Before anyone could stop him, George charged out of the building and onto the sidewalk. Kneeling down, he cocked the Dragoon and squeezed the trigger.

The force of the weapon discharging knocked Hizzoner to the sidewalk. His round missed any outlaw in the bank, the slug traveling clear through the wall and into the hardware store, where it hit the ammunition case and set off several boxes of shotgun shells.

The outlaws in the bank thought they were coming under attack and began shooting in all directions.

George raised to his knees and let bang another round from the Dragoon.

The slug struck an outlaw in the chest and knocked him halfway across the room.

"Clear out!" Tie hollered. "We're blowin' the vault!"

Fifteen seconds later, it seemed the gates to Hell opened up in the little town in New Hampshire.

23

The force of the giant powder exploding sent half the roof flying off and blew one wall completely down. George Mahaffery ended up in Sheriff Poley's lap and the chief of police found himself sitting on a spittoon, with no one really knowing how they got in their present positions.

"I got money in that bank!" a volunteer suddenly realized.

"Hell, so do I!" another called from a rooftop.

"Get 'em boys!" another called.

Then they all, finally, opened up.

"They just blew the bank building," Smoke called.

"Place needed renovating anyway," John returned the call.

Smoke laughed. "You'll do, John. You'll do!"

And John realized his son-in-law had just paid him one of the highest compliments a western man could give.

Smoke heard the pounding of hooves on the street and jerked up his Henry, easing back the hammer. He recognized Glen Moore. Bringing up the butt to his shoulder, Smoke shot the killer through the belly. Moore screamed as the pain struck him, but he managed to stay in the saddle. He galloped on down the street, turning into a side street.

Out of the corner of his eye, Smoke saw Brute Pitman cut in behind the house, galloping across the neatly tended lawn.

"Coming up your way, Sally!" Smoke called, then had no more time to wonder, for the lawn was filled with human scum.

Smoke began pulling and levering at almost point-blank range. Lapeer taking a half-dozen round in his chest. Behind him, Smoke could vaguely hear the sounds of breaking glass and then the booming of a shotgun. An outlaw Smoke did not know was knocked off the porch to his left, half his face blown away.

"Goddamned heathen!" Smoke heard John say. "Come on, you sorry scum!"

Smoke dropped the Henry and jerked out his six-guns just as he heard gunfire from the rear of the house. He heard Brute's roar of pain and the sounds of a horse running hard.

Splinters flew out of a porch post and dug into Smoke's cheek from a bullet. He dropped to one knee and leveled his .44s at Tustin, pulling the triggers. One slug struck the so-called minister in the throat and the other took him in the mouth.

Tustin's preaching days were over. He rolled from his saddle and hit the ground.

"We've beaten them off!" John yelled, excitement in his voice.

"You stay in the house and keep a sharp lookout, John," Smoke called. "Sally! You all right?"

"I'm fine, honey. But Martha and I got lead in that big ugly man."

Brute Pitman.

And Smoke knew his plan to ride into town must wait; he could not leave this house until Brute was dead and Rex and the others were accounted for.

Reloading his guns, Smoke stepped off the porch and began a careful circling of the house and grounds.

Louis took careful aim and ended the outlaw career of Studs Woodenhouse, the slug from Longmont's gun striking the outlaw leader dead center between the eyes. A bit of fine shooting from that distance.

A rifleman from a second-floor window brought down two of Davidson's gang. Another volunteer ended the career of yet another. Several of the men had left their positions, at the calling of Sheriff Poley, and now the townspeople had the outlaws trapped inside the ruined bank.

One tried to make a break for it at the exact time Mayor George stepped out of the office, his Dragoon at the ready. The Dragoon spat fire and smoke and about a half pound of lead, the slug knocking the outlaw from his horse and dropping him dead on the cobblestones.

"Bastard!" George muttered.

Four rounds bouncing off cobblestones sent the mayor scrambling back into the office.

Tie Medley exposed his head once too often and Sheriff Poley shot him between the eyes. The Hog, along with Shorty, Jake, and Red, slipped out through a hole blown in the wall and crept into the hardware store. There, they stuffed their pockets full of cartridges and began chopping a hole in the wall, breaking into a dress shop and then into an apothecary shop. They were far enough away from the bank building then to slip out, locate their horses, and get the hell out of that locale.

"Let's find this Reynolds place!" Shorty said. "I want Jensen."

"Let's go!"

Smoke came face to face with Brute Pitman at the rear of the corner of the house. The man's face was streaked with blood and there was a tiny bullet hole in his left shoulder, put there by Martha's pocket .32.

Smoke started pulling and cocking, each round striking Brute in the chest and belly. The big man sat down on his butt in the grass and stared at Smoke. While Smoke was punching out empty brass and reloading, Brute Pitman toppled over and died with his eyes and mouth open, taking with him and forever sealing the secret to his cache of gold.

Smoke holstered his own .44s and grabbed at Brute's six-guns, checking the loads. He filled both of them up with six and continued his prowling.

Sally and Martha watched as he passed by a rear window, blood staining one side of his face. Then they heard his .44s roar into action, and each listened to the ugly sounds of bullets striking into and tearing flesh.

Glen Moore lay on his back near the wood shed, his chest riddled with .44 slugs.

Smoke tossed Bruce's guns onto the back porch and stepped inside the house.

"You hurt bad?" Sally asked.

"Scratched, that's all." He poured a cup of coffee and carried it with him through the house, stopping by John Reynolds's position in the foyer.

"It didn't go as King Rex planned." Smoke sipped his coffee. "I got a hunch he and Dagget have turned tail and run."

"Then it's over?"

"For now. But I think I know where the outlaws holed up before they hit us."

The gunfire had intensified from the town proper.

"Where?"

"That big house with the huge barn just outside of town."

"That's Jennings Miller's place. Yes. Come to think of it, I believe he went to visit one of his children the other day."

"When this is over, I'll get the sheriff and we'll take a ride over there. Does Dagget still have kin in this town?"

John grimaced. "Unfortunately, yes. The Mansfords. A very disagreeable bunch. They live just north of town. Why do you ask?"

"Probably never be able to prove it, but I'll bet they helped Dagget out in casing the town and telling them the best place to hide."

"I certainly wouldn't put it past them."

The firing had lessened considerably from the town.

"I'll wire the marshal's office first thing after the wires are fixed."

A train whistle cut the waning gunfire.

"I'll ask them to give any reward money to the town. I reckon that bank's gonna be pretty well tore up."

The train whistle tooted shrilly.

John laughed.

Smoke cut his eyes. "What's so funny, John?"

The gunfire had stopped completely; an almost eerie silence lay over the town. The train tooted its whistle several more times.

"I wouldn't worry about the bank building, Son. Like I said, it needed a lot of work done on it anyway."

"Bank president and owners might not see it that way, John."

"I can assure you, Son, the major stockholder in that bank will see it my way."

"Are you the major stockholder, John?"

"No. My father gave his shares to his favorite grand-daughter when she turned twenty-one."

"And who is that?"

"Your wife, Sally."

24

Only two outlaws were hauled out of the bank building unscathed. Several more were wounded, and one of those would die in the local clinic.

Paul Rycroft and Slim Bothwell had managed to weasel out and could not be found.

Almost miraculously, no townspeople had even been seriously hurt in the wild shooting.

Rex Davidson and Dagget, so it appeared, were long gone from the town. The sheriff and his deputy went to the Mansford home and gave it a thorough search, talking with the family members at length. The family was sullen and uncooperative, but the sheriff could not charge anyone. After all, there was no law on the books against being a jackass.

The bodies of the dead were hauled off and the street swept and cleaned up in front of the ruined bank building. The townspeople began gathering around, oohing and aahing and pointing at this and that.

The sheriff had deputized two dozen extra men and sent them off to guard all roads and paths leading out of the town. People could come in, but you had damn well better be known if you wanted to get out.

The telegraph wires had been repaired—they had

been deliberately cut by Davidson's men, so the prisoners had confessed—and they were once more humming. A special train had been ordered from Manchester and Concord, and the small town was rapidly filling up with reporters and photographers.

Pictures were taken of Mayor George Mahaffery, holding his Dragoon, and the sheriff and his deputy and of the chief of police and his men. Smoke, Louis, and York tried to stay out of the spotlight as much as possible.

That ended abruptly when a small boy tugged at Smoke's jacket.

"Yes, son?" Smoke looked down at him.

"Four men at the end of the street, Mr. Smoke," the little boy said, his eyes wide with fear and excitement. "They said they'll meet you and your men in the street in fifteen minutes."

Smoke thanked him, gave him a dollar, and sent him off running. He motioned for the sheriff and for Louis and York.

"Clear the street, Sheriff. We've been challenged, Louis, York." Then he briefed his friends.

"Why, I'll just take a posse and clean them out!" Sheriff Poley said.

Smoke shook his head. "You'll walk into an ambush if you try that, Sheriff. None of us knows where the men are holed up. Just clear the street."

"Yeah," York said. "A showdown ain't agin the law where we come from."

Since they had first met, Martha and York had been keeping close company. Martha stepped out of the crowd and walked to York. She kissed him right on the mouth, right in front of God and everybody—and she was still dressed in men's britches!

"I'll be waiting," she whispered to him.

York blushed furiously and his grin couldn't have been dislodged with an axe.

Louis and Smoke stood back, smiling at the young

woman and the young ranger. Then they checked their guns, Louis saying, "One more time, friend."

"I wish I could say it would be the last time."

"It won't be." Louis spun the cylinder of first his right-hand gun, then the left-hand .44, dropping them into leather. Smoke and York did the same, all conscious of hundreds of eyes on them.

The hundreds of people had moved into stores and ducked into alleyways. Reporters were scribbling as fast as they could and the photographers were ready behind their bulky equipment.

"There they stand," Louis said quietly, cutting his eyes up the street.

"Shorty, Red, Jake, The Hog," Smoke verbally checked them off. He glanced up and down the wide street. It was free of people.

"You boys ready?" York asked.

"Let's do it!" Louis replied grimly.

The citizens of the town and the visiting reporters and photographers had all read about the western-style shoot-outs. But not one among them had ever before witnessed one. The people watched as the outlaws lined up at the far end of the wide street and the lawmen lined up at the other. They began walking slowly toward each other.

"I should have killed you the first day I seen you, Jensen!" Jake called.

Smoke offered no reply.

"I ain't got but one regret about this thing," Jake wouldn't give it up. "I'd have loved to see you eat a pile of horse shit!"

This time Smoke responded. "I'll just give you some lead, Jake. See how you like that."

"I'll take the Hog," York said.

"Shorty's mine," Louis never took his eyes off his intended target.

"Red and Jake belong to me," Smoke tallied it up.

"They're all fast, boys. Some of us just might take some lead this go-around."

"It's not our time yet, Smoke," Louis spoke quietly. "We all have many more trails to ride before we cross that dark river."

"How do you know them things, Louis?" York asked.

Louis smiled in that strange and mysterious manner that was uniquely his. "My mother was a gypsy queen, York."

Smoke glanced quickly at him. "Louis, you tell the biggest whackers this side of Preacher."

The gambler laughed and so did Smoke and York. Those watching and listening did so with open mouths, not understanding the laughter.

The reporters also noted the seemingly high humor as the three men walked toward hot lead and gunsmoke.

"It's a game to them," a reporter murmured. "Nothing more than a game."

"They're savages!" another said. "All of them. The so-called marshals included. They should all be put in cages and publicly displayed."

Martha tapped him on the shoulder. "Mister?"

The reporter turned around.

The young woman slugged him on the side of the jaw, knocking the man sprawling, on his butt, to the floor of the store.

Jordan Reynolds stood with his mouth open, staring in disbelief.

"Good girl," John said.

A man who looked to be near a hundred years old, dressed in an ill-fitting suit, smiled at Martha. He had gotten off the train that morning, accompanied by two other old men also dressed in clothing that did not seem right for them.

Sally looked at the old men and smiled, starting toward them. The old man who had smiled at Martha shook his head minutely.

The three old mountain men stepped back into the crowd and vanished, walking out the rear of the store.

The reporter was struggling to get to his feet.

"Who was that old man, Sally?" Martha asked.

"I don't know," Sally lied. Then she turned to once more watch her man face what many believed he was born to face.

There was fifty feet between them when the outlaws dragged iron. The street erupted in fire and smoke and fast guns and death.

The Hog went down with three of York's .44 slugs in his chest and belly. He struggled to rise and York ended it with a carefully aimed slug between the Hog's piggy eyes.

Shorty managed to clear leather and that was just about all he managed to do before Louis's guns roared and belched lead. Shorty fell forward on his face, his un-fired guns shining in the crisp fall air.

Smoke took out Red first, drawing and firing so fast the man was unable to drag his .45 out of leather. Then Smoke felt the sting of a bullet graze his left shoulder as he cocked and fired, the slug taking Jake directly in the center of his chest. Smoke kept walking and firing as Jake refused to go down. Finally, with five slugs in him, the outlaw dropped to the street, closed his eyes, and died.

"What an ugly sight!" Smoke heard a man say.

He turned to the man, blood running down his arm from the wound in his shoulder. "No uglier than when he was alive," Smoke told him.

And the old man called Preacher chuckled and turned to his friends. "Let's git gone, boys. It was worth the train ride just to see it!"

The reporter that Martha had busted on the jaw was leaning against another reporter, moral and physical support in his time of great stress. "I'll sue you!" he hollered at the young woman.

Martha held up her fists. "You wanna fight instead?"

"Savage bitch!" the man yelled at her.

Lawyer John Reynolds stepped up and belted the reporter on the snoot with a hard straight right. The reporter landed on his butt, a sprawl of arms and legs, blood running down his face from his busted beak.

John smiled and said, "Damn, but that felt good!"

25

BANK ROBBERY ATTEMPT FOILED BY WESTERN GUNSLINGERS screamed one headline.

SAVAGES MEET SAVAGE END IN PEACEFUL NEW HAMPSHIRE TOWN howled another front-page headline.

Smoke glanced at the headlines and then ignored the rest of the stories about him. He was getting antsy, restless; he was ready to get gone, back to the High Lonesome, back to the Sugarloaf.

"Is that reporter really going to sue you, Father?" Sally asked John.

The lawyer laughed. "He says he is."

"You want me to take care of it, John?" Smoke asked with a straight face.

"Oh, no, Son!" John quickly spoke up. "No, I think it will all work out."

Then Smoke smiled, and John realized his son-in-law was only having fun with him. John threw back his head and laughed.

"Son, you have made me realize what a stuffed shirt I had become. And I thank you for it."

Smoke opened his mouth and John waved him silent. "No, let me finish this. I've had to reassess my original opinion of you, Son. I've had to reevaluate many of the beliefs I thought were set in stone. Oh, I still believe very strongly in law and order. And lawyers," he added with a smile. "But I can understand you and men like you much better now."

York was out sparking Miss Martha, and Louis was arranging a private railroad car to transport them all back to Colorado. His way of saying thank you for his namesake.

"I'd like nothing better than to see the day when I can hang up my guns, John," Smoke said after a sip of strong cowboy coffee. "But out where I live, that's still many years down the road, I'm thinking."

"I'd like to visit your ranch someday."

"You'll be welcome anytime, sir."

John leaned forward. "You're leaving soon?"

"Probably day after tomorrow. Louis says he thinks he can have the car here then. About noon."

"And this Rex Davidson and Dagget; the others who got away?"

"We'll meet them down the road, I'm sure. But me and Sally, we're used to watching our backtrail. Used to keeping a gun handy. Don't worry, John, Abigal. If they try to take us on the Sugarloaf, that's where we'll bury them."

"I say," Jordan piped up. "Do you think your town could support another attorney? I've been thinking about it, and I think the West is in need of more good attorneys, don't you, Father?"

His father probably saved his son's life when he said, "Jordan, I need you here."

"Oh! Very well, Father. Perhaps someday."

"When pigs fly," John muttered.

"Beg pardon, sir?" Jordan asked.

"Nothing, Son. Nothing at all."

They pulled out right on schedule, but to Smoke's surprise, the town's band turned up at the depot and were blaring away as the train pulled out.

Louis had not arranged for one private car but for two, so the ladies could have some privacy and the babies could be tended to properly and have some quiet moments to sleep.

"Really, Louis," Sally told him. "I am perfectly capable of paying for these amenities myself."

"Nonsense. I won't hear of it." He looked around to make sure that Smoke and York were not watching or listening, then reached down and tickled his namesake under his chin.

"Goochy, goochy!" the gambler said.

Louis Arthur promptly grabbed hold of the gambler's finger and refused to let go.

They changed engines and crews many times before reaching St. Louis. There, all were tired and Louis insisted upon treating them to the finest hotel in town. A proper nanny was hired to take care of the twins, and Louis contacted the local Pinkerton agency and got several hard-looking and very capable-appearing men to guard the babies and their nanny.

Then they all went out on the town.

They spent two days in the city, the ladies shopping and the men tagging along, appearing to be quite bored with it all. It got very un-boring when York accidentally got lost in the largest and most expensive department store in town and wound up in one of the ladies' dressing rooms . . . with a rather matronly lady dressed only in her drawers.

Smoke and Louis thought the Indians were attacking from all the screaming that reverberated throughout the many-storied building.

After order was restored, York commented. "Gawddamndest sight I ever did see. I thought I was in a room with a buffalo!"

* * *

The train chugged and rumbled across Missouri and into and onto the flat plains of Kansas. It had turned much colder, and snow was common now.

"I worry about taking the babies up into the high country, Smoke," Sally expressed her concern as the train rolled on into Colorado.

"Not to worry," Louis calmed her. "I can arrange for a special coach with a charcoal stove. Everything is going to be all right."

But Louis knew, as did Smoke and York, that the final leg of their journey was when they would be the most vulnerable.

But their worry was needless. Smoke had wired home, telling his friends when they would arrive in Denver. When they stepped out of the private cars, he knew that not even such a hate-filled man as Rex Davidson would dare attack them now.

Monte Carson and two of his men were there, as were Johnny North and Pearlie and a half dozen others from the High Lonesome; all of them men who at one time or another in their lives had been known as gunslingers.

York was going to head south to Arizona and officially turn in his badge and draw his time, then come spring he'd drift back up toward the Sugarloaf. And toward Martha.

This was the end of the line for Louis. He had many business appointments and decisions to make, and then he would head out, probably to France.

"Oh, I'll be back," he assured them all. "I have to check on my namesake every now and then, you know."

Smoke stuck out his hand and the gambler/gunfighter shook it. "Thanks, Louis."

"Anytime, Smoke. Just anytime at all. It isn't over, friend. So watch your back and look after Sally and the kids."

"I figure they'll come after me come spring, Louis."

"So do I. See you, Smoke."

And as he had done before, Louis Longmont turned without another word and walked out of their lives.

Christmas in the high country and it was shut-down-tight time, with snow piled up to the eaves. For the next several months, taking care of the cattle would be back-breakingly hard work for every man able to sit a saddle.

Water holes would have to be chopped out daily so the cattle could drink. Hay would have to be hauled to them so they would not starve. Line cabins would have to be checked and restocked with food so the hands could stay alive. Firewood had to be stacked high, with a lot of it stacked close to the house, for the temperature could drop to thirty below in a matter of a few hours.

This was not a country for the fainthearted or for those who did not thrive on hard brutal work. It was a hard land, and it took hard men to mold it and make it liveable.

It was a brutal time for the men and women in the high country, but it was also a peaceful time for them. It was a time when, after a day's back-breaking and exhausting work, a man could come home to a warm fire and a table laden with hot food. And after supper, a man and woman could sit snug in their home while the wind howled and sang outside, talking of spring while their kids did homework, read or, as in Smoke and Sally's case, laid on the floor, on a bearskin rug in front of the fire, playing with toys their father had carved and shaped and fitted and pegged together with his own strong hands. They could play with dolls their mother had patiently sewn during the long, cold, seemingly endless days of winter.

But as is foretold in the Bible, there is a time for everything, and along about the middle of March, the icy fingers of winter began to loosen their chilly grip on the high country of Colorado.

Smoke and Sally awakened to the steady drip-drop of water.

Martha, who had spent the winter with them and had been a godsend in helping take care of the babies, stuck her head inside their bedroom, her eyes round with wonder.

"Raining?" she asked.

Smoke grinned at her. He and Sally had both tossed off the heavy comforter some time during the night, when the temperature began its steady climb upward.

"Chinooks, Martha," he told her. "Sometimes it means spring is just around the corner. But as often as not, it's a false spring."

"I'll start breakfast," she said.

Smoke pulled on his clothes and belted his guns around him. He stepped outside and smiled at the warm winds. Oh, it was still mighty cool, the temperature in the forties, but it beat the devil out of temperatures forty below.

"Tell Sally I'll milk the cows, Martha. Breakfast ought to be ready when I'm—"

His eyes found the horse standing with head down near the barn. And he knew that horse. It belonged to York.

And York was lying in the muddy snow beside the animal.

Smoke jerked out his .44 and triggered two fast shots into the air. The bunkhouse emptied in fifteen seconds, with cowboys in various stages of undress, mostly in their longhandles, boots, and hats—with guns in their hands.

Sally jerked the front door open. "It's York, and I think he's hard hit . . ."

"Shot in the chest, boss!" a cowboy yelled. "He's bad, too!"

"You, Johnny!" Smoke yelled to a hand. "Get dressed and get Dr. Spalding out here. We can't risk moving York over these bumpy roads." The cowboy darted back inside the bunkhouse. Smoke turned to Sally. "Get some water on to boil and gather up some clean white cloths for bandages." He ran over to where York was sprawled.

Pearlie had placed a jacket under York's head. He met Smoke's eyes. "It don't look good. The only chance he's got is if it missed the lung."

"Get him into the house, boys."

As they moved him as gently as possible, York opened his eyes and looked at Smoke. "Dagget and Davidson and 'bout a dozen others, Smoke. They're here. Ambushed me 'bout fifteen miles down the way. Down near where them beaver got that big dam."

Then he passed out.

Johnny was just swinging into the saddle. "Johnny! Tell the sheriff to get a posse together. Meet me at Little Crick."

The cowboy left, foggy headed.

York was moved into the house, into the new room that had been added while Smoke and Sally were gone east.

Smoke turned to Pearlie. "This weather will probably hold for several days at least. The cattle can make it now. Leave the hands at the lineshacks. You'll come with me. Everybody else stays here, close to the house. And I mean nothing pulls them away. Pass the word."

Smoke walked back into the house and looked in on York. Sally and Martha had pulled off his boots, loosened his belt, and stripped his bloody shirt from him. They had cut off the upper part of his longhandles, exposing the ugly savage wound in his chest.

Sally met her husband's eyes. "It's bad, Smoke, but not as bad as I first thought. The bullet went all the way through. There is no evidence of a lung being nicked; no pink froth. And his breathing is strong and so is his heart."

Smoke nodded, grabbing up a piece of bread and wrapping it around several thick slices of salt meat he picked from the skillet. "I'll get in gear and then Pearlie and me will pull out; join the posse at Little Crick. All the hands have been ordered to stay right here. It would take an army to bust through them."

Sally rose and kissed his lips. "I'll fix you a packet of food."

Smoke roped and saddled a tough mountain horse, a bigger-than-usual Appaloosa, sired by his old Appaloosa, Seven. He lashed down his bedroll behind the saddle and stuffed his saddlebags full of ammo and food and a couple of pairs of clean socks. He swung into the saddle just as Pearlie was swinging into his saddle. Smoke rode over to the front door of the house, where Sally was waiting.

Her eyes were dark with fury. "Finish it, Smoke," she said.

He nodded and swung his horse's head—the horse was named Horse. He waited for Pearlie and the two of them rode slowly down the valley, out of the high country and down toward Little Crick.

By eight o'clock that morning, Smoke and Pearlie had both shucked off their heavy coats and tied them behind their saddles, riding with only light jackets to protect them from the still-cool winds.

They had met Dr. Spalding on the road and told him what they knew about York's wound. The doctor had nodded his head and driven on.

An hour later they were at the beaver dam on Little Crick. Sheriff Monte Carson was waiting with the posse. Smoke swung down from the saddle and walked to where the sheriff was pointing.

"Easy trackin', Smoke. Two men have already gone on ahead. I told them not to get more'un a couple miles ahead of us."

"That's good advice, Monte. These are bad ones. How many you figure?"

"Ground's pretty chewed up, but I'd figure at least a dozen; maybe fifteen of them."

Smoke looked at the men of the posse. He knew them all and was friends with them all. There was Johnny North, at one time one of the most feared and respected of all gunslingers. There was the minister, a man of God but a crack shot with a rifle. Better hit the ground if he ever pulled out a six-shooter, for he couldn't hit the side of a mountain with a short gun. The editor of the paper was there, along with the town's lawyer, both of them heavily armed. There were ranchers and farmers and shopkeepers, and while not all were born men of the West, they had blended in and were solid western men.

Which meant that if you messed with them, they would shoot your butt off.

Smoke shared a few words with all of the men of the posse, making sure they all had ample food and bedrolls and plenty of ammo. It was a needless effort, for all had arrived fully prepared.

Then Smoke briefed them all about the nature of the men they were going to track.

When he had finished, all the men wore looks of pure disgust on their faces. Beaconfield and Garrett, both big ranchers in the area, had quietly noosed ropes while Smoke was talking.

Monte noticed, of course, but said nothing. This was the rough-edged west, where horse thieves were still hanged on the spot, and there was a reason for that: Leave a man without a horse in this country, and that might mean the thief had condemned that man to death.

Tit for tat.

"Judge Proctor out of town?" Smoke asked.

"Gone to a big conference down in Denver," Monte told him.

Beaconfield and Garrett finished noosing the ropes and secured them behind their saddles. They were not uncaring men. No one had ever been turned away from their doors hungry or without proper clothing. Many times, these same men had given a riderless puncher a horse, telling him to pay whenever he could; if he couldn't, that was all right, too.

But western men simply could not abide men like Davidson or Dagget or them that chose to ride with them. The men of the posse lived in a hard land that demanded practicality, short conversations, and swift justice, oftentimes as not, at the point of a gun.

It would change as the years rolled on. But a lot of people would wonder if the change had been for the better.

A lot of people would be wondering the same thing a hundred hears later.

Smoke swung into the saddle. "Let's go stomp on some snakes."

26

The posse caught up with the men who had ranged out front, tracking the outlaws.

"I can't figure them, Sheriff," one of the scouts said. "It's like they don't know they're headin' into a box canyon."

"Maybe they don't," Pearlie suggested.

One of the outriders shook his head. "If they keep on the way they're goin', we're gonna have 'em hemmed in proper in about an hour."

Garrett walked his horse on ahead. "Let's do it, boys. It's a right nice day for a hangin'."

The posse cautiously made their way. In half an hour, they knew that King Rex and Dagget were trapped inside Puma Canyon. They was just absolutely no other way out.

"Two men on foot," Monte ordered. "Rifles. And take it slow and easy up the canyon. Don't move until you've checked all around you and above you. We might have them trapped, but this is one hell of a good place for an ambush. You—"

"Hellooo, the posse!" the call came echoing down the long, narrow canyon. It was clearly audible, so Davidson and his men were not that far away.

Monte waved the two men back and shouted, "We hear you. Give yourselves up. You haven't got a chance."

"Oh, I think not, Sheriff. I think it's going to be a very interesting confrontation."

"Rex Davidson," Smoke said. "I will never forget that voice."

Monte turned to one of his deputies. "Harry, you and Bob ride down yonder about half a mile. There's a way up to the skyline. You'll be able to shoot right down on top of them. Take off."

"This is tricky country," Beaconfield said. "Man can get hisself into a box here 'fore he knows. Took me several years to learn this country and damned if I still don't end up in a blind canyon ever now and then."

They all knew what he meant, for they all had, at one time or the other, done the same them.

"Hellooo, the posse!" the call came again.

"We hear you! What do you want?" Monte yelled, his voice bouncing around the steep canyon walls.

"We seem to have boxed ourselves in. Perhaps we could behave as gentlemen and negotiate some sort of settlement. What do you say about that?"

"Bastard's crazy!" Monte said.

"You noticed," Smoke replied.

Raising his voice, Monte called, "Toss your guns to the ground and ride on out. One hand on the reins, the other hand in the air."

"That offer is totally unacceptable!"

"Then you're going to get lead or a rope. Take your choice!"

"Come on and get us then!" Dagget yelled, laying down the challenge.

"We got three choices," Garrett said, a grimness to his voice. "We can starve them out; but that'd take days. We could try to set this place on fire and burn them out; but I don't want no harm to come to their horses. Or we can go in and dig them out."

Smoke dismounted and led Horse back to a safe pocket at the mouth of the canyon. He stuffed his pockets with .44s and pulled his rifle from the boot.

The others followed suit, taking their horses out of the line of fire and any possible ricocheting bullet. Monte waved the men to his side.

"The only way any of us is gonna take lead this day is if we're stupid or downright unlucky. What we're gonna do is wait until Bob and Harry get into position and start layin' down some lead. Then we can start movin' in. So lets have us a smoke and a drink of water and relax. Relaxin' is something them ol' boys in that box canyon ain't liable to be doin'."

The men squatted down and rolled and licked and shaped and lit. Beaconfield brought out a coffee pot, and Smoke made a small circle of rocks and started a hat-sized fire. The men waited for the coffee to boil.

With a smile on his lips, Smoke walked to the curve of the canyon and shouted, "We're gonna have us some coffee and food, Davidson. We'll be thinking about you boys all hunkered up there in the rocks doing without."

A rifle slug whined wickedly off the rock wall, tearing through the air to thud against the ground.

"This is the Jester, King Rex, Your Majesty!" Smoke shouted. "How about just you and me, your royal pain in the ass?"

"Swine!" Davidson screamed. "You traitor! You turned your back to me after all I'd done for you. I made you welcome in my town and you turned on me like a rattlesnake."

He is insane, Smoke thought. But crazy like that much-talked-about fox.

"That doesn't answer my question, Davidson. How about it? You and me in a face-off?"

"You trust that crud, Smoke?" Johnny North asked, edging close to Smoke.

"No, I just want to see what he'll do."

They all got that answer quickly. All the hemmed-in

outlaws began pumping lead in Smoke's direction. But all they managed to do was waste a lot of lead and powder and hit a lot of air.

"So much for that," Smoke said, after the hard gunfire had ceased.

He had no sooner gotten the words out of his mouth when Harry and Bob opened up from the west side of the canyon wall. Several screams and howls of pain told the posse members the marksmanship of the men on the rim was true.

"That got their attention," Monte said with a grim smile.

They heard the clatter of a falling rifle and knew that at least one of the outlaws had been hard hit and probably killed.

"You have no honor, Jester!" Davidson screamed. "You're a foul person. You're trash, Jester."

"And you're a coward, Davidson!" Smoke called.

"How dare you call me a coward!"

"You hide behind the guns of a child rapist. You're afraid to fight your own battles."

"You talkin' about Dagget?" Johnny asked.

"Yeah."

Johnny grimaced and spat on the ground, as if trying to clear his mouth of a bad taste. "Them kind of people is pure filth. I want him, Smoke."

"He's all mine, Johnny. Personal reasons."

"You got him."

"Dagget!" Smoke yelled. "Do you have any bigger bolas than your cowardly boss?"

There was a long moment of silence. Dagget called out, "Name your poison, Jensen!"

"Face me, Dagget. One on one. I don't think you've got the guts to do it."

Another moment of silence. "How do we work it out, Jensen?"

"You call it, Dagget."

Another period of silence. Longer than the others. Smoke felt that Dagget was talking with Davidson and he soon found that his guess was correct.

"I reckon you boys got ropes already noosed and knotted for us, right, Jensen?" another voice called.

"I reckon."

"Who's that?" Monte asked.

"I think it's Paul Rycroft."

"I ain't lookin' to get hung!" Rycroft yelled.

Smoke said nothing.

"Jensen? Slim Bothwell here. Your snipers got us pegged out and pinned down. Cain't none of us move more'un two/three inches either way without gettin' drilled. It ain't no fittin' way for a man to go out. I got me an idea. You interested?"

"Keep talking, Slim."

"I step out down to the canyon floor. One of your men steps out. One of us, one of you. We do that until we're all facin' each other. Anybody tries anything funny, your men on the ridge can drop them already out. And since I'll be the first one out . . . well, you get the pitcher, don't you?"

Smoke looked back at the posse members. "They're asking for a showdown. But a lot of you men aren't gunslicks. I can't ask you to put your life on the line."

"A lot of them ol' boys in there ain't gunslicks, neither," Beaconfield said. "They're just trash. Let's go for it."

Every member of the posse concurred without hesitation. The minister, Ralph Morrow, was the second to agree.

"All right, Bothwell. You and Rycroft step out with me and Pearlie."

"That's a deal. Let's do 'er."

Each taking a deep breath, Smoke and Pearlie stepped out to face the two outlaws. Several hundred feet separated the men. The others on both sides quickly followed, the outlaws fully aware that if just one of them screwed up, the riflemen on the skyline of the canyon would take a terrible toll.

Davidson and Dagget were the last two down from the rocks. Davidson was giggling as he minced down to the canyon floor.

And Davidson and Dagget positioned themselves so they both were facing Smoke.

"And now we find out something I have always known," Davidson called to Smoke.

"What's that, stupid?" Smoke deliberately needled the man.

"Who's the better man, of course!" Davidson called.

"Hell, Davidson. I've known that since the first time I laid eyes on you. You couldn't shine my boots."

Davidson flushed and waved his hand. "Forward, troops!" he shouted. "Advance and wipe out the mongrels!"

"Loony as a monkey!" Garrett muttered.

"But dangerous as a rattlesnake." Smoke advised. "Let's go, boys."

The lines of men began to walk slowly toward each other, their boots making their progress in the muddy, snowy canyon floor.

The men behind their rifles on the canyon skyline kept the muzzles of their guns trained on the outlaws.

No one called out any signals. No one spoke a word. All knew that when they were about sixty feet apart, it was time to open the dance. Rycroft's hands jerked at the pistol butts and Beaconfield drilled him dead center just as Bothwell grabbed for his guns. Minister Morrow lifted the muzzle of his Henry and shot the outlaw through the belly, levered in another round, and finished the job.

The canyon floor roared and boomed and filled with gunsmoke as the two sides hammered at each other.

Smoke pulled both .44s, his speed enabling him to get off the first and accurate shots.

One slug turned Dagget sideways and the other slug hit Davidson in the hip, striking the big bone and knocking the man to the ground.

Smoke felt the lash of a bullet impact with his left leg. He steadied himself and continued letting the hot lead fly. He saw Dagget go down just as Davidson leveled his six-gun and fired. The bullet clipped Smoke's right arm, stinging and drawing the blood. Smoke leveled his left-hand .44 and shot Davidson in the head, the bullet striking him just about his right eye.

Dagget was down on his knees, still fighting. Smoke walked toward the man, cocking and firing. He was close enough to see the slugs pop dirt from the man's shirt and jacket as they struck.

Dagget suddenly rose up to one knee and his fingers loosened their hold on his guns. He fell forward on his face just as Smoke slumped against a huge boulder, his left leg suddenly aching, unable to hold his weight.

Smoke punched out empties and reloaded as the firing wound down. He watched as Pearlie emptied both Colts into the chests of two men; Minister Morrow knocked yet another outlaw to the ground with fire and lead from his Henry.

And then the canyon floor fell silent.

Somewhere a man coughed and spat. Another man groaned in deep pain. Yet another man tried to get up from the line of fallen outlaws. He tried then gave it up, falling back into the boot-churned mud.

The outlaw line lay bloody and still.

"My wife told me to finish it this morning," Smoke said, his voice seeming unnaturally loud in the sudden stillness.

"Anything my wife tells me to do, I do it," Garrett spoke.

"Looks like we done it," Johnny summed it up.

27

Beaconfield and Garrett called in some of their hands and the outlaws were buried in a mass grave. Reverend Ralph Morrow spoke a few words over the gravesite.

Damn few words.

Smoke tied off the wound in his leg and the men swung into the saddles. This part of Colorado was peaceful again, for a time.

The men turned their horses and headed for home. No one looked back at the now-quiet-but-once-roaring-and-bloody canyon floor. No one would return to mark the massive grave. The men of the posse had left the outlaws' guns on top of the mound of fresh earth.

Marker enough.

York would make it, but it would be a long, slow healing time. But as Dr. Spalding pointed out, Martha would make a fine nurse.

York had been ambushed in the late afternoon, but he'd somehow managed to stay in the saddle and finally made the ranch. He had crawled into some hay by the barn and that had probably saved his life.

"We'll call our ranch the Circle BM," York told her.

Martha thought about that. "No," she said with a smile. "Let's call it the Circle YM. It . . . sounds a little bit better."

Spring came to the High Lonesome, and with the coming of the renewal of the cycle, a peaceful warm breeze blew across the meadows and the canyons and the homes of those who chose to brave the high country, to carve out their destiny, working the land, moving the cattle, raising their families, and trying their best to live their lives as decently and as kindly as the circumstances would permit them.

Martha would be hired as the new schoolmarm, and in the summer, she and York would wed. Her teaching would be interrupted every now and then, for they would have six children.

Six to add to Smoke and Sally's five.

Five?

Yes, but that's another story . . . along the trail of the last mountain man.

GREAT BOOKS,
GREAT SAVINGS!

When You Visit Our Website:
www.kensingtonbooks.com
You Can Save Money Off The Retail Price
Of Any Book You Purchase!

- **All Your Favorite Kensington Authors**
- **New Releases & Timeless Classics**
- **Overnight Shipping Available**
- **eBooks Available For Many Titles**
- **All Major Credit Cards Accepted**

Visit Us Today To Start Saving!
www.kensingtonbooks.com

All Orders Are Subject To Availability.
Shipping and Handling Charges Apply.
Offers and Prices Subject To Change Without Notice.